STAND BY, STAND BY

Chris Ryan

COMPASS PRESS

★ OXFORD ★ MELBOURNE ★

First published in 1996 by Century

Compass Press Large Print Book Series; an imprint of
ISIS Publishing Ltd, Great Britain and Bolinda Press, Australia

Published in Large Print 1997 by ISIS Publishing Ltd,
7 Centremead, Osney Mead, Oxford OX2 0ES,
and Australian Large Print, Audio and Video Pty Ltd
17 Mohr Street, Tullamarine, Victoria 3043
by arrangement with Random House UK Ltd

**British Library Cataloguing in
Publication Data**
Ryan, Chris, 1961–
  Stand by, stand by. – Large print ed.
1. Great Britain. Army. Special Air
Service Regiment – Fiction 2. Special
forces (Military science) – Fiction
3. War stories 4. Large type books
I. Title
823.9'14 [F]

**Australian Cataloguing in
Publication Data**
Ryan, Chris, 1961–
  Stand by, stand by/
Chris Ryan
(Compass Press large print)
book series)
ISBN 1863407200
I. Title
823.914

ISBN 0-7531-5555-9 (ISIS Publishing Ltd)
ISBN 1-86340-720-0 (ALPAV Pty Ltd)

Printed and bound by Hartnolls Ltd, Bodmin, Cornwall

STAND BY, STAND BY

ACKNOWLEDGEMENTS

I wish to give special thanks to someone who shall remain anonymous but without whose editorial help I would never have finished this. To all my family and friends for their patience and understanding. Also to Mark Booth, Liz Rowlinson, Tracy Jennings and Nicky Eaton at Century.

The Castle

As the knights fight in the hall, people stand by
   the wall.
Jokers joke whilst people poke at one another.
Shrieking sounds down below where cellars glow.
The King sits on his throne when people groan.
The Lady who wears silver threads lives in dread of
   the spider and the dead.

by Sarah Ryan, aged 7, 1996

For my mother

GLOSSARY

ASU	IRA Active Service Unit
Basha	Sleeping shelter
Bergen	Rucksack
BG	Bodyguard (noun or verb)
Blue-on-blue	Accidental strike on own forces
Box	General name for intelligence services
Casevac	Casualty evacuation
CAT	Counter-attack team
Comms	Communications
CTR	Close target reconnaissance
DET	Intelligence gathering organization
DAS	Colombian Police
DF	Direction finding
Dicker	IRA scout
Director	Officer commanding special forces, generally a brigadier
DOP	Drop-off point
DPMs	Disruptive pattern material camouflage garments
DZ	Drop zone
EMOE	Explosive method of entry
ERV	Emergency rendezvous
EMU	Encryption device
FMB	Forward mounting base
FOB	Forward operating base

GPS	Global positioning system (navigation aid)
Head-Shed	Headquarters
Incoming	Incoming fire
Int	Intelligence
IO	Intelligence officer
LO	Liaison officer
LUP	Lying-up point
LZ	Landing zone
Magellan	Brand name of GPS
OP	Observation post
PE	Plastic explosive
Phys	Physical exercise
PIRA	Provisional IRA
Player	Terrorist
PNGs	Passive night goggles
PUP	Pick-up point
QRF	Quick reaction force
RTU	Return to unit
Rupert	Officer
SAM	Surface-to-air missile
Satcom	Telephone using satellite transmission
SEAL	Sea, Air and Land — American special forces unit
Shreddies	Army-issue underpants
SOCO	Scene of Crimes Officer
SP	Special Projects
SSM	Squadron sergeant major
RUC	Royal Ulster Constabulary
TACBE	Emergency radio
TCG	Tactical Control Group

Tout	Informer
UCBT	Under-car booby trap
US	Unserviceable
VCP	Vehicle control point
319	VHF radio

WEAPONS

AK 47	Soviet-design 7.62mm short rifle
203	Combination of 7.62mm automatic rifle (top barrel) and 40mm grenade launcher (below)
HK 53	5.56mm automatic rifle
Galil	Israeli-made 7.62mm automatic rifle
G3	7.62mm automatic rifle
Long	Any rifle
L2	Hand grenade
MP 5	5.56mm sub-machine-gun
RPG7	Soviet-made rocket launcher
SA80	7.62mm rifle
Short	Any pistol
Sig	Sigsauer 9mm pistol

CHAPTER
ONE

That night the dream came again. As usual I was being swept forward, unable to control my speed. I felt as though I was on a roller-coaster at a fairground, accelerating bumpily through the cold, dark air. But why were no other passengers riding with me? Why was I alone in this freezing night?

The ride was very rough. OK, I thought, the track's buckled, but I can handle it — and I clung tight to the side-rails to stop myself being flung out. Then something began to drag at my left arm, holding it back, as if that side of the carriage was being left behind. Let go, dickhead! I told myself, but my fingers wouldn't unclamp from the rail. Pain ripped through me. I thought, I'm going down here. I'm going to get torn in half.

The cold was horrendous. The air pouring past me was so frozen it was searing my skin. When I opened my mouth to yell, it drove a fierce pain into the roots of my teeth, so that I had to clamp my lips shut. Then over the black horizon ahead came a gleam of light. I was hurtling towards that bright rim, the rim of the world. All too well I knew what I'd see beyond it. Up and on I went, faster than ever, my arm being torn in half at the elbow.

Then in a split second I was over the top and into the light, diving towards an operating theatre as big as an airport. A wall of heat rushed up to meet me, so that in an instant I was pouring sweat, like down in the sands of Abu Dhabi. Brilliant lamps blazed on to the table, and life-support equipment was ranged alongside: drips, oxygen cylinders, white dishes full of instruments. Attendants in green gowns and masks were waiting, ready — and in the centre stood a tall surgeon with a hypodermic syringe the length of an AK 47, the point of its gleaming needle levelled at my eye. I longed for a gun so I could drop him at a distance, but no: I was going in close. "BASTARDS!" I roared as I hurtled down towards him. "BASTARDS! BASTARDS!"

I woke up. Kath stood in the doorway, the light from the landing shining on her straight fair hair. In the background Tim was crying.

"Geordie," she said quietly. "Are you all right?"

"Yeah, yeah." I tried to turn over, but I found I'd got the bedclothes wound around me so I was trussed like an oven-ready chicken.

Kath came across and put her hand on my forehead. "You're soaking. Better change the sheets. I'll get you a clean pair."

"I'll be OK, thanks. What time is it?"

"Just after three." She sat down on the edge of the bed, silhouetted against the light. With one hand she drew her dressing-gown tight around her neck, and with the other she smoothed out the top sheet. "What time did you get to bed?"

"Not sure. Maybe half one."

"How much did you drink?"

"Not a lot. Two or three more Scotches."

She knew perfectly well that I'd been hitting the booze far worse than I admitted, and going to ridiculous lengths to cover up. She knew that alcohol was becoming a serious problem for me, and several times she'd pleaded with me to seek professional advice.

Now she asked, "What happened? Was it the dream again?"

"Yeah. Was I making a noise?"

"I thought someone was killing you. You were yelling at the top of your voice. It woke Tim."

"I'm sorry."

"It's all right. I meant to ask — did you hear any news about when Tony's coming over to do selection?"

"He'll be here in June, I think. Why?"

"Just wondered."

I knew what she was thinking: that Tony had been my salvation in Iraq, and might again act as a stabilizing influence when he arrived in England. He might help me get the whole Gulf experience squared away. Possibly she was right — but how could anyone know?

"Arm hurting?" she asked.

"No, it's comfortable."

"Headache?"

"A bit."

"Take some Paracetamol, then."

"OK."

She punched a couple of tablets out of a pack on the bedside table and handed them to me, together with a glass of water. I propped myself on one elbow to get them down.

"Thanks. I'll be fine now."

"Sleep well, then."

She ran a hand over my hair, got up, went back to the door and closed it softly. Soon the kid stopped crying, the landing light went out, and I heard the door of our bedroom click shut.

Our bedroom. I should have been sleeping there, in our big double bed. The fact that I was on my own summed everything up. The recurring nightmare was my excuse for sleeping alone; I'd said I'd move out to the spare room because I didn't want to keep waking Kath with my bad dreams. But beneath the surface, something far deeper had gone wrong.

My sheets were clammy. Like most guys in the Regiment I sleep naked — so I got up, rubbed myself down with a towel, opened the window wider and let the cool night air flow in round my body, drying it off. I listened as the wind rustled through the oak tree at the back of the house. An owl hooted, close and loud. Lucky bird — that it should have so little to worry about. A mouse or two a night was all it needed to be happy, and it had no idea of war, no idea of captivity, no idea of death.

After a while I went back to bed, and lay staring upwards with the sheets pulled under my chin. I knew full well that my troubles stemmed from what had happened in the desert and in that shit-heap of a hospital in Iraq.

I thought of Tony, good, tough guy that he was. Tony, who had shared my captivity, and done so much to get me through it, with his indomitable spirit and unfailing sense of humour. His proper name was Antonio Lopez, but ever since he could remember he had been known by the easy abbreviation. As a SEAL (a member of the American Sea, Air and Land special forces unit), he had been through far worse ordeals than I had, especially when that operation had gone tits-up in Panama. He had come out of the Gulf very much in one piece, and now he was about to take the selection course, in the hope of joining the Regiment for a two-year tour. Was I so much inferior to him, that I couldn't stand the strain?

I kept thinking back to what it had been like before, between me and Kath. If anyone had asked, I could have answered truthfully in one word: "Brilliant!" We'd met four years earlier, and we'd been delighted to discover that our twenty-fifth birthdays were both coming up within a week of each other. Now, lying in the dark, I remembered the day we found the house. We'd seen a photo in an estate agent's window, and arranged to borrow the key. The price was right on the limit of what we could afford, but thanks to the generosity of my in-laws we had enough cash for the deposit. The agent warned us that the place was way off the beaten track. "It's another world out there," he said. "Not to worry, I told him, "that's what we're after."

He handed us the keys and we drove out, only fifteen minutes from town. When we saw the house, we looked at each other and grinned. It was old, 150 years at least, and it stood in a perfect position at the end of a lane, in a hollow surrounded by fields. A spinney of oaks ran away up a little valley at the back, with a trickle of water coming down between the trees. Even in winter, with the branches bare, it looked a dream. What would it be like in high summer?

Keeper's Cottage was its name, and that's what it had been: the home of a gamekeeper. Before long we came to call it KC. Over the years the brickwork had mellowed to a soft red — typical Herefordshire — and the previous owners had worked hard to restore and improve the house, so that we were able to move straight in. Outside, the garden had gone to seed, but Kath, who had green fingers, got stuck into that as soon as spring came. Under her direction I did the heavy digging, but it was she who planned and planted everything. She was thrilled to find that several of the trees in the spinney were rowans, or mountain ash — her favourites — which put on a tremendous show of bright-red berries in the autumn. The place and its associations reminded me of my childhood home in the north, where as a boy I was forever ferreting rabbits and walking the hedgerows.

In KC we were as happy as anybody could have been. It was the first time that either of us had lived in a house without a number — in our eyes a big plus, as it made us feel we had the edge over our friends living in towns. The house and rooms were exactly the right size for us, neither too big nor too small. The place was so private that in summer we could sunbathe stark naked on the lawn. Kath got a vegetable patch going, and grew some cracking beans, peas, potatoes and lettuces, and herbs galore. We ate so many fresh salads that our ears started turning green. In winter we were snug as squirrels, because I got permission from the neighbouring farmer to collect firewood from the spinney, and in the living room we kept a Norwegian log-burner on the go day and night. The stove had a back-boiler for boosting the hot water; if I opened up the draught, I could get the tank boiling.

The footpaths and woodland tracks were ideal for running, and I could do my phys — physical training — at home just as well as round the camp. Soon I had two circuits worked out — one of six miles, one of eight. Kath talked of getting a horse . . . if we could persuade the farmer to rent us a paddock, and after the baby had arrived.

Tim was born, on time, in the County Hospital in Hereford. I watched him come into the world, holding Kath's hand and trying to share her pain. He weighed 8 lbs 2 oz, and once he was cleaned up we could see he was going to have hair even fairer and eyes even bluer than his mother's. Kath's parents were so chuffed with their first grandchild that they came straight over from Belfast to see him; they stayed in the cottage, and Meg helped with the baby for a few days, until Kath got her strength back. Den, a retired doctor, didn't do much except offer medical tips — and I don't think he did much at home either, except watch television.

So we carried on, happy with each other. In the summer of 1990 I went to Africa with the squadron, on team training. We were away two months, but I got back to find everything just the same, and Kath and I carried on where we'd left off. It was only when Saddam invaded Kuwait, and D Squadron was deployed to the Gulf, that things began to go belly-up.

Leaving was tough. Before we flew out from Brize Norton at the start of January '91, Kath and I had some emotional moments trying to plan a future for her and Tim, in case I didn't come back. The house would be hers, of course, and she would be free to sell it if she wanted. But I told her it would be my wish that she should marry again, and that the kid should be educated as well she could afford, at some fee-paying school if no good state school was available. Such thoughts brought with them many tears, but we did our best to look the future in the face.

Next day we were gone. Before the war started I was able to phone Kath from time to time, from the R & R centres established in the desert, and everything was OK. The satellite connections were perfect, and it was like talking to her in the room next door. But once we deployed across the border into Iraq at the end of January there was no chance of further communication, and it wasn't until the ninth of April, when members of D Squadron were reunited in Cyprus on our way home, that I spoke to her again. And as it turned out, during those ten weeks — in the desert, in hospital, in prison — I'd been through quite a bit.

On the line to Akrotiri, Kath sounded very much herself — worried about me, lively, loving, full of news about Tim. It was I who had changed.

Like everyone else I looked forward to getting home; for weeks I'd yearned to be back in England. Yet when I reached Hereford, there was something wrong. I didn't go straight home. I didn't want to — couldn't face it. To my shame, I went out on the piss with a couple of the single lads who lived on the block. All *they* wanted was to have a few beers and go downtown to see if they could pick up a girl for the night. For me, things weren't so simple.

By the time I reached the cottage I wasn't making much sense. Kath looked terrific — I could see that in an objective sort of way — but she also looked shocked that I had arrived back in such a state. Tim had grown inches and was starting to talk. She'd taught him to say "Dad", and he brought the word out on cue. I should have been bowled over. Instead I felt nothing. It was extraordinary, but I didn't even feel randy. By then the other guys would have been randy as hell; during the flight they hadn't been able to stop talking about how they were going to screw their bollocks off the moment the Herc touched the tarmac. I should have been the same, but I didn't seem to fancy Kath any more. I couldn't make love to her; I could hardly kiss her on the cheek, or even look her in the eye. As for telling her what had happened to me — I just explained a bit about my arm, and skirted round the rest.

She was hurt, of course. Although she played it down, she couldn't conceal her worry and unhappiness. I think she hoped that time would heal the trouble between us, whatever it was, and after a while things would return to normal.

All along I knew that the fault lay with me, not her, and I tried to say so. But then began the nightmares and the headaches started. I started on the booze — something I'd never much bothered with before — and instead of mending, our relationship went further downhill, until we were making space round each other as we moved about the house, and hardly speaking.

When I went to the Med Centre in camp for checks on my arm I should have told the doc what was happening. But naturally I didn't want to reveal what seemed to be weaknesses. Like everyone in the Regiment, I wanted to get sent on operations: that was the whole point of life. To admit one had psychological problems was the surest way of missing some good trip, or even of blighting one's career completely and being put on the back burner. When the head-shed offered us the services of a shrink, nobody wanted to go near him.

The Paracetamol was starting to take effect. Slowly my head eased and some of the anxieties fell away. I heard the clock in the living room strike four, and that was all.

Next day was bright and brilliant, a glorious May morning. When I came into the kitchen, sunlight was already streaming across the table, and Tim's face, plastered with porridge, was such a sight I couldn't help smiling. But I felt terrible, hung over from the mixture of drinks that I'd poured down myself the night before.

As always, Kath had made proper coffee, and, as I got myself a cup, I announced, "I've come to a decision. I'm going to see the doc."

"Great!" Kath's face lit up. "See what he says. It can't do any harm."

"That's right. If I don't like it, I don't need to take any notice."

I was soon away, driving into town. She'd gone back to her job at the bank in the mornings, and was putting Tim into a tots' playschool. At lunchtime a friend gave them both a lift home, so all I had to do was drop them off on my way to the camp.

At Stirling Lines — named after David Stirling, who founded the SAS as a long-range desert group in Africa during World War Two — the usual two MoD Plods in uniform were on the gate. As I drove towards them they recognized me, waved and raised the barrier. In the car-park I found myself next to a mate from D Squadron, Pat Martin, who was just locking his Scorpio.

"Hi, Pat," I said. "Listen, will you tell Tom that I'm going to the Med Centre? I'll be up the Squadron later."

"No bother. Something the matter?"

"Just checking my arm."

It was coming up to 8.30. The rest of the guys would already be assembling in the Squadron Interest Room for Prayers — properly, roll-call and morning briefing. I knew that Tom Dawson, the sergeant major, would accept my message, and that I could square him later. One of the Old and Bold, he'd done more than fifteen years in the Regiment, and had seen it all — the tail-end of the Dhofar campaign, the Falklands, the Gulf. In the Falklands he'd been one of the few who survived the Sea King crash. Seventeen members of D and G Squadrons and half a dozen others were killed when the chopper went down in the sea on a cross-decking sortie. He'd told me he too suffered nightmares. He'd been unable to sleep in a dark room with the door shut; if ever he woke to find the door closed he'd leap up in a frenzy. His own experiences had made him sympathetic, and I knew he'd support me.

I headed straight for the Med Centre, hoping that Tracy Jordan would be on duty. There were two girls who took turns at the front desk, week on, week off. Sheila was small and dumpy, about as lively as a suet pudding, but Tracy was something else. Nearly six feet in her socks, with wild coppery curls tied in a top-knot that made her look even taller, she was all arms and legs, and at twenty-three or -four, still seemed like an overgrown filly. She was quite a well-known figure about camp because she was athletic, and was often to be seen running with a girl friend in the lunch hour. Rumour had it that she was a demon at squash; apart from being fit, she could stand in the centre of the court and scoop the ball out of the corners without having to move very far.

I knew practically nothing else about her. But I'd often noticed that her eyes carried a hint of suppressed merriment; this, combined with a tendency to make mildly piss-taking remarks, made a lot of the guys fancy her. But she had rumbled the bonk-and-be-off tactics of the Regiment long ago, and stuck to a boyfriend from outside. All the same, reporting sick was less of a drag if Tracy was on duty.

My luck was in. There she sat at her desk, in a snowy sweatshirt and pale blue jeans. Today the ribbon holding her top-knot was emerald green. Did her eyebrows go up as she saw me come in?

"Sergeant Geordie Sharp!" she announced in that

12

faintly mocking voice. "What can I do for you today?"

"Watch yourself," I told her.

"What do you mean?" She wriggled her slim little behind around on her chair in mock indignation.

"Just that," I said. "I need to see Doc Anderson."

"Major Anderson's off. It's Captain Lester."

"OK then."

"There's only one ahead of you. Take a seat. Shouldn't be long."

She rummaged in a filing cupboard for my documents, and handed me the brown manila packet. It didn't worry me that Anderson was away — I'd never got much change out of him. Maybe this new guy would be better.

I waited a couple of minutes, then the light above the door changed from red to green and I went in to find a young, fit-looking man with prematurely grey hair cut very short. He took a quick look at the outside of my packet and said, "Hello, George."

"It's Geordie," I told him. "My Christian name's George, but I never use it. Everyone calls me Geordie. My accent and all."

"OK." He gave a twitch of a grin, opened the packet and began to read the papers. "Injury to your left arm," he said. "Compound fractures of the humerus. Pinned and plated in an Iraqi hospital."

He pulled out an X-ray, fitted it into the front of a light-box on the wall, and studied it for a moment.

"Is that what's giving you trouble?"

"No, no. My arm's fine."

"Can I have a look?"

"Sure." I pulled up the sleeve of my sweater and laid my arm on the desk. He felt it carefully along the line of the scar and looked back at the X-ray.

"Tender?"

"Not too bad."

"Can you use it all right?"

"No bother."

"Turn your hand back and forth . . . open and close your fingers . . . Weights?"

"I've started again with light ones. Just building up."

"I see. How did you do it?"

"Came off my motor bike."

"Ah!" He took my wrist and sat silent for a moment, counting my pulse rate. I liked his direct, no-nonsense manner. Then he asked, "What's the matter, then?"

"Headaches," I said. "They're getting really bad. And I'm having nightmares that scare the shit out of me."

"Did you hit your head in the crash?"

"No — not that I know of. My head never gave any trouble at the time. This only started recently."

"Have you been taking anything?"

"Only the odd aspirin and Paracetamol."

"You're sure you haven't been concocting things out of your med pack? Some of you fellows are buggers for self-help, I know."

"No, no. I don't touch any of that."

"What about booze?"

"Well . . ."

"Are you drinking a lot?"

"A bit."

"How much?"

"Too much."

"OK."

He put me on the couch, brought out his stethoscope and listened to my heart. Then he took my blood pressure with the old arm clamp, looked into my ears and shone lights in my eyes. As he was working he said casually, "How did you come to fall off the bike?"

"It was at night. We were 150 kilometres inside Iraq, behind enemy lines, hitting the comms towers and blowing up fibre-optic lines. And we were on the lookout for mobile Scud launchers. That night the squadron was tasked to move up and find a new lying-up position in which to hide the following day. I was recceing forward on a motorbike. The ground was very rough — a lot of rocks and loose gravel, with sudden deep ditches. We started to see lights in the distance ahead — vehicles moving — and we accelerated to cut them off. I dropped into a bloody great hole — never saw it — and the bike came down on top of me. Smashed my arm against a rock."

"Then what?"

"If you're interested?"

"Sure."

"The guys picked me up and splinted the arm as best they could. Not a pretty sight. One end of the bone was sticking out through the muscle. They put me in the back of a Land Rover and called for a medevac. The head-shed in Saudi was co-ordinating rescue efforts with the Americans. They sent a message to say that a joint operation would be diverted to pick me up. A chopper would come in the following night, to lift me out along with two American casualties."

I paused and looked sideways at the doctor. He still seemed to be interested, so I went on. "That worked fine. We spent the day lying up in a wadi, and soon after dark the heli picked us up on time, with some SEAL guys riding security. But we'd been flying for no more than ten minutes when we were targeted by a SAM. One moment we were cruising steadily, then suddenly everything went crazy. Sirens blasted off, the chopper began to dive and twist in violent evasive manoeuvres, the pilot fired off his chaff in the hope of decoying the missile — but no luck. Suddenly there was this almighty bang. It felt as if the chopper had been hit sideways like a tennis ball. The next thing I knew there was another terrific impact, and we were on the ground. Tony, one of the SEALs, was dragging me out of the wreckage. When we made a check, we found we were the only two alive. The co-pilot had been decapitated. The pilot had lost both arms. What we couldn't understand was how the chopper hadn't caught fire. Soon we saw lights coming at us. Before we could get ourselves together we'd been surrounded by fifty or sixty Iraqis. We could have dropped one or two, but not dozens. So that was us captured."

I stopped. I was still lying on my back on the couch, talking up to the ceiling. I seemed to be out of breath. I realized that I'd been speaking faster and faster. I turned my head to the right and looked at the doc again. He was watching me carefully.

"Carry on," he said.

I looked back at the ceiling.

"I don't remember too much about the next bit. I already had a fever — must have got dirt into my arm, the wound was infected. Also I'd banged one of my morphine syrettes into my leg, and got some more from other guys, so I was quite dopey. They threw us into the back of a truck and drove for the rest of that night. We got to some military camp. They tried to interrogate me — I got slapped around the head a bit — but they could see I wasn't making much sense, and I didn't give them anything but my name and number. I stuck to my pre-arranged cover-story — that I was a medic, and I'd come out as part of a joint Anglo-US team to recover downed air-crew.

"Then we were rolling again, in some other wagon. That part's even hazier. I think I was delirious by that stage. The next thing I remember is lying on an operating table, with guys in green gowns and masks standing round. Jesus! I thought. What are they going to do to me? I tried to get up, but couldn't. I seemed to be strapped to the table. I was fucking terrified.

"Then this tall guy appeared beside me. He had no mask on, so I could see he had a thick, black moustache, just like Saddam. Under it he was smiling — a nasty, thin kind of smile. When he started to talk I was amazed, because he spoke fluent English.

"'I'm going to operate on your injured arm,' he said. 'But don't worry. I know what I am doing. I was trained in England at one of your best hospitals — the John Radcliffe, in Oxford.'

"For a moment I was reassured. I knew the Radcliffe,

and I reckoned the Iraqi must have been there; he couldn't have invented that name out of the blue. I think I said, 'Great!'.

"'Your English medical system is very good,' he went on. 'What is not so good is that you tell us lies about yourself. It is important for us to know which unit you belong to, Sergeant Sharp. Come now — we need to know.'

"I repeated my spiel about being a medic belonging to 22 Para Field Ambulance, the unit I'd invented. I could see he didn't believe me, and after a few other questions he asked sarcastically, 'Where is it based, this famous unit?'

"'Wroughton,' I replied, referring to the tri-service hospital in Wiltshire.

"He'd heard of Wroughton, because he'd been there while at Oxford. It made him pause, but not for long. All this time the lights were blazing down into my face. I was shuddering and sweating with the fever. Then with a sudden movement the Iraqi picked something up from a trolley beside him and held it over me.

"'You see this?' he said, and the half-smile had died from under his black moustache. 'This is a hypodermic syringe, full of anaesthetic. If I plunge the needle into your arm, it will put you out. But if I touch your eyeball with it, you will never see again.'

"'Bastard!' I told him.

"'So, what is your real unit, please?'

"'Bastard!' I shouted again.

"'Sergeant Sharp, this needle is very sharp. You like my little joke? You should laugh, to show you appreciate

Iraqi humour. We are a very humorous people. Now — if the needle goes into your eye, you will not feel much. But afterwards, I promise you, you will not see anything at all. Which is your master eye?'

"I knew what was coming next, so I held my mouth shut.

"'You don't know? Or you won't say? It doesn't matter. We'll assume your right eye is master, and start with that. Perhaps when that is gone, you will see sense with your left.'

"He held the syringe so close in front of my face that I couldn't focus on it any more. I struggled and fought to free my good arm and my legs. I think I shat myself. I yelled at the top of my voice, 'BASTARDS! The whole fucking lot of you are BASTARDS!'"

A noise somewhere close to me brought me back to Hereford. A loud knock had sounded on the door, which now burst open. Tracy's head appeared in the gap. The saucy look had gone from her face, and she was looking quite scared. "You lot all right in here?" she asked. "I thought the doc was getting attacked."

"It's OK." Doc Lester smiled. "The devils are coming out of him."

Tracy withdrew and I apologized for making such a noise. Once again I was soaked in sweat.

"Go on," the doctor said again.

"He did it three or four times. I don't know what happened in the end — whether I passed out, or whether he stuck the needle in my arm. I came round to find the operation done, and my arm in plaster."

"Whoever he was, he did a good job," said the doc. "Plated it, too. The X-rays show a perfect union."

"If ever I see him again I'll make the shit fly out of him."

Doc Lester took my wrist again and counted. "Your pulse-rate's gone from 64 to 180," he remarked. He looked once more at the X-ray. "And then you were in gaol?"

"Yes. Two weeks or so in the hospital, then five weeks in one prison or another, eating crap and feeling like death."

"But no torture?"

"It depends what you mean by torture. There was no systematic interrogation, but every now and then the guards would give us a kicking or a beating. And they'd hit us around with whips. There was one who'd come and tap on my plaster cast with a wooden stick, harder and harder, until I yelled. The worst thing was that we hadn't a clue about what was happening — in the war or anywhere else. The Iraqis kept giving us a load of shit about how the Coalition was losing, but we never heard any proper news."

"Who's 'we'?"

"Myself and Tony Lopez, the American SEAL on the medevac chopper that got shot down. His cover story was similar to mine, and when he stuck to it, the Iraqis eventually put us together. He's a great guy, Tony. Bags of guts. As it happens, he's coming here on selection any time now."

The doctor thought for a minute, then asked, "So now you're getting headaches? When did they start?"

"A couple of weeks ago. Also, I started getting this

recurrent nightmare. It's always more or less the same — a version of that scene in the hospital."

"I'm not surprised." The doc got up and walked to the window looking out. "I think you're suffering from delayed shock. It's stress brought on by what you went through. People in our profession are starting to talk about something called post-traumatic stress. It's to do with the after-effects of wounds and captivity — though nobody knows much about it yet. Have you seen a shrink?"

"No. They offered us one, but none of the guys fancied it."

"How about taking your troubles home? Have you talked to your mum, for instance?"

"I don't have one."

"Or your dad?"

"No. I'm an orphan."

"Oh." He picked up a sheet of paper from the desk and looked at it again. "I see. I'm sorry."

"No sweat."

"What about your wife?"

"That's the trouble." I sat up. "This is it, Doc. I can't talk to her."

"Why not?"

"I don't know. It's not her fault, it's mine. She hasn't changed, but I have. Could they have given me something in the prison?"

"Like what?"

"Something that would put me off her . . . that would kill my sex drive? Bromide or something?"

The doctor laughed, but not unkindly. "If they did they've got drugs the West has never heard of."

"So what's happened, then? I don't even fancy her any more. She gets on my nerves. Everything she says or does seems to jar. I used to love her, but I don't now."

"As I said, it's all down to delayed shock. The stress is catching up on you."

"So what can I do about it? The worst of it is, she's busting herself to look after me, but that only seems to make things worse. I don't want her around the place."

"You need a break. Do you have any children?"

"One. Tim — he's coming up for three."

"Does your wife have a family?"

"Yes. They're across the water, near Belfast."

"Could she go and stay with them for a while?"

"Well, I suppose so." I thought about it for a moment, and asked, "You mean, we have a trial separation?"

"That would make it into a bit of a drama. I wouldn't call it that. Just call it a break. You could try it for two or three weeks. It would give you a chance to sort yourself out. Meanwhile, I'll give you something to take. Two a day." He scribbled out a prescription and handed me the chit. "Take it easy," he said. "You'll be OK in a while. Try and ease off the booze, as well. That'll help."

"Thanks, Doc. Thanks for listening."

"It was a pleasure," he said. "I enjoyed hearing your story."

I stood up and headed for the door.

"That'll be £57.50," Tracy said as I came out.

"I'll send a cheque."

"Seriously, are you OK?" She uncrossed her long legs and stood up. She was almost as tall as me.

22

"More or less. I've been getting these headaches."

She came and stood close to me, looking into my face. "It's what happened over there, isn't it?"

"I guess so."

"Well — I'm sorry. I hope you're better soon. You probably need time to get over it."

"That's what the doc said."

"Good luck, then."

"Thanks, Tracy. Your medicine's as good as anybody's." I was going to give her a peck on the cheek, but at that instant the telephone rang.

After so much emotion, my Spanish course seemed deadlier than ever. There were eight of us studying, and the bait was the possibility that a team job might come up in Colombia, where the forces of law and order were fighting the drug barons in the war against cocaine. The thought of a trip to South America was certainly an incentive, but when it came down to the nitty-gritty — Jesus Christ! (Or, as they would say down there, *¡Jesu-Cristo!*) There I sat, struggling to concentrate on the strange words and pronunciation, while all the time my mind was on Kath and what I was going to tell her. What would my mates in the Squadron say if she went home? Would they write me off as a wanker? I supposed we could invent some problem — it was true that her mother was soon going into hospital for a hip replacement, and would need looking after for a while afterwards . . .

Our instructor was a flabby-looking major from the Education Corps, with thin, fair hair and a poncified accent. He could speak Spanish all right, but it was *quiero hablar* this and *más desfacio, por favor* that, until my headache was worse than ever, in spite of Doc Lester's magic pills. I stuck out the day, but only because the thought of facing Kath was worse.

When I got home that evening, I didn't say much at first. I repeated what the doc had told me about delayed reaction and the after-effects of stress, but I waited till Kath had tucked Tim up in bed before I nerved myself to put the knife in.

I was just going to get another Scotch, but stopped myself. She was standing at one of the units in the kitchen, chopping vegetables on a wooden board. I sat down at the table behind her and said, "Kath, I've had an idea."

"Oh yes?"

I told her what the doc had suggested. For a while she continued chopping. Then the movement of her hand ceased, but she didn't turn round. I thought she was crying. I knew I should go over and comfort her, take her by the shoulders, but the great block that had stifled my emotions wouldn't allow it. I sat there in agony until suddenly she turned on me, eyes blazing.

"So, it's a separation you want," she said bitterly.

"No, no. Just a break."

"A trial separation is what they call it."

"Well — whatever."

"There's only one thing I want to know."

"What's that?"

"Is there someone else?"

24

I was so taken aback I hesitated before answering and, naturally, that made things worse. "No, no!" I insisted. "There's nobody."

"Are you sure?"

"Of course. For God's sake!"

I can't deny that my mind flew straight to Tracy — but nevertheless what I'd said was true.

Kath waited a moment, chopping away again at her vegetables, before she asked, "How do I know Mum will have us? You realize she's going into the Musgrave any moment? She can't put it off — she's been waiting for years."

"Of course. I know. I thought maybe it would be a good idea if you were there to give her a hand when she comes out."

"Big deal! How long am I supposed to go for?"

"It depends. Maybe a month."

"What's everyone going to say?"

"We'll put it round that your mum needs help after her operation."

"I can see you've thought it all out."

"Kath — it's my fault, I know. I'm not blaming you. It's all down to me."

She gave me a strange look. I think she was more scared than angry.

"I'll have to hand in my notice at the bank."

"I know. But that's not the end of the world. I'll be able to send money."

"Who'll look after you if I go?"

"I'll manage. I can get most meals in camp."

When she looked round again, her eyes were full of

tears, and she said, half in pity, half in contempt, "You poor old thing!"

The bank took her resignation in good part, and we arranged for her to go the following Saturday. Her mother positively welcomed the plan, although she didn't know what was behind it, of course. The movements clerk in camp booked air tickets — two out of my allocation of three — so that there was no cost to us. Kath didn't take much luggage — one suitcase for herself and a holdall for Tim. As for Tim, if he'd cried as they were leaving, I think I'd have cracked up; thank God he didn't. We'd told him he was going for a holiday with his Gran, and that chuffed him no end. He began packing his favourite teddies and telling everyone how the aeroplane would lift them up over the water and come down in Gran's house.

We left KC at 6.30 on another lovely morning. Both of us were holding emotion at bay by keeping up a strictly practical front. As Kath got into the car she said, "Don't forget to single the carrots when they're big enough, in about a week. Leave them spaced at one every couple of inches, and push the earth well down afterwards. Otherwise carrot fly will get in."

As we headed for Birmingham, our side of the motorway was almost empty; at the weekend, most people were going south. We didn't talk much, and when I set the two of them down at the departure door of the terminal building, it was just a quick kiss on the cheek and, "We'll speak soon, then". As I drove away I turned my head and saw little Tim waving.

CHAPTER
TWO

Tony was due in from the SEAL base in Florida one evening towards the end of June. The US military flight was scheduled to arrive at RAF Lyneham at 1630, so I borrowed a car from the MT section and drove up the A40 to give him a lift to Hereford. When it turned out that the plane was an hour late, I sat around in the arrivals lounge and had plenty of time to reflect on our conversations in the Iraqi gaol.

Born in Puerto Rico, the son of an electrician, he had one brother. When he was five, his father had decided to take the family to America, in search of a better life for them all. As they were leaving, the father said they were going because America was the land of opportunity. But things didn't work out well for them. They ended up living in a Hispanic area of New York, and after a couple of years Tony's father died, so his mother was left to bring up the two boys on her own. By the time Tony left school he'd been stabbed twice and shot once, all in casual muggings. Prospects of civilian work were zero, so as soon as he was old enough he joined the US Marine Corps, and after two or maybe three years went on into the Navy SEALs.

In 1989 he'd taken part in Operation Just Cause, aimed at removing President Noriega from Panama. A team of four divers was to put explosive charges on Noriega's 65-foot patrol boat, the *Presidente Porras*, so that the vessel couldn't be used to escape. Having left their own ship in two Gemini inflatables, they slipped into the harbour in wetsuits with enough oxygen to give them four hours underwater. Once they'd identified the boat, they hung 24-lb timed charges of plastic explosive over the propellers before returning undetected to their mother ship.

As they were leaving, they heard the explosives go off, and knew the patrol boat was out of action for the duration, if not for ever. The success put them on a high as they flew off by helicopter for their second task — to capture Paitilla airfield, not far from Panama City, and to disable a Lear jet owned by Noriega.

The platoon were so confident about their plan that they saw no need to take heavy weapons; they thought they could accomplish the task by stealth — sneak in, take out a few guards, and have the airfield under their command. But as their choppers approached they started to take incoming fire. Too late they realized that the place was full of Noriega's troops, armed with heavy weapons. The SEALs eventually managed to capture the field, but only at severe cost. In the firefights, which were fearsome, they suffered eleven casualties, four of them dead. Among those four were three of Tony's good mates. And so he learnt how easily an operation can go tits-up, ending in a bag of shit.

At last the tannoy announced the arrival of the flight,

and in came the C-141 from Florida. A few minutes later Tony burst out of the Customs exit, with a pack on his back and a big holdall in his left hand. When he saw me waiting, his face lit up. "Well, I'll be damned!" he exclaimed, hammering me on the shoulder with his free fist.

"You're looking good!" I said.

"You too."

He'd put on weight — which was hardly a surprise, considering he'd been half-starved the last time I saw him. Now he was fit and bronzed, altogether in great shape. His tan accentuated the Puerto Rican elements in his appearance. With his jet-black hair and thick, arched eyebrows he was very dark anyway, almost swarthy; now his skin was even darker, and his teeth, when he grinned, shone even whiter. His hard New York accent was just as I remembered it: "work" came out as "woik", "person" as "poyson".

The OC had asked me to help him settle in, so on his first night I showed him round the camp before leaving him to have a shower and get his head down until the jet-lag wore off. On the second evening I drove him out to Keeper's Cottage, and on the way I decided to break the news about me and Kath. I could have kept up the pretence that she'd gone home to look after her mother, but I'd got to know Tony so well that I didn't feel like trying to deceive him. Of course he'd never seen her, but I'd talked so much about her while we were guests of Saddam that he must have felt he knew her well.

"Hey," he said when he heard. "That's too bad. But you'll get her back over."

It was a statement, rather than a question.

"Maybe," I said. "I've chilled out a good bit since she went away."

"You'll want to see the kid, anyway."

Again I knew he was right.

The rain was pissing down, so KC didn't look its best, but Tony fell for it, drenched as it was. He kept saying, "This is real neat!" and started on about the possibilities of hunting. He seemed surprised I hadn't been out blasting the local wildlife. "Why, I bet you could hunt squirrels right in back here," he said, looking up at the oak spinney.

"Oh, yeah. There's plenty of them. Rabbits too."

"Who's the gardener?" he asked, surveying the unkempt forest of vegetables.

"Kath. I haven't a clue. Every time we speak on the phone she tells me to do this or that — earth up the spuds or thin out the lettuces — but I just don't have the time."

Indoors, the first thing Tony saw was a photo of her and Tim, taken recently in fine weather on the shore of Strangford Lough, with a background of water and smooth green islands. Kath was wearing a blue check dress and Tim, in a pale blue T-shirt and grey shorts, was standing on a stone wall, so his head was nearly level with hers. The picture had arrived only the day before, and I'd stuck it on the mantelpiece in the living room.

"But she's beautiful!" said Tony. "And so's he. Some kid, that. What is he now? Three?"

"And a bit."

"You sure must be proud of them."

I made some noncommittal noise and went into the kitchen to open a window. The whole cottage smelt stuffy. Tony realized the place was in a mess — I watched his dark eyes checking things, saw him run a finger through the dust on the table-top — but he was too tactful to say anything about it. I poured a couple of Scotches and we settled down for some crack.

"So how's things?" he asked.

"Improving. I had a low patch when I couldn't get myself together at all. I was getting bad headaches and recurring nightmares about Iraq. I went on the piss — but I was so zonked I couldn't even bring myself to go downtown with the guys. Instead I was buying cans of Stella, twenty-four at a time, and drinking them here on my own with Scotches in between. But I'm over that now. No more headaches. Nightmares gone. Everything's fine, except for this damned course."

"What's that?"

"This language course. There's a possibility of a team job in Colombia, so there's ten of us learning Spanish."

"No kidding! You realize Spanish is my first language?"

"I knew you spoke it."

"Sure do. My mom and dad always talked Spanish at home, and I grew up with it. I expect it would sound like shit to people in Madrid, but it's Spanish all the same."

Looking out of the window, he fired off a rapid sentence. "Get that?"

"Only that it was something about the weather."

"Correct. I asked if it always pisses with rain during the British summer."

"*¡Siempre!*" I had to think. "*¡Sin falta!*"

"Boy! You got it!"

"I fucking haven't, Tony. That's the trouble. I'm finding it a real hassle. Our final tests are coming up in a couple of weeks, too."

"Well. You just gotta fight and get through them. I guess I've been fighting to survive ever since I was a kid."

Soon we made a plan. Tony was already very fit; on the initial stages of the selection course, over the Welsh mountains, he would have little trouble in purely physical terms. But I knew what a help it would be to him if he learnt the routes over the Brecon Beacons in advance: that way, he would have a big advantage if the weather turned bad or fog came down. So I offered to walk some of the ground with him, and in return, while we were tabbing, he would give me informal Spanish lessons, to increase my fluency and confidence. The deal suited us both.

We were still talking as dusk set in, and I began to wish I'd done something about supper. Over the past few weeks I'd been picking up takeaways on my run home, or else making do with a jacket potato baked in the microwave. Now I remembered that in Iraq, as we ate shitty rice and lusted after our favourite dishes, Tony had described how he liked to cook.

"You hungry?" I asked.

"Sure."

"Want to try your hand in the kitchen? I don't know what there is, but have a look."

A search in the cupboards revealed nothing but a few tins of baked beans and a packet of spaghetti. Fuelled by the Scotch, Tony launched a tirade against my housekeeping.

"Jesus!" he exclaimed. "There ain't enough here to feed a goddam mouse! You can't have been shopping in decades. No garlic. No tomato paste. No chilli. No nothing."

"Our prospects improved when he found a bottle of olive oil and a tin of anchovies in the larder. He went into the garden with a torch and returned with a bucket full of spinach, the dark green leaves glistening with rain. Soon we were eating fishy, oily, peppery spaghetti, which we pretended was a traditional Puerto Rican recipe, and spinach pureed with butter, salt and pepper, which I had to admit was outstanding. Tomorrow, Tony promised, we would pay a joint visit to the supermarket and put the kitchen in order.

Three days later we drove out to the Beacons. In his regular training Tony had started to hump loads in his bergen: he hadn't been used to it, but I told him it was essential to build up slowly to the 55 lbs that he would have to carry during the four weeks of hill-walking which formed the first part of the selection course. For our first recce, however, we took only light day-sacks containing a couple of sandwiches and a waterbottle apiece.

Needless to say, rain was falling, and the clouds were touching the tops of the mountains. I parked the car in a lay-by on the B-road that runs along the side of the Talybont reservoir, so that we could get a look at the map while we were still in the dry. Tony had a hell of a pair of boots — high-leg, black leather Matterhorns lined with Goretex — and as he was lacing them up I twisted the map round until it was aligned with the compass.

"On test week you'll be walking all round this area," I told him, pointing with the blade of my clasp-knife. "We'll start off up the side of the wood here, and get on to these ridges. This is the first part of the Endurance route, and you do it at night, starting out at 0300. Once you get on to the high ground the going's easy. It's just a matter of snaking round the ridges. You're aiming for the summit of Pen-y-Fan . . . here. Highest point in the Beacons, and the centre of our universe. It's said that every guy in the Regiment has the outline of the Fan graven on his heart.

"What we'll do is come round the ridge here, across the feature known as the Windy Gap, then up a horrendous climb known as Jacob's Ladder. You almost have to use your hands to go up. The path's been eroded out of the clay and you're on the edge of some jagged rocks, which fall away to your right. On Endurance you're supposed to average four ks an hour, but on the ladder you come to a grinding halt. That's why you have to run down the hills. In fact, the guys start jogging the moment they get on to any downward slope.

"Anyway, the ladder takes us up the back of the Fan to the summit. Then we drop down here, skirt round the flank of Corn Du and head for the obelisk . . . here. After that we swing away on this path, and come down to the Storey Arms on the main road. Used to be a pub, but now it's an outdoor education centre. Cross the road, and we'll climb up on to Fan Fawr. The spot height there's one of your check-points, and it's quite difficult to find. The course then takes you right away to the Cray Reservoir, in the distance to the west, but we haven't got time for that today.

"This last stretch before the Cray is bloody horrible. First there's miles of moon grass, all tussocks. Then there's this sod of a wood." I pointed to a triangular plantation cradled in a bowl of steep slopes. "It's a hell of a long way round the wood, but going through it's a bugger because of all the drainage ditches. So either way you're in the shit. But, as I say, we won't get that far today. What we'll do is cross the road again at the AA box, here, and climb back over. Then we'll go down through the woods to the reservoir, and the dam on which the route ends."

"Looks like some hike," said Tony.

"It is. Even with our light loads it'll take all day."

We sorted our gear, locked the car and set off. As I expected, Tony moved easily, economically. He could have left me on the climbs, but that day we weren't racing. Going up the steep lower flank of the Fan, we had no breath to spare for talking; Tony's only utterance was one sudden, good-humoured outburst: "Nothing but rain, stone walls and goddam sheep!"

But then, as we came out on to the ridges, the weather began to break. The rain stopped, the clouds parted, and we started to see great green slopes sweeping away below us on either side. Our spirits lifted, and Tony set in to talk Spanish, slowly and methodically, asking questions about the landscape, describing things we could see.

To my surprise, I found I could understand him pretty well, and answers came more easily than I'd expected. Alone with a good friend, and having no reason to feel embarrassed, I found that my confidence built quickly. All the lessons of the past few weeks began to fall into place, and at last the language was making sense. More than that, I found it a pleasure to use.

By the time we'd scrabbled our way up Jacob's Ladder and reached the summit of the Fan the sun had come out, so we sat by the trig stone to eat our sandwiches. When Tony described the scenery as "real pretty" I didn't argue. I realized that, to him, used to the huge open spaces of America, the whole environment seemed dinky and small-scale — and on that hazy summer's day the Brecons were looking their most serene. This, the highest point, might be only 3,000 feet above sea-level, but I knew what the hills could be like when they showed their teeth in the wind and sleet of a winter night. "The obelisk's a memorial to a little boy who died up there one August," I said. "It was in 1900, and he was trying to cross from one farm to another when the fog came down. Tommy Jones, he was called. It was twenty-nine days before they found him, curled up in a hollow where the pillar now stands."

From our vantage-point I explained how important it was to try to maintain our height on the way back across Fan Fawr, before the inevitable steep descent to the checkpoint by the AA box on the main road. "Thereafter, the route to trig-point 642 is really tough, an absolute ball-breaker: whichever way you go, you can't avoid fierce climbs and drops."

We could just make out 642 in the distance to the south. I told Tony that the stone bears a brass plaque in memory of Tony Swerzy, a member of the SAS killed on the Everest expedition of 1984.

And so we went on again, and kept going for the rest of that hazy summer afternoon.

Tony had been allotted a room in camp, but I suggested he might like to spend some nights in the cottage — an offer which he took up with alacrity. Apart from providing cheerful company, he raised culinary standards no end, as baked beans on toast gave way to steaming paella and chilli con carne. He had a heavy hand with the Tabasco, but that suited me fine, and one evening I was inspired to retaliate with the one sure weapon in my armoury, a curry as hot as Hades.

We went up to the Brecons several more times, and spent a couple of weekends walking some of the other routes, including Point-to-Point and Pipeline. We also went over the course for the Heavy Carry day — and with every outing I was improving my fluency in conversational Spanish.

The language course was a tough one, especially for guys like us who were used to a mainly physical existence. Our facilities were good — we had videos, audio-tapes and a separate audio-lab for making tapes of our own if we wanted — but the hours were long, and the lessons demanded a high level of concentration. We kicked off at 9.00 a.m., with the desks in the classroom set out in a horseshoe shape. Round the walls were big posters illustrating various weapons and armoured vehicles, with captions and statistics in Spanish. The poncified major in the Education Corps taught us grammar, and later in the mornings a Colombian professor would come up from Cardiff University to give us conversation. She'd chat to each of us in turn, starting off with *"Buenos dios. ¿Tiene hora?"* and we'd answer, *"Si, señora, son las doce menos cuatro"*, or whatever. The woman was a fearsome age, and knee-high to a piss-pot, but she had a great sense of humour, and generally turned the conversation into areas of interest to us: *"¿Hay un bar por aquí?"* and so on.

By 12.30 everyone would be desperate to clear their heads, so it was into shorts, singlets and trainers and away for a run, five or six miles round the lanes at the back of the camp. On wet days some of the guys preferred a session on the weights in the gym. Then a quick shower, into DPMs again, and a dash down to the NAAFI for a sandwich or a pie, before being back into the classroom for 2 o'clock. By about 3.30 I'd see some of the guys dozing off. They'd have their heads propped in their hands, ostensibly concentrating like hell on their books, but then suddenly a hand would slip and a head would lurch downwards, and the owner would wake up with a start. By the time classes ended at 4.30, we'd all had enough — but then we had a pile of homework to take back with us.

Several months previously I'd applied to go on the Northern Ireland course, and now, one morning after Prayers in the Squadron Interest Room, the SSM said, "Right, as soon as we're finished here, I want to see the following in my office." He read out a list of names, and mine was on it.

In we went, one at a time. Tom was sitting at his desk in one corner of the little room, and the squadron clerk was pattering away at his word-processor in the other.

"OK, Geordie," the SSM began. "You want to go to the NI Troop?"

"Right."

"We've got you down for troop training, starting July twentieth. You OK with that?"

"Yep. That's fine."

"Good. You want to get yourself down to see Johnny Hopton, who's running the course. Find out if there's any particular preparation you can do beforehand. Are you happy with that?"

"That's fine.

"Right, then. You start on the twentieth."

I went out feeling chuffed to bollocks. Everyone wanted to get on the NI course, because a posting to Ulster meant live operations, rather than the endless training which otherwise was the Regiment's lot in peacetime. Ulster meant danger, excitement and the chance to take on a real enemy. I knew that the posting was partly a question of seniority — the head-shed probably needed a couple of sergeants on the course — but I also knew they must have got together and talked about possible candidates, and I was glad to know they hadn't been put off by my low patch after the Gulf.

The idea of a tour in Northern Ireland naturally made me think more than ever of Kath and Tim. What would happen if they were in Belfast and I got posted there?

Would I be able to go and visit them, or would they be out of bounds? The possibility was way off, but I checked — and the answer was that, yes; guys in the troop were allowed to make social visits, provided the area was safe.

The training course would last four months. As I thought of my family, that suddenly began to seem a long time. I found I was missing them, and began to wonder if I should ask Kath to come back. Her mother had had her hip operation in the Musgrave, and it had been a success. The hospital had sent her home after only a week, and Kath's presence had turned out to be a bit of a godsend. But now that Meg was almost fully mobile again, and out of pain, there was no reason from her point of view why Kath shouldn't come home.

I would have to admit to everyone — Kath, her parents, and above all myself — that I'd made a big mistake. It wasn't exactly a question of swallowing my pride; I didn't feel proud at all — anything but. Rather, it was a question of being certain that I wasn't going to make things worse by dragging Kath and Tim home. If they did come back, and I got posted across the water, we'd be separated again anyway for the whole year of the tour . . . The permutations went round and round in my mind. Take action? Or wait some more?

When we sat our final test on the Spanish course, my confidence had built up to a new high, largely because of Tony. Thanks to our conversations, not even the prospect of giving a lecture to the rest of the course could faze me. I stood up and talked for three minutes about the relative merits of Real Madrid and Arsenal as if I was the greatest soccer pundit on the Costa. Besides the talk, we had to answer questions about a video we'd been shown, act as interpreter in a conversation between the Colombian woman and a third party, and write a description of our favourite holiday resort. I chose Corfu, and gave it the works. Next morning, I was amazed to see my name at the top of the list of passes.

That night I phoned Kath and told her the news. She sounded bright and lively, full of the joys of summer. They'd been out somewhere along the coast, and Tim had been paddling in the sea. He was talking a lot now and he'd been asking where his dad was.

As she talked, the idea I'd been holding back for weeks swept over me. On impulse I said, "Listen, Kath. How about coming back?"

I heard her draw in her breath. There was a pause.

"Why not try it?" I urged.

Then she said, "Geordie! You mean it?"

"Of course. I'm a whole lot better. I'm back to normal. Off the booze altogether. Things don't seem right without you."

She must have burst into tears. Half a minute passed, and I could hear snuffling sounds.

"Kath — are you there?"

"Yes. Geordie?"

"What?"

"I'm dying to see you."

"Great! Come on over, then."

"Of course I'll come. But listen."

"What?"

I heard her blow her nose. "Mum's had to go back into hospital. She's been getting pain down her leg. We're hoping it's nothing serious, but the implant could have shifted, and they want her in for a few days' observation. I've told her I'll be here to look after her when she comes out. I won't be able to make it for a couple of weeks."

"Not to worry. I can wait. As long as I know you're on your way."

"Have you pinched the tops off the beans yet?"

"Yes," I said, telling a white lie. "I did that."

"Brilliant," she said. "Lots of love, Geordie."

"Same to you."

As soon as I put the phone down, I whipped out into the vegetable patch. Jesus, I thought, I've boobed here. The fucking beans were nearly up to my shoulder and covered with big white flowers! The smell was enough to stop you in your tracks. What was I supposed to do? Pick the flowers off? No — that would take forever. "Pinch the tops off," she'd said. But where did the top begin? What was top and what was stalk? There seemed to be bunches of buds all the way up. In the end I thought, To hell with it, and went along the rows nipping four or five inches off the top of each plant, and hoping the damn things would survive.

CHAPTER
THREE

The NI course was an eye-opener to all twelve of us who took it. Most of it happened at the Llangwern Army Training Area, known as LATA, just a few miles into Wales. Because it was so close, we carried on living where we were, in and around camp, and drove there and back every day.

On the first morning we went down in a coach, and spent the day getting issued with all manner of fancy kit, not least cars. There was a pool of cars which lived at LATA, and they were handed out to us like toys — one to every two or three of us for the duration of the course. I was given the keys of a dark-blue Cavalier, which I shared with Pat Martin. Like all the other cars, it was quite a sporty beast but inconspicuous; that was the point — it was fast enough to get us out of trouble but didn't stand out or attract attention. The guy who handed it over told me I would be responsible for maintaining it in good nick, and for bringing it into the MT section if any problem needed sorting out. Then he added, "This one goes all right — but wait till you get across the water and try the intercept cars. They're something else."

The other goodies we got on day one included our

waistcoats — one operational, one for civilian clothes. The ops waistcoat was designed to keep everything off the wearer's legs: it had pockets for radio, spare magazines and grenades, and a built-in holder for a secondary weapon, the handgun. There were also places for plasticuffs and torches — all the little knick-knacks — and inside pockets to hold your orange armband and baseball cap with ARMY written on it, so that in any contact you could instantly turn yourself into a member of the security forces.

The civilian waistcoat had a place for a covert radio, which you worked with a small earpiece, a mike taped to your chest, and a pressel switch in one pocket, so that you could communicate without appearing to move. The drill was to carry a pistol — probably a Walther PPK, generally known as your disco gun — about your person. If you wore a T-shirt next to the skin and another shirt over it, a bit loose, nobody would spot anything.

Most of LATA lay on one side of a main road, shielded from passing traffic by a high wire fence and an evergreen hedge. As somebody gleefully pointed out, the designers of the fence had screwed up, tilting the two-foot overhang of barbed wire inwards rather than outwards, as if its function was to stop people getting out, rather than vice-versa. "It's like it used to be in East Fucking Germany," said Pat as he surveyed it contemptuously. "Anything to stop the bastards getting out."

Pat was like that. A big, solidly built fellow much into weight-lifting, he had ruddy cheeks and brown eyes as shiny as horse-chestnuts. He was forever laughing and joking, and never failed to come up with some cheerfully obscene comment — a typical Cockney, always ready with a blast of effing-this and effing-that, enough to startle strangers. Whenever faced with a surprise or setback, his verbal reaction was so explosive that people who didn't know him thought he was volatile and highly-strung. But really that was just his way of letting off steam, and underneath he was as solid as a rock.

His bulk was deceptive, too. At your first sight of him you might think he was muscle-bound. Far from it — he could do 100 metres in 11 seconds, as well as being able to throw small guys over walls and suchlike — a very useful attribute when you're on the counter-terrorist team and things get physical. He and I hadn't had much to do with each other before the course, but at LATA we teamed up and found we could work well as a pair.

The training area itself consisted largely of rough fields running up to meet Prescott's Wood, a big stand of trees that covered the sides and top of a rounded hill, with a road winding through it, ideal for ambushes and illegal VCPs (vehicle control points). The fields looked more or less like neglected farmland, but they included a few surprises. There were several ranges, outdoors and in. The Garaback, for instance, was a two-storey building which had the walls of its rooms lined with steel sheets and rubber matting, so that live rounds would go through the rubber and drop down without ricocheting.

The course began gently with sessions on lock-picking. These took place in a special room packed with locks of every kind — doorlocks, padlocks, everything — plus a key-cutting machine, for us to use to manufacture our own. Outside we learnt to open cars with a slim jim, a long sliver of metal like a ruler, with hooks on it and small sections cut out.

Something else new to me was photography. We were taught to use cameras with short-focus lenses, for recording serial numbers of weapons and suchlike, and also telephoto monsters, for taking covert long-range pictures of people who might be players. We developed, printed and blew up our own shots in the darkroom on site.

At the same time, we did exercises like Kim's game, in which we were each given a bunch of mug-shots to study, and then, in a live parade, asked to identify any of the faces we'd been looking at. It was drummed into us that our lives might depend on recognizing a key player at a key moment.

A more active pursuit was fast driving, for which the police came down and took us out one-to-one. Most of us were already pretty competent, but we all got sharpened up. We put in big mileage on narrow country roads, such as we'd be using in Ireland, and learned to drive fast but safely. Then they took us to a big municipal car-park, empty in the early hours of the morning, where we used vehicles fitted with a special attachment — a frame which was mounted under the car, like a cradle on small wheels, with hydraulic controls that enabled the instructor to take most of the weight off the tyres. My teacher had a dial with a scale of one to five, and at five the Cavalier became like a turd on black ice, spinning at the slightest provocation. Here we learnt J-turns, yanking on the handbrake to spin the car in its own length.

The best session, though, was on the morning the police took us to a breaker's yard and we bought a load of old bangers for about £50 apiece, to practise ramming. To get out of an illegal VCP or knock a hostile vehicle off the road you need to know what you're doing, and for half a day we behaved like lunatics in full-sized dodgems, hammering the shit out of each other.

Another big issue was weaponry, principally the G3s, the Heckler & Koch 7.62mm rifles which are the standard weapon in Northern Ireland. With a magazine holding twenty rounds, and an excellent mechanism that hardly gives any stoppages, the G3 is ideal for firing into cars, since its penetration is far greater than that of the lower-powered Armalite. The longs (rifles are known as "longs", pistols as "shorts") at LATA were numbered with white paint on the butt, and I got No. 7, which I always reckon is lucky for me. Each of us also got an HK 53, a smaller, neater rifle, .556 calibre, good for tucking under the front seat of a car; and a Sig — properly a Sigsauer P 226 — a 9mm pistol, accurate and reliable, and not prone to stoppages. We were told to carry weapons on exercises, just to get used to them, but at night they went into a lock-up in a classroom, and it was the duty-sergeant's job to make certain they were secure.

At that time the situation in Ulster was pretty bad, and almost every day there was news on TV or in the papers of another atrocity. One afternoon not long into the course the daily programme billed a brief on the political background in Northern Ireland, and the way special forces fitted into the fight against terrorism. Before the lecture, nobody seemed to rate the importance of this topic very highly; the afternoon was fine and hot — definitely not the sort of conditions for sitting in a Portakabin classroom — and a couple of the lads tried to skive off on some pretence. But the moment the talk started, everybody was hooked.

The speaker introduced himself as Chief Superintendent James Morrison of the Royal Ulster Constabulary. He was quite an elderly guy, grey haired, grey faced, grey suited, grey all over. Even his voice was grey: a monotone so quiet it was difficult to hear. He perched his arse on the front of the table and spoke without props, notes or gestures; yet what he said had us leaning forward in our seats.

"It's war you're going to," he began. "It's war and nothing else, so it is. It's been going on for twenty-five years, and I've been in it all that time. I still don't understand Northern Ireland, and I never will. But I do believe we'd be doing a lot better if we'd dropped more of the enemy on operations. I wouldn't send somebody out just to shoot three or four of them; but on specific operations, of which we've had knowledge, it would have put a heck of a lot of fear into them if we'd killed a few more. I shouldn't be saying this to yous fellers but, flip, I am."

That had us fairly hooked, and nobody moved as he went on to outline the way special forces fitted into the campaign against terrorism, in combination with the green army, the RUC, Special Branch and various other intelligence organizations. He then sketched in the nature and behaviour of the IRA. He described how the original IRA, known as the Stickies, had turned away from violence and become doves. Today's hawks were the Provisional IRA, or PIRA (in his accent, "Payra"). He sketched their organisation: at the top, the Army Council, and under that the Northern and Southern Commands — one for Ulster, one for the Republic. The task of the Southern Command was to organize terrorist attacks on the mainland. In the north there were three brigades, sub-divided into small cells known as ASUs, or Active Service Units, which formed the core of IRA activity.

Fragmentation was the name of their game, he said. Each cell probably consisted of only three or four people: a bomber, a shooter, a driver, and maybe one other. Very often they did not know each other; they didn't even know their colleagues' names. The intention was that if anyone was caught, it was impossible for him to give anyone else away. Fragmentation also made life more difficult for the informers — or touts — who might squeal on one phase of a job, but would rarely be able to find out about the operation as a whole.

Morrison told us how the players spent their lives targeting policemen, endlessly trying to pick them up as they left work and follow them back to their homes. "I tell you — just the other day they targeted one of my officers. I'll call him John. The man came home from work at eleven o'clock at night. He hadn't been indoors a minute before a call came from a friend in Special Branch. 'Look, John,' says the caller, 'close your curtains. There's somebody in your back garden. Don't worry — they're ours. If anyone comes to your front door in the next few minutes, let them in, and they'll look after you.'

"Sure enough, more people came. They stayed the night. They told John that some form of attack on him was imminent. They expected it to be a UCBT — an under-car booby trap — and they had people outside ready to grab the bomber. They waited all night, and no one came. Something had spooked them. All the same, John had to move house . . . "

On and on went the hypnotic voice, telling us about deep hides, concreted over or sealed into houses behind false walls, where quartermasters would store weapons and ammunition for months or even years. We heard of transit hides, less elaborate caches, where one man would deposit a weapon and another would collect it to do a particular shooting. He told us how the IRA staged burglaries to decoy the police into killing areas, and how they themselves would never risk firing a rifle or a rocket from a position that didn't afford them a clear escape route.

"There's another thing as well now: they're into drugs. I know this won't really concern yous guys — it's the business of other agencies — but you'd better be aware of it. The PIRA always needs money, for weapons and explosives and whatever, and, as you know, there's tremendous money in drugs. So they're into narcotics too, bringing in drugs from the south, and distributing them on."

The chief paused, looking round at all of us, and then said by way of summing up: "Oh yes, they're the most cunning bastards on earth. They're good bastards in their way and, flip, you underestimate those feckers at your peril."

He stopped, and everyone sat silent. Then a voice from the floor asked, "Do you hate them?"

"Hate them?" The speaker seemed to reflect for a moment, then his voice grew suddenly louder. "Yes, I truly hate them, the murdering, treacherous, lying bastards. I've seen one of my young officers cut down by them in the prime of his life. I've heard his little boy asking when his daddy's coming home, and somebody telling him his daddy won't be getting up anymore, because he's there in his coffin. When that happens to a family, it's terrible, and you don't ever forget it."

The speaker was staying that night in the officers' mess in camp, and after the talk he was invited there for a drink. We drove back to Hereford, showered, changed, and piled into the mess for a couple of beers and some polite conversation. With no particular motive — merely to socialize — I asked the chief if by any chance he'd met my father-in-law, who was quite well-known as a GP around his area of East Belfast. It turned out that the two hadn't come across each other, and there was no connection; but in the long-term that chance contact was to have far-reaching effects.

The brief on Northern Ireland had brought the course into sharp focus, and when we began doing car-drills for VCPs and ambushes; the guys went into everything with new fervour. Reg Brown, our new instructor (himself from the Regiment), drummed into us the fact that when we drove towards a normal VCP, dressed in civilian clothes and in a civilian car, the green soldiers manning the barrier would naturally take us for Irishmen. It was therefore necessary to have all weapons stowed well out of sight, and to let the guys know covertly that we were from the security forces. The way to do this was to keep our ID cards inside our Northern Ireland driving licences, so that when a driver showed his licence the guard would open it up and see the card. Then, if he was properly trained, he would chat for a minute, say, "Fine," and hand the licence back, and we'd be smoothly on our way. Anyone watching would take us for normal punters.

That was the drill for a normal VCP. But it was also likely, Reg told us, that we would come across illegal check-points, set up by the players in Catholic areas as shows of strength, to demonstrate to the locals that they were in charge. "If you see it early enough," he told us, "spin out and disappear. If you're already into it, keep calm, drive on, but slow down as if you're going to stop. Stay in low gear, and make sure your pistol's to hand in the right-hand door-well. As the guy comes towards you, to ask who you are, wind the window down, grab the pistol and whack him. Then, if there's no barrier ahead, accelerate hard and use the car as a weapon to hit any other players who may be on the road.

"If the road's blocked, start off the same. The driver drops the first guy, but at the same time the passenger starts putting down a massive amount of fire on his side. The two guys in the back debus, go wide, and put down more fire. The front two jump out, move back through the others, and put down rounds themselves. All four of you pepperpot back into a line, and then assess the situation. If you've taken out two or three of the players, and there are only four or five altogether, the commander may take the decision to move forward and finish them off. Also, of course, you've got your radios, and by now you will have called for assistance . . ."

Much of our training took place in Prescott's Wood, where everything was pretty realistic. We built OPs by digging in, carefully disposing of the soil, and meticulously roofing the hides with branches, turf, dead grass and leaves so that no sign of disturbance was visible. From those vantage points we had to keep watch on spots like culverts, in which (according to one scenario) a bomb had been hidden, and report any activity that had taken place in the area. We also had to fight our way out of ambushes laid on by guys from the Regiment, who would open the proceedings by throwing a petrol bomb into the road in front of our car.

Often we were out in the countryside, away from LATA altogether. Many of the farmers round Hereford were really on side, and were glad to let us use their land and buildings. Once an arrangement was in place, someone would tell them that if they saw movement round an outlying barn, or in one of their hedges, on a particular day, not to worry; they were to carry on with their normal activities. Our scenario would lay down that some players were using the barn as a transit hide; we'd build an OP in a spot overlooking it, and go to ground there, watching for business to develop. Since much of the land was similar to the ground in Northern Ireland — undulating fields divided by thick hedges — it was ideal for training.

On top of all this there was a good deal of physical

activity. The guys went for their normal daily runs or sessions in the gym, and twice a week an instructor from the Bodyguard Wing took us for unarmed combat. Although quite a small guy, he had a reputation for being able to deck even the biggest lads, and he taught us the holds for disabling people or taking them out. "It's easy enough to kill someone," he said cheerily. "All you need do is use your hand to push their nose-bone up into their brain. Or you can rip their wind-pipe out. But the best thing in a life-threatening situation is just to break the neck." He instructed us to take each other on and learn the moves in slow time, encouraging us to fight dirty by gouging eyes, going for the crotch and so on.

All in all, the course was pretty demanding, but good fun. I felt I was putting a lot into it, but also getting a lot out of it, learning all the time.

Then one morning everything went to rat-shit. We were firing pistols at about ten o'clock when a call came through to the range house, and someone shouted, "Geordie, you're wanted on the phone." Puzzled, I went in and picked up the receiver. There on the line was the adjutant's clerk, calling from camp.

"Is that Geordie Sharp?"

"Yep."

"There's a bit of an emergency. The adjutant needs to see you urgently."

"What's it about?"

"I'm afraid I don't know. That's the only message: you've got to get right back."

Christ! I thought, now what have I done? I must be in for a fearsome bollocking.

I looked round for someone to take charge of my weapons, and the nearest guy was Pat Martin. "Hey, Pat, I've got to head back to the Lines. Will you make sure my weapons and kit-bag go back in the locker?"

"No problem," he answered. "What's the matter? Have you dropped a bollock?"

"Not that I know of." I shrugged and I handed him my pistol, told him my HK 53 was in the hut, and said I'd take the grey admin Sierra.

I drove fast, unable to think of anything I'd done wrong. In a few minutes I was back at camp, parked up and hurrying to the adjutant's office. When I saw the SSM standing in the room, by the Rupert's desk, and also John Stone, who'd been best man at my wedding, I knew something was very wrong.

The adjutant stood up awkwardly as I came in: another sign of big trouble. In that warm weather he was wearing his DPMs, with the sleeves of his shirt rolled up.

"Sit down, Geordie," he said, waving at a chair, and then: "Listen, I'm afraid I've got bad news for you. Your wife's been killed."

"Oh no!" I remember I sat forward with my elbows on my thighs, my hands clasped tight together.

"Yes. We got a signal an hour ago. A bomb went off in a shopping centre in Belfast this morning. It seems to have been an own-goal; the bomber was blown to pieces, but he took out five civilians as well."

My ears heard the words the adjutant was saying, but my brain hardly seemed to take them in. My mind and body had gone numb. I could not move or speak. I sat and stared at the front of the desk, just ahead of me, as if I had turned to stone.

"The rest of the course is being informed," he went on. "We want you to take a couple of days off to make up your mind what you'd like to do."

My voice came back in a kind of croak. "What happened?"

"She'd gone shopping. That's all the information we have so far. She was outside, on the pavement, when the explosion occurred. She was killed instantly. Can't have known anything."

"What time was it?"

"Just after 9.30."

"What about the kid?"

"He was at playschool."

"Thank God for that." I put my face in my hands.

"You'll need time to chill out," the adjutant was saying. "There's no pressure on you to complete the NI course. After this, you may not want to go over there at all. If that's what you decide, everyone will understand. You don't have to go on the operational tour. If you'd prefer it, you can go back to the squadron, and we can look for a posting elsewhere. See how you feel in a couple of days."

"She was coming back!" I said bitterly. And then again, before I could stop myself, I almost shouted, *"She was coming back!"*

"I know, Geordie. Everyone knows that. Everyone's with you." He cleared his throat and went on, "As I say, take a couple of days off. If there's anything you need — help with organizing the funeral — come and

56

tell us. Get it sorted out with the boss and SSM. Now — John can give you a lift home."

I took a deep breath to get hold of myself then stood up and nodded to the adjutant. John put a hand on my shoulder and steered me towards the door. Outside, he said, "Will I take you back?" I nodded again, and walked blindly to his car. As he drove I noticed how tanned he was and asked where he'd been. "Africa," was the answer. "Just come back from an exercise in Botswana."

"What was it like?"

He began to answer, but I could hardly listen. I realized I'd only asked the question in an attempt to keep my mind off my private horror. I seemed to be short of breath, and had to inhale deeply to steady myself.

At the cottage John came into the kitchen with me and said loudly, "Let's have a brew. Where's the kettle?"

"There." I pointed. "There's milk in the fridge." Then I sat down at the table, staring out of the window straight into the vegetable garden, mind in a whirl of guilt and remorse. The kettle began to sing, and presently I heard John say something.

"What was that?"

"I see you've got a bottle of Scotch. Would a quick one help?"

"No, no. Tea'll be fine."

I shivered with cold. When John handed me a mug, I piled three spoonfuls of sugar into it, and as I drank it, I felt a hot flush rising through me.

"Jesus Christ!" I said. "Why her? Why did it have to be her?"

John shook his head and looked down into his tea. Then, noticing the strange kit in one corner, he said, "Whose is that?"

"It belongs to Tony Lopez, the SEAL guy who's trying to join the squadron. He's been staying here."

"Oh — that's the guy who was in the nick with you?"

"That's him."

"How's he doing?"

"Terrific. One of the best."

"Will he pass selection?"

"He'll walk it. He's fitter than the rest put together, and he's got most of the necessary skills already. Been in the jungle, for instance."

"He must be crazy to leave the SEALs. Train in the sun . . . all the assets you want . . . Does he realize what hard work he's letting himself in for?"

"I don't know. It's only for a couple of years."

"Rather him than me. I dread the thought of walking over those hills with a fifty-five-pound bergen." John looked at me and said, "You'd better phone Kath's parents."

"In a minute."

My mind flew to the spacious house in Helen's Bay — a safe and smart residental resort a few miles north-east of Belfast, on the shore of Belfast Lough — with its big gardens and handsome trees and stunning views of the sea. Kath's mother always kept the family home immaculate: never a speck of dust, never a cushion out of place. I'd always supposed that this obsession with cleanliness had something to do with the fact that

58

Kath's father, Den, had been a doctor. Often in the past few weeks I'd wondered what Tim had made of it, dropping bits of food and scattering his toys about the fitted Wilton carpets.

I nerved myself to make the call. Then I said, "Better do it," and went to the telephone.

A strange voice answered: a man, with a strong Belfast accent.

"Who's that?"

"Sergeant Harris, RUC."

"Can I speak to Mrs O'Brien?"

"I'm sorry. She's not very well just now."

"Doctor O'Brien, then."

"Who's calling?"

"His son-in-law."

There was a pause before Den came on, sounding very shaken. "We can't believe it," he said. "We just can't take it in."

"Me neither. How's Mum?"

"She's in shock. We've given her some sedation."

"Look, I'll come over as soon as I can. Tomorrow, probably."

"Thanks, Geordie."

"Den — where is she?"

"Who?"

"Kath."

"Browns are collecting her from the hospital."

"Browns?"

"The funeral directors."

"Have you seen her?"

"No. She was . . . she was . . . The damage was

pretty bad. They identified her from her credit cards and driving licence."

"Oh God! What about Tim?"

"He doesn't know yet. Geordie, are you all right?"

"More or less. I've a friend with me here at the cottage. I'll be there tomorrow. Give my love to Mum."

"So I will."

I rang off.

Little by little I felt anger starting to burn inside me. Once again I heard old Morrison, the RUC chief, saying, "I hate those bastards. I truly do," and suddenly I too felt hatred for the IRA, furious personal hatred for the man who had sent the bomber on his murderous errand.

"Fuck them!" I said, so loudly that it made John start.

"Who?"

"The IRA. Whoever killed her. I'll get that bastard somehow, if it's the last thing I do."

The next two days were a nightmare, and I stumbled through them as though I was half awake. The only mercy was that delayed shock seemed to be numbing my sensibilities and keeping grief at bay.

Early on the Tuesday morning I drove up the M5 to Birmingham Airport, exactly as I had on the day I sent Kath off. The head-shed had fixed me up with an open return to Belfast, but I had yet to collect the ticket. Moving on autopilot, I put the car in the long-term park, walked to the terminal building, found the ticket desk and checked in, all in a mechanical, unfeeling way. It was only when I reached the security check and some dickhead challenged me about where I was going that I really came round. There must have been something about my face that made him pick me out. Suddenly he was demanding to know my name and address in Belfast. When he asked the purpose of my visit, I gave it to him straight, in the most hostile voice I could manage: "I'm going . . . to . . . bury . . . my . . . wife." That stopped him in his tracks — but he was such a turd that he didn't have the grace to apologize. He just said, "All right," and motioned me on.

The plane was only half full, and the flight seemed incredibly short. Nevertheless, it gave me time to think through the security implications of my visit. Kath and I were married in Hereford; the wedding had never been reported in the Northern Ireland papers, and nobody over there knew that she had been associated with the British forces. In the list of bomb victims, her name had been given as Mrs Sharp, a Belfast housewife — again, there had been no mention of her husband. If anyone asked my profession, I would tell them I was an aircraft fitter, working in Bristol. Provided I didn't stray into the hard areas of West Belfast there should be no trouble.

In forty minutes we had landed at Belfast City Airport, and I was walking out through the funny, old-fashioned building which looked as though it dated from the fifties. I grabbed a taxi and gave the driver the address, dreading the moment of arrival and yet wanting to be there quickly.

It was Tim who saved the day from being a disaster. Too young to know what had happened, he was carrying on as normal. When he saw me come in the door, he took one look and ran at me with a yell of "Dad!" I held him up against me — a hefty, warm, live bundle, bigger than I remembered — and found that dealing with him defused the tension of seeing Kath's parents again. All the same, I was upset by their appearance. They had both put on ten years. Meg in particular looked very frail, and when I went to kiss her on the cheek, she was all bones. She was still limping a little, but in a different way from before her operation, and claimed that her hip was now fine; it was just the leg muscles that needed strengthening.

Tim apart, the best thing was their attitude to me. They could easily have blamed me for the tragedy. In fact they went out of their way to show that they understood the problems our marriage had been through, and that they didn't hold it against me for behaving as I had. Whenever I made attempts to apologize they brushed them gently aside.

In the evening, after tea, Den asked about Kath's financial arrangements — whether she'd made a will or had any life insurance. I couldn't answer his questions, because she had always been the family banker — and I'd been so stunned by the news of her death that I hadn't had time to check.

That afternoon he and I went to Browns, the undertakers, to make arrangements. The middle-aged man on duty did his best to put us at our ease, but he threw me completely when he asked how we proposed to carry Kath's coffin out of the church after the service. "I take it you'll be one of the bearer party," he said.

"What? Me? I thought your people took care of that."

"No, sir. It's the custom here for the family to provide the bearers."

"That's right," said Den gently. "Most people do that."

"Well . . ." I was left struggling. I couldn't face the thought of being so close to her, of carrying her remains. "I'm sorry," I said. "I don't think I can do that."

"It's all right." Den raised a hand as if signalling to the undertaker that he would deal with the point in a moment, and went on to ask about the service at the crematorium. I felt terrible, burning with shame that I couldn't do the decent, normal thing.

Then I heard the kindly voice asking if I would like to have a tree for her.

"Where?"

"In the cemetery at Roselawn. Many people do have trees as memorials, rather than a stone. We can arrange to have one for you."

I thought for a moment. I'd never liked big, heavy gravestones. A living memorial seemed a better idea. So I said, "Yes, please."

"What kind of tree? We have beech and ash saplings newly planted."

I was going to ask for an ash, but at the last moment I remembered the trees that she had loved in the spinney behind KC. "Could it be a rowan, a mountain ash?"

"Yes, of course. We can arrange a rowan. And would you like to have a plaque at the foot?"

"Yes, please."

"What wording would you like on the plaque?"

I closed my eyes to concentrate, and cleared my throat. "'In loving memory of Kathleen Sharp. From George.'" Then I added hurriedly, "No: 'From George and Tim.'"

The day of the funeral was as tough as any I could remember. After breakfast I drove Meg and Tim to the playschool he'd been attending, and we dropped him there. All he'd been told about his mum, so far, was that she had gone away for a few days. At some point we would have to break the news to him, but it seemed better to wait until we had all had a chance to get hold of ourselves.

The church service was set for 11.30 in the morning, but members of the family began arriving at the house an hour before that. Meg and Kath's younger sister Angela were busy in the kitchen, preparing sandwiches and rolls for the wake; and as they wouldn't let other mourners come in there, I had to hold the fort with Den in the living room. Some of the people I knew, some I didn't. I forced myself to make small talk with all of them. The saving grace was the picture window which took up most of one wall and looked straight down over the sea. Birds were busy about the rocks, and every now and then a boat would come into sight, providing a blessed distraction and a new subject for conversation. For a few wonderful moments a fishing trawler, on its way out, appeared to have caught fire. Black smoke poured from its funnel, and the little ship steamed round in a circle, and everyone became quite excited by its apparent distress; but then suddenly the smoke was doused and the boat went on its way.

At last it was time to go. Two big, black Daimlers took the main family party, with the rest following in vehicles of their own. At the church the coffin, covered with flowers, was already in place on trestles at the head of the aisle. I found myself consciously trying not to think of what lay inside it. Suddenly I saw the bodies of the pilot and co-pilot of the helicopter that came down in the Iraqi desert, their limbs twisted and ripped off. I told myself to remember what she'd been like, but I found that small things were irritating me: the church was much too big for a congregation this size, we filled only the middle of the first few pews; the minister was young and nervous and kept stumbling over his words; the first hymn was one I'd never heard of. But then, in what seemed like no time at all we'd sung "Oh God, Our Help In Ages Past", and the bearers were lifting the coffin on to their shoulders, to carry it down the aisle. To my shame, I didn't even know them. Cousins? Friends of the family? Whoever they were, Den had recruited them, and they all looked fairly young. Along with everyone else, I stood and waited till they had cleared the church door. Then we were back into the funeral car and following the hearse out of the city, up to the Roselawn cemetery, high on a rounded hill. We drove through an impressive pair of gates and into the biggest graveyard I'd ever seen — hundreds upon hundreds of tombstones and other memorials, set in straight lines over the hillsides, with neatly mown grass all round, and the road sweeping back and forth between. There were also thousands of trees, mostly young, planted in copses and bigger stands, the ground beneath them covered in wood-chips to keep down the weeds. I saw several places where I would like Kath's rowan to be.

At the top of the hill we came to the crematorium, a low, brick building set among sculpted grass banks and beds of flowers. The fact that everything was so perfectly kept seemed to make it more of an ordeal, rather than lessen it. There was a short delay while we waited for the party ahead of us to clear. Then it was our turn to file into the plain little chapel. As if from a great distance, I heard the priest say, "Man that is born of woman hath but a short time to live, and is full of misery. He cometh up, and is cut down like a flower; he fleeth as it were a shadow and never continueth in one stay." It was all I could do to endure until the end, the dreadful moment when the coffin descended through a hole in the floor and Kath was gone.

Outside again, looking down, I realized that the cemetery had a huge view over Belfast, lying below us to the north-west. At the back of my mind I felt it was wrong that my thoughts should be turning so swiftly from the past to the future, but that is what they were doing. "Whoever he is, he's down there somewhere," I told myself. "And wherever he is, I'll get him."

CHAPTER
FOUR

There was no question of my quitting the course. On the contrary, I couldn't wait to rejoin it. Early on Friday morning I nipped into camp and left a message for the adjutant saying I was back on side, then got myself straight down to LATA, determined to make up whatever ground I had lost through being away.

For the first couple of days the guys treated me rather strangely. There was none of the usual banter and piss-taking; instead, their attitude was respectful. Were they anxious not to hurt my feelings? Looking back, I can see that they expected me to be in pieces and were trying to handle me gently. But at the time I found it annoying. Outside the course I had one or two close mates — Tony and John Stone — who knew how hard I had been hit, and I was glad of their help; Pat Martin was another bulwark for me. The rest of the course may well have thought I was an unfeeling bastard, and didn't care much about what had happened. If that was the score, all the better, because I didn't want anyone to know what I had in mind. What nobody realized was that the agony of losing Kath had transformed itself into a ferocious desire for revenge. Grief had turned into anger, despair into steely determination. Far from being in distress, I came back on fire with new motivation.

I'd read in some newspaper that the own-goal bomber had been given a full-scale military funeral in West Belfast. Never mind that his incompetence had led to the deaths of five innocent civilians, or that a Protestant riot had broken out while he was being buried, with thousands of pounds' worth of damage caused. In the twisted minds of the IRA he had died on active service, and was a martyr, a hero. Brilliant!

To focus my animosity, I had given my target a name. Because he was obviously a leading player, I had called him Gary, after Gary Player, the golfer. In my mind's eye Gary had reddish hair and beard, and sly, piglike eyes. He was of medium height, and sloppily dressed — altogether a scruffy individual, dirty and slovenly — but cunning, and bigoted as hell, a dirty fighter and a dangerous customer. Trying to work out the position he might occupy in the IRA hierarchy, I had done my best to reconstruct events. The bomber had been an unemployed twenty-two-year-old. No doubt he had been a member of some ASU, which also included a shooter and a driver. Probably the bomber had been given orders to pick up from Point A the device which was to kill him, and deposit it at Point B. But who had given the orders? That was the key question. According to our instructor Reg Brown, who'd already done a tour in Northern Ireland, it would almost certainly have been an ops officer or a quartermaster in the Belfast brigade.

Maybe I was deluding myself, but I felt sure that fate was pointing me in the direction of my enemy. Already we were into August. Provided I got through the rest of the course OK: I would be posted to Belfast in October, only two months off and then, for a year, I would be on the man's doorstep, trained, armed, and furnished with every pretext for taking terrorists out. When, in the middle of August, Loyalist gunmen killed seven people in eight days, and the IRA responded in kind, I persuaded myself that nobody would notice one more apparently sectarian killing.

On the domestic front, things were under control, if not great. After a family discussion we had agreed that it would be best for me to leave Tim with his Gran. Meg had pulled up again after her operation, and said she could manage. When I came across in the autumn, at least I'd be able to see something of the kid. In England there was no one to look after him.

At Keeper's Cottage I'd left Kath's things exactly as they were — clothes, shoes, hats, a few bits of jewellery. I could have given everything to Oxfam but somehow I didn't want to, so I shut the wardrobe doors, left her dressing table as it was, and deferred action indefinitely.

At the end of August a 1,000lb bomb went off outside the RUC station at Markethill in County Armagh. Miraculously, no one was hurt, but the explosion further sharpened our eagerness to get across the water. Down at LATA we were into the most fascinating part of the course: surveillance, or the art of following a target, either on foot or by car, without being seen. In this, for the first time, we became fully aware of the role that was going to be played in our lives by the shadowy organization known as the "Det". Short for "Detachment", the name referred to the undercover intelligence-gathering unit that worked alongside our guys across the water. Whereas our role was reactive, theirs was passive: watching, spotting faces, gathering information, learning about the enemy.

The Det was made up of guys drawn from all corners of the forces; within the SAS they were known as "Walts". Some had come from the Regiment, but others were from all sections of the British services, and as far as work went, the whole lot kept themselves very much to themselves. In Belfast our guys shared a canteen and bar with them, and we were told that they were friendly enough off-duty; at LATA, whenever I saw some of them, I noticed how totally unremarkable they looked. I'm sure they'd been picked partly for their anonymous appearance, and for the fact that they had no distinguishing features. They were neither too tall nor too short, neither too fat nor spectacularly thin. None of them was particularly good-looking, but no one was all that ugly either. They all seemed to be uniform and neutral, so that they would blend effortlessly into a crowd anywhere in Northern Europe, and if you saw a couple of them in a car you wouldn't look twice. But we soon realized that they were highly trained, and an indispensable weapon in the fight against terrorism.

Until we tried it, I don't think any of us had realized what an elaborate business surveillance was — a team of eight or ten men or women tracking a single target, all in immediate touch with each other by covert radio, all speaking a special language. The radios were secure, and scrambling devices made it impossible for outsiders to listen in. The jargon wasn't designed to baffle anyone: rather, its aim was to achieve economy and precision — to cut down time on the air and eliminate misunderstandings. Thus "Bravo" was any man, "Echo" any woman, "Charlie" any car. "Foxtrot" meant on the move on foot, "Mobile" in a car. "Complete" signified that a person had gone into a house or a car. "Getting a trigger" meant getting your eyes on the target or the place where he was last seen.

To give us an idea, the instructor set up a scenario on the magic board — the big sheet of white-enamelled metal that covered most of the front wall of the classroom. Switching on a projector, he put a blown-up street-plan on the board and placed a few magnetic counters on it. One was black — the target — and the others white. Also on the plan were some coloured spots — red, green and blue, with numbers on them. Each of these, he explained, was used to identify a particular area. It was far easier and quicker to say "Green One" than "The crossroads at the intersection of River Street and Upper Richmond Way", or give the place's grid-reference.

"Now," he began, "the most important guy in any surveillance operation is the one running it from the ops room. He's sat there with all his radios on, a couple of helpers, and a blown-up map of the area you're in. One big plus about this part of your training is that it gets you shit-hot on the radio. You've got to be really slick in reporting the target's movements. If you're slow, you're too late — he's gone round a corner and you've lost him.

"Now, what happens if the target goes to ground in a house? Well, it's up to the controller to bring people in to box the site." He moved four white counters on to street junctions around the black blob. "There you are. You sit on corners, in cafés or bars, waiting for the target to reappear. If you do your job properly, he can't get out of the box without one of you seeing him.

"If you think he's seen you, the golden rule is: peel off. Tell everyone else and get lost. Things go tits-up when somebody *thinks* he's OK and carries on. If you do that, all you manage to do is confirm to the target that surveillance is on him, and he may go to ground for weeks. OK, then, listen to this."

He switched on an audio-tape — a hissing, crackly recording of a live operation. Every time a new voice came in he moved the corresponding white counter, and after every report he shifted the black target to a new position, all the time throwing in explanations of his own.

"I've got the trigger on Bravo One's house," said the first voice. "At the moment he's complete."

"In other words, he's indoors," said the instructor.

Then, a moment later, the voice said, "Standby, standby. The door's open. Oh no. Nothing. It's his wife going to the bins." Another pause. Then, "Standby, standby. That's Bravo One leaving. He's foxtrot northwards."

"He's walking up this street here," the instructor explained, sliding the black counter upwards.

The voice came in again. "He's wearing black on blue.

Heading for the Drover's Arms on the corner. Now he's turning right . . ."

Another voice, a Scottish accent: "Yeah, I've got him. I can take him down Commercial Street. He's foxtrot eastwards. Now he's joined up with Bravo Two. They've both gone complete in Charlie One, a bronze Escort. Can't get the number."

"Both targets are in the car," said the instructor, placing a yellow disc on the board.

A few seconds passed, and the Scots voice returned: "Charlie One mobile eastwards towards Green Three."

Then came another voice, measured, authoritative, the controller: "Steve, are you covering Green Three?"

"On Green Three, facing north."

"Prepare to take over Charlie One . . ."

As I listened, I felt the hairs on my neck rise up. The process was fascinating in itself, but in my mind's eye I was part of a team in West Belfast, tracking two players through the seedy Nationalist areas — maybe the Falls Road or Andersontown. The guys in the car were leading us towards Gary Player and a major contact. Any moment I might set eyes on my No. 1 enemy.

The soundtrack fell silent. "If you're driving," the instructor said, "the one place you don't want to be is in the car behind the target. Keep two or three cars back. If people are doing something they didn't ought to be doing, they're forever looking behind them in their mirrors. If you do find yourself behind, for Christ's sake peel off at the first opportunity and get someone else to take over."

"Stop, stop, stop!" called a new voice from the tape.

"Charlie One has pulled up in a lay-by at 489346. Bravo Two is foxtrot towards a telephone kiosk . . ."

The lads were getting excited by the idea of going across, and enthusiasm rose still higher whenever guys came back with stories of live operations. Several concerned the ace sniper who was doing shoots in the border area and in Belfast, taking soldiers out with a .50 rifle — a fearsome weapon which could put a round straight through a man's chest, flak jacket and all, at five or six hundred metres. The sniper was highly skilled and well organized. From the way he operated, the Det concluded that he had been trained in America. He had a lot of dickers — lookouts — who would check that an area was clear before he ventured forth. Then, if all was well, he'd come out and do a shoot on an army patrol. The only man known to have survived an attack from him was a soldier who'd been on patrol in West Belfast. The incoming round hit his SA 80, which he was holding across his chest. The weapon disintegrated, and parts of it (or of the .50 bullet) flew upwards, ripping chunks out of his face; but at least he wasn't killed.

The Regiment had set out to get the sniper by staging a come-on, posing as a green army patrol. The idea was to egg him on and keep him on the air so that the radio specialists could DF him and find out where he was based. It was dicey as hell, but it nearly worked. A few of the Regiment guys dressed up as ordinary soldiers and went through the motions of mounting a patrol. As they came into the target area, through their earpieces they could hear a dicker commentating on their progress.

"OK," said this Ulster voice, "there's a patrol coming down the road. They'll be in your field of view in about thirty seconds."

The sniper did not answer. There was a pause, then a sudden change of emphasis. "Jaysus!" said the Ulster voice. "There's something wrong here. They've got the wrong fecking weapons. They've got G3s, not SA 80s. The fellers are older, as well. They don't look like squaddies at all."

The sniper realized immediately that the patrol was an SAS one. All he said was, "I'm pulling off." With that he fell silent, and the attempt at DFing him failed.

That wasn't the end of it, though. The Regiment tried again; this time they went to the lengths of taking a black fellow over, to make the patrol look still more realistic. They carried SA 80s, so that everything seemed pukka. It was quite an elaborate operation, with some guys airborne in a chopper and others deployed on the ground around the periphery, to block the sniper in if they got a line on where he was set up.

Again the patrol was listening out as the dickers commentated on their approach, but this time, to their consternation, they heard the shooter say, "Right, I'm ready to fire. I'll take the second fecker from the front." At that they did a bomb-burst, and every man hit the deck in a different direction. Then they upped and ran like stags, all over the place. They didn't collect back at the emergency rendezvous for more than an hour, and by then the gunman had once again melted into the night.

Of all our training, it was the range practices that I enjoyed most. Partly it was because I had become quite good with a pistol; but beyond that, in putting down live rounds I felt I was getting closer to my objective than on any of the rest of our activities, realistic though they were.

For pistol training we'd head out to the range at 0900. A couple of the guys were detailed to collect ammunition from the stores and lug the heavy metal boxes to the range hut. One man would go round putting up the red flags, to show that live firing was in progress, and the rest of us would sort out the targets.

The range had high stop-banks of soil thrown up in a horseshoe shape, so that you could fire at targets round three sides of it. Old railway sleepers were set into the ground, with holes drilled into them so that targets could easily be set up. We'd start by firing off two or three magazines just to get comfortable. Everyone had used pistols earlier in their training, so they all knew which their master eye was and how to take up a proper, easy stance: semi-crouching, with — for a right-hander — the left hand cupped round the outside of the right, supporting it.

If rounds started going low, you knew you were snatching at the trigger — and the instructors had a special drill for correcting that fault. One of them would say, "Hey, try doing the old ball and dummy with me." Then he'd stand behind the shooter and load his pistol for him, sometimes putting live rounds in the magazine, sometimes leaving it empty, so that the man pulling the trigger didn't know if it was going to go off or not. That way, if he *was* flinching and snatching, the instructor could see the end of the barrel dip, and try to rectify the fault.

After the guys had sorted themselves out and got their eyes in, everyone would have a brew from the urn by the target shed. Then the instructor would move on to drawing from holsters. He'd line up the lads in front of the targets and call, "UP!" Everyone would draw, fire a quick double-tap, then re-holster the pistol. Then we'd turn through ninety degrees to the right or left, and at the second command we'd draw, swivel and fire. Next we'd turn the other way, shoot from that position, and finally face backwards, so that we had to spin through 180 degrees.

Then we'd do some walking practice — maybe four of us at a time. The aim was to get everybody nice and confident, walking with their hands at their sides, in a relaxed attitude. Then at the command "UP!" we'd stop, draw whip round and fire, all in a split second. If the targets were numbered, and we were walking in pairs, the instructor might yell "ONE AND FOUR!" whereupon we'd have to engage those two targets. When each practice finished, the instructor would say, "OK, guys, paste up," and we'd go forward to stick coloured patches over the bullet holes.

At some stage, as we were firing, he'd yell "Stoppage!" and we'd go down on one knee, hitting the release button of the magazine as we went; we'd whip the magazine out, slot another in, and be firing again as we came back up. In a contact, our lives might depend on the speed with which we reacted, and I practised until I could do the change in less than three seconds.

Speed and accuracy were everything. With the Hun's Head targets — the silhouette of a German soldier's head and trunk — it was always the head we aimed at, and up to twenty paces I reckoned I could put a double-tap straight through the middle of the forehead ten times out of ten. With the bigger Figure 11 targets we stuck on small white patches to give us precise aiming marks.

I found it odd that the lads who weren't actually firing would show little interest in what was going on. They'd sit on the bench outside the hut, chit-chatting away — the young ones would be on about the old trout they'd been humping the night before, the older guys about the extensions they were putting on their houses. As for me, I couldn't get enough of it. I had grown fanatically determined that if ever my chance came across the water, I wasn't going to flunk it. I'm sure some of the guys thought I was becoming obsessive, and I suppose I was — but only for a reason about which I couldn't enlighten them.

All our training emphasized the need for restraint and split-second timing. Many times in the past (we heard), our predecessors had had to wait until players were actually levelling weapons in front of them before they themselves could fire; if they'd shot sooner, before they were under immediate threat, they could have ended up in court charged with murder. It seemed ridiculous that the dice should be so heavily loaded in the terrorists' favour — yet that was the way things stood.

I recalled part of old Morrison's tirade, in which he had lambasted the excessive restraints under which the security forces had to work: "When we've brought a murderer into the station," he'd said, "if I so much as cuff him on the ear, that'll guarantee to put me in court. If I kick the chair from under him, that's an assault. Even if I lean over the table to emphasize a point, that's threatening him, and the interview's stopped because it's being monitored by the chief inspector sitting in the back."

In some irrational way, I felt that the normal restrictions did not apply to me. Gary Player had already committed murder, and that was sufficient justification for my taking him out, never mind any further crimes he might commit. At the back of my mind I realized that in planning a personal vendetta I was stepping out of line. The essence of any SAS operation is teamwork, and here I was, trying to crack something on my own.

Working solo, without mates to cover my movements, would expose me to a far greater risk of getting shot or captured. Normally, working in pairs, you cover each other, and you can shoot your way out of trouble. Alone, without a partner, I could easily end up in the shit. I never really faced up to the thought of what might happen if I was captured. Very few of the guys ever did. Deep down, they knew perfectly well that if the IRA got them, they would be whipped south of the border and would probably never see the light of day again. They would die — but not before they had suffered unspeakable tortures. For this reason, some of them privately admitted that if things looked really bad they'd shoot themselves; but most preferred to believe they would come out fighting. I was one of that majority.

Apart from survival, there was also the little matter of identifying my victim. How in hell was I to find out who he was? And even if I did discover his name, how was I to track him down? Such was the force of my anger that I had no doubt I would find him somehow.

One morning a couple of weeks before the end of the course, I was due to have my arm checked by a specialist in the tri-service hospital at Wroughton. By then I was so hyped up that the thought of losing half a day's training quite pissed me off — but I scented possible compensation in the fact that Tracy might be on duty when I clocked in at the camp Med Centre to pick up my X-rays.

She was. When I appeared, she was on the phone, but before I'd taken two steps into the room she banged down the receiver with a loud cry of "SHIT!"

"Something the matter?"

"It's our effing landlord. He's throwing us out."

"That's tough. What happened?"

She told me she'd been living with a friend, Susan, in a flat on the outskirts of town. They had no proper security of tenure, and now the owner of the house was going abroad and wanted to let the whole place as a single unit. He had given the girls a fortnight to pack their bags.

Listening to Tracy talk, watching her, I thought she had changed. Her face was lit up with indignation, but she seemed more mature, less wild and tarty than I remembered her. Maybe I was influenced by the fact that she'd been very sweet about Kath the first time I'd seen her after the disaster. In any case, *I* now felt sorry for *her*.

Even so, it wasn't until I was in the minibus, half-way to Wroughton, that the idea hit me. For some time I'd been worrying what would happen to Keeper's Cottage when I went to Belfast. Tony was about to go off on the jungle phase of his selection course; in any case, he wouldn't want to live out in the country on his own while I was away. I could simply lock the door and go, but I didn't want the place to stand empty for months on end.

So why not offer the house to Tracy and Susan? I didn't know whether or not Susan had a car, but Tracy certainly had one, and could easily commute in and out. As long as being out in the wilds didn't spook them, they could live in the cottage rent-free, look after things till I got back, and give themselves time to find permanent accommodation elsewhere.

At Wroughton there was the usual delay. A backlog of patients had built up, and I was told I'd have to wait half an hour; so I went down the corridor to the pay-phone and called the Med Centre's reception.

"Hi," I began. "It's me, Geordie."

"What's happened now? Left your head behind?"

"Listen — I've had an idea about a place for you and Susan. You can have my house. It's going to be empty from the end of the month, for the best part of a year."

"Where is it?"

"Off the Madley road, about four miles out."

"How much d'you want for it?"

"Nothing. I just need to have it looked after."

"Well . . ."

I could practically see her squirming her neat little arse about on her chair.

"Tell you what — I could pick you up tonight and take you out to have a look. Susan as well; you'd better both see it. It's pretty much out in the wilds, on its own. What do you think?"

"Are you sure?"

"Of course. I wouldn't be ringing otherwise."

"What time, then?"

"Wait one. I'll be back up from LATA about half-seven. Say half-eight. What's your address?"

She gave it, and then said, "There's no strings attached to this, are there?"

"Of course not."

I was there five minutes early, showered and changed. Naturally I'd said nothing to the guys on the course, but all day I'd been haunted by a peculiar feeling, half guilt, half anticipation. Was I being disloyal to Kath's memory? There was no denying that I found Tracy attractive. But then I told myself, Hell — I'm just trying to fix up a business arrangement, of mutual benefit.

Or so I thought — until she came flying down the steps of the house, all legs and arms.

"Where's Susan?" I asked.

"She had a date already. But she likes the idea, and she's given me power of attorney to do what I think fit. Anyway, her job means she is away a lot, travelling."

"Let's go, then."

She was wearing a silver-grey track suit, and had a small bag hung over one shoulder. From the scent that wafted off her in the car I didn't think she'd been running. I had a good look at her profile for the first time, and saw that it matched her manner exactly, being rather pert and perky. On our way out she asked about Tim, and I explained he was with his Gran in Belfast.

"Is he OK?"

I turned to look at her, and saw her looking steadily, seriously, back at me.

"I think so. Lucky he's so young."

"That's right."

She fell silent for a couple of minutes. But then, as I turned down the lane to the cottage, she exclaimed, "Gawd! You said it!"

"What?"

"Buried away."

"D'you mind that?"

"I dunno. I've never lived in a place like this."

When we got out of the car she shuddered and said in an aggrieved voice, "It's dark!"

"What did you expect? It's night-time."

"I mean, there are no lights anywhere."

"This is the country. You don't have lights in the country. Don't need any. If you eat plenty of carrots, you can see in the dark."

"You're kidding."

"Honest!"

"There could be people lurking about out here."

"What sort of people?"

"Rapists. Homicidal maniacs."

"There are far more of them in towns. This isn't the environment for people like that."

For a few seconds I thought she was going to throw a wobbly, especially when an owl sounded off close by. But in fact things went the other way. Once inside, she responded strongly to the place. She was a city kid all right, but her mind was open, and she was prepared to learn and adapt. She loved the house, saw the mess, gave me a mild bollocking, said she'd take over, and set straight in to clear up the kitchen.

"Eh," I said, "You can't do that."

"Stop me."

"You'd better have a drink, then. Glass of wine?"

"Thanks."

One thing very soon led to another. She offered to cook something for supper. I suggested that we go out to the pub in the village, which served a reasonable evening meal. She said, "No, that would be a waste of money." Suddenly I heard myself say, "You mean the waste of an opportunity?" The next thing I knew we were in the bedroom, and I saw an immensely long flash of thigh as she pulled off her jogging pants.

"Jesus!" I cried. "This is crazy. I haven't any — er . . ."

"I have!" She made a grab for the little bag she'd brought with her. "Isn't that the Boy Scouts' motto? 'Be prepared'?"

84

* * *

In the morning, as we sat having a cup of coffee in the kitchen, I said, "I should never have brought you here like this."

"I'm glad you did."

"I feel guilty."

"Why? You're on your own. You've no one else."

"No — but it's so soon after Kath."

"You never messed about when she was alive."

"No."

"I've been worrying about you for weeks."

"You didn't show it much."

"How could I?"

"I know."

She shook her head and put her hand over mine. I looked up into her face and said, "Somehow, with you, I feel myself. I feel normal — comfortable, like."

"Same here." She smiled, producing tiny creases down her cheeks.

"What will people think, though?" I asked.

"They won't think anything. They needn't know I've spent the night here. As long as we don't walk into work wrapped round each other."

"Jesus, no! I'll run you home round the back way, and go in on my own."

"And then —" Tracy went on with her own line of thought — "when Susan and I move in, it'll look like a straightforward business arrangement."

"What about when I come back?"

"Tonight, you mean?"

"No, no — from across the water."

"I'll be waiting here for you."

"You mean that?"

"If you want me."

The course ended with two big exercises, one out in the country and one mainly in town. In the first, we were told that a bomb had been planted in a certain culvert, under a country lane, out in the middle of a large estate. According to the scenario, command wires had been spotted running up a hedge to a firing point in the corner of an old quarry. Good intelligence had been received to the effect that terrorists were coming back at night to detonate the bomb when a vehicle patrol went past. I was detailed to command an operation to take them out.

There was no time for an on-site recce. For an hour we pored over the 1:50,000 map, planning covert approaches to the spot marked as the target. Then, as dark was coming on, we bussed out to a drop-off point, tabbed in across country, over the back of a hill, and prepared to lie up in wait. In the last of the light we found the command wires and traced the top end of them to a drain beside a gate-post, where the fence coming up from the culvert reached one corner of the quarry.

It was a filthy night, pissing with rain. The gate-post was nearly at the summit of the hill, and from it we could look down on the lane, which ran along the contour below us, across our front. Having set the rest of the patrol to cover us, Pat and I worked our way down the command wires, to make sure they were connected to the device. Crafty bastards, the terrorists had coupled them up to the barbed wire, so that for most of the run the fence itself would act as a conductor: that way, no extra wires were needed, and there was nothing unusual to be seen. At the bottom end we picked up the special circuit again and followed it to an old milk churn under the little bridge.

That was good enough. Back near the firing-point, I deployed two pairs of guys left and right, as cut-offs, in case Pat and I — the killer group — missed the players and they tried to run out sideways. Then we settled into a small hollow thirty metres from the gate-post. There were a couple of more obvious hiding places, closer to the target; but the depression was just deep enough to cover us, especially in the dark, and it wasn't the kind of feature that would attract anyone's attention. I set the bipod of the G3 on the front of the dip, and wriggled around until it was at a comfortable height.

As the night wore on our hollow gradually filled with water, until we were lying in a couple of inches of liquid mud. The moon was three-quarters full, but because of the clouds its light was very faint, and I wished we'd had time to set out ambush lights. In the event, I had to keep switching on the kite-sight of my G3 to get a good view of the culvert area. In the grey-green glow of the sight the fence posts along the road showed up clearly, but when I looked with the naked eye I could scarcely make them out.

I was finding it hard to concentrate. Half the time my mind was slipping away to Tracy, and the way she'd wrapped her great long legs round me, first round my waist, then round my neck. What a night! And how fantastic that she was hell-bent on taking root in the cottage. To bring myself back to earth, I tried to imagine that I was no longer in the safe, soft Herefordshire countryside, but in some godforsaken corner of Ulster, with fanatical murderers lurking behind every hedge, and Gary Player himself coming to detonate the bomb.

Our magazines might have been loaded with blanks, but all the other details of the exercise were as real as could be. We knew the Det trainees were out as well, tracking the alleged players, but apart from occasional checks on the comms net, nothing happened until about 2.30 a.m. By then the rain had cleared and the night had gone very quiet. Suddenly, a gun-shot cracked off in the woods on the slopes opposite, and echoes rolled away down the valley to our right.

I had my radio in the special pocket of my ops waistcoat, down the left side of my chest. Two small throat-mikes were held in position either side of my Adam's apple by a choker of elastic. The pressel-switch, or transmission button, was a small rubber dome clipped on to the front of my windproof smock. If ever I found myself so close to the enemy that I couldn't speak, Control would interrogate me through my earpiece, and I would answer by using different numbers of presses — one for no, two for yes — which came across at the other end as quick bursts of static.

Now I gave it one blip to alert Control.

"Zero Alpha," came the voice of the boss, who I knew was in a command vehicle a couple of miles down the road.

"Bravo Five-One," I said quietly. "There's been a

shot fired approximately five hundred metres north of our location."

"Roger. Checking. Wait out."

Before I could say anything else, two more shots rang out. Pat, a yard to my left, came out with, "Fucking hell! It's Arma-fucking-geddon!" Then, way off in the distance, torches began to flash. A pair of headlights flicked on, and a vehicle went haring along a woodland ride, the beams whipping wildly up and down. Men shouted, and a big dog, maybe a German Shepherd, barked. The sounds were all faint with distance, but clearly coming towards us.

"Bravo Five-One to all callsigns," I said. "I think it's poachers at the squire's pheasants. Nothing to do with us. But it could be a come-on. Just sit tight."

Gradually the commotion died down. The vehicle drove off and silence returned. A few minutes later I picked up some movement below. I nudged Pat and brought the butt of the G3 up to my shoulder. But all the kite-sight revealed was a fox, padding up the hedge towards us. The animal came right to the firing-point, stopped, sniffed and cocked its leg against the gate-post. Then it turned through the gate and disappeared to our left.

"Well I'm buggered!" muttered Pat. "One fox foxtrot towards target!"

At last, soon after three, the Det came on the air. "Two X-rays, foxtrot towards your location, nearing zero six zero," said a Scottish voice. "Three hundred metres from firing-point."

"Bravo Five-One, roger."

My neck crawled. The baddies were not doing anything as straightforward as coming along the lane to the culvert and up the hedge towards us; rather, they were moving in across country, from behind our left shoulders. The slope of the ground meant that we wouldn't be able to see them until the last moment.

"X-rays still foxtrot," said the Det Scot. "Two hundred metres."

A couple of minutes ticked by. Then, "Zero Alpha," came the boss's voice in my ear. "Have you got eyes on the X-rays?"

By then they could have been almost on top of us, too close for me to speak. I gave a single punch on my pressel to signify "No".

I lay like a stone, holding my breath, listening. A minute passed, then another. The boss called again and asked the same question. Again I gave him one press.

Where the hell were they? With the utmost caution I turned my head until it was facing backwards like an owl's. Nobody in sight. Obviously they were waiting out, somewhere very close. We knew that they were there, and they knew that we were there. They were trying to wind us up and push us into making a mistake.

Sod them. On the net I heard the boss asking the Det to check the bearing-to-target they had given. The answer came back confirming it. Still no movement near us.

Then Pat reached out and touched my left arm.

There they were — two black heads and torsos showing against the sky, a few yards off to our left. The pair moved forward in a crouching attitude, so close I could hear the rustle of their clothes.

90

Gently I raised the butt of the G3 to my shoulder and looked through the kite-sight. The figures showed up in every detail. One was carrying a weapon, a long, and the other had a box-like object slung from his left hand. As I watched they went to ground by the gate-post.

I gave a touch on the pressel.

"Zero Alpha," said the boss. "Have you got X-rays on target?"

Two presses.

"Are they armed?"

Two presses.

"How far off are they? Less than thirty metres?"

Two presses.

"Twenty metres?"

Two presses.

"Three patrol Charlies mobile, direction target," said the Det voice. "Have you got eyes on them?"

One press. But a moment later I saw them — three Land Rovers driving on sidelights up the lane. This, for me, was the moment of decision. Yes, I told myself, these two guys were definitely a threat. The patrol was within seconds of passing over the culvert. The terrorists were on the firing-point. If we didn't drop them immediately they'd detonate their bomb, possibly with disastrous results.

"Standby, standby," I whispered to Pat. I sensed, rather than saw, him bring the butt of his weapon up into his shoulder. My own rifle sat steady on its bipod. I pushed the safety catch forward to "Automatic". Then at the top of my voice I yelled, "ARMY! ARMY, ARMY! HALT OR I FIRE!"

Instantly the pair split, one running right, one left. At the first movement I let rip at the right-hand figure with three short bursts. Pat did the same at the left (I was aware of flame spurting from the muzzle of his rifle). Both players went down and lay still. I gave mine another burst, on the ground, to make sure of him, waited a few seconds, and got back on the radio.

"Bravo Five-One. Contact! Two terrorists dead. No casualties ourselves. Checking the area. Wait out."

We had a quick look round, made sure none of the other guys had seen anyone. Then I reported, "No other terrorists on target," and asked for the QRF — a green army team — to move up to the prearranged rendezvous. I deputed Pat to meet them and explain exactly what had happened. Then I saw that the rest of my team got the hell out; the instructors had hammered into us the fact that in Northern Ireland a crowd gathers immediately at the scene of any incident, and it is bad news if locals see the faces of members of the special forces.

Soon we were away back to base in a couple of the Land Rovers that had acted as the threatened patrol. Behind, on the ground, the alleged terrorists would still be lying where they had fallen, until a photographer had taken pictures of them. Also on the scene would be one of the Regiment acting as the LO (or Liaison Officer) — he'd be directing the QRF who would cordon off the whole area. Nobody else would be allowed until the arrival of the SOCO, the Scene of Crimes Officer, who was from the RUC. He would measure distances and angles, collect up the cartridge cases and make notes for his report.

After a wash-up, we got our heads down, but not for long, because the exercise continued in the morning with a full-scale inquiry. Not only did a proper judge preside in court, with real-life barristers holding forth; the Regiment brought down about sixty cooks and bottle-washers from the squadron, to act as audience and sit there heckling. We'd been told how easy it would be to let ourselves down by getting details wrong when we gave our accounts of what had happened, or by giving away more information than necessary; so we briefed ourselves carefully beforehand, and in the event got the whole incident well squared away. The best bit of the morning came when one of the cooks, Jimmy Bell, went way over the top. We didn't know whether he'd had a couple of pints on the way down or what, but he became so obnoxious with his heckling and his shouts of "Order! Order!" that the judge ordered him removed from the court, and it was all we could do to sit there with straight faces.

Maybe because of my upbringing in the country, I felt more at home operating out on farms and in the woods than in towns. But the next event on our programme was a four-day spell in Lydd and Hythe, the mock village on the Kent coast purpose-built for training. That is an eye-opener, because there are video cameras set up on every corner, and after a house assault you could run the tape and see exactly what everyone had done. If someone had behaved like a prat it was useless for him to deny it, because there he was on the video, pissing about for all to see.

Our final exercise — a joint one with the MI5 — was

mostly urban. The scenario was that two major players had just come across the water and gone to ground in Birmingham. MI5 trainees followed them to a house in Solihull, where they were supposed to have secreted some weapons in a garage. It fell to Pat and myself to do a CTR, and exercise our newly acquired skills as lock-pickers by breaking into the garage at night to verify the information. Sure enough, we found a cache of two dummy AK 47s and some bomb-making equipment. We reported the find and pulled off taking care to remove all traces of our entry, and left a couple of guys in an OP that covered both house and garage.

MI5, meanwhile, was continuing its own surveillance, boxing the area to make sure that the villains didn't slip away unobserved. But it was our guys in the OP who saw the players loading their weapons into a car next morning. By then we were all pretty professional at keeping up a running commentary, and this one came over without hesitation: "OK. Bravos One and Two are in garage. They've got the weapons. Now they're loading them into Charlie One. Weapons definitely in boot of car. Standby, standby. Bravos One and Two mobile towards Blue Three."

Seconds later the MI5 boys came up with, "OK, I have Charlie One at Blue Three mobile towards Blue Two."

So it went on. Charlie One, a battered old blue Montego estate, was followed to a deserted farmhouse in the hills outside Kidderminster. This was the base from which they were going to mount their operation. Again our troop went in at night to put an OP on the farm, and when the baddies turned up to collect their weapons we ambushed them, in theory killing the lot. In fact (according to the scenario) one escaped, and moved north to join an ASU in Wolverhampton — so the exercise continued in pursuit of him, and the action moved up there.

When the course ended, we had a couple of beers at the bar in LATA, then went back for a Chinese meal in Hereford. After that we felt we'd taken enough fried rice and crispy noodles on board to soak up a few more beers, so we went on to the Falcon, one of the Regiment's regular haunts. By then we'd all grown our hair fairly long, as part of our preparation for Northern Ireland, but we were all of much the same age, size and physique, and it wasn't difficult for outsiders to tell where we came from.

As usual we stood around together, occupying what we regarded as our own territory, at one end of the main bar, and before long we began to get aggro from a gang of town lads in the opposite corner. At first they were just making the odd sarcastic remark, more or less loud enough for us to hear. Then one of them, as he came past on his way to the bar, deliberately barged into me with his shoulder. He was quite a big lad, with straw-coloured hair shaved flat at the top to make an Elvis-type quiff.

"Hey," I said. "What's the matter with you? Bog off, before you get hurt."

He mouthed some obscenity, then turned to the barman. I could see that he was drunk enough to behave stupidly, but not so drunk that he couldn't do somebody serious damage. When he came back with two pints of lager, I stood well aside. Apart from anything else, Fred, the landlord, had recently installed closed-circuit TV, so that if anything did start he would have the evidence on tape — and in the event of trouble, he'd be straight up the camp next morning.

Nothing more happened for a while; but when I went for a slash, out of the corner of my eye I saw the fellow get up and start after me. Then, as I stood at the communal urinal, he came and took up position right beside me, not having a piss himself, but peering down at my midriff in the most offensive fashion.

"Look," I said, "I told you to fuck off."

"Not much to bloody write home about, is it?" he said contemptuously. "Can't think what she sees in it."

I saw his right hand moving down towards his pocket, so I didn't wait any longer, but dropped him where he stood. He slid down the enamel face and finished up lying on his left side with his head in the trough. Just the place for him. I made a quick grab into his trouser pocket. Sure enough, he had a flick-knife. In a second I had lifted the lid of the flushing cistern and dropped it in. Maybe in a few years' time, if rusty water started coming down the system, somebody would have a look and discover its corroded remains.

Back in the bar I muttered, "Time to thin out, lads. We could have a problem. I'll see you."

"Where's your admirer?" asked Pat.

"Just having a little nap."

With that I said good-night to Fred and moved off casually. On the way home I tried to make sense of the yobbo's aggression. Tracy had said something about

recently breaking up with a boyfriend . . . but no —
she would never have been friends with a turd like
that. And anyway, how could he possibly associate me
with her? She and I had never been seen together in
town. I decided that there was no connection; it was
just normal jealousy of the Regiment coming out. All
the same, the incident made me realize how much the
girl was on my mind.

CHAPTER
FIVE

A few days before we left, at the start of December, we heard on the grapevine that 500 men of the First Glosters had been sent to Ulster in response to the latest upsurge of violence. It certainly sounded as though we were going to get some action.

Several of the lads went berserk over their packing, insisting that they take almost every single object they possessed. We knew that our accommodation was going to be basic — no more than a series of Portakabins inside a warehouse — yet they seemed hell-bent on having their fridges, TV sets, microwaves and God-knows-what with them. There was no limit on what we were allowed to take — the bulk items went ahead by road and ferry, leaving us with only our ops kit — all the same, I didn't go in for much heavy stuff for one thing, I didn't think I'd need it, and for another, I didn't want to strip the cottage just as the girls moved in. In the end all I took was my Technics stereo system, minus the speakers, because I reckoned they'd piss off my neighbours in a close-quarter environment, and in any case I'd recently invested in a pair of Stax headphones whose sound quality put the speakers in the shade.

A Puma came into camp on the Monday afternoon, and

lifted the twelve of us away over the Welsh mountains. Looking across the cabin, I was glad to see the grizzled, close-cropped head of Tom Dawson, the sergeant major, who was coming as our second-in-command on the final posting of his career. I suppose that in a way he was a father figure to us all, and, maybe because I had no parents of my own, I'd benefited more than most of the guys from his wisdom and long experience.

We put down to refuel in a shit-hole of a depot on the coast, and then did a flit across the sea. The crossing gave me time to reflect on the set-up at home. Tracy and Susan had moved their things in the day before, and we'd piled Kath's clothes into the small spare bedroom. The three of us had spent that night in separate rooms, as proper as could be. In the morning I'd shown the girls how to work the central heating system and how to manage the wood-burning stove. I'd amassed a big store of logs, so they had plenty of fuel. "For God's sake don't burn the place down," I told Tracy. "That's the only rule."

At that stage I don't think she'd said anything to Susan about her long-term plans; all Susan knew was that they had somewhere to live for the next few months. But when we were alone for a moment Tracy said again, "When you come back, I'll be waiting for you." That gave me a big kick, of course, but I was still disturbed by the speed at which everything had happened. Kath had been killed on 28 July, and we were now only just into December. Four months. I kept telling myself that it wasn't me who had written Kath off. I hadn't done anything to get rid of her. Fate, or whatever, had snatched her.

My soul-searching didn't last long. Soon we were

over the coast and landing in the camp on the outskirts of Belfast. Inside the warehouse, the first thing we saw was a man with pink hair. "For fuck's sake!" cried Pat. "What's this? A poofters' convention?" But an old SAS hand, who'd been there for a couple of months already, assured us that it was only one of the Det guys who'd tried to dye his fair hair brown but had got the mixture wrong. The senior wrangler explained that it was perfectly legitimate for members of the Det to change their appearance for cover purposes. This fellow however, was going to have to stay out of sight for a few days, until he got himself sorted.

Apart from the pink-head, our immediate surroundings weren't that cheerful, but Pat and I got cabins next to each other and soon settled ourselves in. Some previous occupant of mine must have been a freak for Pirelli calendars, because it was tits and bums on every wall. Rather than rip them down and have bare cream-coloured panels all round, I left them where they were, gradually persuading myself that in some respects the June bird looked remarkably like Tracy.

The best that could be said for our set-up was that everything was under one roof: not only our cabins, but also the briefing room, armoury, MT depot, canteen, bar, showers and bogs were situated within the warehouse. To me it had a claustrophobic air, but the guys who handed over to us assured us that you soon got used to it. One feature nobody had warned us about was the rats. That first evening a sudden yell of outrage went up, and we ran out of our cabins to see a guy called Ginger Norris pointing up into the roof.

100

"Look at that!" he roared. "The biggest fucking rat you've ever seen!"

Sure enough, there on one of the girders perched a vast rat, a real monster, and, when a volley of trainers went up at it, all it did was move a tier higher and sit there polishing its whiskers, cool as a pint of Stella. "Jesus Christ!" cried Ginger. "Never mind the PIRA or anybody else, the next thing'll be we'll all go down with lepto-fucking-spirosis." He was all for taking out the rat with his Sig, until somebody pointed out that we'd be even worse off if he shot the roof full of holes and let the rain through.

"It's those wankers of cooks," explained one of the old hands. "They sling all the leftover food in open bins out the back of the cookhouse, and the rats eat themselves stupid. It's like giving them a free run of the menu at the Dorchester."

"Why don't we get some cats?" I suggested.

"Cats?" said Ginger derisively. "Cats? Rats this size would have them for breakfast."

Our first couple of days were spent on orientation, getting to know Belfast itself. Even though I'd made several visits to my in-laws in Helen's Bay, and had come into the city centre from the east, I'd never been in West Belfast, and now I was appalled by the sheer squalor of the place. I'd seen endless pictures of it on television, of course, and I was familiar with the crude murals of black-hooded figures painted on the sides of buildings; but nothing had quite prepared me for the pure grot — the scruffiness, the meanness, the ugliness, the filth.

Our own senior guys drove us around the softer areas of the city in unmarked cars; but the hard areas were out of bounds to such vehicles, and the only way we could get a look at them was by courtesy of the RUC, who gave us tours, two at a time, in the back of their armoured Land Rovers.

That meant, first of all, getting infiltrated into one of the fortified police stations — an experience in itself. The one Pat and I went to was defended like Fort Knox with high, anti-rocket wire-mesh screens, mortar-proof walls of reinforced concrete, and closed-circuit television cameras bristling from every rooftop. Driving in, we passed through three separate manned gateways; then, to enter the building, we went round a couple of corners — thick walls set at right-angles to each other to cut down the chance of blast penetration.

Inside, a sergeant gave us a quick tour, mainly of the ops room, where radios crackled and the walls were covered with large-scale maps dotted with coloured pins. This station, said our guide, had been attacked more than a hundred times, with rockets, mortars, sniper fire and coffee-jar devices, or petrol bombs. "They fired an RPG7 from the distilleries into the canteen, so they did," he told us. "There were no fatalities, but quite a few people were injured. Then they tried to float a bomb down the stream which passes under the station in a tunnel. We have a cage on either end, and cameras, but still they were going to try it. Luckily the Special Branch got wind of what was happening, and they aborted the attempt.

From one of the sangars — high, fortified towers — we had a great view over the city. Everything looked peaceful enough, yet still our guide could speak of nothing but attacks. One great merit of the station's position, he explained, was that it had a school and a housing estate right behind it. These made the PIRA reluctant to fire mortars in that direction, because the weapons were notoriously unreliable, and an overshoot that caused civilian casualties would create very bad publicity.

We ventured out on patrol in a police Land Rover. A constable drove, and a sergeant called Martin kept up a running commentary from the passenger seat. We crouched in the back, craning forward to peer out through the armoured glass of the windscreen, with a third RUC man scanning through the small aperture in one of the rear doors.

Here, on this corner, a rocket attack on a police Land Rover had cut an RUC sergeant nearly in half. Here a lad had tried to throw a bomb over the wall into a police station, but he'd dropped it, and it blew off his arm. Here, on the Falls Road, was the infamous Rock Bar, where members of the PIRA would meet for a pint. Here they had staged a burglary on a library, and as a policeman approached to investigate they'd opened up on him with an M 60 machine-gun. Here was Rose Cottage, inhabited by a harmless old pensioner. Under the pretence of befriending him, IRA men had offered to decorate a room for him, and in the course of doing so they had built a false wall, shortening the room by about five feet and creating a major weapons hide, later discovered by the Royal Marines.

We were patrolling as a pair, in company with a second vehicle, never far from it, in case one or other suddenly needed help. Martin was frequently on his radio: "Six Five, roger. We're just going to Sebastopol . . . We're passing Berlin." Every now and then our partner vehicle would drive past in the opposite direction, as the pair wove intricate patterns through the sordid, run-down streets. Again and again Martin said, "The whole of this road is divided, Green Nationalists on one side, Orange Protestants on the other." But he kept emphasizing that most of the population was perfectly normal: "There's so many decent people here. The proportion of bad ones is very small." Nevertheless, he agreed that he was constantly on the lookout for familiar faces, trying to spot known players and work out their patterns of movement, and after an hour I felt the entire place was poisoned by hatred.

Back in the station, Pat and I went off to have a piss. The nearest gents was tucked away on the floor below, and Martin came down to show us the route, leaving us to find our own way back. As we emerged, a man in civvies was coming along the corridor towards us — quite an old guy, with grey hair — and as I glanced at him I felt a prickle of recognition. In the same instant his face gave a flicker as he recognized me.

"Hello," he said. "I know you, surely."

"Yes — we met in Hereford."

It was Chief Superintendent Morrison, the RUC man who'd talked to our course at LATA.

"Geordie Sharp," I said, "and this is a colleague, Pat."

We all shook hands, and Morrison said, "Have you a moment for a chat? This is my office, right here."

He pointed at a door beside us. Instinctively I said, "D'you want to go on up, Pat? I'll be with you in a couple of minutes."

Pat got the message and thinned out. The chief ushered me into his office, large but bare, and gestured at a chair in front of the desk. "Take a seat. Just come over?"

"That's right."

"Well, I hope you have a successful tour."

I wasn't quite sure what he meant by that. Was it just innocent good wishes? I said, "Thanks."

He started fiddling with a glass paperweight. Then, looking steadily at me across the desk, he said, "I believe you lost your wife in the Queensfield bomb."

"That's right."

"I'm so sorry. I know it was an own-goal, but there's no consolation in that. Very likely the device would have killed even more people if it had gone off where they meant it to. I think I told you over in England, we're up against real bastards here, evil bastards. What I didn't say to your course was that I've lost my own brother to them, and his son, my nephew. So I can imagine how you feel."

"Thanks," I repeated.

"Sympathy's not much use. I've learnt that over the years. But you have mine, and if there's anything I can do to help, you'll let me know."

Even as he spoke, an idea was opening up in my mind.

"That's very good of you," I said, and then I added casually, "I don't suppose you know who did it — who was responsible for the bomb?"

"I'd have to check. Why?" His lined, grey face softened into a smile. "D'you fancy going after them or something?"

"No, no." I forced a smile in return. "I just thought it might help somehow, to know."

"Of course. And if I did find out any information, what would I do with it?"

"Maybe you could send it care of my father-in-law. That would be the safest." I gave him the address in Helen's Bay.

"Good enough. And now maybe you'd better rejoin your colleague. I'm pleased to have seen you again."

I went back to the ops room feeling like a conspirator, busy with my own thoughts — only to find that the others were talking about a subject of intense interest to me: the way in which leading players protected their houses. Many had closed-circuit TV cover front and back, Martin was saying, and most reinforced their front doors with steel plates and big, heavy, old-fashioned iron bars which could be swung or slotted into place at night, making it impossible to force an entry. Often they'd have an inner door as well, with an air-lock between the two in which they could scrutinize visitors. Then, at the bottom of the stairs, they'd have a cage or grille of heavyweight weldmesh, so that they could seal off the upper floor. That way, they were safe from all but the most determined attacks.

The troop's eight intercept cars were monsters in disguise. They looked quite ordinary, but under their sedate exterior lurked mighty engines and any number

106

of refinements. Some of the engines had merely been hotted-up, but others had been replaced by more powerful units altogether. The extra punch was needed because the cars were carrying a huge amount of weight in the form of armour — at the front, along the side-panels, and behind the two back seats. To manage all this, as well as four blokes and their gear, rifles, shotguns, assault kits, door-charges and so on, the springs and shock-absorbers had been uprated. Even so, the belly-plates were liable to ground when you went over bumps like sleeping policemen, sending out showers of sparks.

Inside each car there was a comprehensive comms system, with the radio tucked away in the glove compartment, a pressel switch down by the handbrake, and a microphone slotted into the sun visor. For normal covert operations we'd listen through our earpieces, but there was also a loudspeaker fitted into the glove compartment for when the shit hit the fan. "If you get into a chase, and the villains know you're after them, there's no point in trying to stay covert, so you switch to the speaker," somebody explained. "Equally, if you start to take incoming, and the windscreen goes, your earpieces are the last thing you need."

I didn't appreciate quite what the cars would do until I went out for a familiarization drive. The one I had was an old Rover 2000 known as the Bluesmobile. It looked drab and decrepit, as if it was well past its scrap-by date, and when we started out I thought I was driving a tank, so heavy did it feel. But as soon as I got out on to the ring road and put my foot down — that was something else. In a few seconds we were doing 150 m.p.h., with a good bit in hand, and only a build-up of traffic far ahead made me ease off. Thereafter I took things more steadily and concentrated on getting familiar with the radio system. One lesson I learnt from the run is that a G3 is a brute of a weapon to take in a car: too long to fit down neatly beside the driver's seat, and difficult to bring up quickly. I'd already heard of an occasion when a G3 had slipped so that the muzzle landed on the accelerator pedal, and the driver suddenly found himself heading off into the sunset at a great rate of knots. Now I saw the wisdom of bringing an HK 53, which would fit comfortably under the seat.

Our familiarization was supposed to last for the first couple of weeks, but in the event things turned out less leisurely. One evening I was in my cabin, with Eric Clapton keeping the world at bay, when through the music I heard a call on the tannoy: "Standby team into the briefing room."

In half a minute all ten of us had assembled.

Tom Dawson, the second-in-command, was in charge. "Right, lads," he began. "We've got a fast ball. Operation Eggshell. It's a babysitting job, with a few strings attached. There's a hit going down on a senior political figure, timed for 2230 tonight. The boss is at TCG, getting details. Basically it's a city job, in East Belfast. We need four guys to babysit and six to deploy in the intercept cars."

He turned to me. "Geordie, you're to command the house party. The address is Knocklofty Park. There's no time for an on-site recce, so you'll need to take a good

108

look at the map and get your arses down there a.s.a.p. Covert approach from wasteground behind. If you want to grab something to eat you've got twenty minutes. Final briefing at 2000, and roll immediately after."

Because I'd already eaten, I had plenty of time to sort and check my kit: HK 53, side-arm, magazines for both, torch, knife, wire-cutters, covert radio. We'd go in wearing civilian clothes, but with our ops waistcoats on. I told all my guys to bring a pair of clean trainers for when we got inside the house; even if the people you're looking after are about to be blown to kingdom come, they don't take it kindly if you mess up their carpets. I also packed a roll of heavy-duty polythene and one of lightweight black cloth, for doctoring up a lookout room when we established ourselves in the target. With film slanted across a room from ceiling to floor and the back wall blacked out, you can move around without somebody outside being able to see you.) Then I thought, If the old people are going to be in the house, we'd better take flak-jackets for them, just in case shrapnel comes through the floor or one of the doors. Also we needed a couple of big medical packs.

At 2000 the boss, Captain John Mason, was still down at TCG, so our final briefing came from Tom.

"Just to confirm details," he began. "The PIRA's target is Freddy Quinlan, the Unionist MP. He's already at home with his wife. He's been offered the chance to leave, but he's declined. He's that way: doesn't rate the opposition, stupid bugger. Normally he has no security on the house whatever, not even any cameras. But that's his lookout.

"Our information is that the PIRA are planning a rocket attack. Probably a drive-past. They'll launch an RPG7 to take out the front door, then follow up on foot to finish off anyone who has survived. That means your guys, Geordie, will want to be upstairs with the family. At the same time, it's vital that you preserve an impression of normal activity. The curtains will be drawn, but we want people to move around the house naturally for as long as possible. OK?"

I nodded, and he went on, pushing a large-scale town plan across the table towards me, "Your covert approach will be through wasteland behind the house. It's the former grounds of a mansion, gone to seed. We'll get you dropped off here" — he pointed with a pencil — "and it'll only be a short walk in, three hundred metres at the outside. Between the edge of the park and the back garden is a wooden panel fence. Don't go over that, in case the players have eyes-on from behind one of the adjacent properties. Get under it, or through the bottom. The back door of the house will be open for you. OK?"

Again I nodded. "How do we recognize the house and garden from the back?"

"There's a World Wildlife Fund panda symbol hung over the outside of the fence."

"What about the telephone? Is the line bugged?"

"Possibly. Special Branch have told Quinlan to carry on taking normal calls, but obviously not to mention the operation."

"Fair enough."

"Anything else?"

110

"A rocket will probably blow the hell out of the electrics and leave the house dark. We'd better take some ambush lights as an emergency back-up."

"Good thinking."

Tom went on to brief the car-teams and the QRF. I listened with half an ear, studying the map. The old park or garden showed up as a sizeable green blob in the middle of massed streets and houses, but there was nothing to be learnt about it from where we were. The drop-off point was on the far side of the park from our destination, so all we needed to do was cross the wasteground in an easterly direction.

As soon as Tom finished, the signals corporal went through his own plan. The boss's callsign for the night was Zero Alpha, and our house team was designated Hotel One. We were also assigned a chatter-net on a different frequency, so that if necessary we could talk to each other without cluttering up the main channel. Our car units were Mobile One, Mobile Two and so on. The house was designated "the target", the back door was "Red" and the front door "White". Some of our guys were to mount an OP in a garden across the road — that party had the callsign Whisky. The Det, with various Delta numbers, were already out on surveillance.

A few minutes after eight a grey van pulled into the warehouse. The legend on the panel said, "NORTHERN IRELAND ELECTRICITY VAN — Engineering Department", and the vehicle had a big sliding side door, excellent for an unobtrusive exit. My house team piled in and set off. With the pair of ambush lights and power-pack, my bergen was going to be quite a burden, even though we were going on such a short operation. I'm sure Pat spoke for all of us when he said, "I don't like the thought of this fucking rocket coming in."

"Neither do I," I told him. "But as long as the house is reasonably substantial we'll be OK upstairs."

Peering forward through the windscreen, I said to Titch, the driver, "You will bring us in with the door on the kerb-side, won't you?"

"No sweat."

Twenty minutes of twisting and turning through the city brought us to our objective.

"Here's the park now," said Titch. "I'm just running down the side of it. The lay-by's a couple of hundred yards farther on. Stand by to debus."

The moment he stopped I hit the handle, slid the door and was outside, landing in a shallow puddle. I took a quick look round. It was pretty good: a smallish recess at the edge of the suburban road, screened by bushes. Some traffic was passing, but none very close. Immediately behind us were the old iron railings of the mansion's grounds, topped by two strands of barbed wire. Rather than risk getting hung up I cut through them, peeled them back and went over the railings, quickly followed by the other three. Titch had got out and opened the bonnet of the van. I saw him peering about under it with a torch, tugging at electric leads as if checking for a fault. As soon as we were clear he slammed the bonnet shut and drove off. I was pretty sure nobody had seen us.

Inside the park it was like being on an island, dark

112

and peaceful, with the city traffic roaring and grinding round in the distance outside. As I waited for my eyes to acclimatize, one of the Det guys came up on the radio with, "Delta Two, a dicker's just walked down the street past White."

"Sounds like the job's going down OK," I whispered. "We'd better get in there."

Round the perimeter of the park ran a belt of mature trees, some of them pines. The air was full of the smell of evergreens and ivy. Once through the trees, we came out on to open grass. At the edge of the cover I paused for a look round. Away to our left, a couple of hundred yards off on the crest of a rise, stood the old mansion, dark as dark, a heavy-looking Victorian building with turrets and pointed eaves. The grass we were on must once have been the lawn. Some lawn! Three or four acres, at least. We moved swiftly across it, towards more high trees on the far side. Ahead of us, between the trunks, lights were showing — the backs of the houses in our target road.

The ground beneath the second belt of trees was choked by undergrowth — diabolical bramble bushes, five or six feet high, interlaced with elder. Rather than crash through the thicket, we tried to pick a way between, only to find ourselves on the edge of a flooded area, perhaps an old pond. Pulling off, we made another approach, and soon came to a six-foot wooden fence along the backs of the gardens. A quick cast to the right brought us face-to-face with the reassuring black-and-white shape of the panda badge.

"Pity to carve this up," I whispered, feeling the wooden panels.

"It's OK," answered Jimmy Adair. "There's a drain running under it."

He'd found a kind of culvert, and with a few jabs from our collapsible shovel we enlarged it enough for us to wriggle through. The back of the house was only ten metres off: whitewashed walls, several windows, the back-door conveniently screened by a projecting outhouse. A light was showing upstairs, but the curtains of that room were drawn.

We stood in the shadows by the fence. I held in my pressel switch and said softly, "Hotel One. On Red now."

"Zero Alpha, roger," answered the boss.

As promised, the door was open. We slipped into a short corridor and locked up behind us, shooting home the bolts at the top and bottom. A smell of cooking hung in the air. We took off our boots, stacked them in a neat heap and put on our clean trainers. Then, leaving the others to cover me, I went quietly forward, HK 53 at the ready, past the kitchen and into the hall.

The TV was on in one of the front rooms. I knocked on the door, pushed it open a foot or so and showed myself in the gap. The woman saw me first — a small, elderly person with white hair swept back in a bun. She gave a bit of a cry and stood up.

"It's all right," I said. "We're here to look after you."

The husband was a fierce-looking little fellow, with curly silver hair, dark eyebrows, and thick-rimmed glasses; he was wearing a fawn cardigan and matching slippers, like any retired professional. As soon as I saw him, I recognized his face from news bulletins and the papers.

From the darkness of the hall I asked him if the front curtains were fully drawn.

"Sure they are," he said testily. "That was the first thing your people told us. We've got the old blackout blind pulled down as well." As he came towards me he said, "This is ridiculous," but not in a voice that carried much conviction. I caught a trace of whisky on his breath. He was easily old enough to be my father, so I didn't feel I could give him too many orders, still less pull him around physically if he became difficult. I was glad to find that his irritation was only bluff when I assured him that the threat was not only real but imminent, he agreed to move upstairs.

"What I don't understand is this," he said. "If you know they're coming, why the heck can't you intercept them before they get here?"

"The trouble is, we don't know where they're coming from. We have other units outside, and with a bit of luck, they may get to the villains before they do any damage to the house. But we can't take chances with your safety."

Before I could stop her, his wife switched off the television.

"Sorry," I said. "We'd better leave that on."

She gave me a look, but went back to the channel they'd been on.

It turned out that the couple slept at the back of the house — the room in which we'd seen the light — and had another set in their bedroom. As quickly as we could, we got them safely in there, and told them that if they needed to go to the bathroom they mustn't switch on any more lights.

"Here," I said, getting out the flak-jackets. "If you don't mind, put these on. They're a bit heavy and uncomfortable, but they could just save your lives." Then I took the medical packs into the bathroom and opened them up so that the IV kits were immediately to hand.

Next we took a look round downstairs. The house was solidly built, with floors that didn't bounce, and walls which felt good when you hit them. The whole place was tidy as could be. I found it hard to believe that the shit was about to be blown out of it. The front door was locked and bolted, but only medium-strong, and it had a half-moon of frosted glass above it. The thought of an RPG7 rocket coming through it was not amusing. The weapon was developed by the Russians more than thirty years ago, in the depths of the Cold War, for the express purpose of taking out British or American tanks; though extremely simple, it was capable of destroying any armoured vehicle, let alone an ordinary car or somebody's front door. The chances were that if one came through into the hall, it would blow out the back wall of the house as well.

The only firefighting equipment was one ancient-looking extinguisher, but I put this ready, just inside the kitchen. Luckily the stairs started from the back of the hall and came forward towards the front, so that if we did get a rocket through the door, the main blast would be directed through the kitchen and out of the back door, rather than upwards. "Let's get our boots out of the line of fire, anyway," said Pat, and we shifted them into a scullery.

Upstairs again, I saw that the landing ran across the back of the stairwell. Kneeling behind the white-painted wooden banisters, we could cover the whole of the hall. If any assault party tried to follow up a rocket, we could take them out from there, no bother.

I checked all the doors, and once I'd got the layout I detailed Jimmy to remain in the back bedroom with our hosts, in case anyone started trying to come through the rear window. In the front bedroom on the left, facing forwards, we slung a sheet of polythene at a forty-five degree angle, fixing it to the walls with drawing-pins brought for the purpose, so that we could look through the window without being visible from outside. To complete the optical illusion, we pinned our thin black cloth over the rear wall, cutting out background reflection.

Hardly had we done that when Pat, who was looking out, said, "Hey, there's someone coming past."

In the patchy illumination of the street-lamps we saw a young man in what looked like jeans and a black donkey jacket walk past from right to left. He was trying to maintain a nonchalant appearance, but we saw him take a sideways glance at the target.

"One of their dickers, I bet," said Jimmy.

Sure enough, a moment later the Det came up with "Delta Two. That same dicker's gone back the other way."

"Hotel One," I called. "Established on target."

"Roger," answered the boss. "Stand by."

I was still new enough to the game to be surprised by the immediacy with which our team's voices jumped out of the night. I knew that the boss was miles away, at the desk, and that the Det guys were spread out all over town. But from the speed with which people came up on the air, they might have been in a tight ring round the target.

I decided that when, or if the attack came, we'd go to ground in the blacked-out bedroom and close the door. Then, immediately after the explosion, we'd whip out on to the landing so that we could drop anyone who came into the hall below. We therefore constructed a kind of shelter out of the two single beds, tipping them on edge and tilting the tops inwards against each other, like a tent, with the mattresses on the floor to give some protection from below and room for us to crawl in so that we had cover in case the ceiling came down. Then I set the two ambush lights out, one on either side of the landing, so that if anyone fired up at them, the rounds would go well clear of our own position. I ran the wires round the landing so that the switch was at the point where I intended to be.

Waiting was no joke. We'd turned up the sound of the TV a bit, so that we could hear it burbling away, and the ever-changing light from the screen flickered out into the hall. Occasionally one of us went down to open or close the living-room door a bit, so that any watcher would see a change in the light showing through the frosted glass over the front door, and conclude that Quinlan and his wife were in and out of the room. When I went down for the last time I left the door shut, as if they were both in the room. Each of those trips downstairs made my hair crawl. What if the players had given the Det the slip, and were lining their rocket-launcher up at that very moment?

In fact, we had plenty of radio chat to keep us abreast of the situation. At 2215 the same dicker made a third pass. He'd taken the trouble to go round in a big circle, so that he came by in the same direction as on his earlier appearance, and gave the casual impression of being another walker going the same way. But the Det knew him too well, and reported a definite sighting. After that, though, no other pedestrians showed, and we guessed the strike was coming up. Our intercept cars had taken up strategic positions in surrounding streets, in case the hit-car escaped immediate ambush, and they too came on the air occasionally, with callsigns India One, India Two and so on.

From time to time I briefed our landlord on the latest situation. At 2220 the lady of the house offered us a brew made from an upstairs kettle, which we gratefully accepted, one at a time. "So long as you don't damage anything," she kept repeating. I promised her that we'd be as careful as we could, but said that I couldn't vouch for our friends on the other side.

Minute by minute, the time ticked on. My mind was flying round in circles: Kath, Tim, Tracy, Gary Player . . . It was too much to hope that he would have been assigned to carry out tonight's hit. Almost certainly he was too senior to take part at the front: he'd be sitting back safely in some command post. But by God, if *any* player appeared down there in the hall, there was only one way he'd ever leave the building, and that was feet first, in a bag.

Then at 2235, came the call we'd been expecting. "Delta Three. Suspect black Volvo mobile towards target. Sun roof is open, so anticipate drive-past rocket attack. Estimate time to target one minute."

"Roger," answered Delta Control.

Then it was our boss: "Zero Alpha. Assault imminent. Confirm prepared."

"Hotel One," I answered. "Roger."

"Delta Two," came a Welsh voice. "Confirm Volvo mobile to target. Westwards down Craven Avenue. Estimate thirty seconds."

"Zero Alpha to Hotel One," said the boss. "Standby, standby."

"Hotel One, roger."

I nipped into the back bedroom. "On the floor, please," I said. "They're coming."

There was something pathetic about seeing the old couple go stiffly down on their knees on their double mattress, then lie flat, tucking themselves in against the flank of their own bed. Jimmy yanked another mattress off the bed so that it covered them, then lay down on the outside of the pair, a human wall.

I dived into the front bedroom, closed the door and laid my HK 53 along the wainscoting, where I could put my hand on it in the dark. The other two guys were already on their backs in the makeshift sangar.

I don't know how many seconds passed. I imagined the rocketeer climbing to his feet in the passenger seat, head through the sun-roof opening, bracing himself as the wagon swung round a corner. In my mind I saw him bring up the awkwardly long launcher and settle it into his shoulder. Suddenly I thought of a German friend who loathed all Volvos, and, whenever he saw one, shouted, "*SCHEISSAUTO!*" This one was a shit-car, all right.

I caught one more Det report, calling the Volvo into the start of our road. Then I closed my eyes and clamped my hands over my ears.

I just heard the car engine, screaming at high revs in some low gear. Then came the *whoosh* of a rocket being fired, and an almighty, earth-moving *BANG!* I felt the floor flex beneath me. The door of our room flew open and smacked back against the end of one bed. From hall and landing came the sound of plaster falling. My instinct was to yell at the top of my voice, to let out the tension, but I fought down the impulse.

The lights had gone out. The television had been silenced. In a second all three of us were at the banister rail, weapons trained on the hall. The air down there was full of smoke or dust or both. Through it I saw that the front door had gone, and street-lights were showing through an open rectangle. I had my hand on the switch of the ambush lights, but something made me hesitate. If there were any rats incoming, I wanted them well in the trap. But were there any? From outside came a sudden hammer of rounds going down, then more, and more. Then a screech of tyres followed by a heavy impact. We'd got the car, for sure.

From somewhere under us at the back of the hall came a flicker of ruddy light. Fire. Nothing serious as yet; just enough to give useful illumination. But already

I'd come down a notch or two from my peak of tension. The shots outside, and the noise of the crash — everything suggested that the gunmen had gone under.

Not at all. Movement in the doorway. Two dark, hooded figures ran in, kicked the door of the living room wide and opened up through the gap with sub-machine-guns, spraying the room with uncontrolled bursts. In the confines of the house the noise was shattering, and the players themselves were adding to it. No silence for them. High on adrenalin, they were roaring obscenities fit to bust: fecking this and fecking that. When one of them flashed a torch round the room and found there was nobody in it, they yelled even louder.

All this had taken maybe four seconds. By the time they ran back into the hall, the flames below us were bigger and giving better light. They illuminated our targets just enough. The range was point blank, and they never even looked up. Two short bursts from each of us, and down they went. In the flickering light I'd gone for the mass of their upper chests, but one of them caught it in the head as well when he fell forward. I saw the armour-piercing rounds rip his balaclava open, and pieces of skull fly out.

Another volley of rounds spurted from the other man's weapon, but only because in going down he'd pulled the trigger inadvertently, and the rounds smacked harmlessly into the wall at floor level. As he crumpled on to the carpet, I gave him a quick double-tap in the head. The body gave a couple of violent jerks, then lay still.

122

For several seconds we didn't move. We were safe in the smoky darkness, and in a brilliant position. If fifty players had followed the first two in we could have dropped them all. The reek of cordite filled the air. Suddenly there was noise and movement above us — a creak, a snap, a rustle, a tearing sound. I faced upwards to see a big chunk of plasterboard fall away from the ceiling and plummet on to the stairs, where it burst and bounced down in smaller pieces, raising another cloud of dust, as if a shell had landed.

"Jimmy!" I yelled.

"Aye," he called from the back bedroom.

"Your people all right?"

"Fine."

"Keep them there a minute."

Now I did turn on the ambush lights, so that they illuminated the hall and caught the smoke, which was rising in clouds. Through it I could see the two bodies lying hunched against the wainscoting, one either side, and the blood seeping out over the pale carpet. Both men had fallen on their weapons, which were buried beneath them. I felt for my pressel with shaking fingers.

"Hotel One. Two X-rays dead on target. White demolished. No home casualties. Get the QRF up!" I knew I was shouting, but I couldn't help it.

The leader of the fire-party was also shouting. Everyone was trying to get on the air at once.

"Zero Alpha," said the boss firmly. "EVERYBODY WAIT OUT! Now. Hotel One. Is your area secure?"

"Hotel One, roger. Area secure."

"Roger. Hotel Two. Is *your* area secure?"

"Hotel Two. Two dead X-rays. One RPG. One side-arm. This area is now secure."

"Zero Alpha. Inform all stations. QRF coming in now. Stand by for pick-up."

Covered by the other two, I stepped cautiously down the stairs. The shreds of the front door hung from its hinges, but the centre of it had been blown clean out. Cold air was wafting in through the hole, and carrying with it the rising wail of an ambulance or fire engine.

My immediate concern was to stop the house burning down. Luckily it turned out that the only things on fire were some old newspapers and magazines, and the extinguisher, ancient as it was, soon put them out.

The Quinlans were amazingly resilient. They stumbled out of their bedroom looking like startled owls, white-faced, hair on end, eyes wide. "So long as you don't damage anything," the old girl had said. Now their hall and everything in it had been destroyed. Pictures had been torn from the walls and blown into a heap of shattered frames and glass at the far end. The grandfather clock had been reduced to matchwood. Two chairs and a table were fit only for the fire. Plaster and paper had been ripped out of the walls in horizontal strips. The kitchen, also, was a wreck. I suppose the old people were in shock, but they seemed incredibly philosophical about the damage.

With their directions, using our torches, we found the fuse boxes and trip switches in the kitchen, but the system must have suffered major damage because it wouldn't come alive again. Perhaps it was just as well.

All of a sudden Pat began to laugh. "No fucking damage!" he gasped. "Fucking roll on!" He was laughing

124

so much he had to sit down. In a couple of seconds I was helpless as well, doubled up, in hysterics. I knew it was a reaction to release of tension, caused by an excess of adrenalin, but that didn't help me stop. I realized that the Quinlans must think us incredibly callous, or crazy, or both — but again, that was no deterrent. Only when an RUC officer stuck his head round the door and said, "What's so bloody funny, then?" did we manage to pull ourselves together.

The QRF arrived, cleared the street and cordoned it off. Suddenly the house was full of people, among them a couple of firemen, and the Scene of Crimes Officer, who began taking measurements and statements, and chalking on to the landing carpet the positions from which we'd fired. A photographer took pictures of the bodies. They weren't looking all that pretty. One had the skull split clean down the middle, over the cranium. The armour-piercing rounds had opened up his head like a melon. Grey brain was showing through the gap, and the scalp had slid over to one side, crumpling the face into folds. The eyeballs were bulging out of their sockets. Brain and blood were spattered over the wall behind. Both terrorists looked very young. As the bodies were being bundled into bags I asked the RUC man if he knew who they were, but he shook his head. "From the Lisburn ASU, by all accounts," he said, "but beyond that, I've no idea."

Back in the warehouse we held a big debriefing. It turned out that our own reactive OP had nailed the Volvo, killing both the driver and the guy who fired the rocket. They'd captured not only the rocket launcher, but two AK 47s and a couple of side-arms as well.

At first we were baffled about how the two-man assault party had escaped detection, and where they'd come from. The car had not stopped or even slowed down, so they couldn't have been in it. The mystery was solved by a search of the front garden, which revealed that they'd lain up in the shrubs either side of the front path. They must have slipped in there immediately after dark, before our surveillance was in place, and stuck it out for nearly five hours.

In any case, the bag for the night was four, and everyone was really chuffed that the operation had gone down. Alter the wash-up we all got in the bar together — RUC, the Det and us — for a few celebratory beers. By then the Det and the RUC between them had identified the dead terrorists, but the names meant nothing to me.

Among those celebrating was the guy with pink hair. When I got close to him, I began to think I'd seen him somewhere before.

"Listen," I said, "I'm sure I know you. Where could it have been?"

"Two Para," he said immediately, with a grin. "Aldershot."

"Right, right!"

Suddenly we were on net. His name was Mike Grigson, and though we'd never really met we'd been in the same company for a brief spell. We began to exchange chit-chat, and hit it off well. He'd done a year with the Det already, and obviously knew the score. For the past few days he'd been taken off outside duties and given

126

some role in the head-shed, until he was fit to appear in public again.

"What went wrong?" I asked.

"Duffed up the fucking mixture, didn't I?" he said cheerfully. "That's the trouble with being fair-haired — I stand out in a bloody crowd. I was trying to do something about it."

As for myself I couldn't make out whether I was on a high or a low. One moment everything seemed terrific, because it had all gone according to the book; the next, I felt terrible at having killed, or helped to kill, two people. Yet perhaps the worst thing was the realization of how difficult my self-appointed task was going to be. A major operation, with all the stops out, had accounted for four lowly paddies. How was I ever going to get near Mr Big on my own?

A couple of pints later I bought Pink Mike a drink and asked casually, "So, who were those players tonight?"

"Nobody much. Rank and file from the Lisburn ASU."

"Had you seen them before?"

"The two in the car, yes. The driver and the rocketeer. Not the others."

"How d'you recognize them?"

"We're out looking for them all the time. That's our job. Besides, we've got dozens of mug-shots in the ops room. Covert pictures, but some of them pretty good."

"Could I have a look at them sometime?"

"You're not supposed to, really. But maybe we could fix it. Why?"

"Just curious, that's all."

CHAPTER
SIX

Ten days or so after that, just before Christmas, I had the evening off and drove out to Helen's Bay to see the family. It was easy enough to get away — all I had to do was clock myself out and enter my business as "Socializing". I booked out one of the admin cars on the wall-chart in the ops room — a dark-blue, two-litre Sierra with the callsign Tango Four — and marked up my destination and time out, which was 1735. The car had normal covert comms; in the event of an emergency while I was out in the vehicle, the head-shed would still have the means to recall me, in the form of a bleeper which I carried in my trouser pocket. If that went off, I was to contact base immediately. The device had a switch that could be put on to "Pulse", so that if a call came in a tight situation you could feel it rather than hear it, and no one else's attention would be attracted. As an extra precaution I took along my Walther PPK; there seemed practically no chance that I would need it, but out there you can never tell.

It was already dark when I pulled out of the base and set off north-eastwards. The rush-hour traffic was heavy, and to make matters worse the bypass had been closed;

at the time I assumed it was the result of an accident, but later I heard that there had been a punishment shooting incident which had left vehicles strewn all over the main road. Rather than be late, I took a risk and cut through a hard area which I knew was out of bounds. I realized this was a stupid thing to do, but I thought I could get away with it for once.

My luck was out. Travelling down the Falls Road, I saw a street protest ahead. Twenty or thirty people with placards were demanding political status for prisoners. I didn't fancy the look of the crowd, or the thought of the dickers who might be hanging round its fringes, so I took a right into Beechmount Drive and Ballymurphy Street, across Beechmount Avenue ("RPG Avenue" to its fans), and so back into the Falls and Divis Street, before making my way out to the Sydenham bypass and the Bangor road.

As I drove, my mind was on recent events. Operation Eggshell had been followed by an inquest, very similar to the one staged at LATA, at which we'd given evidence from behind a screen. Our training had stood us in good stead. The terrorists had been caught fair and square; three had actually fired weapons, and the fourth had had an AK 47 in his possession, as well as a Browning pistol. So we had no trouble justifying the action we took. Oddly enough, the stress of the operation had brought on a recurrence of my nightmare, but the dream came only once, and in a less frightening form than before. All through it I remained aware that it was only a dream, and at the back of my mind I knew I was in control.

Tango Four was quite speedy when it got going, but

none too quick off the mark. On the floor in front of the passenger seat I had a present for Tim — a box-kit of solid wooden figures, pieces and blocks with sockets cut out of them which built up into a fire engine, with a crew riding on top and a ladder perched above them. The smooth solidity of the kit appealed to me, and I felt sure he'd like it too. My only worry was that it might be a bit young for him, he was growing up that fast. I'd managed to go over several times, and I could see him changing from week to week.

Maybe I was thinking too much about him, or about the procedures in court. Maybe I had just dropped my guard because I was off duty. Either way, I had reached Holywood, only a few miles short of my destination, before I became aware that I was being followed. For some time I'd been half-noticing an odd pair of headlights behind me, the left hand or kerb light showing much yellower than the right. Sometimes they were one car behind, sometimes two. Suddenly I realized that they had been there for an unhealthy length of time.

I thought, Shit — I should never have taken that short-cut. Whoever they are, they must have picked me up in West Belfast. Ahead on my left I saw the bright lights of a line of shops, facing on to the main drag but set back from it in a small road of its own. I flipped on the indicator, pulled in and cruised slowly along, peering out sideways as if in search of some particular shop. Several had closed already, but a few were still open.

The uneven lights copied my move. The car came into the lay-by and crawled along, hanging back. Out on the main road again I accelerated hard, only to see a big roundabout ahead. I went into it fast, using gears and engine to brake. As I decelerated, the lights closed rapidly from behind. Instead of going straight on — as I'd been planning — or turning off I held the gear-lever in second and kept the car in a tight right-hand turn, tyres squealing, all the way round. Glancing to my right across the mound of the roundabout, I caught a side-on glimpse of my tail. Under the street lights it looked a sickly mid-green, and pretty much beaten up — an old banger. It could have been a Cortina, but I wasn't sure. There were two guys in the front.

As I popped out on the Bangor road again, the lights were still behind me. No doubt about it now. Bloody hell! My neck began to crawl. I was after them — or rather, one of them — but also they were after me.

What were they trying to achieve? The simplest explanation was that they hoped to find out where I was going. That ditched my evening's programme, for a start. Maybe the registration number had been blown, and they'd picked me up from that. Like all the troop's cars, this one had five or six sets of plates for use in different areas. But still they could have recognized the number I had on that day. Another possibility was that I'd been spotted as I came close to the demo in the Falls Road. Or maybe these were just two dickers at large, up to their usual bullying tricks. If they spotted a car which they thought was new to an area, they might easily harass it, purely to annoy the driver. They might also try to overtake and stop me, just for the pleasure of telling me to fuck off. The worst scenario was that they were organized players, with colleagues up ahead, and that they were already trying to position a second car for an ambush.

I felt for the pressel switch of the radio, down by the gear-lever, and called, "Tango Four".

"Zero Alpha," the desk answered.

"Tango Four. I'm out past Holywood and getting a hard follow. Can you help with a back-up?"

"Roger. What's your location?"

"On the A2, inland from Helen's Bay. Heading eastwards for Red Seven. Just past Craigavad."

"Roger. Stand by." Then, a moment later, "I have two Indians on orientation training not far south of you. Are you sure you've got a tail?"

"Absolutely. I've just done a 360 round a roundabout, and they're still behind me. I don't know if they're trying to lift me or what, but I can't get rid of them."

"Roger. Keep heading for Red Seven, and whatever you do, stay on the main."

"Roger." Red Seven was the next big junction ahead, on the outskirts of Bangor, the seaside town. I could either carry on into the town or hang a right, heading south for Newtownards. My instinct was to keep out of built-up areas until I got help. The Indians were our intercept cars, and once they were in support, things would be different. On my own I didn't fancy getting lost in a maze of side-streets. Even to be held up at traffic lights would be bad news. Above all, I didn't want to get caught in a cul-de-sac.

For the time being I drove steadily, to show no sign of panic. A few seconds later I called, "Tango Four. Proposing to turn right at Red Seven."

132

"Zero Alpha," replied the desk. "Affirmative. Turn right, and right again at Red Eight."

"Roger."

"Confirm two Indians mobile towards you. What make of car are we looking for?"

"It's a crappy old banger. Mid-green. Could be a Cortina, but I'm not sure. I'm identifying it from its uneven lights. The kerb-side headlight's yellow, the outer one white. You can't mistake it if you get ahead."

"Roger."

As I drove with one hand, I was holding the map over the wheel with the other and trying to check my route. It was dangerous and difficult, because the interior light tended to dazzle one and reduce forward visibility.

Still, in the mirror, I could see the lights two vehicles back. I thought I'd better stand down my in-laws before things got any hotter. I felt for my mobile phone, dialled, waited, and got Den.

"Hi, Den. It's me, Geordie. I'm sorry, but I've had a call-out. I'm going to have to postpone my visit."

"Oh, that's too bad. Tim was really looking forward to it."

"I know. So was I. Tomorrow, maybe?"

"Everything all right?"

"Yeah, yeah. Everything's fine."

"You in a car?"

"That's right. Why?"

"It sounds noisy."

"It is. Look, I'll speak to you soon. Sorry about this. Give Tim a hug from me."

Everything was far from all right. I came to Red Eight, another big roundabout, and took the main road to the right. The lights stayed with me.

"Tango Four," I called. "Passing Red Eight now."

"Roger," came the answer. "You've got Red Nine a mile ahead. Hang another right there, for Newtownards. Confirm two Indians closing on your location."

"Roger, and thanks."

So far I hadn't heard the desk talking to the Intercepts, who must have been on a different net. But suddenly they switched over and came through loud and clear. The first thing I heard was India One calling his location as Red One Six. I recognized the voice: it was Matt Matthews, a long, thin Yorkshireman. I couldn't get a proper look at the map, but as far as I remembered, that was the junction in Comber, a small place five miles south of Newtownards. Then he confirmed, "India One mobile towards Red-One-Five." That was in the centre of Newtownards. They were heading straight towards me. I thought of them as a pair of cheetahs, coming up country in immense bounds.

I managed a quick glance at the map, and saw that a left turn in Newtownards would take me out towards the shore of Strangford Lough, away from civilization.

"Tango Four to India One," I called. "I'm mobile southwards towards Red-One-Two. Proposing turn left there, on to the shore road. Can you get something planned down there soonest?"

"India One," said Matt. "Wait out."

"Tango Four. Now passing Conlig. I still have the tail, but they don't seem to be trying to close."

"India One. Roger. If you can, slow down. We need to get ahead of you."

Slow down! Hell! I eased off the accelerator until I was doing only forty-five. The crazy lights came surging up behind. Reaching across with my right hand, I drew my PPK from its shoulder holster. Some guys, when driving off duty would sit on their pistols or keep them stuffed down between their legs. But I always thought that if I got rammed or had a crash the gun might fly forward off the seat and disappear under it or beneath the pedals. A shoulder holster was safer. With the PPK in my hand, I brought a round into the breech and slipped the pistol into the pocket on the inside of the driver's door.

To my amazement I heard India One call, "Red-One-Five now." Jesus! I thought. He's in Newtownards already. He must have been going like shit off a shovel. Seconds later he called, "Red-One-Four," and I knew he was safely through ahead of me, turning on to the lough road.

The lights had dropped back again. Already I could see the beginning of the town ahead.

"Tango Four. Hitting the outskirts of Newtownards."

"Zero Alpha, carry on to Red-One-Four. Left there."

"Roger."

The Indians and the desk began an urgent discussion — something about a parking place. I couldn't look at the map long enough to pick up the one they were talking about. At the 30 m.p.h. limit I eased down to about thirty-five. More cars were heading north out of town than going in.

Then I saw traffic lights in the distance ahead. Shit!

I did *not* want to stop. Timing was critical. As I approached, the lights were green; now, if I got it right, I might be able to shoot them as yellow changed to red and cut off the pursuit.

I hung back, hung back, then at the last instant slammed into second and hit the accelerator. Done it! I thought. I should have known better. From behind came a squeal of brakes and angry hooting. The lights swerved wildly, left and right, then steadied again. Bastards — they'd got across on the red.

"Tango Four. Approaching Red-One-Four."

"India One. Roger. One k and a bit past it, you'll come out beside the lough, on your right. The road's right by the water. Another k and there's a parking place on the right, between the road and the water. We're complete at the far end of the parking place. Dive in here at the last minute, and give us a flash as you come in. Over."

"Tango Four. Roger."

"India One. If the baddies follow you in, drive straight through, out the other end and back on to the highway. Then we'll follow and take them out. If they go past, all the better. We'll take them out anyway."

"Roger."

At the T-junction a left-hand filter let me through without stopping, and I accelerated away.

As I did so, India One called the desk. "Intercept imminent. Permission to proceed on own initiative."

"Zero Alpha. Roger. At your discretion. If the situation's life-threatening, go ahead."

In a few seconds I had the water of the lough on

my right. I pushed my speed up to sixty, then to sixty-five.

"Tango Four," I called. "Beside the water."

"India One. Keep coming."

"Estimate fifty seconds to park-place. Forty, thirty . . ."

"India One, we've got you. And the tail. Keep coming."

"Tango Four. Twenty seconds. I've got the sign. Turning in . . . NOW!"

Thank God there was nothing coming the other way. At the last instant, without giving any signal or braking, I wrenched the wheel hard to the right. The Sierra heeled and slewed with a screech of tyres. Rocking and twitching, I shot into the parking area, a long strip just above the water, with a low stone wall along its outer edge.

The manoeuvre took the tail by surprise. Before the driver could react he had passed the opening. I saw his brake-lights flash for an instant, then the car sped up again. At the far end of the park two cars sat waiting. Both were dark, but I had no doubt that they were hot to trot, with engines running. Sure enough, as the tail car went by the exit, both leapt forward and out on to the highway.

Headlights blazed up as they gave chase. Oncoming drivers flashed at them in vain. Everything had happened so fast that I had never stopped, never even slowed down much. I simply put my foot down again, came back on to the road and joined the pursuit.

The dickers (or whoever they were) must have realized

something was wrong. They must have known they were in the shit, because they began to drive like hell. Eighty was about the most their wagon would do, but they held that speed through some fearsome bends, and it was all I could do to keep the Sierra on the road.

The lead Indian was our big Audi Quattro, with its crab-like grip of the road transmitted through all four wheels, and its engine souped up to give it the acceleration of a Ferrari. There was no way the dickers could escape it. But equally, for the moment, there was no way it could get past them.

"India One," called Matt. "Taking command of the intercept. We're mobile behind the target towards Yellow Eight. We'll grab the first chance to overtake."

"India Two," came a new voice. "The road widens out below the park at Mount Stewart, three ks ahead. That's your best chance."

"India One. Roger. We'll try it."

Suddenly everything slowed dramatically. The target had come up behind another car, an innocent red Mini. Oncoming traffic was preventing anyone overtaking. Now the target was well illuminated by the Audi's lights and sure enough, it was an old Cortina.

India One was crowding up behind it, hoping to unnerve the driver with the blaze of light. But then, as the oncoming traffic cleared, the Cortina whipped out and overtook the dawdling Mini.

"Standby, standby," called Matt. "Going . . . NOW!"

The Cortina driver made the mistake of hanging over on the right-hand side of the road after he'd overtaken.

With a fierce surge of power the Audi was past the Mini and pulling up on the left-hand side of the target. The second Intercept car, a Rover, was there too, a couple of feet from the Cortina's back bumper.

From my tail-end-Charlie position I saw it all as if in slow motion. The Audi cut in hard across the Cortina's left front wing. The dicker driver stood on his brakes, but the big car hit his front end a glancing blow that threw the vehicle sideways against a stone wall, stopping it dead. A second later the driver of the Rover deliberately rammed into the back of it, to shock the inhabitants for a couple of seconds while the team from the Audi jumped out. In an instant the road was full of our guys, all crouching behind their own cars with weapons levelled over the roofs and bonnets.

I slid the Sierra to a halt and leapt out. Somehow the red Mini had squeezed through the gap behind the Audi's tail, but it had come to rest a hundred metres down the road, as if the driver was busy having a heart attack.

"OUT!" yelled Matt. "Out! Hands on the roof! Move!"

This was a dicey moment. If the villains had weapons, they might be desperate enough to use them. But because we didn't know for sure that they were armed, we couldn't open fire.

At last the passenger door of the Cortina opened, and a shaven-headed youth looked out, blinking.

"Fucking OUT!" roared Matt.

The youth struggled out. A second later he was spreadeagled over the bonnet of the Cortina, face down. A rapid body-search, and he was flat on his face in the road with a knee in his back, his driver the same. The driver had a cut on his right temple, where his head had hit the door in the crash, but it was nothing serious.

A preliminary search of the car revealed no weapons, but while it was going on I vaulted over the wall to have a look beyond. From my position behind the Cortina at the moment of the crash, I thought I'd seen a flash as something flew out of the driver's window and over the wall. Sure enough, my foot now hit something heavy — and up came a Luger 9mm automatic. I was about to yell out that I'd found it, but a sixth sense made me hold my tongue. In that instant I realized that the weapon could come in handy. I'd already worked out that if I did manage to close in on Gary Player and drop him, I must make it look like a sectarian killing. Therefore it would be brilliant to use a weapon that was common among the players. If the forensic boys managed to establish what kind of pistol had fired the fatal round, there'd be no chance of them tracing it back to me. On the contrary, if it had been used in previous shootings, it would probably be traced back to the IRA, and the police would conclude that the latest murder was the result of internecine feuding. And so, instead of crowing about my discovery, I stuffed the Luger down inside my waistband and hopped back over the wall.

Matt was taking no chances. Through the head-shed he called out not only the RUC and the Liaison Officer, but also a flatbed truck, so that the car could be taken away for forensic examination and a thorough search. At the least it would yield fingerprints; at best, it might turn out to have secret compartments, with weapons, traces of explosive or other incriminating evidence in them. In any case, the Cortina was undrivable, as its right front wheel had buckled under the impact with the wall. The Audi, in contrast, had suffered nothing but superficial dents.

We drove back to base in a discreet, well-spaced convoy, with the Sierra in the middle and the Intercept cars fore and aft. That was the last journey the Sierra would make for the troop. Now it had been blown, it would have to be binned, at any rate from Ulster. The only future for it was to be sent back to England and used as a range car. The Intercept cars would probably go in for a paint job.

The entire incident had lasted less than an hour. We reached base without further trouble, but I found that in the warehouse the atmosphere wasn't very sweet. "Hey, Geordie," one of the senior guys said as I was going to dump kit in my room, "you want to watch yourself. This place has been in fucking uproar since you sent the balloon up. You sure you haven't been somewhere you had no business to be? Better get your story right, or you'll be deep in it."

The wash-up was pretty hostile. The sergeant major couldn't make out how I'd been picked up. As far as anyone knew the Sierra hadn't been blown before I took it out. There was a strong suspicion that I'd been somewhere out of bounds, but I denied it strenuously, inventing a fictitious route round the edges of the city. I think I got away with it, but the debrief left me with the feeling that I'd almost dropped a colossal bollock. It also left me disturbed by the fact that I'd been forced into telling lies — something that I never like doing, least of all to my mates. Yet another worry was the sheer number of the enemy. The bastards seemed to be everywhere, with nothing to do but lurk about and look for targets. The one big consolation was that I hadn't led them to my inlaws' home. To have done that would have been a disaster of the first magnitude.

As soon as things had settled, I phoned them and got Meg.

"I'm really sorry about that," I began.

"What happened?"

"It was just that a job came up suddenly."

"Well — it's a bit late now. Tim's asleep already."

"No, no — I wasn't meaning I'd come out now. I only called to apologize. I had a present for Tim, too."

"You couldn't help it, I'm sure. There's always another day. But you ought to come and see him more often. He's getting to be a bit of a handful."

"Oh, like what?"

"He doesn't always want to do what I tell him. He's inclined to lose his temper, too. I'm not saying I can't manage him, but the more he sees of his father the better it will be." She broke off for a moment and then added, "By the way, a letter came for you."

"Really? What is it?"

"I don't know. It doesn't look very exciting. A small brown envelope, typed — that's all."

A prickle went up my neck. Maybe Chief Superintendent Morrison had surfaced.

"It can't be anything important," I said casually. "Why not open it and tell me what it says?"

"All right, then. Hold on while I get it."

142

There was a pause. Then I heard rustling, ripping noises.

"Well!" said Meg in her most superior voice. "It's nothing much at all. Just one typed line, in fact."

"What does it say?"

"'Your man is Declan Farrell.'"

"What? Say that again. At least, no — wait one while I get a pencil. Hold on."

I was in the public phone booth outside the canteen, and had to make a dash for the ops room to borrow paper and pencil from the duty clerk. Back at the booth, I grabbed the receiver and said, "Hello? Yes?"

"What's the matter with you?" said Meg. "You sound all flustered."

"No, no. I'm fine. Just had to grab a pencil. What's the name again?"

She repeated it, and spelt it out.

"Fine. Got it."

"Does it mean anything to you?"

"Not a lot. But I'll work it out. Thanks anyway."

In the morning I phoned Morrison on his direct line to ask if I could go and see him.

"You got my note, then?"

"That's right."

"D'you know a pub called the Old Bell, out on the Comber road?"

"I'll find it."

"Fine. It's on your right going out. I'll meet you there at seven-thirty tonight."

* * *

Settled in a quiet corner, the chief could have been any old businessman having a pint on his way home after work. But what he had to say related to business far beyond most ordinary people. Basically, he was trying to warn me not to tangle with Farrell, because of the sheer nastiness of the character.

"You'd be the better for leaving him alone," he said, "For instance, when two harmless young lads were caught trying to nick his car for joyriding, he had them brought to him, and rather than crippling them in the traditional way, using an electric drill, he had them held down while he himself used a hand drill to perforate their kneecaps. So pleased was he with this arbitrary sentence that he went straight out and gave himself a lavish dinner."

Morrison took a swig from his pint of stout and went on in his quiet, tired voice, "And did you hear about the young woman they battered to death this time last year? You remember that one? No? Well, Farrell thought she was a Protestant informer, or working for us. So they grabbed her. Of course she couldn't tell them anything, because she didn't know anything. She was perfectly innocent, not involved at all. First she was raped, then they took her out behind a pub and beat her to a pulp with hammers. When they found they couldn't kill her by stamping on her, they finished her off by hurling a breeze-block down on her head. That's Farrell for you. There's nothing subtle about IRA torture; it's just the most basic and brutal thuggery.

He went on to say that Farrell was one of the IRA's chief extortionists, and that he raised many thousands of pounds a year from running protection rackets. "He'll

144

go to the manager of a big building site and say, 'Look, if you don't want your machinery to go missing, or you don't want your walls to fall down, it'll cost you a couple of hundred a week.' Security firms — that's another racket. The IRA charge for seven or eight men to guard a factory, when in fact there are only two working. The irony is that, with the IRA on the scene, the place isn't going to get raided anyway; one thing thieves can do without is getting kneecapped.

"The same thing with drug-dealers. The PIRA limit the number who are allowed to operate, either on the streets or in clubs, and they take a percentage of their profits."

Morrison stopped, giving me a steady look. "Your man Farrell has his finger in every fecking pie — and if anyone else tries to get a hand in, he doesn't hesitate to cut it off."

CHAPTER
SEVEN

In the morning I happened to see Pink Mike crossing the warehouse on his way back from the bog. He was looking pleased with himself, as if he'd had a monumental shit. His hair was on the mend, too — it had gone a kind of rich auburn.

"Hey," I called, "got a minute?"

"Sure. What is it?"

"Have you heard of a player called Declan Farrell?"

"Christ, have I!"

"What d'you mean?"

"It's like asking if I've heard of the Pope. He's one of the big bastards."

"Really! D'you have any info about him?"

"There's a bloody great file that lists all his villainies. What do you want to know?"

"Anything about him — what he looks like, where he hangs out."

"What's your interest?"

"I heard someone talking about him. He sounds a vicious sod."

"He is. I'll sort you out something. Where will you be?"

"I'm on standby, so unless something breaks I'll be around the warehouse. I'm going to the gym now for an hour. Then I'll be in my cabin."

"I'll be over, then."

Never had the weights seemed lighter. I suppose it was the flow of adrenalin that pepped me up, but I found myself going through the lifts with incredible ease. It was my day for back and chest. Before the injury to my arm I'd been a member of the 220 Club, bench-pressing four big 55-lb Olympic discs on the bar — and even though that was no big deal in real weight-lifting terms, I'd only recently climbed back to it. Some days I still found it a strain, but that morning an hour flew past. Then I did twenty minutes on one of the stationary bikes, and after a shower and a dhobi session in the laundromat, I was bouncing around the cabin when Mike reappeared.

Under one arm he was carrying a rolled-up towel, out of which he produced a big brown envelope. "For Christ's sake be careful," he said, handing it over. "This stuff is highly classified. It's not supposed to leave our ops room. The most up-to-date sheet is missing, because Box have borrowed it, but everything else is there. I'll come back for it after lunch."

With him gone, I closed the door and pushed a wedge under the inside, silently praying that we didn't get a call-out in the next hour. Then I opened the envelope.

The first things I saw were two photographs, mug-shots, taken with a telephoto lens but well focused — good, clear pictures. I stared at them in consternation. I'd been seeing Gary Player in my mind so clearly that I had his likeness firmly in my head — and this wasn't him.

It took me a few moments to sweep away the figment of my imagination and concentrate on reality.

In place of the scruffy, tousled, sandy-haired fellow I'd invented for myself, here was someone dark and definitely good-looking, in his thirties. Far from having thuggish, Neanderthal features, the face was rather distinguished: high forehead, thick eyebrows, dark hair well cut and neatly brushed back, and a strong, square jaw. The eyes were dark as well, and, even in those unflattering photos, lively. At some stage the nose had been broken and left with a slight flattening at the bridge, but that only added to the appeal of the face.

If the man's appearance disconcerted me, the notes on his career and character gave me still more of a shock.

TERRORIST SUSPECT NO. 608

Name:	FARRELL, Declan Ambrose
Date of Birth:	1958
Place:	Fruithill Park, Andersonstown Road, Belfast.
Education:	Christian Brothers' School, Glen Road, Belfast.
	8 O levels.
	3 A levels B B B.
	Queen's University Belfast.
	2nd Class degree, Mechanical Engineering, 1979.
	Rugby, trial for University XV.
	Wing forward.

Religion:	Catholic.
Height:	6' 2"
Build:	Broad shoulders, good figure.
Appearance:	Tends to dress well. Wears suits.
Weight:	210 lbs approx.
Distinguishing Features:	Nose broken while boxing as boy. Flattening at bridge. Limps slightly on left foot as a result of car accident.
Politics:	Fanatical nationalist.
Cover Occupations:	Has sometimes posed as Consulting Engineer.
Finances:	No special sources known.
Aliases:	Seamus Malone. Has also used the name Fearn.

I had to read these details several times to make them
sink in. No moron, this. On the contrary, he was far
better educated than me, with three A levels and a
university degree. Bigger, too — an inch taller, and
a lot heavier. A physical sort of guy, he'd played
rugger almost at university standard. A boxer as well.
A big, strong fellow, aggressive, by the sound of it.
Sure enough, the accompanying notes described him
as "aggressive, assertive, likes to throw his weight
about. In his youth, much given to fighting in public."
(In the margin somebody had added in pencil, "Still
likes a fight. The Black Barrel brawl, 1988".) He was
said to have a sadistic streak, and to favour torturing
prisoners. Once, it was reputed, he had tied an enemy

up and cut him to pieces with a chain-saw. At home he kept dogs, generally big ones — Rottweilers, Rhodesian Ridgebacks or Pit Bulls.

His career in terrorism was poorly charted, because he had always been too clever to be caught, or even to leave clear traces of his activity. His involvement in incidents was usually recorded as "suspected" rather than "confirmed". For a time he had been active around South Armagh, near the Border, and it seemed that he preferred rural operations to those in towns. But later he had concentrated on Belfast, and now, at the latest entry on the sheets, he was down as the adjutant of the PIRA's West Belfast Brigade. Although the dossier listed several specific incidents which he was thought to have orchestrated, it did not mention the Queensfield bomb; this, I assumed, was because the incident had taken place after my last sheet had run out, and it would appear on the page which Mike had said was missing. I didn't stop to think why Box — our name for MI5 — should have borrowed it. I just assumed they were investigating some aspect of Farrell's career.

Alongside the heading "Address", several lines had been entered and crossed out. Evidently he had moved around a good deal. The latest entry said simply, "Ballyconvil". It looked as though that was where he had last been heard of. Altogether, he seemed to be in the same category as many IRA suspects: the authorities knew who he was, and where he was, but so far hadn't been able to pin anything major on him. I remembered Chief Superintendent Morrison saying, "We know who the feckers are, so we do — if only we could just go and get them."

150

Ballyconvil was the only name on any of the sheets that I needed to remember. I made a note of it on a slip of paper, and sat staring at the photograph until the face had burned into my mind. Yes — on more thorough inspection, the mouth was thin and cruel. The eyes could well be the same. But why in hell had a man of such intelligence chosen to become a scumbag? What had turned him into a terrorist?

My study of the dossier left me feeling personally threatened. Inadvertently, I had chosen to take on a hell of an opponent. Farrell sounded a powerful man in all senses of the word. Yet in a way all his attributes only strengthened my feeling of enmity. Before I'd known anything about him I'd hated him. Now I felt jealous of him, too. It was a useful combination.

I got the file back to Mike without incident, and went straight to the big gazetteer in our ops room. It gave several Ballyconvils, but there was one which stood out from all others as the most likely: a village on the back of the hills just to the north of West Belfast. From there anyone could drop on to the motorway, and in less than ten minutes be safe in the Republican fastnesses of the Falls or the Ardoyne.

Before I could do any more research, another operation came up. Once again, through a tout, the Det got wind of an attempt to shoot a prominent Unionist, this one a farmer who served as a part-time volunteer in the Ulster Defence Force. Like Quinlan, he had openly defied the PIRA for years, and lived in his isolated farmhouse with very little security. Now, when the tip-off came, it was clear that he urgently needed a team of babysitters.

At the same time, we got word that the weapons for the shoot would be deposited in a transit hide some ten kilometres from the target. The hide was in an old barn, part of a property that had been on the market for a year or more. Because we didn't have a precise date or time for the shoot, the head-shed decided to put an OP on the barn, so that we could keep an eye on what was happening, and warn the babysitters when the villains were on their way. There was also the chance that we might catch them in possession of weapons when they returned from their hit.

Guess who was detailed to man the OP? Yours truly. It didn't worry me, because I enjoy that sort of job. What did worry me a bit was when I heard that I'd got to take a Det guy in with me, because the head-shed wanted some experienced observer to get a good look at this particular bunch of terrorists, to see if he could identify any of them. Some of the Det boys could be real tossers when it came to any sort of hardship, so when I learnt that my companion was to be Mike Grigson I was relieved. Having been in the Paras, he knew how to carry on in an OP and could look after himself.

At the preliminary briefing, the boss detailed Pat Martin and myself to carry out a preliminary recce of the place. It turned out that the property consisted of a semi-derelict cottage as well as the barn, and ran to some six acres. It was out in the hills south-west of the city, and as we pored over the map on the ops room table, I found myself thinking that a shitehawk could fly over the mountains from there to Ballyconvil in five minutes or less.

"One pass only," the boss was saying. "There's so little traffic down that road it's not worth risking a second look. There could easily be eyes on. Just a straight drive past. Don't even slow down."

"Right," I said. "What do we know about the house?"

"It's up for sale. The agents say it's empty, but we're not sure. Somebody could be using it."

"If we want to do a thorough recce," said Pat, "why doesn't one of us put on a suit and pose as a potential buyer? Get the keys from the agents and go along all pukka?"

"Good suggestion," said the boss, "but again, it's not worth the risk. If there is a player inside, he'll probably have a video lined up on the entrance. There's iron gates across the approach, secured with a padlock and chain. While you're tinkering with that they'll get a nice film of you, from which they can take mug-shots for their files."

"Normal OP then," I said. "What's this? Looks like a wall or hedge round the farmyard." I pointed to a faint mark on the 1:25,000 map, a dotted line which seemed to define the property. "It could be a ditch as well. The best thing might be to dig in out in the field — here — and then to move in close at night. Where's the hide supposed to be?"

The boss consulted a note. "As you face the barn, in the right-hand back corner. A 45-gallon polythene water-butt has been dug into the ground, top flush with the floor, and covered with straw."

"So, to get a view of anyone putting a weapon into it, or taking one out, we'll need to be about . . . here." I picked a spot in the hedge or ditch that looked as though it should give a view into the barn.

"That's right." The boss straightened up with a muttered curse. He'd hurt his back parachuting a few months before, and it was still giving him gyp. "You'd be very close to the action there — have to take it easy. Well, there's not much more we can tell from the map. You might as well be on your way."

"Fine. We should be back by four."

Operation Deadlock was under way. Pat and I took the scruffiest, least remarkable of the ops cars, a green Marina covered with dust and grime, and set off by a roundabout route for the high country to the south-west. Our target, Ballyduff, had been advertised by the selling agents as "in need of refurbishment". It sounded just the sort of place that players would use as a transit hide: well isolated and out in the country, yet only twenty minutes from the IRA heartlands of West Belfast.

Pat drove while I read the map. "Hang a left here," I said as we came over a shallow crest. "Then it's straight down."

Up there on the hills the farmland was rough as rough could be. The hairy-looking fields sprouted clumps of rushes, and rocks poked up through the coarse grass. In the depths of winter the whole landscape was dun-coloured and dead-looking. Rusty barbed-wire fences sagged, and in the hedgerows a few stunted trees were all bent in the same direction by the prevailing west wind. Puddles of water glistened in every depression of that upland bog. It was the exact equivalent of West Belfast in rural terms — scruffy, clapped out, a shit-heap, ideally matched to the mentality and habits of the PIRA.

"Glad I'm not a bloody cow up here," said Pat.

"You'd need to be able to live on pure grot. Look out, now — the house'll be down here on our right."

We were on a minor road, marked yellow on the map, which ran gently downhill. Though straight as a ruler, it wouldn't be any use for overtaking in a chase because it was about seven feet wide, with ditches on either side.

"You'd never get past," said Pat, reading my thoughts.

"Not a chance. Here we are, now. Ease off a touch, but keep rolling."

For moments like this, when there wasn't much time, I had trained myself to concentrate intently, so that my mind took a series of snapshots. Now in quick succession I got the following: along the back of the property, a line of bare trees; a long, low, whitewashed bungalow facing away from us, downhill; rusting corrugated iron roof, no windows in the back; beyond it, farther from the road and to our right, a sizeable barn, set at right-angles to the house, corrugated iron walls as well as roof, barn thirty metres from the far end of cottage; front of cottage decrepit, some window panes broken and boarded; pale blue door, same colour as wrought-iron entrance gates; gates chained together — old chain, but shiny new padlock; grounds gone to seed.

Ten metres out from the front of house, and parallel to it, a line of ash trees ran along an overgrown ditch — the feature I'd picked out on the map. Outside the ditch, rough pasture sloped down into the distance. Maybe there was a stream across the bottom.

In four or five seconds we were past.

"Notice anything particular?" I asked.

"Brand-new padlock. I bet they've put it on there until they've done the job."

"Looks like it."

"No mains electricity."

"I don't reckon it's got mains water, either. See that hand-pump outside the door?"

"Yep. Good place for a CTR, that ditch under the trees."

"Perfect. I'll come in up that field."

"The front door of the house wasn't properly shut," Pat added. "I reckon someone's been using it." Then he mimicked a la-di-da estate agent's voice as he quoted derisively, "'In need of refurbishment'. I should fucking well think so! The place'd fall down if you farted."

Two miles further on we came to a small crossroads and turned right. Already the short winter afternoon was dying, and in the dusk the fields looked even wilder.

"Anywhere here would do for the drop-off," I said. "We've got a junction coming up, a lane in from the left. Let's make it there." I took a note of the grid reference, and we headed for base.

Back in the warehouse, the babysitting party were getting their kit sorted. They'd done a recce of their own, and had picked a drop-off point from which they could infiltrate over fields and slip into the target's house through the back garden.

Mike and I had no arguments about what kit we would take. He was well equipped anyway, with his own G3 and kite-sight. The only item he needed to borrow was an all-in-one sniper suit, Goretex-lined and covered in DPM material. Those things are great for keeping you warm and dry; the only trouble is that you can't run in them. But it didn't look to me as though we were going to do much running. The important thing was to make sure we had everything we might need for a stay of several days: food, obviously, and water, but also such extras as cling-film to crap into, and plastic bags in which to seal the said crap. Also a spare water bottle for pissing into. You might think that to piss a couple of times in the middle of a boggy field would make no difference, but you'd be surprised how it starts to stink. The point was, nobody could be sure how long we might have to spend in the OP. Also it was vitally important to write WATER clearly on water bottles and PISS clearly on the others.

Apart from those basics, we needed food — mainly boil-in-the-bag rations, which could be eaten cold — spare shirt, sleeping-bag, torch, collapsible shovel, wire netting for the roof of the OP, spotter-scope, and so on. It all made up into a considerable load.

At 1800 we held a final briefing. The Det would be out in force with six or eight cars. Four of our own Intercept cars would be deployed, but they would hang well back so as not to arouse suspicion. Our callsigns for the night were all Sierras. Sierra One was the babysitter group, Sierra Two ourselves, and the rest of our cars Sierras with higher numbers. The main locations were designated Black: Black One was the target house, Black Two the hide, Black Three the babysitters' drop-off point, Black Four ours. The last two doubled as emergency rendezvous points, in case anything went wrong.

Pat drove us out to Black Four. As we approached, he flipped the switch which cut out the brake-lights. At the instant he pulled up for the major road, Mike and I whipped open our doors and slipped out to right and left. The car carried on without stopping, to turn left and disappear over the hill.

We gave it five minutes, listening, watching. The night was soft and still. No other traffic was moving. Reassured, we crossed the road, climbed a barbed-wire fence, and set off uphill across the field on a bearing of 160 mils, moving slowly over the damp grass, with myself in front and Mike watching the rear.

All around us, at ground level, the night was completely dark, not a gleam from house or car. Only in the sky to the north-east was there a faint glow, rising from the lights of Belfast. But as our eyes slowly adjusted to night vision, we could see well enough.

In three-quarters of a mile we crossed six fences or hedges, the last of them on a slight rise. From there, I calculated, the cottage should be in view across a shallow depression. No problem. The kite-sight picked it out well, the house and barn showing through a line of trees. I waited to check the wind: a breath fanned against our faces, wafting down from the north-east, taking our scent back the way we had come.

158

My aim was to approach within two hundred metres of the perimeter fence, and establish our OP in a suitable hollow out in the field. Three hundred metres off, I whispered to Mike to wait and cover me while I recced forward. There was no shortage of possible locations. The field was exceedingly rough, and I found plenty of holes three or four feet deep where the peaty soil had been eroded away and rock was showing through. I chose a depression with a front wall of rock some two feet high, topped with peaty soil and tussocks of grass, and went back to bring Mike up. The site was almost a natural slit-trench. Working as silently as we could, we pitched a sloping roof of wire netting, anchored it with pins top and bottom, and covered it with sods of turf sliced out of a nearby hollow. Some handfuls of long dead grass scattered over the top completed our roof, which tapered down almost to ground level at one side, leaving room at the other so that we could roll out sideways. At the top of the front wall, in the centre, I cut out a notch of turf to make a lookout aperture.

"Safe as Fort Knox," I told Mike. "We'll call the place that." Then I went through to the desk: "Sierra Two, OP established. Going forward to choose site for CTR."

We peeled off our sniper suits and left everything we didn't immediately need packed in our bergens, in case anything happened and we had to run for it. The night was reasonably warm, so it was no hardship, and we moved forward wearing only our ops waistcoats and windproofs on top of ordinary DPMs.

The field was so uneven that walking over it in the dark was awkward. We kept stumbling into holes, and we had to take it slowly. A couple of times I heard scuttling noises just in front of us, but I assumed that they were being made by rabbits. A sweep with the kite-sight revealed that the field was full of them.

Remembering the position of the barn door, and the angle I needed, I made a cautious approach to the hedge right opposite the front door of the cottage. A dry ditch, some brambles and the trunks of a couple of ash trees gave us all the cover we needed. With careful movements I cleared a space round us, cutting away any bramble shoots that might snag our clothes, and settled down to wait.

The cottage door was ten metres away, the barn door about thirty. The time was 2130. According to our tout, the delivery of arms was planned for 2300. As close in to the target as that, I didn't want to speak, so I waited for the desk to come up and ask if we were in position, and replied with a couple of jabs on my pressel.

The minutes ticked slowly past. I heard the reports of the Det guys moving around, but there seemed to be no enemy activity. Then at 2210 Delta Four, who was somewhere down the lanes behind us, came up with, "Stand by. There's a vehicle mobile towards Black Two." Soon its headlights appeared, but they went straight past the gates at speed.

A moment later I froze. Until then I had thought the place was deserted. Now, through the kite-sight, I saw a figure standing in the door of the barn. Evidently the man had been alerted by the car; he'd come out, maybe thinking this was his delivery. I was disconcerted to think that he'd been there all the time without my realizing it.

Luckily our discipline had been good, and we hadn't made a sound. I nudged Mike, pointing at the barn. As if reading my thoughts, the desk came up with, "Sierra Two, do you have X-rays on target?" and I gave him another double touch on the pressel.

"How many? More than one?"

A single press.

The desk began to ask more questions. It was impossible to answer them by buzzes. I reckoned the barn was far enough away for it to be safe to speak softly, so I got my head right down in the ditch and pulled the hood of my windproof round so that it was covering my face. That way, my throat mikes were unimpeded but my voice wouldn't carry any distance. I explained what was happening, and was told to stand by.

The drop-off time came and went. "As usual, the Paddy Factor's operating," Mike whispered.

Yes — the Paddy Factor. The sheer unreliability of the players made our job even more difficult. Clever and cunning as the bastards were, they could also be totally undisciplined. Already, in my short time in the province, I'd heard of one case in which two men were on their way to murder a policeman, but decided to drop in at a pub for a pint to stiffen their morale. Six pints apiece later they were still in the bar, pissed as owls, their mission forgotten. Another time two fellows heading for a shoot had an argument with each other; they ended up fighting each other to a standstill, and again the mission went by the board. So tonight maybe our crowd wouldn't come at all.

Well past midnight, the man in the barn emerged for a

stroll. He walked right past us, three metres away, and on to the gates, where he took a piss. The night was so still that we could hear every drop falling. Then he fiddled with the padlock — whoever might have put the new lock on, he had the right key — dropped the chain, and pulled the gates open one at a time. Hinges squealed and metal scraped over the gravel of the drive. That done, the man came sauntering back to pass us again and return to the barn. I guessed he was a guard, a kind of dicker, stationed there to make sure nobody else approached the place. I reckoned he was quite dedicated, as he'd been hanging around for hours in the dark, and had never showed so much as a gleam of light.

As if his little promenade had stirred the weather, the wind began to blow, drifting down the hill into our faces, and swirling round the cottage. In a few minutes it had become quite gusty, and I was glad because the noise of it made me feel less exposed.

At last, at about 0130, the Det reported another vehicle heading our way. Again the headlights came up from behind us, but this time they swung in through the gates, illuminating the cottage for a second before the driver snapped them off. He came past us on sidelights only — a van — and rolled on until he was almost inside the barn. Two men jumped out and called a quiet greeting to their waiting colleague. The kite-sight gave me a clear picture of all three.

I gave a jab on the pressel switch.

"Zero Alpha. Have you X-rays on target?"

Talking into my hood, I whispered, "Sierra Two, affirmative. Two X-rays arrived by van. Just about to unload into the barn. Wait one. Yes — one man has two longs. So has the other. Four longs into the barn. Can't see much in there. Wait one — better now. They have a torch on in the back right-hand corner. Longs being lowered into hole below ground level. There's straw round it. All four longs complete in hide . . . X-rays returning to rear of vehicle. Lifting out a heavy box. Two — two boxes. They look like ammunition, from the weight. Two boxes into barn, into cache. Ammo also complete."

They didn't hang about. I saw them lowering some form of lid and raking loose straw back into position; then all three came out and boarded the van. It looked as though there was a partition between front and back, because they had to put one man in through the rear doors and close him in. At the gates, one of them got out to fasten the padlock and chain behind them.

"X-rays complete in van and mobile northwards," I reported. "Propose making CTR of barn itself."

"Zero Alpha," answered the desk. "Are you certain it's clear?"

"Looks good."

"At your discretion, then."

"Roger. Wait out."

"Did you get a look at any faces?" I asked Mike.

"Not really. Not enough light. But I wasn't expecting anything much from tonight. These guys who move the weapons around are only minor players. It's the shooters I'd like to see."

"Well, hang on here and cover me while I suss out the barn. If anything happens, start putting rounds through the roof. Then RV back at Fort Knox. Switch to the chatter-net for the time being."

I was pretty confident that everyone had gone, but I took no chances. I stood at the barn door and listened for a while before I went in. Then I switched on my infra-red torch, invisible to the naked eye. Through my passive night goggles the interior of the barn showed up as light as day.

There was a good deal of loose straw piled in the far right-hand corner, and a low stack of bales to the right, only a couple of layers high. From the indentation on top of them, I could see that someone had been sleeping there. The floor was beaten earth. In the middle of it stood a wooden trestle table, with a frying pan and some plates on it, all dirty with old grease. There were also two tin-openers and an intact can of Pal dog-food. Jesus, I thought, these must be some low-level Paddies if that's what they're living on. The rest of the stuff in the barn was junk: a pile of old sacks; an ancient hay-cutter, rusted to hell; a couple of buckets, full of holes, with twisted handles, a ruined armchair with springs and stuffing bursting through dark-red upholstery.

I picked up a broken pitch-fork handle and began sounding the floor beneath the straw. At the fourth or fifth prod I got a hollow thump. Down on one knee, I drew the straw aside to reveal a circular sheet of heavy marine plywood, like the end of a beer barrel, with a piece of two-by-two nailed to the middle of it to form a makeshift handle. Fingers under one edge, fiddle around, lift gently. I couldn't see or feel any booby-trap device.

Up came the board. Beneath it, the lid of a black plastic dustbin. Up came that too — and there, glinting in the torch-light, were four AK 47s, standing on their butts, muzzles uppermost. Beside them, two black ammunition boxes were stacked end on end. Holding the barrel carefully with a gloved hand, I lifted one of the rifles, and saw it had had plenty of use — the metal was scratched, and the woodwork of the butt and foreend was chipped and scraped. The PNGs didn't give enough clarity for me to see fine detail, so I pushed them up on to my forehead, whipped out my pencil torch and shone the fine beam on to the lettering beside the breech. The script was Chinese — no doubt that was where the weapon had come from. I lowered it carefully into place and flipped up the lid of one ammunition box. It was filled to the top with loose live rounds, but through them I saw something green and glinting. A quick rummage revealed two L2 hand-grenades, smooth green spheres about the size of a fist with a yellow band round them, and the inscription L2-A2. How the hell had the bastards got *them* — standard British Army issue?

Having checked the cache mentally, I replaced the box, the lid, the board, the straw, and withdrew, making sure not to step in any bare patch that might take a footprint. At the door of the barn I searched with my kite-sight for our OP in the ditch, and was glad to find that I couldn't see any sign of Mike. But he was there all right — and once we'd reported to the desk that the hide was complete, we pulled off to our basha in the field.

All through the next day we lay low sharing stags, two

hours on and two off. We had the spotter scope trained on the cottage, and at that range the field of view took in the gates as well. Apart from the odd car passing up and down the road, the only event was the arrival of a party of potential buyers to look at the house in the middle of the morning.

Mike was having a kip, but I woke him up. "Now," I said, "watch this. If it was the dickers who put that new lock on the gates, they've fucked up. They obviously weren't expecting any customers."

A middle-aged gent in a dark suit got out of the car and went to undo the padlock. He tried for a couple of minutes, gave it a big shake, scratched his head, looked back at the car and tried again. Finally he turned and said something through the car window. Out got a young-looking couple, the bird a not-bad-looking blonde in a tight, short skirt. There was no way they could approach the home of their dreams except by climbing over the stone wall beside the gate. Fatty Estate Agent went first, and reached back to give the blonde a hand. Up she came, arse-on to us, with her skirt riding hallway up her kidneys, and displaying a pair of outrageous mauve knickers.

"Phworrrhh!" went Mike.

"What's the matter? You desperate?"

"You haven't been out here for a fucking year, mate."

The clients straightened themselves out, walked up the drive and in through the front door. As Pat had noticed on our initial recce, it wasn't locked, and the agent pushed it straight open. The visit wasn't a success. In about thirty seconds the party was out again and off back towards the car; they never went behind the house or anywhere near the barn. One look at the cottage was enough for them. Then it was back over the wall, a repeat flash of the royal purple, and another dying groan from Mike. "Phworrrhh!" he went again, as if someone had stuck a knife in his guts. The agent took one final, disgusted look at the padlock and drove off.

Somewhere, sometime, I'd seen knickers that colour before. Suddenly I got it: Singapore, on an exercise. We'd done a drop into Changhi airfield, and afterwards we were invited into the RAF officers' mess for a drink. There in a glass-fronted showcase on the wall was a pair of purple satin pants, exactly the colour of the ones we'd just seen, and underneath, the legend: "SUPERSONIC KNICKERS. These knickers were wrested from GLORIA in the JACARANDA NIGHT CLUB on January 1976, and flown at Mach 1.5 in a Mk 3 Phantom of 43 Squadron, by Squadron Leader Jeremy Turner, the following morning. RIP."

I told Mike the story, and he struck back with one about how a colleague of his in the Det had started going out with this slapper from Belfast. Everyone knew that her brother was in the PIRA, and told him for Christ's sake to be careful. His only concession was to ask a couple of his mates to follow him in a second vehicle when he went to pick her up. He'd hardly got her on board when they saw something fly out of the passenger's window. Afterwards, when they asked him what it was, he explained, "I said to her, 'Ey — last time you weren't wearing any knickers. What you got some on now for?' Whereupon she made a grab and *rrripppp*, away they went, and there's her saying, 'Not any more, I haven't!'"

Talk of knickers whiled away an enjoyable few minutes, but still we had six more hours of daylight to get through. All day long rain had threatened but held off. It was lucky for us that there were no cattle on the ground, either in our field or in any of the ones adjoining. That meant there was no reason for the local farmer to come out and look around. A shepherd with a collie would have been the worst, but there were no sheep either. With the wind blowing steadily from the cottage and away down the open country behind us, it was safe to have the occasional brew and to boil up a couple of hot meals. As I'd expected, Mike's manners in the OP were pretty good; once the stink of his aftershave had worn off — no joke, a potential danger — there wasn't a lot I could criticize.

As always on that kind of job, the prime enemy was boredom. After a couple of hours with no activity or movement, I was bored out of my mind. My thoughts went round and round in circles, but kept coming back to two subjects. The nice one was Tracy, the less pleasant was the edginess in my mother-in-law's voice. It wasn't like her to be as sharp as that.

At least, when Mike and I were both awake, we could chat. As casually as possible, I brought up the subject of Declan Farrell. I'd pretended I'd heard about the chain-saw incident earlier, from someone else, and wondered what sort of a man he might be. "He must be a right hard bugger, to do a thing like that."

"He is," Mike agreed. "He's supposed to have a filthy temper. I don't know how many people he's kneecapped."

"What drives him? I mean, what makes him do it?"

"What makes any of them do it? It's bred into them from infancy. You've heard those street kids of three and four effing and blinding. You've seen them throwing stones at the patrols. It's in their blood. They grow up knowing nothing else."

"Have you ever seen Farrell?"

"A couple of times. He's quite an impressive-looking guy, I have to admit."

"But he'd never actually do an operation now? Too senior?"

"I dunno. They've lost a lot of lower-grade operators lately. They may be thin on the ground. Besides, he likes getting involved. Also, he's that arrogant, he might come out just to show the lads how things should be done. If they've fucked up on the last couple of jobs — as they have — he might fancy giving a lead himself."

"You don't think he'll come tonight?"

"Could do. Why — you scared?"

I forced myself to laugh. "No, just curious." Suddenly I realized I'd used that expression before, and disciplined myself never to use it again.

There was no change of plan during the day. Every time the desk came through the message was the same: "NTR — Nothing to Report." In the absence of any more news from the touts, we assumed that the shoot would go down at 2200 that night.

On that dull winter afternoon, soon after five, we moved forward again to take up the same position in the ditch. I noticed that the wind was dropping and the temperature falling, but paid no particular attention.

From the net we knew that the babysitting team had stayed *in situ*, like us, and that the Det were moving out into the country again. So were our Intercept cars. Across a wide area of the countryside, the trap was being set.

This time the players were early — and where they came from, nobody could say. We got no warning; somehow they eluded the Det. Suddenly, at only 2120, there were lights coming up the road from behind us. I managed to put a call through while the vehicle was still at the gate and somebody was undoing the lock, but then, as it cruised in past us, we had to go quiet.

This time it was a car — an old two-litre Rover, superficially similar to our own Interceptor. The driver swung round to the right beside the end of the cottage, then backed out and came forward again, to stop, facing the road, almost in front of us. Close as we were, we couldn't see the registration number, which looked as if it had been deliberately caked with cowshit. Four men got out and slammed the doors, not bothering to keep the noise down. I guessed they'd all had a couple of pints. Then one opened the boot, lifted out a bundle, and all four walked across to the barn. Seconds later somebody struck a match and a gas pressure-lamp hissed into action.

A harsh yellow glare flooded the inside of the building. One of the men seemed to realize that they were being careless, because he came back to the threshold, looking

170

to right and left, and said loudly, "This fecking barn's supposed to have doors on it, too. Whatever happened to them?"

"Bollocks to the doors," said another voice. "Get feckin changed."

From the bundle somebody sorted out long black garments, and all four began to pull them on.

In Mike's ear I whispered, "Recognize anyone?"

He nodded twice, staring intently.

"Farrell?"

He shook his head.

In a minute or so the four men were encased in black from head to foot. One of them had opened up the hide, and was handing out the rifles and loaded magazines. I heard magazines clicking home.

I felt my heart going like a hammer, and took a couple of deep breaths. Jesus! I had the G3 set on automatic, and levelled at the group, thirty metres off. I could wallop them all.

One man, the shortest in the group, walked round the other three, giving them a cursory inspection. Then he doused the lamp, and all four walked to the car.

The moment they were rolling, I got on the radio. "Sierra Two. Four X-rays have collected weapons and ammunition from Black Two. Four AK 47s. Now complete in dark-green Rover 2000. Mobile northwards from my location."

"Zero Alpha," answered the desk. "Roger."

"Fuck it!" I gasped. "Why didn't we drop the bastards?"

"I know. It drives you up the bloody wall."

Mike stood up and shook himself, as if to throw off the weight of frustration. Then he called, "Delta Eight. Those four X-rays — two unknown to me, but the others are Eamonn O'Reilly and Jonty Best. Over."

For the next half-hour all we could do was listen as the hit team moved in erratically on its target. We heard the Det cars reporting the Rover forward, from Green Five to Green Four and Green Three. From there it was only four or five hundred metres to the target, but for some reason the players veered off into open country and disappeared for twenty minutes. Then at last they were picked up again, heading back to Green Three. This time we reckoned the raid would go down within the next few seconds. But then came an unexpected twist: instead of stopping at the farmhouse, the assault vehicle went straight past. One of the Intercept teams requested permission to take it out, but the head-shed refused. The desk wanted to let things develop and see what was going to happen.

Mike and I waited tensely, wound up on full alert. I imagined all our people being in the same state — some in the farmhouse, as I'd been a few days back, some in an OP outside the house; most in cars, all poised to react. Had something spooked the players? Time and again a job collapsed when they took fright at the last moment. Maybe they'd spotted one of our cars lurking in a strange place. Maybe they'd seen something at the house itself. We listened out, expecting to hear a report from the agency monitoring CB radio, which normally caught what the players were saying to each other.

Half an hour went by. Then suddenly somebody picked

up the Rover again, incoming towards the farmhouse, apparently making another run. This time the desk decided on action, and scrambled two Intercept teams to take it out before it reached the target. After a quick manoeuvre they trapped it, by the simple expedient of placing one car to block the lane ahead of it, and sending another up behind.

Then came another twist. The trapped Rover wasn't carrying the hit team. The two men in it were unarmed, dressed in ordinary clothes, and claimed to be on their way home from a session in the pub. A preliminary search of the car revealed no weapons. The vehicle seemed to be completely clean.

Consternation. Was this the hit car, emptied out? Or was it a lookalike decoy? Suddenly, as I listened to the exchanges, I realized that the desk was calling me, asking again if I'd got the number of the car we'd reported.

"Sierra Two, negative," I replied.

The desk ordered the two men to be brought in for questioning, and the car detained for forensic examination. Was that it for the night, then?

Not for us. It was Mike who saw the lights coming at high speed from the north.

"Look out!" he said. "They're back."

The car came screaming down the narrow road. The driver was in either a great hurry or a great rage. He flung the Rover right-handed through the gates, roared past us and scorched to a halt with the nose of the car in the barn doorway and the headlights still on. The illumination was so good that binoculars were more use than kite-sights. The same four men leapt out, all effing and blinding at the tops of their voices, and began to unload their weapons. One kicked the straw away from the top of the hide and lifted the cover, but they were all furious for a few moments and stood arguing.

"Sierra Two," I reported urgently. "Four X-rays back at Black Two. They still have their weapons. We could smack them all. Permission to open fire. Over."

"Zero Alpha," the desk answered. "Roger. Wait one." Then, "Zero Alpha to Sierra Two. Negative — no permission. Don't do anything. Let them go. Over."

"Sierra Two, roger."

"Oh for fuck's sake!" whispered Mike in my ear.

Such was the commotion that until the very last moment the players didn't realize another car had arrived. Nor did we. It must have come very quietly, maybe without headlights. All at once it was in through the gate and sliding past us, to stop behind the Rover. Two men got out, leaving the doors open, and strode towards the shemozzle in the barn. Something made me focus on the driver, a big man with a slight limp. As he advanced he called out in a deep voice, "What the feck's going on here? Cunts! Get a hold of yourselves."

The instant he reached the light and I saw his face, I knew.

So did Mike. "Fucking Farrell!" he exclaimed. "There he is!"

"Sierra Two," I called again. "Two more X-rays now on location. One is Declan Farrell, repeat Farrell. Request permission to fire. Over."

Again the answer was negative. I couldn't believe it. I had the crosshairs of the sight steady on the side of the bastard's head. My finger was on the trigger. One touch, and Kath's death would be avenged. Between the two of us, Mike and I could have dropped all six terrorists where they stood. Not one of them would even have got out of the barn.

Then suddenly we found we had an urgent problem of our own. As I lowered my G3, I noticed Farrell's car rock on its springs, as if someone was shifting around inside it. The car rocked again. Against the dim light I saw something leap over the back of the front seat, and out of the driver's door came not another player, but a bloody great dog, a Rotty.

"Jesus!" I breathed. "Now we're in it."

The blessed north wind of the day had died away, and odd puffs were coming from all directions. The dog trotted across to the front of the cottage and lifted his leg against the door-post. Then he began sniffing along the front wall. If we moved we'd be bound to attract his attention, but if we lay still he'd get us anyway. It would only be a matter of seconds before he picked up our scent.

"Come on," I hissed at Mike, "we've got to pull out."

Too late. The dog stopped, lifted his head and stood staring in our direction. Then he let fly a volley of barks and lunged forward. We lay flat. He pulled up two feet away, dancing high on his toes, barking and snarling like hell.

"BUSTER!" yelled Farrell from the barn. "Quiet, you bastard! Come here!"

The dog's only response was to bark even louder. He

began really doing his nut. Gobs of spit were flying out of his chops and landing on us. His barks would have wakened the dead. We were in an impossible position. If we kept still, someone would be over to see what he was going mad about (perhaps even Farrell himself — this at least could provide me with an excuse to take him out). But then again, if we shifted, the dog would go for us.

All this went through my mind in about half a second. I tried to slide my right hand down my side to bring my knife out of its sheath, but even that slight movement was enough to trigger an attack. With a thump like a sack of cement landing, the dog was on top of us, gnashing viciously. His jaws closed on Mike's right forearm, and he was growling thunderously. Still I wanted to get the knife into him, but the instant I moved he let go and bit again, this time Mike's shoulder. The dog was bracing his rear legs and twitching his arse about as he got pressure on and tried to drag backwards. There was only one thing for it. I rammed the muzzle of the G3 against the dog's ribs and put one round through his chest. The report was slightly muffled, but still there was a loud, dull *boom*.

The impact of the shot lifted the creature clean off us and threw his body on to the bank, where he lay twitching, with a few last noises, half-barks, half-grunts, choking out of his mouth.

"Run!" I hissed.

We scrambled backwards out of the ditch and stumbled into the boggy field. For a second the voices in the barn had fallen silent. Then the men began to yell. We ran as best we could, tripping over the tussocks. Through the screen of trees we saw figures pour out of the barn. A moment later there came a rattle of automatic fire, and rounds went cracking over our heads. We dropped into a hole, about fifty metres back from the ditch. In the dark we were reasonably safe. A second rifle opened up. We heard rounds smacking into the ground away to our right. Obviously the players thought we had come in from the road and were going back that way. They fired wildly, whole magazines full, in that direction.

As soon as they stopped, we ran again, aiming for Fort Knox. In the confusion we lost our markers, and had to cast out, right and left, to find it. In the shelter of the rock bank at last, we stopped to get our breath.

"How's the arm?"

"I can feel it's bleeding, but not too bad. Hand's working OK."

"Sierra Two," I called. "We've been compromised. No casualties, but we need an urgent pick-up. We'll be at Black Four one-five minutes from now."

"Zero Alpha," the desk answered. "Roger."

"Sierra Two. We've stirred up a hornet's nest at Black Two, so I recommend all units steer clear of it."

Still the villains were convinced that we'd come in from the road. They were poncing down the drive with flashlights, loosing off into the dark. I thought of the purple knickers going over that wall.

It took us about a minute to collect all our gear and destroy the OP. Once we'd recovered the ground-pegs and dragged off the wire-netting, the turf-and-grass roof collapsed in a heap, leaving little sign that anybody had been there. As a final touch, I kicked away the edges of the observation notch that we'd cut in the bank so that it would look like a natural hollow.

Ten minutes later we were back at our dropping-off point, lurking behind a convenient stone wall. We'd hardly got into position when Pat came up on the radio to say that he was closing on the location. I acknowledged, and we emerged into the road. Almost at once we saw headlights coming up the hill, and within seconds we were safe in the back of the car, heading for home.

CHAPTER
EIGHT

After that fiasco it took me three or four days to chill
out. My big disappointment was not so much that the
PIRA had pulled out of their operation; what pissed
me off was the fact that I'd missed — or rather, been
deprived of — a golden chance of settling my personal
score. The whole business could have been squared away.
If Mike and I had opened fire, we'd have had little trouble
afterwards establishing that we'd used reasonable force;
having been faced with four armed men, we would have
had no difficulty in maintaining that our lives had been
in jeopardy.

The wash-up didn't provide any clues as to why the
players had quit, but it did reveal why the desk had
forbidden us to shoot. We learnt that one of the four
gunmen was a key tout, and that his continued existence
was considered of paramount importance. Better him
alive than Farrell dead — at least, that was what we
were told at the time. Later, I came to wonder if that
was the whole truth.

This setback made me do some hard thinking. Farrell
had lost his dog, but he probably thought Buster had
saved his life. There was no way he could pinpoint the

179

identity of the would-be assassin who'd tried to nail him, but he would certainly guess that it had been a member of the security forces. After such a close shave, he surely wouldn't risk himself in the field again for a while. My own time in Ulster was rapidly ticking away. It followed that, if I was going to get Farrell, I must go after him on my own.

The idea excited me, because I knew how dangerous a solo mission would be. Of course I'd just had another illustration of how vital it was to work in pairs. If that dog had got hold of me on my own I could easily have ended up getting captured. The risks of a one-man operation were all too obvious. But there was something about Farrell's arrogance that goaded me on: the way he'd yelled at his own guys as he arrived at the barn — even those few words had made him sound a real bully-boy.

Already I'd formed the outline of a plan. I'd find out where he lived, set up an OP on his house, observe his movements in and out, and then, once I had him sussed, take him out with my secretly confiscated 9mm Luger. I'd fired so many thousands of rounds on the range that I was confident I could put a double-tap into his head from fifteen or twenty metres — and that would be the end of him. My main difficulty was to get enough time off. To find the house might take several recces; to establish the pattern of his movements would need several more. I could take the odd evening off and pretend to be socializing with my in-laws, but sooner or later I would surely get caught by some emergency — a call would go out, pulling all the guys back, and I wouldn't be there to answer it. Instead, I'd be stuck out in the middle of some godforsaken bog, waiting for Mr Big-Boy to come home.

The next time I visited Kath's parents was for Christmas lunch. We had a fine meal with all the trimmings, and then the traditional handing-out of presents from under the decorated tree. Tim, being easily the youngest person present, got the job of messenger, taking each package to the right person. As long as he was the centre of attention he behaved perfectly, but later he threw a tantrum for no visible reason, and I could see he was becoming too much for his gran. I think he was reacting to the loss of his mother and the break-up of his home. Apparently these rages were becoming quite frequent. Suddenly he'd let fly with a scream and refuse to co-operate. No wonder he was getting on Meg's nerves — and on mine.

Lying in my cabin one night, unable to sleep, I started thinking about Tracy (as usual). I'd been phoning her most evenings, and had sent an expensive silver bracelet as a Christmas present. Our relationship was going great guns — as far as it could while we were a few hundred miles apart. I had no doubt we were going to stick together when I got home, and I was pretty sure she'd take Tim over, as if he were her own. She had only ever seen him as a baby, when he'd been brought into the Med Centre in Hereford, but that didn't seem to worry her.

Now I had a brainwave. Partly because I'd volunteered to work over Christmas, I had a week's leave coming up, and I'd been planning to go home. But if I did the opposite, bringing Tracy over, I could take local leave, and have a chance to pursue my own devious plans in the province. At the same time, she could start getting to know Tim. Furthermore — my mind ran on — we could have a kind of premature honeymoon at my in-laws' holiday cottage on the north coast. The place was standing empty, and it was in a safe enough area. We'd take Tim with us, and at the very least give Meg a break. Afterwards, if all had gone well, Tracy might take him back with her to Keepers Cottage and start getting our family settled there — maybe not after this first visit, but some time later.

For once the tide seemed to be running in my favour. Three phone calls fixed everything: one to Tracy, one to Meg, one to the airline. The great thing about Tracy — or one of the great things about her — was the positive way she reacted to new ideas. I can't stand people with negative attitudes, who reject suggestions on principle before they've even thought about them. Tracy's outlook was the opposite of that: everything new was fun, or likely to be — and so it turned out when I suggested that she might come over. "Great!" was her reaction. Susan could hold the fort at KC. She herself could take a week off work any time, she said. Her only question was, "When?"

Meg was almost equally enthusiastic. I put over the idea that Tracy was a trained nurse, and fully capable of looking after a young child. I said, truthfully enough, that her elder sister had two young boys of her own, and that Tracy had helped look after them. I'm sure my in-laws must have seen the way things were going. They'd known that I'd left Tracy in possession of the house in England,

and when I said she was coming over, no doubt they put two and two together; but they were too sensible to criticize my arrangements. As for the troop — instead of having to creep out on surreptitious expeditions, I merely said that I was proposing to spend my leave in a holiday cottage on the north coast.

After its last little dust-up the Sierra had been smartly retired from our stable of cars, and in its place I had a Cavalier. This time I drove with one eye permanently on the rear mirror, and once I'd come off the M2 at Junction Four, I made a couple of unnecessary stops — one at a garage to buy some peppermints, one in a lay-by to check under the bonnet for some imaginary engine fault. Satisfied that I had no tail, I headed up round the edge of the hills towards the village of Ballyconvil.

The place was so small that when I saw it my heart sank. Four, five, six little houses straggling along the road — and that was it. One, with "LIAM'S" painted white-on-green above the door, was a bar cum general store, and the others were ordinary dwellings, so poor and mean I couldn't imagine Farrell setting foot inside any of them, let alone living there. If the village had been anywhere at home, I'd have gone into the pub for a pint and made casual inquiries about the neighbourhood; but here I knew the appearance of a stranger speaking with an English accent would immediately raise an alert. Word would go round in a flash; everybody would be talking and on the lookout.

All I could do was drive straight through the place and on up the hill. But as I glanced back to my left, I realized that there was one more house, set apart from the rest of the hamlet on higher ground. It was hidden from the road directly below it by the fact that it stood back on a ledge, and remained out of view until anybody passing was clear of the other houses. The place looked like a farm, with a couple of barns set round a yard, but even a fleeting glimpse gave the impression that it wasn't a run-of-the-mill ramshackle farmhouse. The old buildings had been renovated in the past year or two: the roofs were tidy and straight, the windows in the house new. The set-up looked too smart to be a working farm. Right, I thought, that can only be him.

I drove on for twenty minutes, stopped in a lay-by and watched the mirror for ten minutes between intervals of studying my 1:50,000 map. Very few cars passed, and none gave me any cause to worry. Obviously I wouldn't be able to park in the village when I did my CTRs; I needed somewhere secure to leave the car. My eye fastened on some blocks of forestry, green on the map. The one nearest to Ballyconvil was round the back of the hill from the farm, but only one kilometre or so away across country. It was worth a look, anyway.

A short drive brought me into sight of it. As I expected, it was a dense conifer plantation which climbed the hillside and swept round into a big bowl. The public road followed the contour-line below it, and a barbed-wire fence bounded its lower edge. After a few hundred metres I came to the entrance, a gravelled drive leading up into the trees and turning left. Following the road, I came to a barrier in the form of a heavy wooden pole, hinged on a pivot at one end and padlocked with a chain to a post at the other. No supersonic knickers here — only a sign saying: "FORESTRY COMMISSION. NO ADMISSION TO UNAUTHORIZED PERSONS."

I got out and had a look round. The gates were nicely out of sight of the main road. The gravel was clean and hard, so that tyres left no mark on it. A careful check of the chain, the padlock and the ground showed that the entrance had not been opened for some time. Evidently there was no work going on in the wood, no thinning or felling. The set-up seemed ideal for my purposes. After my lock-picking course at LATA, the barrier would present no problem. Once inside, I could drive up to a convenient point in the forest, hide the car, and go in round the shoulder of the hill on foot. If, by ill chance, someone came across the vehicle while I was away and reported it, I'd say that it had been nicked, and must have been dumped up there by the villains.

With that settled, I turned round and drove back along the same road. My second pass through Ballyconvil confirmed earlier impressions. The farmhouse came into view as I approached the village, and I saw that its walls had been freshly painted white. The window frames were new and made of dark wood. The roof was as it should be — traditional slate. At the back, a stretch of high-wire fence was showing. Somebody had spent a lot of money on the place. But there was no car outside the door, and no sign of any activity.

That second pass also gave me a chance to look at the background. Behind the house, rough grass fields sloped away up the flank of the hill, with much the same texture as the one in which Mike and I made our

OP; but after only one field's width the farmland gave out and the mountain proper began. The cut-off was a fence running horizontally round the contour; above it, thickets of gorse grew among the bracken, and higher still the bracken gave way to heather. It looked as though the gorse would be perfect for an OP — prickly, but brilliant cover, within less than two hundred yards of the target.

On the morning Tracy was due in, I got Pat to lift me out to the City Airport, and I was there in time to pick up a hire-car before the flight from Birmingham landed. When the car-hire girl told me all she had left was a red Datsun I nearly flipped. Red! That was the last colour I wanted. Especially in the forest — it would show for miles. But then I told myself, "Come on, you're a civvy tourist for the week. Behave like one." So I paid with my Visa card, gave my in-laws' address, and signed for the Datsun.

When Tracy appeared in the scruffy arrival area, we ran straight to each other and held on tight without speaking. I think other people could feel the high current of emotion flowing between us, because they kept away and didn't even look in our direction. Through her shiny blue shell-suit she felt slim and fit.

"You've lost weight," she said.

"I know. Things are pretty tense over here."

"It suits you, though."

"Good!"

This was her first visit to Belfast, and as we headed out for Helen's Bay I explained that we were already on the north-eastern edge of the city, well away from all the nasties in the West. The holiday cottage, I said, was even farther from the centre of the troubles, so that there was no need to worry.

Tracy went over big with both my in-laws — she said all the right things, and made an immediate hit. Den told her she was too thin, and said she should eat more; in particular, he insisted she should have another piece of the lemon cake which Meg had made and put out with the coffee. As for Tim — Tracy started straight in, playing with his train set and talking to him as if he was an adult. I couldn't believe it. After about thirty seconds they were having a serious discussion about why the signals went green for go and red for stop.

It didn't seem the right moment for a talk about long-term plans, so we packed up and got going, on the basis that all three of us would be away for the week. Den had bought Tim a new car-seat because he'd outgrown his old one, and we fixed that in the back of the Datsun. As we drove off I realized what great cover it was to look like a regular family on holiday in a hire-car, innocent and harmless as could be. Only I knew that the Luger was in the boot. We stopped once to stock up from a little supermarket in a village, and the entire journey took not much more than an hour.

The cottage wasn't quite what I'd been expecting. I'd been imagining something tucked away on its own — but I hadn't known the address: No. 1 Coastguard Row. It was one of four, built for the local coastguards, and stood at the end of a little terrace overlooking the sea, perched above the road so that you had to leave the car down below and walk up a flight of stone steps to the front garden. I immediately thought, Ah, this is handy, because the houses were out of sight of the road, and nobody would spot a car coming or going at odd hours of the night or early morning.

Inside everything was fine. Meg had phoned a friendly neighbour, who kept a spare key, and got her to switch on the underfloor heating, so that the place was warm and welcoming. Tim had been there before, so of course he considered himself an expert on the house's layout, and showed us which rooms were which.

It was a good job we had him with us, otherwise we'd have spent all day in bed, as well as all night.

With a fire going in the front room the house became a cocoon, cradling our little family, and there wasn't much temptation to go outside. All the same, that first afternoon we walked along the shingly beach. The tide was coming in, and the sea was flat and calm, with only the tiniest waves turning over as they hit the shore. I showed Tim how to choose flat stones and give them an underarm flick so that they did ducks-and-drakes across the water. At that stage he wasn't much good at throwing, and he spun himself round in circles with his efforts to get more leverage on to his arm. I noticed that there was plenty of driftwood on the high-tide line, so on the way back I collected an armful for the store in the shed behind the cottage.

All the time I was thinking of the white farmhouse at Ballyconvil and the dark forest on the hill. How was I going to account for my need to be absent for hours at a time? Why should I want to disappear in the middle of what was, in effect, our honeymoon?

I'd already tried to explain to Tracy that guys in the Regiment habitually told their wives and girlfriends as little as possible about what they were doing. It was plain good sense and good security, I said, to restrict knowledge to a minimum. With her knack of going straight to the point, she'd come back with, "Well, *that* doesn't sound great. If you're not coming clean about your work, how am I to know what else you may be covering up?" She was right, of course. Secrecy breeds distrust — and now with our relationship hardly started, I was going to have to start deceiving her.

I said nothing that day. While she was getting supper on the go I walked down to the pub at the other end of the village. Den had told me that out there, in tourist country, it was safe enough, especially as he and Meg were well known locally. The place was called the Spanish Galleon, and the walls were covered with mementoes of the Armada, mostly pictures of fantastic gold jewellery recovered from the *Girona*, which was wrecked off the coast in the autumn of 1588. I bought myself a pint of stout and explained to the landlord that we'd come to the cottage for the week. I couldn't tell whether or not he knew about Kath, so we just had a general chat, mostly about fishing. A fellow about my age, who was already at the bar, said he had a friend who owned a fishing boat at some place nearby. After a while I bought a bottle of plonk for supper and set off home.

In the morning, before it was fully light, Tim came bursting into our room in his pyjamas. "Why are the beds pushed together?" he demanded.

"So we can have a cuddle," said Tracy.

"Gran and Grandad don't have them like that."

"Well — come on in and have a cuddle anyway."

Next thing, he was in between us, wriggling like a ferret.

"Why are you bare?" he asked accusingly.

Jesus! I couldn't help laughing.

"This duvet's nice and warm," said Tracy. "We don't need pyjamas."

So it went on. She was brilliant with him, especially when he started in about God.

"Who's God?" he wanted to know.

"He's like a big father, up there in heaven."

"Why can't I see him, then?"

"He's like the wind. You can feel the wind, but you can't see it. You know? God's like that."

"What does he feel like?"

"Sort of warm. Like if someone's kind to you. He feels good."

"Is Mummy in heaven?"

"Yes. I'm sure she is."

"Why did she have to go there?"

"I expect God wanted her."

"What did he want her *for*?"

"Because she was a very good person."

"Can I go and see her?"

"Not really . . ."

The inquisition was relentless, but Tracy was equal to it; she never lost her cool or cut Tim short with an unsympathetic answer. By the end of breakfast there was a terrific bond between the two of them. Altogether we were a happy family that morning.

190

It was all the harder, then, to break the news that I had to go off in the afternoon to do a job of work. Tracy looked really pissed off. "But I thought you were on leave," she said. "That's the whole point of my being here."

"I know," I prevaricated, "But there were a couple of things outstanding. I promised the lads I'd get them done."

She knew I was being deliberately evasive, but because of the earlier conversations we'd had about security she didn't press for more information. When I said I'd be back after dark, she just said, "Take care. You'll find supper waiting."

It was less than an hour's drive to Ballyconvil. But I didn't go to the village at all. Navigating with the help of the big-scale map, I took a swing out right-handed, to the west, and came up to the forestry plantation from the opposite direction. Once again the entrance was deserted. A quick check confirmed that nobody had moved it since my last visit. Pulling on a pair of thin silk gloves, I brought out my little collection of bent levers and spikes, and in a minute I had the padlock open. The barrier-pole swung up easily, with the lump of concrete on its end acting as a counterweight. With the car through, I closed the gates and put the padlock back in position.

Inside the plantation, the road climbed to the left in a wide curve. The spruces on either side were quite large — maybe thirty years old and fifty feet tall — and they'd never been thinned, so that they were growing in a solid mass. Nobody could look into the forest from a distance and see a car moving. Half a kilometre up, I reached a fork and took the left, along the contour, in the direction I wanted. Round a corner the road suddenly came to an end in an apron of gravel, a spread big enough for timber-trucks to turn. Uphill, above it, was a small patch of bare ground under the first rows of trees; I got out and checked that it was firm, then backed the car as far under the branches as it would go, out of sight of any passing helicopter. I'd thought about cutting branches and covering it completely, but decided that, if I did, it would be too obvious that somebody had tried to hide it. Instead, I relied on an element of bluff. On the front passenger seat I left a book that I'd sent away for: *Field Guide to the Birds of the British Isles*. (I'd taken some stick when that arrived in the warehouse and was opened by Security in case it was a bomb — "Fucking hell, there's only one kind of bird that Geordie's interested in," and so on. Very witty.) Now, I hoped, it might come into its own.

I locked up, settled my day-sack on my back and set off along a fire-break that continued the line of the hard road. It felt odd to be moving operationally in the open without a G3 or a covert radio. It felt even odder to be on my own, without at least one partner in immediate contact. All I had in the way of equipment, apart from the Luger and the kite-sight, was my knife, wire-cutters, secateurs, a torch and a pair of binoculars. While planning the sortie I'd thought hard about borrowing one of the troop cameras, so that I could take pictures of Farrell, develop them myself and make certain I had the right man. After a while, though, I'd abandoned the idea. One problem was that I couldn't take a camera away for a whole week without its absence being noticed — and in any case, I knew well enough what Farrell looked like. What with Pink Mike's photos and our live sighting at the transit hide, there was no chance I could mistake him.

Heather and rough grass had grown across the ride, but along the middle a narrow path had remained open, and the going was easy. About two hundred metres from the turning-place it bent to the right. As soon as I was out of sight of the car I dropped down and crawled into the wood, coming round in a half-circle under the trees and putting in a few minutes' covert observation to make sure nobody had followed me up.

That was easier said than done. The lower branches of the trees had all died from lack of light, but they were still stiff and spiky, the lowest of them growing to within a couple of feet of the ground. Even when I tried to crawl along the smooth carpet of old pine needles; my day-sack kept catching. In most places the only remedy was to belly-crawl, right down flat. Even as I was worming my way back to the path I thought how impossible it would be to make any speed through a plantation as dense as this.

Like a snake, I wriggled carefully up to the edge of the ride, and for fifteen minutes I lay there watching the car through binoculars. Nothing moved, and gradually I relaxed. Maybe I was being excessively cautious — but you never know.

Emerging again, I shook the spruce needles out of my

shirt collar and went on along the track. In a few minutes I came to the boundary fence — a two-metre-high barrier of squared wire — and looked cautiously out. Ahead was the slope of the open hill, falling from right to left: wide stretches of heather, patches of dead-looking grass, clumps of gorse. Unless there was somebody up on the hill itself which seemed unlikely, I felt confident no one would see me, because the nearest farmland and houses were way down over the brow. In any case, I had done my best to dress up as a hiker or bird-watcher, in a dull-coloured windproof and thick grey Norwegian stockings pulled up to the knees over my jeans, like plus fours.

Take it easy, though, I told myself. Don't rush it. I gave myself a couple of minutes inside the fence, then climbed over and took another look round. Somehow I needed to mark my entry-point, for when I came back in the dark. To have tied a handkerchief to the fence would have been too obvious. Looking back into the wood, I saw a bare dead branch, stripped of its bark and nearly white. I climbed back in, threaded it into the mesh near the top of the wire at an angle, as if it had blown there, and climbed out again.

On the move in the open, I worked my way round the contour. Only ten minutes later I stuck my head cautiously over a rise and found I could see down to the farm. A short belly-crawl brought me into a dry stream-bed, and that in turn led down to a clump of gorse just above the highest field. Having crept round the edge of the bushes, I cut away some of the lower branches and scraped the ground beneath them clear of prickles to make a comfortable nest. With minimum effort I'd fashioned myself a perfect OP.

The farmhouse and its outbuildings were less than 200 metres below me. The house — to the right as I looked — was long and low, and ranged with its back to the hill, which rose in a mown grass bank immediately behind, so that the top of the bank was only a few feet from the gutter of the slate roof. House and bank were separated by a path no more than a yard wide. There were only two windows in the back of the house, and both were small — lavatories or bathrooms, I guessed. The left-hand end of the house jutted forward, away from the hill, like the foot of a blunt L, and there, in the middle of the end wall, in my full view, was the front door, with a little pitched roof over a porch.

To me, the house was of secondary interest. Far more important was the high mesh fence which bounded the property and abutted the ends of the farm buildings, so that the entire establishment was enclosed by wire or stone; it took me a few moments to work out that the area surrounding the house was one huge dog-run. The drive came in through gates a couple of metres high on the side farthest from me. Any doubt about this being Farrell's place was dispelled when a dog suddenly came into view sniffing along the perimeter fence. The animal was a hefty-looking Rottweiler, no doubt the partner of the late and unlamented Buster.

Scanning for details, I spotted a video camera on one corner of the house, covering the approach, and what looked like a security light high on the wall. At first I imagined that the light would be activated by infra-red sensors, but then I realized that if a dog was loose in the compound outside, the system would drive people crazy by popping on and off all night.

There appeared to be nobody at home; certainly there was no car standing outside. Then, as I lay watching, I heard a cow bellow and I realized that at least one of the barns was still in use for its original purpose. That was a surprise. From the high standard to which the outbuildings had been renovated, I'd assumed that farming had gone out of the window. Then I thought, Maybe keeping cattle is a form of cover, a pretence of normality designed to draw attention away from other activities.

The afternoon passed slowly. At about 3.30 light rain began to fall, so I pulled on my waterproof. The temptation to doze off was strong, especially after our energetic sessions during the night. To stay awake, I kept trying to work out how I would drop Farrell if or when he came home. By far the easiest would be to get him with a G3 or a hunting rifle from up the hill, above the compound and outside it. But since I couldn't sneak a G3 out of the warehouse (or lay my hands on a hunting rifle), I was going to have to go in close and use the Luger. Because the dog was constantly on the move around its patch, that was going to be difficult. I tried to measure the distance between the porch, where Farrell would probably get out of his car, and the nearest point of the top fence from which I'd have a clear view of him: twenty-five metres at least. I'd want to be closer than that to make sure.

At least the Luger was in good shape. When I first

got it, I saw that it was old but in immaculate order, as we generally found with PIRA weapons. Someone had really looked after it — but all the same I'd stripped it down, cleaned it thoroughly and given it a good oiling. One afternoon, when a gale was blowing and the noise of the wind was enough to cover the shots, I'd managed to take it out into an old gravel pit and put twenty or thirty rounds through it, so I knew it wouldn't let me down.

Just after four o'clock there came a surprise. Up the drive wandered an old crone, a real bog peasant, with a black scarf round her head, an ancient overcoat nearly down to her ankles, buttoned-up boots, and smoking a pipe. The dog ran to meet her, and as she let herself in through the gates it jumped up with its paws on her shoulders. She gave it a kiss and slipped it some tit-bit, after which it went with her as she headed into the farmyard. Through the binoculars I watched her take the pipe from her mouth and put it down on what looked like an old stand for milk-churns. Then she disappeared into one of the sheds and came out with a bucket. A steel gate clanged as she went into the open-fronted barn, presumably feeding the cattle in there. Later she brought an armful of hay across the yard and dumped that in the same area. All the time the dog was at her heels, clearly glad of her company. Then she picked up her pipe and vanished round the far side of the house, where I guessed she was feeding the dog. Finally she went back out through the gates. This time I saw that they opened automatically, presumably worked by pressure pads under the road.

Darkness fell soon after the old girl had disappeared

down the hill. I wanted to move in closer, but the wind was dangerous; I could feel what there was of it eddying past me from above — and after our experience at the transit hide, I didn't want to blow things by stirring up the dog. So I stayed where I was and waited.

My reward arrived just after six o'clock. Headlights came blazing up the hill and a car swept in towards the gates, which opened in front of it. I saw the Rotty rush out and leap around as the car cruised forward and pulled up outside the door. On went the security light, and out got three men. I saw straight away that the driver was Farrell, but I could make nothing of the other two. The car was a Mercedes estate, and before any of the men entered the house they opened the tail-gate, took out some heavy-looking suitcases, two apiece, and staggered across to the nearest outbuilding. From the way they were buckling at the knees I could tell they had a fair weight on board. When they reached the outhouse Farrell produced a bunch of keys, with which he unlocked a door. Once the suitcases were stashed inside, the men went over to the house, and soon several lights were showing as they settled down inside.

That was enough for day one of my campaign. I'd established that the farmhouse was Farrell's, and that he was using it. All I had to do now was devise some means of getting in close. As I walked back up the hill in the dark, my mind was already working on it.

At the forest gate I put on my gloves again to close the padlock, once again leaving it cocked at a particular angle, so when I returned I would see if anyone else had been through.

In bed that night we were still lying entwined, with Tracy's back towards me, when she said, "Geordie, what are you doing?"

I was half asleep, and muttered, "What?"

"Out there, with that gun."

"What gun?"

"The pistol. I found it under that pile of clothes."

"Oh, that. I need it for self-protection. That's all."

She went quiet for a minute, then said, "You're going after someone, aren't you?"

I tried to keep myself relaxed. If I let myself tense up, she'd be bound to feel it. I was in a real spot. If I tried to bluff it out, she'd know I was lying — she had a tremendous sense for that. And if I did start telling lies, I'd undermine our relationship right at the beginning.

"Don't worry," I said. "It'll be all right."

"It's the person who killed Kath, isn't it?"

"Trace!" Now I did tense and pull away from her. "How the hell did you know that?"

"I guessed it. I've had the whole afternoon to think about it. I reckoned, Either he's on leave, or he isn't. He can't be half-working. I know you lot don't work alone. It's always in pairs, isn't it?"

I nodded. My forehead was still against the back of her head, and, although she couldn't see me she could feel the movement.

"Well? You're trying to kill him?"

I nodded again.

"Why?"

"He killed Kath. That's why."

"I don't suppose he meant to."

"He sent the bomber to kill *some*body. He's killed plenty of others, too. He's a murdering bastard."

"An eye for an eye."

"That's right."

"Why not just leave him?"

"Trace, this is nothing to do with you."

"Of course it is!" She suddenly turned over to face me and said angrily, "If we're going together, I'm part of everything you do."

I wanted to tell her gently that she couldn't be, that my profession made any such arrangement impossible. But I sidestepped, and said I'd reconsider things when we were fresh in the morning.

"The trouble with you," she said, "is that you're a loner. You know that, don't you? You're always wanting to do things on your own."

Next day, Tuesday, the weather gave me a breathing space. A westerly gale brought in tremendous rainstorms, which continued on and off until dark, and made it no sort of a day for lying out in the open. After lunch we went for a drive up the coast and walked along part of the Giant's Causeway. Tim loved the amazing formations of rock, like chopped-off pillars, and jumped tirelessly from one to another until another storm drove us back into the car. I suspected Tracy thought she'd won the argument — although I hadn't made any definite promise to lay off, I didn't seem to be taking any further action.

In fact my mind was working full-time on the problem of how to get in close on Ballyconvil farmhouse.

Wire-cutters would see to the perimeter fence all right, and if I came along the back of the house, between the grass bank and the building, I could position myself at the corner, only two or three metres from where Farrell had got out of the Merc. But what about the ruddy dog? If I bought a pound of steak, or liver, and doctored it up, there was little doubt that the Rotty would wolf it down. But if I put the dog under before Farrell returned home, he would immediately notice something was wrong if the beast didn't run out to greet him. Worse still, it might freak out in front of the house, where he'd be bound to see it. And what if he arrived back with a couple of other guys, as he had before? Would I have to take them out as well to make my getaway?

When Wednesday dawned fine, I decided I would have to have another go. Tracy was upset, of course, and we had our first real row; but I limited the damage by promising that I was only going on another recce — which was true up to a point. I needed to check Farrell's movements at least once more before committing myself.

This time I started later, and didn't reach the forestry gates until 1600. I took a careful look at the padlock, decided it hadn't moved since my last visit, drove through and up to the same parking place. Once again I saw nobody on my way to the OP, and I was there in time to watch the old peasant-lady going about her evening business. The dog was loose as before; it followed her about, and from the pattern of their movements I reckoned she fed it at the same place, out of my sight. That could be a problem: after its meal, it would be less hungry.

With the clear sky, the light was hanging on for a few extra minutes, and full dark didn't come down until after five. By then the wind had turned to the north, straight in my face, and I reckoned it was safe to move down to a position only fifty metres above the wire. There I lay down behind a solitary gorse bush, studying the farmyard with the kite-sight. The dog must have laid up somewhere, because I couldn't see it, and in the hour that followed I had nothing to do but think. In particular I thought about the amazing contrast between being cocooned in the light and warmth of the family one minute, and lying alone on a cold, black hill the next, trying to light the forces of darkness single-handed. Maybe Tracy was right? Maybe I was a loner?

The Merc came up the drive at almost exactly the same time as before, just after six. Was this another delivery of weapons or whatever? Once again the dog raced out to meet the car and danced attendance as it moved up to the front door, but this time only two people got out: Farrell and a woman. Through my binoculars she looked young and smartly dressed, in a pale jacket and skirt and carrying a handbag that must have been made of patent leather, because it flashed in the security lights. This time I got a good sight of him, too. He'd put on weight since those photographs; I could see it about the jowls. There was his limp again, too — a small dip on the left foot — but still he moved quite sharply. I watched him unlock the door and hold it open for his companion. Then the house came to life as the interior lights went on one by one and the security lamps were doused.

"You think you're safe in there," I said quietly. I

held in an imaginary pressel switch and said, "Tango One, target complete in house. Permission to proceed. Over." Then I told myself to stop pissing about, and set off for the car.

I was back at the cottage by eight o'clock. Tim was already asleep, and a good smell of supper filled the air. I sat down at the kitchen table, preparing to relax, but Tracy pulled me up sharp. "A man called to see you" she said.

"Jesus! What sort of a man?"

"I dunno. About your age. Quite scruffy."

"Irish?"

"Yes, of course."

"What did he want?"

"He said, were you the man who's mad after the fishing?" She put on an Ulster accent, rather well.

"Oh — right. It was that guy from the pub, then." I remembered I'd talked to a man in the Spanish Galleon about the possibility of going out in one of the local boats — but I hadn't made any arrangement.

"He was wearing earrings," Tracy said.

"Not my fellow then. Someone else."

"Don't look so worried."

"Listen!" I stood up. "We've got to get out of here."

"What — now?"

"Yes, right away."

"Why? You keep telling me this is a safe area."

"Yes, but now the bastards have found me."

"Oh, Geordie — come on! Your imagination's running

away from you. The man was friendly enough. Relax. Sit down and have a drink."

I sat down again, and took a sip from the glass of red wine she'd poured for me. But I wasn't feeling relaxed in the slightest.

"What did he say?"

"He asked how long we were staying."

"What did you tell him?"

"To the end of the week."

"Then what?"

"He said he'd call back tomorrow."

"Hell!"

The inquiry could have been genuine, but the conversation in the pub had been so casual it didn't seem likely. Or was Tracy right? Was I becoming the victim of my own fantasies, seeing enemies everywhere?

Once you're in that state of mind, getting out of it is very difficult, and I couldn't shake it off. I did settle enough to decide we'd stay in the cottage that night, but first I took two of the wooden chairs from the kitchen and jammed one at an angle under the handle of the front door, the other at the back. I also dug the Luger out of my day-sack and kept it handy, wherever I was. Tracy thought I was overreacting, I know, but she saw how serious I was, and didn't say much.

After supper I said, "Look — I've got a plan. You don't have to go along with it. It's up to you."

"Go on, then."

"They've seen me here. They've seen you with me. Someone has. Therefore, the quicker we get you back to England, the better. In the morning we'll pull out of here, back to Belfast, and I'll put you on the plane."

She reached across the corner of the table and put her hand over mine. Her eyes were swimming.

"I'm sorry, love." I said, "But that's the safest."

Still she looked at me.

"There's something else," I went on. "I think you should take Tim with you. If you will."

That was too much. She burst into tears, head down on the table. I held on tightly to her hand.

"Don't cry. As I said, you don't have to."

"No, no!" she said fiercely, sitting bolt upright. "It isn't that. It's the opposite. I want to have Tim with me. But I want you too. I want all of us to be together, somewhere safe."

The night passed without incident, but in the morning I inspected the car with the utmost care, checking the wheels for any sign of a trigger device, and lying flat on my back in the road to wriggle underneath and scan for booby traps. When I found nothing, I wondered again whether I wasn't creating a drama about nothing.

We closed down the cottage and handed the key back to the neighbour, making up some excuse for leaving early. Then, from a call-box in the next village, I phoned my in-laws to warn them that we were on our way back. I didn't try to explain that Tracy was going to take Tim to England with her — better to leave that one until we could talk it through in person. Over the phone, our decision might have sounded like an insult — as though we didn't trust Meg to look after the boy properly.

As soon as we knew we'd got tickets on the afternoon

plane, Tracy packed up Tim's kit and stuck it out in the hall. Then we all had a cheerful lunch, with everybody in good spirits. Far from there being any tears, Tim was thrilled by the prospect of another flight, and of going back to Keeper's Cottage. Looking at him, and thinking how like Kath he was becoming, I reckoned he had inherited something of her steady nature: as long as people were kind to him, he didn't seem to mind who he was with. And of course Tracy had been wonderful with him from the start. It may have been wishful thinking, but I honestly felt that he was already seeing her as his mother.

With only three days of leave left, it was hardly worth my going to England. On my way to the airport I promised not to go chasing after personal enemies any more. From now on, I said, I'd just keep my head down.

It was two-thirty when we reached the terminal, for the three-fifteen flight. I helped them check in, and waved goodbye as they disappeared into the security area, with promises I'd phone that evening to make sure they were safe home.

As soon as they had gone, I hustled back to the short-term car-park. I'm afraid I'd told Tracy that I was going to turn the hire-car in and get one of the guys in the troop to come out and lift me back to camp. In fact I never went near the car-hire office. I drove the red Datsun out of the airport and headed straight for Ballyconvil.

CHAPTER
NINE

I reached the forestry gate without incident. This was later than either of my previous visits, and by the time I'd parked the car in its usual spot dusk had thickened among the trees which didn't worry me — if Farrell ran true to form, he wouldn't be home for at least another hour and a half. On the way over I'd bought a big steak from a village supermarket and stopped in a lay-by to doctor it. I slit it open to form a sandwich and gave it a good filling of barbiturate powder.

I'd decided the best option was to wait for full darkness, then cut through the wire on the bank behind the house. Once into the compound, I'd lie up by the back corner of the building, within four or five yards of where the Merc should come to rest. If the wind direction made it possible, I'd leave the dog alone. If he detected my presence I'd have to throw him the meat. When I fired the shots to drop Farrell, the dog might come for me, but if necessary I could drop him too.

I just hoped that the boss didn't come back with a whole troop of admirers. The snag about the Luger was that I only had a single magazine, holding eight rounds. Once I'd fired them, it would take maybe twenty seconds to reload. If Farrell had that bird with him it would be tough on her, but that was just too bad. With the shooting over, I'd be back through the fence and away.

If the dog came for me at that point, I could still try the meat — and if he ignored it I could whack him with a bullet.

All this was going through my head as I locked up the car and did a mental check: pistol, spare rounds, knife, torch, binoculars, wire-cutters, meat. With everything either about my person or in my day-sack, there was no reason to wait any longer. But at the last moment I realized I was shivering with excitement or anticipation, or both. I said to myself, "Chill out."

Taking a deep breath, I set off along the forest track between the high, dark trees. The wind was light and in my face; as far as I could tell from this distance, that meant it should be blowing from the house to the hill. That was good.

I was nearly at the forestry fence before I sensed something wrong. Suddenly I got a strong feeling I wasn't alone. I stopped. I hadn't heard or seen anything, but a message had reached me somehow. I stood still, the blood pounding in my ears. Sniffing the air, I smelt nothing except the clean breath of the spruce. My normal senses produced no evidence of trouble, but my sixth sense was saying "Look out!" loud and clear.

I took one step closer to the edge of the ride and again stood still, invisible in the blackness, waiting to see if anything moved. The wind stirred faintly through the tops of the spruce, but that was the only sound. What the hell was wrong? Normally I never get spooked. I regard the night as a friend, not as a foe or anything to be frightened of. But here something was definitely amiss.

I gave it a couple of minutes, struggling to get hold of myself. I could pull out, obviously — but that would be pitsville, an almighty waste. All day, all week, I'd been psyching myself up to get the job over and done with, and this was my best chance. I knew that if I quit now, I'd never forgive myself.

Gradually, as I stood there, I got the feeling that there was somebody ahead of me on the ride, between me and the forest boundary. Again I had no physical evidence, just the feeling. Then I thought that maybe it was a poacher. There were probably fallow deer in the wood, and some local could easily be after them. He might have seen my car come up, and be waiting for the coast to clear. Well, if we did have a clash, it needn't be anything serious.

Time was passing. I couldn't hang about much longer, or Farrell would be back and safely inside before I reached my firing position. Nor could I see much future in trying to work round to my objective some other way. I hadn't checked out the other tracks inside the forest, and if I started trying to work them out now, I might easily finish up getting lost.

I gave a shudder, half involuntary, half deliberate, as if a good shake would throw off my doubts. Then I went forward.

Fifty yards farther on, I knew too late that my instinct had been right. All at once there *was* somebody on the track ahead — and not one person, but two. Two dark figures, blacker than the night. For a split second I still thought they might be poachers. Then, from the way they came at me, I knew they couldn't be.

I turned back and started to run, only to see a torch flash on ahead of me. I'd been followed as well. Cut off. There was only one way to go: sideways, downhill, straight into the trees. I dived to my right, aiming to plunge under the lowest branches and slither or crawl down the smooth carpet of needles on the ground. But it didn't work. Immediately a branch snagged on my day-sack. Another jabbed into my left temple, ripping my skin. Behind me I heard the bark of a big, heavy dog.

I found myself in a bit of a clearing. Two more dark figures loomed in front of me. I lowered my head, charged forward and nutted the left-hand one properly, dropping him in his tracks. The second took a dive at my legs and brought me down. I kneed him in the crotch and hit out with my left fist, struggling to get at the Luger with my right hand. Then a heavy animal came crashing through the trees and a second later jaws closed on my right ankle.

Suddenly there were men all round me, hammering at me with sticks. I tried to shield my head, but took some damaging blows about the neck. My shoulders and kidneys got a battering, and I couldn't get up because of the dog. I started to feel sick. Then a torch blazed down into my face and a voice said, "OK, come on out of it!" I tried to get up and run, but somebody else crashed into me from the side, knocking me back to the ground. Next second I was face-down in the pine needles with a knee in my back and another guy sitting on my head.

For a few horrible moments I was shitting myself. I thought I'd been grabbed by the PIRA. In the gleams of torchlight I saw that my attackers were dressed darkly and wearing ski-masks. Fucking hell, I thought, Farrell's got wind of my movements. I really thought I was going down.

Then I realized that the voices I could hear were relatively cultured. Somebody dragged my arms back and snapped a pair of cuffs round my wrists. The guy who'd sat on my head stood up and said, "On your feet!" The dog had let go of me, but it was still jumping around. Then someone tied a cord to my wrists, and two of them hustled me back through the stiff lower branches of the trees to the open ride.

By then a whole load of torches were bobbing about. There seemed to be guys everywhere. When I moved my feet a couple of inches, one of them snapped, "If you don't want a big clog stuck on yer, stand still."

The next thing was a body search, expertly carried out. Two men shone torches in my face while a third ran his hands over me. He soon found the Luger and my sheath-knife; of course my day-sack wouldn't slip off with my hands locked together, so he had to undo its straps.

Then a different man came up in front of me — some sort of boss, I guessed — and said, "What the hell d'you think you're doing up here?"

From the odd glint of metal about his shoulders I got the impression that this figure was in uniform. But, not knowing who he was, I reckoned it best to keep quiet. Then, behind him, I saw something white, and a second later two fellows dragged a big bag down over my head. At the top end was a hood with an elasticated drawstring, which settled tight round my face, leaving my vision clear. The bottom end was pulled in close round my knees, with my arms and hands inside. I felt humiliated to be trussed and bundled like that, but it gave me a clue about the identity of my captors. Those white bags are what the RUC use to cocoon prisoners, so that traces of explosives or gunpowder or blood or any other tell-tale substance aren't rubbed or washed off on the way to the station. I'd been lifted not by the PIRA, but by some arm of the security forces, probably HMSU, the Headquarters Mobile Support Unit, the RUC's equivalent of the SAS.

"Look," I said to nobody in particular. "I don't know who you guys are, but I'm SAS."

"SAS?" said an Ulster voice incredulously. "With a fucking Luger? Bollocks. Think of something better — and get moving."

A shove in the back started me off along the ride towards where I'd left the car. A man with a torch lit the way, but on the uneven track, and with my hands behind me, it was difficult to balance, and I kept stumbling. Ahead, I saw headlights sweeping up the hard road, and by the time we reached the turning-place several vehicles had assembled, the gargle of radios burbling out of them.

At the back of a long-wheel-base Land Rover someone yanked open the door and propelled me in, telling me to lie on the floor. Two other guys climbed in and sat on the side-benches, one with his boots right in my face. The door slammed, and immediately we set off downhill.

That was one hell of a journey. I was getting my right shoulder, elbow, hip and ankle well battered on the bare steel of the floor as we went over bumps; but more agonizing was the mental torture I was suffering. In the space of a few minutes, my whole life and career had gone tits-up. That was me finished in the SAS, I felt certain — it was inevitable I'd be RTU'd. Probably that was me finished with Tracy, too. When she found I'd gone straight back on the job after promising to lay off, she might well ditch me.

Almost worse of all, that was the end of my attempt to level the score with Farrell. I couldn't imagine I'd ever get another chance. And how in hell had these people cottoned on to me? Perhaps someone had seen the Datsun going up into the forest and reported it?

I wasn't going to show weakness by asking more questions; in any case, I was sure nobody would answer if I did speak. I felt certain we were heading back into Belfast, and after half an hour I began to see orange street-lamps above us as I peered up through the back window. There was a good deal of stopping and starting at traffic-lights. Then we went slowly through three successive pairs of high mesh gates into what I guessed must be a police station.

The driver backed fast up some sort of ramp and came to an abrupt halt. The back door was opened from outside, my two escorts scrambled out and dragged me after them. I got a quick impression of high brick walls forming a narrow cul-de-sac, before being bundled in through a door at the end.

Inside a brightly lit office an RUC sergeant was sitting at a desk.

"I'm Sergeant West," announced one of the men holding me. "We've arrested this man under Section Fourteen. He was found in possession of a weapon in suspicious circumstances in the forest above Ballyconvil, suspected of being a terrorist."

"Fine," said the custody sergeant. "Put him in there, and get the bag off him."

He nodded towards the first room across the corridor, which was a cell, bare but clean and smelling of disinfectant.

In there, with the door securely shut, my two attendants pulled the white bag over my head and one of them released the handcuffs. "Right," he said. "Get your clothes off."

"Wait a minute . . ."

"Get 'em off. Everything except socks and pants." The door opened, and someone handed in a grey track suit. The sergeant who'd arrested me dropped it on to the bed, which was a raised concrete bench. "You can put that on afterwards."

"Look," I snapped. "I'm not a fucking criminal. I'm in the SAS."

"Yes," said the sergeant, equably enough. "And I'm the Colonel-in-Chief of the Coldstream Guards. So just do as I say, and put your clothes in there."

He held out a black plastic bin-liner and reluctantly I started to strip off.

I saw the sergeant staring at me. "What happened to your face?" he asked.

"Nothing — why?"

"You've blood all down your right side, looks like a cut on your forehead."

I put my hand up and felt a matt surface down my cheek. Until that moment I'd felt nothing. "Oh, that. I ran into a tree."

"Nobody hit you, then?"

"No." I dropped my clothes into the bag and pulled on the track suit, which stank of mothballs.

The sergeant left the bag on the floor and went out saying, "The Scene of Crimes Officer will be with you in a moment."

I sat down on the bed feeling stunned. I knew I'd be deep in the shit with the Regiment. But all the same, my overwhelming desire was to get out of this gaol and back to the troop, among my own people, as soon as possible.

The door of the cell opened, and in came not the SOCO, but the custody sergeant holding a paste-board and a biro. "I've given you the custody number one-oh-two," he said. "What's your name?"

"Sharp. Geordie Sharp. Sergeant in 22nd SAS."

He gave me a hard look and said, "Are you suffering from any illness?"

"No."

"Do you need any medication?"

"No."

"Are you injured in any way?"

"Only this cut." I pointed at my head. "And I got a load of bruises. And a bite in the ankle from a dog. But I don't think it's serious."

"Do you want anyone informed of your arrest?"

"Yes, I do." I gave him the name and number of Tom Dawson, the sergeant major, troop second-in-command, and asked if I could speak to him.

"No," was the answer. "I'll speak to him myself."

The custody sergeant went out, and the cell door clanged shut again. Next man in was the SOCO, a thin, lugubrious-looking fellow with a ferrety face, carrying a white tray with instruments on it.

"I need to take some samples," he said.

"What for?"

"It's routine."

"Bloody hell!"

"Nothing to worry about. Hold out your hands, one at a time."

Like a robot, I did as I was told, watching with a mixture of fascination and revulsion as he wiped swabs of cotton wool carefully over my fingers and palms, then used a flat-ended gouge to dig out minute scrapings of dirt from under my fingernails. Finally he took a pair of scissors and cut some hair from my forelock, which was short enough anyway.

As he worked, I felt myself getting more and more steamed up. In the end I came out with, "This is bloody ridiculous! I haven't done anything."

"I've heard that before," said the SOCO mildly. "None of them has ever done anything. They're all as innocent as lambs, so they are."

Just as he was finishing, the custody sergeant reappeared and said, "Right, you're wanted for questioning."

He took me across the corridor into an interview room, where a table was set out with one chair on the far side of it and several in front. We sat down briefly, waiting for someone. I'd already decided to say as little as possible until one of my own people turned up; but suddenly an idea occurred to me.

"What station is this?" I asked.

"I'm not allowed to tell you."

"Does Chief Superintendent Morrison work here?"

"Morrison?" The sergeant was obviously surprised that I knew the name. I'd scored a point. But he said, "No. Not here."

"Well, can you get a message to him? Tell him I'm here?"

The sergeant looked at his watch. "He's probably off duty now. It's after eight."

"How about calling him at home, then?"

"I don't think he'd welcome being disturbed. He's probably at his tea."

"At least he could authenticate who I am . . ."

The door opened, and in came a chief superintendent, a small, neat, sandy-haired man, who sat down on the far side of the table and said, "Now, I need to ask you a few questions."

He was quietly spoken and courteous, but I knew that every word I said was being recorded, so I said as few as possible. I tried to give away nothing beyond my name, rank and number, and kept repeating that I was a member of the SAS. But when the chief asked, "Are you saying that you were taking part in some official operation?" I had to answer, "No."

"What *were* you doing, then?"

"I can't say."

"Where did you get the Luger?"

"Pass."

"It's not one of your unit's normal weapons."

"No."

All the time my mind was in the warehouse, in the ops room. I kept thinking of the consternation that news of my arrest must be causing, the acute embarrassment at having one of the guys go off his trolley. I hoped to hell that someone was already on his way across to rescue me. Further, I hoped it would be Tom, rather than Peter Ailles, the troop boss, whom I hardly knew. That wasn't his fault; it was just that he spent so much time at TCG, liaising, that the guys in the troop saw very little of him.

After a while the chief ran out of questions, so I asked a couple myself.

"What's happened to the hire-car?"

"Don't worry. It'll be taken care of."

"The keys were in the pocket of my windproof."

"Yes. We found them."

"Have you informed my people that I'm here?"

He picked up a telephone and spoke briefly. "Yes," he said, "they know. There's someone on the way over. Meanwhile, we'll get the doctor to clean up that cut. When did you last have anything to eat?"

I stared at him. Was he offering me food? What was this place? A fucking hotel with cells? I had to think back. Of course — we'd had lunch with my in-laws. "About one o'clock."

"Do you want something now?"

I shook my head. I couldn't have eaten a thing. "No, thanks."

The custody sergeant took me along to the medical

218

room, where a doctor cleaned the rip on my temple, declared that it didn't need stitching, sprayed it with disinfectant, and put a dressing over it. He also took a look at the puncture-marks on my ankle and gave them similar treatment.

"I don't think you'll get rabies," he said, "but you'd better have an anti-tet." When he saw the bruises on my shoulders he said, "You may be glad to know that you've got one broken police nose to your credit."

Back in the cell, I sat on the bed with my mind spinning. There was no way I could start telling lies within the Regiment. The only thing to do would be to admit the truth. But, Jesus — the humiliation of it! Not only had I broken all the rules and tried to take out a target on my own, but I'd failed to carry out the operation efficiently. I'd failed to recce the ground properly, failed to notice that I was under surveillance, failed in everything.

The minutes crawled past, and I felt sick with remorse. Nine o'clock. Tracy would be home by now. Suddenly I wanted contact with her. I'd promised to call.

I pressed the button beside the door, to sound the buzzer. Presently the hatch opened and a face appeared outside the grille.

"Is it possible to make a telephone call?"

"Afraid not."

"Can you make a call on my behalf?"

"Only to inform someone that you're in custody."

Bloody hell! That was the last thing I wanted her to hear. So I said, "Forget it, then," and tried to settle down.

At last, about 9.30, there was a stir out in the corridor,

and I heard several pairs of boots on the floor. The door of the cell swung open, and my heart jumped. There was Tom, a bit haggard and drawn, but big and reassuring all the same. I could have embraced the old bugger, I was so glad to see him.

"Is this him?" asked the custody sergeant.

"It is."

"D'you want to have a word with him?"

"Sure."

They ushered Tom into the cell and closed the door. For a few seconds he stood looking at me as if I was a ghost. Then he said, "For fuck's sake, Geordie, what's this about?"

I glanced round the shiny yellow walls. "Tom, I can't talk in here. I'm sure the place is bugged. For Christ's sake get me out."

"Yes, but what the bloody hell have you been doing? You've dropped a king-sized bollock, I can tell you. The shit's hit the fan in a big way. You're a fucking disgrace to the Regiment."

That was the nearest I'd ever heard Tom come to shouting. Then he calmed down a bit and said, "Don't worry. We're going. You're not under arrest. But what the hell have you done?"

"Nothing. I haven't killed anybody. I haven't threatened anybody. I haven't damaged any property. Nothing."

"What's the problem, then?"

"I'll tell you when we get out of here. There's one thing, though."

"What's that?"

"The bastards here have entered me in their records.

I saw them doing it. We'll need to get the entry erased."

"Don't worry. That's in hand. This has gone right to the head-shed in Hereford."

"Already?"

"Yep. They're closing everything down in double time. If any mention of it gets out, you'll really be in it. Meanwhile, I've got to take responsibility for you. Let's get you out of those fucking pyjamas, for a start."

Tom banged on the door until someone opened it, then called for my kit to be returned. While I was dressing he went out to deal with the chief superintendent. I don't know what arrangement he made, but somehow he got things well enough squared away to take me with him. The hire-car was still on my mind; I felt in the pocket of my windproof, and found that the keys had gone. I had visions of the Datsun sitting in the wood for weeks, and a phenomenal bill from the hire company winging in my direction. But when I mentioned the problem to the custody sergeant, he said the same thing as before: the car had been dealt with.

Tom had brought two vehicles, for mutual back-up, but as I rode back across the city in his company we couldn't talk, because the driver was from the pool and possibly insecure. Only when we reached the ops room was it possible to open up.

By then it was eleven o'clock. The boss had come in, or stayed up, specially to see me. He sat at a desk, with me in front of him and Tom beside me, together with a clerk to take notes and work the tape recorder. I was relieved to find the atmosphere reasonably sympathetic; everybody was puzzled and worried, but not too hostile.

"You look knackered, Geordie," the boss began. "Have you had anything to eat?"

"Not since lunch."

"What about a cup of tea?"

"Great."

"And a sandwich? Yes." He called through the open door, "Get us a sandwich and a cup of tea, will you?"

As somebody went off to the canteen, he said, "By rights I should be sending you down to Lisburn, but there's something big on there and they can't deal with you. I can't deal with you either, but I've been told to take down a preliminary statement. So — what happened?"

I told them everything — that I'd found out that Farrell was behind the bomb that killed Kath, and that I'd tracked him down and stalked him. When the boss asked how I'd got my information, I just said, "From the RUC." Then Tom asked where the Luger had come from, and I had to admit that I'd nicked it after the car hit. Everything I said seemed to sound flat and ordinary. There was nothing impressive about my performance, and I finished up lamely by saying, "I suppose I got a bit obsessed."

"You can say that again." Tom scratched his grizzled head. "You went off your bloody rocker."

Somebody brought the sandwich and mug of tea, and I got them down me. I felt curiously calm, as if everything was now over and done with. I said, "Can I ask something?"

222

"Go ahead."

"How was it I got lifted?"

The boss gave a wry smile. "I checked with the Det, and it appears you weren't the only person chasing that target. People have been watching him for a couple of months. You're right that he's one of the leading players, and now he's getting into drugs. Apparently our little plans are maturing nicely — so the last thing they wanted was to have Farrell topped just as he was about to lead them on to something hot. When you came on the scene, they weren't very pleased."

I sat silent as this information sank in, remembering how, on my first CTR, Farrell and his two companions had staggered from the Mercedes to the barn with those heavy cases. I thought, Should I mention that now? Then I decided not to, as I didn't want to start being cross-examined by RUC agents. The boss jolted me back to the present by saying, "Well, I don't know what's going to happen. All I can say is that you're off back to Hereford first thing in the morning."

I looked at Tom, as if to question the ruling, but he only said, "That's you finished in Northern Ireland, right enough. You'd better shift your arse and get packed, because the chopper's coming in at nine o'clock."

It felt extraordinary to be back in camp so suddenly, so far ahead of expectations. People I knew were surprised to see me, and asked what was up. I took refuge in simple evasions — "Just back for a few days," and so on. In theory I could have been on leave, as guys from the troop got a week's leave every month. But if I was on leave, why was I hanging around the Lines?

By the end of my first day back I'd had bollockings aplenty. But on the whole the mood was sombre rather than angry; there was no screaming and shouting, more puzzlement. When I went in on CO's orders, I was sat down and told how stupid I'd been. "Surely you realize by now that we do things in small teams," the colonel said. "That's the whole basis of the Regiment." He had very clear, pale blue eyes that penetrated like lasers, and now I was getting the full glare.

"What we do not do is bugger off and try to carry out idiotic missions on our own. For all you knew — for all the checking you'd done — we could have been running an operation of our own against Farrell. You could have ended up shooting some of your own mates, or vice versa. It's bad enough to have fallen foul of the HMSU. It makes us look a load of pricks. An own-goal would have been that much worse."

I nodded. There was nothing I could say.

The CO leafed through some papers on his desk. "The pity of it is, you were doing very well until then. I've got some positive reports here. You were making an excellent comeback after your various problems. Now you've gone and blown it."

He put his thumbs to his cheekbones and his fingers to his temples, staring down at the desk-top as though his head was aching. "If I RTU'd you, you wouldn't have a leg to stand on. Would you?"

I shook my head.

"By rights, you should be RTU'd. If a thing like this got out it could do tremendous damage to the Regiment. But in view of what you went through in

224

the Gulf and losing your wife, we're prepared to give you another chance. At the same time, to show I'm not condoning what you did, I'm putting you on a three months' warning. As you know, any slip-ups during that period, and you'll be out.

"Also, I'm going to fine you heavily. I've discussed your case with the Director in London, and he's instructed me to fine you £2,500. I've got no alternative. Is there anything you want to say?"

Again I shook my head. The fine was fearsome — a whole month's pay, which I knew would be stopped at source. That month, there'd simply be nothing coming into my account.

"You're to take a week off, while things settle down," the CO was saying. "You live out, don't you? Well, keep out of camp for that time. The most important thing is that nobody else should know what has happened. If you have to say anything, say there was a personality clash, as a result of which you had to come home. If what you did leaks out, that'll constitute an offence under your three months' warning. Understood?"

"Fair enough."

"Don't forget: the bottom line is that you've got to pull yourself together properly. From now on you're really going to be watched. If you want to survive, you'll have to get your finger out."

By the time all that was over, it was early afternoon. I reckoned Tracy would already be back at Keeper's Cottage, so I phoned her there. She was amazed to hear that I was in Hereford. "What's happened?" she asked. "Come over for a day?"

"For good," I said. "Things have changed a bit. I'll tell you when I see you. I'm heading out now."

"Why didn't you phone last night?"

"I couldn't. Tell you in a minute."

It seemed incredible that I'd said goodbye to her at Belfast City Airport less than twenty-four hours earlier. Half my life seemed to have gone by since then.

I was going to call for a taxi. Then I thought about my fine and changed my mind. After a while I managed to press one of the cooks into making a diversion on his way home and giving me lift. I even made him stop at a flower shop while I ran in. There I had to curb my natural extravagance again, and forgo the big bouquet that I fancied most. Hounded by the thought of my empty bank balance, I settled for six red roses.

The first thing Tracy said to me was, "You went back after him, didn't you?"

"Yes."

"And you got lifted."

"How on earth d'you know that?"

"It's written all over your face."

"It'd better not be. I've been sworn to silence about what happened."

"You can tell me, anyway."

I told her. The hardest thing was to admit that I'd deliberately deceived her about my intentions, that I'd been planning to go back on the attack even before she and Tim had left. Although I didn't say it, I felt it was nearly as bad as if I'd gone off and screwed some other woman the second she was out of my sight. All I could do was apologize, and promise that that was the end of deception between us.

Tracy was fantastically forgiving — even if there was a touch of the schoolmarm in her when she said, "Well, that'll teach you to mess about." Then she took me to see Tim, who was playing in the sitting room. "Look!" she called out cheerfully. "Here's your dad come home. Isn't that lovely!"

CHAPER
TEN

All through the next week I was way up and way down. Part of the time I felt incredible relief at being clear of Northern Ireland, at having escaped from that cesspool of hatred and fear. It felt great to be away from the dark, horrible, underhand warfare practised by the scumbags of the PIRA.

At other times I was desolate at having let my mates down. I kept thinking of Pat, stuck over the water for another nine months, and Mike, no longer pink or punk, but still bearing the scars of Farrell's Rotty on his right shoulder.

The fact that the head-shed had been lenient with me didn't lessen my feeling of shame and degradation. Privately, I reckoned the mainspring of their attitude was fear that, if they did get rid of me, I would start mouthing off about the Regiment to outsiders. They'd calculated that it would be safer all round to keep me where I was.

The last thing I wanted was to go back to my parent unit, the Parachute Regiment. For a couple of days I seriously considered leaving the army altogether, and to test the water about civilian jobs I phoned two guys who'd got out the year before. Neither was particularly encouraging. Both had gone into forms of BG work — bodyguarding — but both said that, although the jobs were well paid, they were also boring as hell.

One was retained by an Arab sheikh, and although he spent most of his time twiddling his thumbs he had to be prepared to take off for any corner of the globe the instant the phone rang. The other had signed up with a crazy Dutch family of millionaires who lived in mortal fear of having their two boys kidnapped. Father and mother were both nutty as fruitcakes, constantly feuding with each other, but it sounded as if the kids needed a shrink even worse than the parents. They refused to do what they were told, couldn't sleep in the dark, ate junk food at all hours of the day and night, and did nothing but lie around watching videos, the more violent the better. The idea of working for people like that turned me right off, and as I had no other ideas about what I could do, I decided I'd better stay put.

More than that, I realized how much the Regiment meant to me — how hard it had been to get in, how much I had put into the years of training, how much I'd lose if I left. Before I'd gone off the rails my prospects had been excellent — and now I became determined to do my best for myself, as well as repay the trust the Regiment had put in me. That meant ditching all thoughts of becoming a rogue warrior and consigning my idea of revenge to the past. Besides, what would I achieve if I did drop Farrell? I'd have a murder on my hands — and it wouldn't bring Kath back.

Two people in particular made me determined to

soldier on. One was Tracy, who was emerging as more and more of a star with every day that passed. On the surface she carried on as if nothing had happened — going in to work at the Med Centre, taking Tim to the camp playschool, cooking for us in the evening — but underneath the surface she was giving me phenomenal moral support. I know it sounds stupid, but I was amazed that someone of such slender physique and sunny personality could have such resources of strength inside her. It made me feel humble, first that I had made such a boob myself, and second that I had underrated her.

My other saviour was Tony. As I'd predicted, he had sailed through selection, and was now a fully-fledged member of D Squadron. He immediately heard on the grapevine that I'd come back, and blew into the cottage for coffee on Sunday morning. There was no way I could conceal what had happened from him, so we went for a hike through the woods around one of my jogging circuits, and I told him the story.

His reaction was positive, to say the least. Far from criticizing what I'd done, he lamented the fact that I hadn't quite succeeded. "Maybe I could go get him for you," he suggested, when I described the layout of the forest, the OP in the gorse, the perimeter fence and the house. "Now we know exactly where he is, maybe I should line up a deer-hunting trip over there. You said there are deer in those woods? OK. I get a hunting permit and go over. Then I have the right weapon to take him out from up the hill, without going near the house. What about that?"

But we agreed to let the idea of a hunting trip ride,

meanwhile, we resorted to the age-old SAS formula for sorting out personal troubles: we drove out to Talybont, parked in the lay-by, and tabbed it as hard as we could to summit of Pen-y-Fan. No matter that it was a miserable day, with rainstorms sweeping across the bare mountains: the physical challenge and the grandeur of the hills wrought their usual magic, and I came home with my confidence at least partially restored. Of course I would carry on with the Regiment.

On the Monday morning when I went back to work, things took a turn for the better. At Morning Prayers in the Squadron Interest Room the sergeant major asked me to see him in his office immediately afterwards, and when I went in there he said, "Geordie, I'm glad to say you're in luck. You don't fucking deserve it, but there's a slot come up for you. Geoff Hunt, who's been on the SP team, fell off a pissy little wall on Friday and broke his ankle. That means we need a guy to take his place. You're a trained assaulter, so in you go."

"Fine," I replied. "How long will it be for?"

"There's six weeks of the squadron's tour left. After that, we'll find you something else."

"Great!"

My enthusiasm wasn't just for show. I'd been dreading the possibility that they were going to make me ops sergeant — the worst job around, as it amounted to sitting on your backside in the ops room and being little more than tea-boy for the head-shed, with endless paperwork. I was genuinely glad to go back into the Special Projects (or Counter-Terrorist) Team for a spell.

I'd already done one tour with them and enjoyed it, so it was no trouble to slip back into harness.

The task of the unit was to respond instantaneously to any terrorist attack, such as the hijack of an aircraft or seizure of a building. Of the two teams, Red and Blue, one was always at thirty minutes' readiness, with vehicles loaded, ready to roll, and the other at three hours. In fact the first team was often capable of taking off within ten minutes of an alert.

Life on the SP team could be quite exciting. If a call-out came, you could never be sure whether it was an exercise or a genuine emergency. One of the Regiment's greatest ever hits — the siege at the Iranian Embassy in London in 1980 — began in just such uncertainty. On the morning of 30 May, a former member of the Regiment, Dusty Gray, phoned the head-shed from Heathrow Airport and tipped them off that all the Metropolitan Police's terrorist dogs had suddenly been whipped away to London.

It so happened that at that moment a major exercise was getting under way. According to the scenario, there'd been a hijack attempt at an airfield in the north-east, and the SP team was about to deploy in response. Then in came this call from Dusty Gray. At first the CO thought it was someone trying to take the piss and screw up the start of the exercise by feeding him duff information, but then he decided it was for real. Before any official notification came in, he said, "Bugger the exercise," and deployed the SP team to a holding location on the way to London. The result was that when the media later came and camped outside the gates to watch for warriors departing, they saw fuck-all — until six days later, when every television screen in the country showed our guys abseiling down from the Embassy roof in their black kit and taking the villains out. Twelve years on from that historic event, the terrorist threat remained much the same, and the head-shed often sprang an exercise without any warning to keep the guys on their toes.

In between, we were ceaselessly training. The thirty-minute team had to stay within easy range of camp and train locally, but the rest were free to go up country and do things like practise aircraft-entry and visit prominent buildings that might become targets for terrorist take-over.

Being on the team meant that I could carry on living at home, because my address was easily within the thirty-minute limit. At night, when the roads were clear, I could be inside the warehouse within eleven minutes. Like everyone else, I carried a bleeper wherever I went. If all the numbers appearing on its screen were one, I knew it was a practice call-out; what we wanted was all the nines — the real thing.

There were sixteen of us assaulters on the Blue Team, and for me it was a bit of a comedown to be merely one of the pack. On my earlier tour I'd been Sniper Team Commander — in effect the third in command of the whole outfit, under the boss (a captain) and a staff sergeant. But any active employment was better than being stuck behind the desk in the ops room.

We usually began our day at 0830 with an hour's fitness training. Then we'd practise abseiling, fast-roping out of helicopters, climbing glass walls with suckers, entry into rooms — all pretty physical stuff. I enjoyed the challenge of getting really fit again, and put in extra hours at the gym; in that role you need all the strength you can muster — you're forever lifting people, pulling them about or restraining them. You're also carrying a lot of extra weight — apart from the MP 5 sub-machine-gun and pistol, there's the body armour, kevlar helmet and ops waistcoat (loaded with axe, stun grenades and ammunition). For all these reasons, upper-body strength is a real asset.

The other thing we did was fire pistols. We fired pistols until we were almost out of our minds. Hundreds of rounds a day. Sometimes at Hun's Head targets on the camp's own range, sometimes in the Killing House, sometimes in the Garaback down at LATA. It would have been easy to go stale, get bored of it, but I concentrated by imagining (still) that my target was Farrell, and telling myself that somewhere, sometime, all these practice rounds would pay off.

Inevitably, our training was repetitive. We fast-roped until we could do it in our sleep. We practised entry into rooms until it was second nature. I had an advantage, coming in towards the end of the tour — I hadn't been doing these things for such a long time. I could see that some of the guys were already bored witless. They'd begun to take outrageous risks, like urging the chopper pilot to go in at a higher speed when we were about to fast-rope down to the top of the building, or even dispensing with the rope altogether, jumping instead. This, apparently, was where my predecessor had come unstuck: the head-shed had been led to believe he'd hurt himself jumping off a wall, but in fact he'd been attempting an unscheduled, ropeless descent from a helicopter.

With a month of the SP tour to go, a new buzz-word suddenly started circulating: Colombia. A fastball job had come up: the squadron had been tasked to send out a team at short notice to train the president's bodyguard.

"Colombia?" said Murdo McFarlane, the redheaded Jock, in the canteen one lunchtime. "Is that in Canada?"

"Is it bollocks," big Johnny Ellis said. "That's Columbia with a U, twat. This one's in South America. It's a hotbed of drugs and fucking corruption. Cocaine pours out of it like water out of the Amazon. That's why El Presidente needs so much guarding: the drug barons spend their lives trying to top the bastard."

"How d'you know so much about it?" I asked. "Have you been out there?"

"No, I just saw a video."

"Spanish-speaking, I suppose?"

"*Absolutamente.*"

The gossip set me thinking. Maybe, with my good result in the Spanish course, I would be in with a chance of getting on board.

A couple more days passed, then up went a list on the Orderly Room notice board, headed "Operation Bluebird". The ten-man bodyguard training team, it announced, would be commanded by Captain Peter Black; second in command would be Sergeant Geordie Sharp. Specially attached as interpreter and liaison officer would be Sergeant Tony Lopez (US SEALS, now of D Squadron). The team would deploy via RAF Brize Norton on 10 March 1992 — barely three weeks away. That meant we had to start sorting ourselves out straight away.

On the day after the announcement I had a preliminary meeting with the Rupert. I'd seen him about the camp — a tall, slim, fair-haired fellow, only twenty-five or so — but I hadn't had any real contact with him. Rumour reported that he'd been to Eton, and that he seemed only a little the worse for the experience; certainly he'd come from the Grenadier Guards. Whatever else, he was quite a physical sort of guy, and ran like the wind; he'd played as a winger for the squadron's Rugby XV, and had scored a good few tries. Anyone who could do that and survive had my admiration, because the methods used in those matches are horrendous — real caveman stuff. But I'd been warned about him by one of the sergeants in Training Wing, who'd described him as "a flaming idiot", able to talk his way out of anything but lacking in any soldiering skills. On the range he'd proved positively dangerous. The safest place to be when he was firing a weapon was straight in front of him. Under the stress of using live rounds his command and control went out the window. On the other hand, when giving a briefing or appreciation, he could sound quite impressive. No doubt that was why he'd passed Officers' Week on selection.

So I had severe reservations about him. My antipathy was increased by a factor of which nobody in the head-shed could possibly be aware. At a Christmas party in the officers" mess, to which civilian staff from

236

the camp had been invited, he'd come on strong with Tracy and tried to take her back to his room. When she refused he kept on at her, not just that evening but on several later occasions as well — so much so that I almost went round and briefed him up to keep away.

The result was that, when we met formally in the Squadron OC's office, I was fairly cool.

"Geordie," the OC said, "have you met Peter Black? He joined the squadron while you were away. He's going to command Air Troop."

"Hi," I said. "Yeah — I've seen you around." We shook hands and sat down in front of the OC's desk.

The boss then ran through the arrangements for the forthcoming team job. I was to be in command, and Black was to act as our liaison link between the British Embassy and the Colombians, for administrative purposes.

"Peter," he said, "Geordie's had plenty of experience, so if you have any problems, it'll be best to consult him first."

"I expect we'll manage," Black replied, but I could see the OC's remark had pissed him off.

There were a few more general points to be settled, and when the boss had finished, Black and I went into the Squadron Interest Room to work out details.

He certainly had a posh accent, and his eyes were set rather too close together in his narrow face.

"What do you know about Colombia?" he asked.

"Fuck-all, to put it bluntly."

"That makes two of us." He grinned. "There's a briefing laid on for tomorrow, so we'll start learning then. You've been in the Regiment more years than I have months, and you know a hell of a lot more about it. So I'm going to be leaning on you for advice."

"Fair enough."

"Now. When we get out there, the team's going to be based at a Colombian army camp at a place called Santa Rosa, about 250 ks south of Bogotá. You'll be there — obviously — and Tony Lopez will be helping liaise with the Colombians locally. But it looks as though I'm going to be stuck mostly in Bogotá itself, liaising with the British Embassy . . ."

He went on to ask my opinion of the other guys nominated for the team, and we assigned each one a particular lesson that he would teach: personal security, residential security, hotel security, vehicle anti-ambush drill, counter-attack team drill, movement by helicopter and so on — about twenty in all.

"What about Ellis?" he asked. "What's his special strength?"

"Johnny Ellis? His advantage is just that: strength. He's built like a bloody gorilla; a really hard man. He's the guy for the physical training and unarmed combat. He'll sort out the Colombians, no bother. Him and Murdo."

"Is that McFarlane?"

"Right. If Johnny's a gorilla, Murdo's a yeti. The only difference between them is their colour. One's got fair hair, the other red."

"Is it Murdo who plays the pipes?"

"It is, and it's a fucking disaster. You can't stop him."

Gradually, we got everyone sorted. Other key members

of the team were Stewart McQuarrie (also a Jock) and Mel Scott, both in their mid-twenties and fairly new to the Regiment. Stew was another very physical guy, strong and quick on his feet — a free-fall specialist who liked walking out on to the wings of bi-planes and dropping off. We nominated him to take charge of the close-protection training, on which he'd done a lot of work and contributed some new ideas. Mel, who came from Liverpool, was small, and rather quiet, though given to occasional lightning repartee. He was also an excellent instructor with a gift for putting things over in a clear, amusing way — and off-duty he was one of the squadron's leading piss-artists.

I myself opted for weapon and demolition training, at which I'd had a good deal of experience. All of us, of course, were primarily fighting men, trained to kill, but we looked forward to sharing some of our skills with other people. Closer acquaintance with Black didn't improve my opinion of him. Just as his face was a little ferrety, with its close-set eyes and pointed nose, so there was something of the ferret in his approach to things. He kept asking quick, sharp questions, and seemed insatiable in his quest for information. Whether or not he was going to use it sensibly was another matter. I felt I was going to have to keep a close eye on him — I hoped he wouldn't do anything stupid while he was at the embassy. Ruperts on their own, away from the guys and with a captive audience, are notorious for adopting James Bond attitudes and telling tall stories about the Regiment.

One of the most important features of team jobs

overseas is discretion. The SAS quietly trains special units in countries all over the world, and our guys depend on the British embassies for liaison with foreign governments. I'd seen this in practice in Africa, when one of the lads had a car accident. Because of the good relationship between the team and the embassy, everything was quickly sorted out, and the driver escaped a dose of prison. Instead of losing a member — which would have disrupted the training programme — the team remained intact.

I think there are a lot of misconceptions about the roles of officers and men within the SAS. In most Regiments the lower ranks automatically salute an officer as a form of respect. In the SAS nobody salutes. Respect is not necessarily accorded to rank: it has to be won. This doesn't mean that the other ranks look down on the officers. Far from it — there are plenty of first-class Ruperts. Unfortunately, there are also plenty of pricks; and now it looked as though I'd been landed with one of them.

Next day, in the evening, we had a briefing on Colombia and its problems, given by an Int officer who had come down from London. He was a good, articulate speaker, and knew his stuff, but a lot of the political complications he mentioned went over our heads. Naturally our main interest centred on drugs — to be precise, on cocaine.

"Now, it's not my job to tell you fellows how to carry on," he began, "but I do suggest very strongly that you don't get involved in drugs of any kind. You're bound to be offered them in towns, but for God's sake don't touch them. The vendors may easily be trying to set you up; they may even be plain-clothes police.

"As I'm sure you know, pure cocaine comes in the form of fine white powder. But in Colombia there's also stuff called *basuco*, the base from which cocaine is refined. It's coarser and greyer — looks a bit like granulated sugar. Another drug to be aware of is *burundanga*, which removes your will to resist. I know it sounds ridiculous, but that's just what it does. Villains put it into food or drinks, and then, when they ask for your wallet or your car keys, you just hand them over. As *burundanga* has no taste or smell, the only way to make sure you avoid it is to keep reasonable company."

He paused, took a drink of water, and went on: "Fortunately, you're going to be working with, and for, DAS, the secret police. They're by far the most powerful official organization in the country. Everyone else lives in fear of them — they do what they want, and they can even order the army about. They're a bit like the Gestapo in Nazi Germany, or the Savak in Iran under the Shah.

"The sheer scale of the drug problem is difficult to grasp. If I say that Colombia controls eighty per cent of the world market in cocaine, it doesn't mean much. But look at it this way: the drug barons are so rich and powerful that they have their own ocean-going ships, their own jet aircraft, their own *islands*, even, for moving their products around the world. If they want to eliminate some enemy, they don't hesitate to blow up a civilian airliner in flight and kill everybody on board. A hundred and fifty innocent people murdered — that's nothing to them, provided they get their man. On the ground, by the way, a favourite method of dealing with an opponent is to give him the Colombian neck-tie: they cut his throat, and leave him with his tongue hanging out through the slit."

That made all the guys pay attention. This was getting interesting. It reminded me of the day at LATA when Morrison began to talk about the PIRA and its methods.

The drug business, our visitor went on, was controlled by a few regional mafias, known as cartels. During the 1980s the strongest of these had been the Medellin cartel, centred round the city of that name to the north-west of Bogotá. When the government tried to take it on, the cartel responded with a long-running campaign, during which the Minister of Justice, the publisher of the leading newspaper *El Espectador*, and the Attorney General were all assassinated.

When the president declared all-out war in 1989, government forces seized nearly a thousand buildings and ranches, more than 350 aircraft, numerous boats, over a thousand weapons and 30,000 rounds of ammunition. The cartel retaliated by downing an aircraft belonging to the national airline Avianca on a scheduled flight from Bogotá to Cali, with the loss of everyone on board. They also blew up the newspaper offices and police headquarters in the capital. Eventually a colossal man-hunt ended with the death of one of the Medellin leaders, Gonzalo Rodriguez Gacha, known as "El Mexicano". Subsequently most of his former colleagues gave themselves up, including the notorious Pablo Escobar.

That name rang a loud bell for me. I remembered being fascinated by a newspaper picture of a sleek young guy with thick black wavy hair and a lazy right eye, described as the richest criminal in the world.

"As usual in Colombia," said the speaker, "it was a colossal fix. In effect the drug barons surrendered on their own terms. They were given token sentences, and allowed to serve them in a purpose-built prison at Envigado, Escobar's home town, where they're living in luxury.

"When they were put away, the power of the Medellin cartel declined, and narco-terrorism subsided for some time. But all that happened was that the Cali cartel came up in its place, and the drug trade kept on growing. Cocaine paste continued to pour in from Peru and Bolivia. The Colombians refined it at clandestine laboratories hidden deep in the jungle, and exported pure cocaine to countries all over the world, but mainly to North America.

"In the early days, couriers called *mulas* — mules — were used to smuggle the drug out in small quantities, but now that's all gone by the board. Today, it's big time. The Cali cartel has developed a system of flying planeloads out to islands in the Caribbean, then loading ships destined for Europe.

"As I said, the scale of it defies imagination. In the mid-eighties Escobar alone was reckoned to be worth two billion dollars. The funny thing is, he grew up the happiest kid you could imagine, in a strongly religious home. But then he got expelled from school and drifted into crime — stealing tombstones, stealing cars. Before he was twenty he was into contract killing. Then he started driving coca paste from the Andes to the laboratories in Medellin. He made so much money that by the time he was thirty he'd bought a hacienda for over sixty million dollars.

"The irony of it is that at the height of his criminality he was seen as a great philanthropist. He built hundreds of new houses for slum-dwellers in his area, and they all thought he was a saint. A very complex guy, by the sound of it: with one hand he was building hospitals for the poor, and with the other he was having whole families assassinated. One of his favourite methods of killing a man was by forcing a red-hot spike into his brain."

He paused, looking round at our group often. Then he added, "That's Colombia for you. Of course, none of this is directly relevant to your mission. You're not going to be fighting the Cali cartel or chasing Escobar. At least, I hope not." He laughed.

"Apart from the drug cartels, there are a number of terrorist organizations battling for purely political ends. In other words, Colombia is not an easy country to govern. The president, Cesar Gaviria, has just announced an entirely new constitution, but that doesn't by any means guarantee stability. In fact, he has every need of a highly efficient bodyguard — and no doubt that's why he's called upon your Regiment for assistance."

The next couple of weeks were pretty hectic. I was still on the SP Team, of course, and still training every day, half-expecting a call-out. In the intervals, I was working out what we needed in the way of stores and equipment, and the other guys on the team were going up to the

Team Tasks' Cell in camp to sort out the materials they would need for teaching the various lessons. Videos, slides, diagrams, paperwork — everything was stored in made-up packs, stacked in pigeon-holes that stretched from floor to ceiling. We also had a talk from the MO on the various filthy diseases to which we might be exposed: yellow fever, typhus, tetanus and rabies, to say nothing of AIDS.

In the evenings there was a special refresher course in Spanish, and the teacher from Cardiff who'd helped us earlier came up a couple of times to give us a flying start. In particular, she put us right on some of the ways in which Colombian Spanish differs from the language on the mainland — for instance, that *ll* is pronounced as *y*, rather than *ly*, and that a *c* before an *i* or an *e* sounds like *s* rather than *th*. She also produced some cracking local expressions, like *cayajo* (shit), *jincho* (pissed) and *cabron* (arsehole or jerk). Of course, Tony could have told us these and a lot more, but coming from old Maria, they made a great impression. I told everybody to get stuck into their Spanish, because I knew that an important element in Operation Bluebird would be winning the hearts and minds of the Colombians. If we could communicate with them properly on a person-to-person basis, and establish good relations, the chances of their government ordering British arms and equipment some time in the future would be that much greater.

We seemed to need a mountain of kit. For our personal weapons we took MP 5 Kurtzes — the short-barrelled version of the sub-machine-gun — as well as Beretta pistols, a couple of 53s and a couple of 203s —

combination weapons with an automatic rifle in the top barrel and 40mm grenade launcher below. We also loaded up a terrific amount of ammunition, because we'd heard there was a shortage out there. Also, we'd heard that the Colombian jundis — the ordinary soldiers — couldn't shoot for pussy, and needed a lot of training purely in weapon skills. So I signed for pallets full of ammunition boxes — 7.62 rounds for their Galil rifles, and 9mm for the MP 5s and Berettas — as well as a load of PE4 plastic explosive, and saw it all packed into steel Lacon boxes along with hundreds of targets and our personal heavy gear. If we'd known what was going to happen we'd have taken jungle kit — but as far as we could tell at that point, we were merely going to spend six or seven weeks in a reasonably civilized camp. I don't know what it was that made me pack my Magellan GPS — the hand-held global positioning system that communicates with satellites and tells you your location on the face of the earth to within a few feet. Maybe I thought I would show off the miracles of western technology to our students in the jungle.

The best feature of our preparation was that each of us got an extra payment of £3,000 in travellers" cheques. Described as an overseas allowance, it was an addition to our normal pay — a kind of bonus for going abroad. For me it came just in time, as the loss of a month's pay had left me struggling, and I put all but £500 straight into the bank. The money also consolidated the feeling that I was back in the fold.

Several of the other guys also stashed their unexpected loot, but a couple kept all the money on them, determined to blow it in the night-spots of Bogotá and buy emeralds, which were rumoured to be incredibly cheap. They were the financially incurables. As somebody remarked, "Giving that amount of money to fucking Johnny's like giving whisky to an Indian." When Johnny announced that in Bogotá night clubs the girls danced on the tables and didn't wear knickers, the place was in an uproar. What with the money, the promise of a hot climate, and the language, the lads were getting a bit above themselves. As they went about the camp I could hear the most outrageous greetings: "*Buenos tardes*, Shitface. *¿Como esta?*" and "On your *bicicleta, cabron*."

On the day we were due to fly, Tracy took the morning off so that we could spend some time together, and we had a scene uncomfortably like the one with Kath before I went to the Gulf.

"It's only for two months," I said, "and there's nothing dangerous about it. All the same, we'd better know were we stand. Don't get upset, but I've changed my will."

"So?"

"If I'm run over by a bus in Bogotá, you get everything, including the house. Except for Tim's trust fund. That stays the same."

"That's fantastic. But, Geordie?"

"What?" I saw Tracy looking at me in a peculiar way.

"Don't do anything stupid this time. It's not fair on me and Tim."

"Of course I won't."

Still she was looking at me with a strange expression. "Geordie," she said, "I want you to have this." She reached into the pocket of her jeans and brought out a blue velvet box.

I took it and opened it. Inside was a little silver figure on a chain, small, but heavy and solid for its size.

"Wear it round your neck," she said.

"Who is it?"

"St Christopher. The patron saint of travellers. He'll bring you luck. He'll bring you back safe."

"But where did you get it?"

"I bought it, stupid!"

"You shouldn't have bothered."

"I wanted to. Put it on."

I slipped it over my head and gave her a kiss.

"There's something I need to tell you," she said.

"What's that, love?"

"It's just that I seem to be pregnant."

CHAPTER
ELEVEN

It's an old joke in the RAF that Lockheed, manufacturers of the Hercules C 130 transport, solved the aircraft's noise problem by putting it all inside. When you hear a Herc fly over it doesn't sound too bad, and even at close quarters the scream of the four turbo-props is tolerable. Inside the back, though, its a different matter. The high, penetrating whine bores into your head, and after seven or eight hours even ear-plugs and defenders can't keep it out of your brain.

That was what we had to contend with — three consecutive marathon flights of eight, eight and five hours respectively. The pull-down seats along the sides of the fuselage are impossible to sit on for more than a few minutes, so the guys slung their parachute-silk hammocks and crashed out in them, swinging along to the rhythm of the aircraft. Most RAF crews would have gone ballistic at people taking such liberties with their aircraft, but our particular crew was dedicated to special forces missions, and we knew several of them personally, so more or less anything went. It was also possible to make the odd comfortable nest among our Lacon boxes. Looking at the steel trunks, all padlocked and labelled and held down by heavy-duty netting, I reflected on the weight of the kit we were taking. The boxes of ammunition were four-man carries, and many of the others weren't much lighter.

From Brize Norton the plane lumbered across the Atlantic to Gander, in Newfoundland, where it went tits-up on the runway, so that we had to kill time while its load was transferred to another. The next hop took us to Belize, north of Panama, where it was stinking hot. Finally we flew down to a military airfield somewhere in the west of Colombia, the flight being timed so that we came in at the dead of night, when nobody would see us.

After so many hours cooped up, the lads were pissed off to find that they weren't allowed to leave the aircraft. Instead, some immigration official came on board to stamp our passports. When we heard that we had to fly on for another couple of hours to a little-used military airfield way out in the country, the pilots were even more pissed off, as they'd never seen the place before, and it had no proper runway lights. But in the end there was no problem, and we finally staggered out into the warm tropical darkness at about 0400, just in time for a shower and a nap before breakfast.

Daylight revealed that the camp was built on level ground, and that the perimeter fence enclosed a large area of maybe fifty acres. Beyond the wire, scrub had been cleared back for another hundred yards or so, and then dense secondary jungle took over. In the far distance, above the trees, we could see bare rocky mountains. The buildings were all new, made of concrete, and reasonably well finished, with mosquito screens over the windows, doors that fitted, and showers that worked. The only trouble was, the place was alive with flies, big spiders and geckos; instead of rats, as in Belfast, it was lizards, going like smoke up and down the walls, racing across the walkways and disappearing into holes among the rocks.

We spent most of day one sorting ourselves out. We went for a run round the perimeter and did a bit of phys to get the flight out of our systems. The dry season, known as the *verrano*, was coming to an end, but the weather seemed to be holding up. Early morning was relatively cool, but by eleven or so the heat had built into the high eighties, even though we were 3,000 feet above sea-level, and for us, not yet acclimatized, the temperature was quite oppressive. That didn't stop the guys lying out after lunch and sunbathing in their shreddies. They'd immediately spotted the possibility of acquiring a serious tan; I also saw the possibility of getting seriously burnt, and I let it be known that if anyone was careless enough to roast himself, he'd be seriously fined. Because we didn't want to make ourselves conspicuous by wearing any kind of uniform, we'd decided to go for shorts and T-shirts, and that in itself presented a problem, as our necks and knees were glaringly white.

Another plus was the big swimming pool, which we could use whenever we wanted. The canteen, which we shared with the Colombians, was an attractive, airy place, but at first most of the guys couldn't take the food at all. It seemed to be beans and chillis with everything, and by the end of the day most of us were racing for the bog. As everyone was expressly ordered to put used paper into a bin, rather than down the pan, the shit-house was not a place in which to sit thinking fine thoughts.

Peter Black spent that day with us to see us in, and came with me and Tony to meet his opposite number, Captain Jaime Ortiga — a smooth guy, dark and Indian-looking, with a pencil-thin moustache. He was all smiles as he ushered us into his office. The room was bare, with whitewashed walls and a single big fan turning slowly overhead. The only decoration was a colour photograph, mounted and framed, on the wall behind the boss's desk. It showed a middle-aged guy in a peaked cap with a red band, and about three hundredweight of medals on his chest.

Have a go, I thought. Break the ice. So, summoning my best accent, I asked, *¿Hay el Presidente?"*

Captain Jaime looked hellishly startled. He spun round as if someone had driven a pin into his arse, saw the photo, and suddenly realized what I had said. The moustache spread out in a wide smile.

"*¡Si, si! El Presidente Gaviria! ¿Hablar castellano?"*

"*Un poco.*"

"*¡Muy bien!*"

That little exchange put him in high good humour, and, with Tony interpreting, he gave us a very civil welcome to the base. I was pleased to find that I could understand almost everything he said, even if I got a bit tongue-tied when trying to answer questions. I heard him ask Tony how he came to have such fluent Spanish, and Tony kept out of trouble by saying that he'd learnt it as a child.

252

The captain told us that the group he wanted us to train consisted of forty-two DAS officers. Some were new to bodyguard work, but others had already been partially trained by the Americans. Suddenly he broke into English to say: "We no like Americans. British better! British tactic better!" No doubt he meant it as a compliment. I was watching Tony's face, and saw one eyebrow go up by about two millimetres.

It was agreed that we would start training next morning. With the preliminaries settled, Black set off for Bogotá in a Land Cruiser, together with his diplomatic bag, the radio codes and so on. The drive was said to take about four hours. He told us he was going to be based in the Hostal Bonavento, a small hotel near the British Embassy in the northern quarter of the city. He reckoned he'd be spending a good deal of time at the embassy, in the office of the defence attaché, which had a direct satellite link with the UK. Since we had a portable satcom set with us, keeping in touch with him would present no problem.

Training started on day two. Startled out of their wits by Murdo McFarlane's reveille, the home team shambled out on to the barrack square at 0630, all shapes and sizes in white T-shirts with little DAS logos on them and dark-blue trousers.

We formed them up in three ranks, comprising three groups of fifteen, fifteen and twelve. At my request, Tony put over a little spiel about the requirement for physical fitness and strength in BC work, and the need to be able to heave bodies around in quick time. I could see one or two of the Colombians looking fairly sick, and when we set them running round the perimeter wire, the fatties soon fell away behind. By the time we'd given them a dose of circuit-training they looked about done-for; but after a shower and breakfast they came out spruce enough for training proper. We were hoping to pass them all out in the end, so we wanted to nurse them along.

At an early stage we explained to them that the team which eventually emerged would have two elements: the bodyguard itself, which would surround the president and give him close protection, and the counterattack squad, which would range out ahead of him whenever he was on the move, making a show of its weapons and letting everyone know that it had real teeth. I'd expected the majority of them to prefer the second option, and I was surprised to find that most of them thought it was the BC work that was really macho. They thought they were defending God, and all wanted to be the man who saved the president's life — i.e. in the bodyguard itself. The idea of going CAT really pissed them off. At a later stage we planned to split the course into two main streams, but for the time being we tried to teach all of them a bit of everything.

They certainly needed some instruction, most of all in the use of weapons. Some were OK with their pistols, but when it came to rifles and machine-guns they were useless. I could see that they were actually scared of the weapons, and sometimes shut their eyes when they pulled the trigger. They were also excitable, and inclined to be bloody dangerous. There was one short-arsed guy considered even by his mates to be a bit cracked in the head. His name was Alejandro, but they referred to him openly as *"El Loco"* — the loony — so we did the same. One day I had him firing his Galil on automatic when suddenly he gave a yell and dropped the weapon, which went on blasting off of its own accord, leaping about on the ground and sending rounds winging away into sundry parts of Colombia. Fortunately there were only half a dozen rounds left in the magazine and nobody got hurt. When I tore into him for letting go, El Loco protested that the gun wouldn't stop firing when he released the trigger — and when we stripped it down, we found that the sear had indeed broken.

To sharpen up their powers of observation, we laid out a special lane through the jungle surrounding the camp, putting down things like compasses, small pieces of map, matchboxes and other objects that wouldn't normally have been there. We then made them walk down the lane, one at a time, taking notes of what they'd spotted. To keep them on the ball we made a few booby traps out of trip-wires connected to thunderflashes.

I also gingered them up with a few little explosive. The aim of working with plastic explosive was to make them aware of the damage a car-bomb could do, and to teach them what to look for when they were clearing an area — to keep eyes open for suspicious packages or anything out of the ordinary. They were fascinated when I broke some eight-ounce sticks of explosive out of their wrapping paper and started to knead them in my hands. When I proposed to set fire to a lump of the stuff they were poised for the off; and when I did ignite it, they disappeared like shit off a shovel into the jungle, because PE 4 burns with a merry roar and an intense orange flame. They weren't to know that it can't explode if ignited, unless it's in a bloody great lump of thirty pounds or more. Later we got the wreck of an old car out into an area surrounded by rocks, and, working on the principle of P for Plenty, I put a charge of nearly five pounds underneath the chassis. When the students saw the whole thing rise to the height of the tree-tops, they were chuffed to bollocks.

That helped bring them on side. But it was when we started on car drills that we really got a good spirit going. Until then the Colombians tended to feign indifference, especially the ones who'd already had some training from the Yanks. They thought they knew it all, and weren't interested in learning anything new. But when they heard what we were actually saying, and saw that our methods were far superior, they came over to us in a big way. For instance, the Americans had taught them that if they got attacked from one side, all they had to do was turn in that direction and assault the enemy. When we showed them how to pepperpot outwards, and come in from different angles under covering fire, they were mightily impressed.

The other thing that chuffed them was unarmed combat. At first they were laughing at Murdo because of the dark-red colour of his hair and moustache, and the tattoos which covered him from the neck down. (When he showed them the pair of eyes on his arse, they fell down laughing.) Soon they were calling him *"El Mono"* — the ape. But when he invited them to attack him, one after another, he decked the lot, or tied them in such knots that they were very soon crying for mercy. Then he started to divulge a few secrets of holds and so on, and their respect for him became enormous.

What they didn't realize was that Murdo was one of the few Jocks never known to take a drink; to him, fitness was a creed, and his obsession with it gave him a strong practical interest in medicine. On this trip he acted as our medic, treating several of the Colombians for minor injuries — most of which he'd inflicted himself. All this made him very popular with the locals.

Another cause of amazement to the Colombians was Marky Springer, generally known as Sparky because he was our principal signaller. Over six foot tall, thin as a piece of wire, and covered in dense black hair, Sparky looked like a bloody great spider. He didn't drink either, and, unlike Murdo, he was fanatically mean about money. Tight as a gnat's arsehole, he hoarded every penny, and never went out to celebrate. Yet he, too, was a first-class operator, able to turn his hand to many skills.

Driving techniques and range-work were taught by Stew McQuarrie, one of the ugliest members of D Squadron, and a renowned piss-artist, given to drowning his sorrows in case he should catch sight of himself in the mirror. With his wiry bleached hair and permanently wrinkled forehead, he looked a picture of misery. The great thing about Stew, though, was that even if he got smashed out of his mind one evening, he'd be there on the dot in the morning, ready to give his all. In spite of the beer he put away, he had the steadiest of hands, and was one of our best marksmen.

As I walked round watching the lads at work, and listening to them teaching, I felt pleased with the way things were going. But the experience also made me realize that, competent as they all were, there is no such thing as a typical SAS guy: they are all individuals, all very different.

As for the Colombians, they liked it best when we started showing them close-protection formations, such as the closed box (in which they formed tightly round the main man) or the open V (with two guys watching for any threat from the front, ready to stop anyone coming inside, and another guy always on the main man's shoulder).

By the end of the first week our guys had settled in well. Everyone was walking around saying "*¡Carajo!*" instead of "Shit!" and "*Jodido*" in place of "It's fucked". At the start of a lesson they'd crack off with "OK, *para bolas!*" rather than "Pay attention", and they'd learnt that "*mamar gallo*" meant to take the piss out of somebody.

After work, the trainees talked endlessly about drugs. The fact that Escobar was in the nick had them well wound up, and they kept telling stories about him: how in his prime he'd been earning a million dollars a day; how he'd established a full-scale zoo, with rhinos and elephants, at his *estancia*; and how he'd mounted one of his early cocaine-running aircraft on top of an arch over the road leading to his house, as a kind of trophy.

The drug war was on everybody's mind, and one evening we had another brief, this time from an officer of the Colombian anti-narcotics unit. A lot of what he said was already familiar to us, but when he got down to the nitty-gritty he became much more interesting.

Talking of Escobar, for instance, he described a telephone conversation in which the drug baron had been speaking to his wife. When she protested about screams she could hear in the background, Escobar shouted, "Just keep that fellow quiet until I've finished my conversation." It transpired that the man yelling was losing his fingers, one by one, to a pair of bolt-croppers, because he was suspected of having lifted a few thousand dollars from one of the bulk payments. If that fellow erred again, the narcotics officer told us, not only he, but his whole family, would be executed — children, wife, parents, the lot.

"Yes," said the officer, in his fractured English, "I am sorry, but life is a little cheap in Colombia. You know, last year the narcos want to kill one *sapo* — an informer, literally a toad. They hear he is in the police station. Next to it is some apartments. So what do they do? They bring a truck full of explosive. Park it outside. Big bang. End of police station. End of apartments. One informer dead. Also two hundred other persons dead. *¡Maravilloso!*"

He also said they'd recently caught a notorious torturer called Gonzales whose speciality was sawing off his victims' heads in front of their families. It wasn't that he wanted to conceal anybody's identity, just that he enjoyed dismemberment.

We didn't have much in the way of entertainment, but while everything was relatively new that hardly mattered. One advantage was that there seemed to be no threat from guerrillas or other nasties, so that security was totally relaxed. In the evenings we could stroll down the road to the nearest village, where there was a bar cum restaurant which served incredibly cheap meals. For the equivalent

259

of about fifty pence we could eat to bursting point, and the local beer was about fifteen pence a bottle. We could tell from the label that the stuff was brewed just down the road, and it cleared your gut like paint-stripper; but you could get nicely wrecked on it just the same.

For our first few days we reckoned the national sport must be cycling. Every time we went out of camp we saw streams of *fanaticos* flying down the road like the clappers on racing bikes. Then one evening we went to the pub and found that a big soccer match was on. A huge television screen had gone up in one corner of the bar; the picture was diabolical, and so was the sound, which was turned up to about 2,000 decibels, but the place was packed with fans, roaring like lunatics. By the time the right team won, they were dancing on the tables. This led to our discovery that the nation was soccer-mad, and that Captain Jaime was a keen supporter of the team he called "Espurs". Unfortunately none of our lads could match his knowledge or answer his questions about the club's latest exploits, but soccer always made a good subject for casual conversation. At least we'd heard of Captain Jaime's hero "Gary Leeneker", Spurs' skipper, and when the local radio station reported that his team had been defeated by Nottingham Forest in the semi-final of the Rumbelow's League Cup, we were able to sympathize.

It was at the end of our second week that we went up to Bogotá. When work finished on Thursday night, we declared a long weekend and prepared to head for the bright lights. Many of our trainees came from the capital, and they couldn't wait to get back there, so they set off ahead of us in their own cars, promising to meet us at our hotel and show us the best places to buy emeralds and leather goods.

Peter Black had been down to see us once, but he'd called off a second visit on the pretext that the international situation was difficult, and that he needed to be in the embassy. He'd booked us into the Hostal Bonavento for the nights of Friday and Saturday.

We set off in two Land Cruisers early on Friday morning, with Colombian drivers, in high spirits and full of expectation. After two weeks on the edge of the jungle, everyone was ready for a bit of the old *vida regalada*, or, as some call it, high life. Everyone, that is, except Sparky Springer, who preferred to stay in camp on his own, eating shit, and refused to spend a single centavo if he could avoid it. Since he was easily the most proficient guy on the 319 radio, it was no bad thing that he stayed on site.

By third-world standards the road was pretty good, with only the odd mega pothole to double up the Toyota's springs, and the main obstacles to progress were pack-animals and buses. Donkeys and mules were plodding along under huge burdens, often with loads so wide that they took up as much space as a car. The peasants leading or riding them mostly wore dark-coloured hats like pork pies, with little turned-up rims, although some of the women had their heads swathed in black scarves.

The buses were going faster than the carts and donkeys, but not much. Just to look at, they were quite an eyeful, because every square inch of the bodywork was painted in brilliant colours, hot reds, yellows and blues. A lot of the decoration was in formal patterns, but often, in the middle of a panel, there'd be an elaborate picture — a view of mountains, a stretch of coastline, a church or a bridge. Every vehicle must have taken hundreds of hours to paint. They were grossly overloaded, stuffed to the gills with passengers, and most were leaning drunkenly to right or left, with half the suspension knackered. Black diesel smoke poured from their exhausts, and the slightest uphill incline dragged them down to about 20 m.p.h., if not to a halt.

Some of the hilly country we went through was farmed, but thousands of acres were still scrub. Beside the road peasants were selling fruit and bottled drinks from little shacks made of corrugated tin. Every village had a whitewashed church with a big cross above it, and all along the roadside were shrines to the Virgin Mary, with statues set in little arched recesses. As we progressed through a mountain pass, we saw that some of the shrines were hacked out of the living rock. Everything looked primitive and peaceful, and it was hard to imagine that the country was in the grip of narco-war.

As we trundled along I tried to think forward. The Colombians wanted the grand finale of our training to take place in Bogotá. The idea was that a team of our best recruits would show off their newly learnt skills by taking the president himself, or maybe his deputy, straight through the centre of the capital in a three-car motorcade, with a big, armoured limo in the centre, to the national stadium. Even though that great event was still a month or more ahead, I was keen to see some of the course over which it would take place.

For almost all our four-hour journey we were climbing, so the air became progressively cooler. Peter Black had warned us that we might feel faint at first, because the city's nearly 9,000 feet above sea-level, and if you go up to that height quickly you can suffer from lack of oxygen. Maybe the drive had been slow enough to allow us to acclimatize; whatever, we simply felt relieved to escape from the heat.

The run-in to Bogotá was across a level plain, with a haze of smog ahead of us, and big mountains dominating the eastern skyline. Our first sight of the city was a severe let-down. Along the sides of the road there was a straggle of tumbledown shacks, which gradually thickened up into a vast and incredibly sordid jumble. Corrugated tin, parts of old cars, wooden boards, inverted bathtubs, doors, canvas, sheets of metal, plywood and cardboard — you name it, the Colombians had used it to run up their hovels. Mangy-looking dogs were nosing about the heaps of garbage. Tethered donkeys stood around, eyes shut, ears back. "Shitsville!" cried someone — and so it was. These were the notorious *barrios*, or slums, that people had kept telling us about. Even passing through with the car windows closed, we got the impression that the place must stink to high heaven.

Soon, though, we were through the worst, and into an area that was still poor but at least had proper buildings. Our driver, Simon, who spoke a few words of English, had been proposing to head round the western outskirts to our destination in the northern quarter, but I told him to go right through the centre, so that we could get a look at it. Shiny high-rise blocks loomed ahead, and after a few more minutes we came to the centre itself. Another world. Suddenly we could have been in any prosperous European or American city — Frankfurt, Brussels, Chicago. Gleaming skyscrapers of glass and steel soared into the sky, and at street level the shops were as glossy as could be, full of expensive clothes, furniture, video cameras, hi-fi and other electronic equipment. Cafés, bars, restaurants and cinemas jostled in between. The contrast with the slums was incredible.

The city had been built on a grid system, with the main streets running north and south; but every one was jammed solid by cars and buses. With so many engines ticking over, the pollution was horrendous. The combination of smog and altitude made it difficult to breathe. Whenever lights changed and a mass of traffic surged forward, every driver clapped his hand on the horn and kept it there, so that the noise was outrageous as well.

"We'll need to watch ourselves here," I said as an old woman narrowly escaped death under the wheels of a cement truck. "They don't give a flying monkey's for pedestrians."

"Sure don't," Tony replied. "And the other thing you need to watch out for is pickpockets. See all those kids — those street urchins? *Gamines*. They're partly beggars, partly thieves. While one's accosting you, another slides up and tries to snatch your wallet."

Soon I realized that the system of street names, or rather numbers, could hardly have been simpler. All the big roads running north and south, parallel with the mountains, were called *carreras*, or avenues. The streets running across them at right-angles were *calles*. We were heading north on Carrera Septima, and the further we went, the higher the number of the *calles* became, rising from single figures in the centre. As we inched our way forward, Simon kept up a running commentary, pointing out sights of interest.

On one corner, where crowds of people were milling about among some stalls on the pavement, he pointed and said, "These men selling *esmeralda*."

"Emeralds in the street?"

"*Ciertamente*," said Simon indignantly. "Every day."

I had a sudden vision of an emerald necklace flashing on Tracy's skin. Wouldn't green stones look fabulous on her freckled neck, framed by that chestnut hair?

The Calle numbers kept rising, through the twenties, into the thirties and forties. Our hotel, the Bonavento, was way out on Calle 93, but conveniently placed within a few blocks of the British Embassy on 98. The further north we drove, the ritzier the surroundings became; from the number of big houses set back inside walled compounds, it was clear that we were entering the smart residential area of the city. There were also fancy-looking restaurants by the dozen.

The Hostal Bonavento turned out smaller than I'd expected, and they tried to pack us in three to a room; but I insisted that we got four rooms altogether. That meant one lot of three and three pairs, and I went into a room with Tony. We dumped our kit, had a wash and went for a quick lunch. I'd already arranged to go round to the embassy at 2.30, and I wanted Tony to come with me; but I told everyone else that they could fix their own programmes, provided they were back at the hotel and fit to travel in time for our return journey at lunchtime on Sunday.

I think at the back of my mind I'd been hoping that the embassy would be a beautiful old colonial building, standing in the middle of a walled garden. Far from it. It was merely a suite of offices on the fourth floor of a modern tower block, with the amazing name the Torre Propaganda Sancho. Having sat on our arses for four hours we opted to walk round there rather than take a taxi.

The air was thin, all right. Even tabbing at a normal pace made us pant. Because we'd heard that the Colombians clocked visitors as they went into the embassy we'd decided not to turn up together; so a couple of blocks away we split and I went on ahead.

Inside the foyer of the propaganda tower a receptionist took my details, gave me a visitor's badge, and directed me into the lift. "Embajada Británica" said the elaborate gold writing outside the door on the fourth-floor landing. I rang the bell and waited, not quite knowing what to expect. There was quite a long pause before anything happened, and I was on the point of ringing again when the security system clicked into life and a woman's voice said, "Can I help you?"

"Sergeant Sharp to see Captain Black."

A buzzer sounded and the door opened. Inside, waiting to receive me, stood an amazingly attractive woman, simply dressed in a white shirt and black skirt, with long, dark hair and a distinctly Spanish look about her oval face, olive skin and black eyes. She was older than me, I reckoned, but not much.

"Hello," she said, smiling and holding out an elegant hand, "I'm Luisa Bolton. I'm sorry to have kept you waiting, but our receptionist's off sick, and I'm having to double."

Her English was perfect, but with a slight Spanish intonation. I introduced myself and explained that Tony would be with us in a moment. Then I asked, "What do you do normally, then?"

"Communications — that's my job. Come in, anyway. Peter's with the ambassador for the moment. Will you have some coffee?"

She led the way into an ultra-modern office, leaving a trail of some weird perfume behind her, and I perched awkwardly on a swivel chair among the fax-machines, teleprinters and word-processors while she went into a little annexe and set a coffee percolator on the go. A plate-glass window gave a dramatic view of the nearby mountains to the east, with expensive-looking properties clinging to their lower slopes. On the opposite wall the only decoration was a huge coloured print of a condor with its wings outstretched. The picture must have been ten feet wide, nearly life-size.

Soon, another delicious smell was mingling with the perfume: fresh, home-grown coffee. It was odd, but this woman was reminding me strongly of Tracy. Her colouring was quite different, and her legs weren't so long, but there was something about her movements and mannerisms that was familiar and enticing. I realized

I was watching her with more than just professional interest. I gave myself a sharp mental bollocking. Hands off! For one thing, Tracy had been fantastic in taking on both my house and my child. For another, I knew that any involvement with a member of the embassy staff might lead to serious complications — especially as I was still on a warning order from the Regiment, and needed to play everything straight.

In a couple of minutes Tony arrived, and I introduced him. As Luisa organized cups and saucers, she asked questions about our journey up, and we answered politely. But all the time I was thinking, "There's something going on here. It was that one word which had tipped me off: the way she'd referred to the Rupert simply as "Peter". In a flash of intuition I felt certain he was humping her. Why else would she refer to him in that familiar way, by his first name only? That was why he'd suddenly cancelled his second visit to the camp: he'd got straight into a legover engagement and was having too good a time in Bogotá.

I wondered if I ought to have a word with him straight away, tell him to screw the nut. This was his first team job. In the past, plenty of jobs had been ruined by one guy not being able to keep his pecker in his pants. I realized though that if I said anything, it might lead to a major confrontation to the detriment of the team. Already there was an atmosphere between us, and any criticism from me would be bound to make it worse.

As Luisa came back carrying the cups, I got a look at her left hand. No rings. I slipped a look at Tony. He was fancying her something torrid, but he hadn't heard what I had.

"Milk?" she asked.

"Thanks."

"Sugar?"

"No, thank you."

I stirred my cup and said innocently, "Have you been out here long?"

"Most of my life." She gave that dazzling smile again. "My family settled here at the beginning of the century. They were Spanish. Then, in the fifties, my father came from England, married my mother, and settled down here. So I'm half Spanish, but have an English surname. And no 'o' in my Luisa."

"How are comms with the UK?" I asked.

"They're terrific now," she answered. "The telephone used to be terrible. The lines were always jammed, and if you did get through, the interference was impossible. But with satellites, it's fantastic. We can talk to London as if it were next door. And of course your own satellite phone is incredible."

We made small talk for a few minutes. Then we heard movement outside, and a solid, stocky man appeared in the doorway, holding a sheaf of papers. He was in his early forties, I guessed, overweight, with neck bulging over collar and gut over waistband.

"Hello," he said. "I'm John Palmer, Defence Attaché."

Black was with him, and all four of us went into Palmer's office. There was nothing difficult to discuss. I reported that everything was going fine down at the camp; apart from the odd attack of gut-rot, all our guys were well and enjoying themselves. There was no friction with the natives. On the contrary, the locals were friendly.

Our trainees were responding well to a bit of pressure and would make up into a reasonable BC team. I could see no particular problems coming up.

The news from the other end was less promising. The DA revealed that diplomatic relations between Britain and Colombia were under strain, after the arrest of a Colombian student at Essex University on charges of drug-smuggling. There had been verbal fisticuffs between the two governments, and threats to expel embassy staff at both ends. All this made our own position precarious; it was therefore essential that we did nothing to make the ill-feeling worse.

"Of course, your presence in the country is entirely unofficial," the DA told me. "Things might get very difficult if the media reported that you were here."

"Don't worry," I told him. "Nobody's planning to sell his story to the *Espectador*. Our lads are all fairly sensible." Privately I was thinking, What sort of a prick is this? What's he trying to tell me?

After half an hour of rather uneasy chat, we pulled out. As we were leaving, Luisa gave me a card with all the embassy phone numbers on it, including an emergency number, a home number for herself, and one for Major J. R. Palmer, Defence Attaché. On our way out Tony said, as a parting shot, "No chance of your keeping us company at supper, I suppose? Show us the sights a bit?"

Again she nearly killed him with that smile, "That would be wonderful", she said. "But as it happens we've got a reception on here. I'm on duty. That puts me out, I'm afraid."

"Oh well — not to worry. Another time, perhaps."

Black came down in the lift with us, and on the way I said, "I presume you're invited to the party tonight."

The light was rather dim, but I'm sure he blushed. "Actually," he said, "I am."

We'd decided not to piss about leaving the tower separately. As we started walking, Tony didn't make any comment for a moment, but then he said, "He's screwing her."

"I wondered if I should say something to him. He could fuck up the whole operation."

"How did he get into the Regiment?" Tony asked.

"They must have been short of officers when he came along."

It was the prospect of belly-dancing that made Tony and I choose the Four Seasons restaurant: authentic Colombian food, and a bit of entertainment thrown in. By seven-thirty we were definitely hungry, so we called up one of the black-and-yellow taxis and rode it into town. The other guys had long since disappeared like water into sand. I predicted that Mel, for one, would come back shit-faced and minus his wallet.

Our own idea was probably much the same as everyone else's: to have a good meal, suss out the belly-dancing and then head on for some of the hotter night-spots. Unfortunately it didn't work out.

The restaurant was fine. A couple of photos in the window had been unpromising — the dancer, Carmencita, looked more like a Michelin ad than a great seducer — but we had a beer in the bar, and then chose a table beside the small dance floor. We both had the same main course — *tamales*, maize pancakes with a terrific, spicy filling of chopped meat and vegetables. The filling was delicious, but so hot that we needed several more drinks to swill it down, and we hit the Carlsberg Specials.

We were just sitting back anticipating that action might soon start up, when the thunderbolt struck. Our table gave us a good view of everyone who came in and out, but I wasn't paying much attention. A party of four men sat down at the table next to ours. Then, looking straight past Tony, over his left shoulder, I froze.

"Hey!" Tony was leaning forward. "What's the matter? You look as though you've seen a ghost."

"I have. Let's get the hell out of here."

Forcing myself to move my hand casually, I signalled a passing waiter and made motions for him to write out our bill. But when I picked up my glass to finish the beer, my hand was shaking — because there, barely ten feet away, sat Declan Farrell.

"What is it?" said Tony. "You look real sick. You've gone white as paint."

"Talk in Spanish," I muttered. "Talk about football. Anything."

He looked at me as though I was crazy, but he started in. I hardly heard what he was saying, because I was desperately trying to collect my wits. It's OK, I kept telling myself. You're in no danger, because Farrell has never seen you. He's never set eyes on you. He hasn't a clue what you look like. If you don't do anything crazy, he can't possibly pick you out. Reason told me that Tony and I were not particularly conspicuous. Plenty of other people in the restaurant were dressed like us in casual shirts and jeans. Farrell, in contrast, was wearing a smart lightweight jacket and tie. One of his companions was the same; the other two had leather jackets and open-necked shirts. Without letting my eyes linger on them, I tried to assess who was who. All were dark haired, Farrell as dark as any. I guessed the second tie-wearer, who had pale skin, was Irish, and the other two Colombian.

With Tony still making the odd remark in Spanish, I got out my wallet and pushed it across the table. "You pay," I muttered. "I'm going to use the phone."

The telephone was round a corner and in a kind of cupboard on the way to the gents — private enough, provided nobody walked past. The equipment was modern, with one slot for cards and another for coins. I brought out a handful of change and surveyed it. The rate of exchange was about 1,000 pesos to the pound. A 100-peso coin seemed about right for a local call, so I lifted the receiver, fed one in and dialled Luisa's office number. I reckoned the reception would still be in progress, and I just hoped it was going on within earshot.

The number rang and rang, ten, twenty, thirty times, before at last someone answered, a man. "*¿Digame?*"

"Captain Black, *por favor*."

"*¿Quien?*"

"Captain Black."

"*No conocer.*"

"Major Palmer, then."

"*Momento.*"

He put down the receiver, and through it I could hear faint party noises. My mind was in overdrive. Farrell being watched in Ballyconvil because he was into drugs. Farrell staggering home to his outhouse with heavy suitcases. Farrell now in Bogotá. Morrison's story was that the PIRA was into Colombia in a big way. I'd known they had been taking percentages from dealers on the street in Belfast, but this was another league: their involvement could be world-wide, and might increase their power to buy weapons to a fantastic degree.

At last someone came to the phone.

"Palmer here. Who's that?"

"Geordie Sharp."

"Who?"

I repeated my name.

"Sorry, old boy. I don't think I know you."

Jesus! I thought. The guy's half-pissed. Taking care to keep my voice even, I said, "We met this afternoon. Can I speak to Peter Black, please?"

"Good God yes, I know who you are. The SAS chappie. Up from the savannah. What did you want?"

"To speak to Peter Black. Urgently."

"Black? Black? I'm not sure I can find him. Can't I deal with it? What time is it? Where are you, anyway?"

"*Please . . . find . . . him!*" I ground the words out as if I was speaking to a child.

"Oh, all right. Hang on then."

The telephone began to beep. Feverishly I dredged up more coins and stuffed a couple into the slot. Somebody came along the passage and went past me: none of the Farrell party. I waited, shifting from one foot to the

274

other, and hoping to hell that Black was more sober than the DA.

At last he came on the line. "Yes?" he said. "What's happening, Geordie? Have you got a problem?"

"Yes. A big one. The PIRA are in town."

"Are you trying to take the piss out of me?"

"No I'm not. It's Farrell."

"Bloody hell!"

"He's with some Colombians."

"Where is he?"

"Where I'm speaking from. It's a restaurant called the Four Seasons. On Carrera 15, 84-22."

"I know it. *Bloody hell!*"

"Exactly."

"Who are you with?"

"Tony Lopez."

"You'd better get out of there."

"Don't worry. We're on our way back to the hotel."

"OK. Where are the rest of the lads?"

"Christ knows. They've gone on the piss all over town."

"You can't get them back?"

"Not a chance."

"I want you all out of Bogotá as soon as possible."

"Well, we can't go before tomorrow."

"That'll have to do."

"Will you alert Hereford about this?"

"Of course."

"Great. I'll see you back at the hotel."

I returned to our table slowly, loitering to see if I could overhear any conversation from our neighbours.

Sure enough, one of Farrell's companions was speaking with an Ulster accent. "That'll be fine," was all I got, but the "fine" came out as *fayeen*.

Tony had already settled the bill. "Everything all right?" he asked.

"No. Let's get a taxi."

"Where are we going?"

"Back to the hotel."

"Don't you want to walk?"

"Not now."

"What about the belly-dancer?"

"She can stuff herself."

Knowing Farrell, I felt sure he would have dickers out on the street, watching his arse for him, and I didn't want one of them to spot me. Even in the taxi I thought it safer not to talk, in case the driver was a plant and could understand English. Not until we were back in our hotel room could I enlighten Tony about what had happened.

"Sure it was him?" he asked.

"Absolutely. One hundred per cent. I'd know him anywhere. He was the big guy right behind you."

"You should have stuck a knife in his back there and then."

"We would have been lynched."

"What in hell's he doing here?"

"He's got to be trying to set up some big drugs deal. Or buying weapons. Or both. Both probably."

"You don't think it's something to do with the fact that our guys are out here?"

"Can't be. There's no way he could know about us."

*   *   *

Bill Egerton was tall, thin, bespectacled, and in his early thirties, a scholarly-looking fellow with a long, pale indoor face, but wonderfully quick to grasp the point.

"Yes," he agreed immediately. "You'd better call Hereford. England's five hours ahead of us, so it's 4.15 a.m. over there. Is that all right?"

"It'll have to be."

I was carrying the camp emergency number in my wallet, and I knew the orderly officer would be on duty in the guardroom. The call had hardly gone through before it was answered. Reception was perfect, and by a stroke of luck I recognized the voice.

"Chalky? It's Geordie Sharp."

"Fucking hell! I wasn't expecting you just now."

"Well, listen. We're in the shit. Who's the duty officer?"

"It's Bob Keeling."

"OK. I need to speak to him."

"Now? It's half past four in the morning."

"I know. This is urgent."

"OK. I'll wake him up."

I waited a minute. In the pause I saw the guardroom, with all the lists pinned on the notice board and the bunches of keys on their hooks. Then, close at hand, I heard another phone ring. Egerton picked it up, said a few words and put it down. "Your American colleague's checked the restaurant. They aren't there. The other party's gone as well."

"Thanks."

The secure circuit came alive again.

"Yes?" Bob Keeling sounded sleepy and slow.

"Geordie Sharp in Bogotá. There's been a lift. Two British diplomats and our own Rupert, Peter Black."

"Say that again."

I repeated it.

"Christ!" exclaimed Keeling, coming fully alert. "When did this happen?"

"About half an hour ago."

"I'll get the ops officer in right away."

"Fine. You've got my number."

"He'll call you back."

I rang off and saw Egerton staring at me. "Were you at the party?" I asked.

"Yes — but because I was on duty, I was only drinking orange juice."

"I don't want to be offensive, but the DA sounded pissed."

Egerton twitched. "Yes. He overdoes it a bit."

I sat thinking for a minute. Then I said, "If this *is* drug-related, what will they do with them?"

"If they were only narcos, they'd demand a ransom. That happens all the time. But if the IRA's involved — I don't know. I've no experience of that organization."

"Where are they likely to take them?"

"Out of town somewhere. Probably into the jungle."

"How do we track them down, then?"

"Ah!" Egerton gave a very slight smile. "Our sources of information are quite good. Unofficially, we're in touch with people known as *sapos*."

"Toads," I said.

"You've heard of them. For quite a small consideration

from the slush fund — say 25,000 pesos — they produce very useful intelligence." Then he added, "Of course, it's nothing to what can be got from high-tech equipment."

"Such as?"

"You know how they found the laboratories at Tranquilandia?"

He saw that I wasn't with him, and explained: "The biggest cocaine factory there's ever been. It had a dozen laboratories turning out over three tons of the stuff every month. The narcos practically built a town there for their workers — houses, roads, a landing strip, everything, in the middle of the jungle. That was back a bit, in the eighties, when the Medellin cartel was at its height.

"The United States Drug Enforcement Agency found the place by putting tracking devices into a couple of drums of ether, which is one of the agents used in the manufacture of cocaine. Satellites tracked the drums right down into the Amazon basin."

"You know a lot about this."

"Well, I got interested."

"Is it true that DAS really run the country?"

"You could say that. They're extremely powerful. Most people live in fear of them."

"And you have contact with them?"

"Very much so. The Commander-in-Chief's a personal friend. Why?"

"I was thinking we may need their help."

"You could get help from the DEA, I'm sure. They've got people here all the time. Also there's the Colombian Police's own anti-narcotics unit."

"We need to keep this in the family. If some big

organization goes in with guns blazing, the first thing the narcos will do is top their hostages. Our own speciality is covert approach and surprise."

Minutes ticked away. Then the secure line rang and I grabbed the receiver.

"Geordie? You have a problem?" Far from sounding annoyed at having been dragged out of bed, Alan Andrews, the ops officer, was all lit up.

"Sorry to get you in," I said.

"Not to worry. What is it?"

"I'm in Bogotá and we've got a fastball. Peter Black's been lifted by the PIRA, or by Colombians, or both." I told him what had happened, cutting everything short.

"I'll inform the Director immediately," he said. "He'll be round to the Foreign Office as soon as they're in business. We'll get a squadron on standby."

"Great. The question is, what do I do now? The earliest I can collect the guys together is tomorrow morning. I'd like to get everyone back to our training camp, but it's four hours out of town."

"What time is it now?"

"Quarter to midnight. We're five hours behind you."

"Wait one. I'll speak to the CO and call you back."

Five minutes later he came on again. "I've talked to the CO," he said. "Recovery of the personnel is the number one priority. Everything else has to give place to it. You'll have to suspend the training course, or cancel it if need be."

"Roger. We'll keep this phone manned from now on. It's the best comms base by far."

"Good. The other thing is, this whole saga needs

282

to stay under wraps. Officially, you aren't there. The diplomatic shit's already stirring over the guy at Essex University, so it's essential you keep your head down, if you can."

"That's fine by me."

I rang off. "As I thought, they don't want the Colombians involved," I told Egerton. "Is that going to make things awkward for you?"

"We'll have to see what happens. If the DA doesn't reappear fairly soon, we'll have to report his absence. But we can give it a few hours anyway. The Ambassador's gone off for the weekend; if we can avoid having to drag him back, all the better."

"Listen," I said. "This is really very good of you. Don't let me land you in it too."

"That's all right. I had a brother in your Regiment, so it's a pleasure to help."

CHAPTER
TWELVE

Egerton announced that he was going to stay over, and called his wife to tell her. Then he revealed that there were a couple of bedrooms behind the offices, and offered me one of them. As this seemed a better option than returning to the hotel, I took it. Before I turned in, I phoned Tony again and brought him up to date. I said he should get his head down.

I tried to do the same, but couldn't. I was half-listening through the open door for the phone, half-cursing the way things had gone to ratshit. In a way it was my fault. If I hadn't recognized Farrell and reported his presence, nothing would have happened. On the other hand, I couldn't have ignored him and left him to carry on with whatever villainy he was engaged in. If the PIRA were into drug-running to the extent of sending him to Bogatá, it was really bad news for the province, and something that ought to be tackled right away.

I think I lay awake most of the night, imagining various scenarios; but in fact I must have gone to sleep, because suddenly I became aware of Egerton standing over me with a brew of tea. It was 6 o'clock in the morning.

"Things are moving," he said. "We've had a police

report of a disturbance outside your restaurant, so I guess that was it. Also, I made a couple of calls. They should produce results within an hour."

"Brilliant. Is there a back way out of the building?"

"Certainly. If you carry on down to the lower garage level in the lift, you can walk out of the pedestrian exit."

"Great. I want to nip back to the hotel to square things away. Now that this has happened, there's bound to be someone watching the embassy, and I don't want to be seen."

"Fair enough."

By then it was mid-morning in England. I called Hereford again, and was put straight on to the CO.

"No positive news yet?" he asked.

"No, but things are on the move. What do you advise about our location? I could send the team back to camp, but that's more than four hours out of town. I'd rather have them on hand in case we have to head off somewhere quickly."

"I understand. Are they in a secure place?"

"Reasonably. The hotel think we're hydro engineers."

"Keep them there for the moment, then. If you find out where the hostages have been taken, you'll need to set up a forward mounting base in the area, and get your people into it."

"Fine."

"We've been looking at ways of getting a squadron out to back you up. It's been to Defence Minister and Foreign Minister level. We're just waiting for clearance from the FO."

"Good. We're OK for the moment. I'm getting first-class support in the embassy." As Bill was temporarily out of earshot I asked, "Do you know of a guy in the Regiment called Egerton?"

"Donald? Don Egerton. Of course. He was a star. Killed on an exercise in Africa four or five years ago."

"Oh — right. I thought the name was familiar. It's his brother in charge here."

"Glad to hear it."

I hung up and glanced at my watch. I knew that, whatever might be said officially, ways would be found to get reinforcements out to us. Once the Regiment's involved in an operation of this kind, obstructions tend to fall away.

Then . . . there was a good chance that on this Saturday morning Tracy would be at home. Worth a try, anyway.

I dialled — and there she was.

"Geordie! What's happening?"

"Nothing. Everything's cool. I just got a chance to call."

"Well, great. Where are you?"

"In Bogatá."

"How's the weather?"

"All right. Not as hot as in camp. We're 9,000 feet above sea-level. What about there?"

"Typical March — cold and wet."

"How's Tim?"

"On top form. He's got a friend here for the day — Alex Kirkby, from the village."

"Oh, great. Everything all right, then?"

"Yes. Well . . . it was funny. A man rang last night."

"What did he want?"

"He just asked how you were enjoying yourself in the sun."

"Nothing else?"

"No. I asked what he meant, but he rang off."

I felt a stab of anxiety. "What sort of a voice did he have?"

"Nothing special. I couldn't place it."

"Not Irish?"

"I wouldn't say so."

"Listen. If it happens again, call the police. OK?"

"OK."

"And don't worry. It was probably just some nutter."

I said goodbye and rang off. Although I'd pretended to be nonchalant, I was disturbed. Outside the Regiment, nobody was supposed to know where we were. Who'd passed word around that I was in Colombia?

Before I had time to start worrying, Bill Egerton returned and showed me the way out via the fire-stairs, lending me a key so that I could come back in the same way.

I ran down to the lower garage floor and came out of the door cautiously. The car-park was three-quarters empty, and there was nobody in sight. The rear of the block was deserted, too. I turned to the right and set off, noticing for the first time that the building was flanked by a garden full of spectacularly bright flowers.

I walked the short leg to the hotel without picking up a tail. Tony had dragged everyone out of bed, and I got them all into the room he and I had been sharing. Most of them were looking rough. As I predicted, Mel had lost his money. He still had his wallet, but he'd got so smashed that someone had nicked all his cash from it without him noticing. The only things he had left were some emeralds he'd bought from a guy in the street and stashed in a pocket of his jeans. At least, he thought they were emeralds. The others reckoned they were bits of green glass.

"Listen," I said. "The shit's hit the fan."

I told them the score, then said, "We're to stay put for the moment. Then, if we find out where the hostages are, we'll go in and get them out. Meanwhile, I'm going to phone Captain Jaime and tell him the course is suspended for a couple of days. I'm heading back to the embassy now. Tony'll follow me, to man the secure phone. The rest of you are going to have to stick it out here in the hotel. OK?"

At the sniff of an operation their hangovers fell away, and everyone gladly ditched their plans to buy leather jackets. Those could wait. I had a shave and a shower and got some breakfast down me, then grabbed a taxi to the back of the embassy. Egerton was certainly well organized. His wife had come in, bringing his shaving kit and some weekend clothes.

"Progress," he began. "We've got a lead. Word is that the party's flown out to a brand-new refinery in the jungle on the Rio Caquetá."

"Where's that?"

"Way down south, in the Amazonas, near the border with Peru."

"How do you get there?"

"Not easy. There are no roads. The only way's to fly."

"In that case we're definitely going to need help from your friends in DAS. Will your friend fix things for us?"

"I think so." He picked up a telephone, dialled and began speaking rapidly in Spanish. He glanced at me a couple of times as he was talking, and ended with, "Si, si. Muchas gracias."

He turned to me. "He wants to see you."

"When?"

"Now. A car will collect you in a few minutes."

"Does he speak English?"

"Perfectly. He went to Harvard."

"What's his name?"

"General Felipe Nariño."

At that moment the door-buzzer sounded and Tony arrived. "The guys are standing by to move," he announced. "I've called Captain Jaime at the camp and told him the course is suspended for the time being. Also, I spoke to Sparky and put him in the picture."

"We'd better get our arses back down there," I said.

Egerton cleared his throat. "I think you'll find you've got air transport at your disposal. You'll need to go back to get your kit and presumably the camp you've been at has a landing strip?"

"Sure."

"Then it might pay you not to send anyone off by road. Hang on until you've seen the general."

Five minutes later I was in the back of an air-conditioned Mercedes 500 with smoked-out windows, sweeping through the outskirts of the city towards the palatial establishments perched on the slopes of the mountain. I didn't feel by any means secure. It wasn't beyond the bounds of possibility that I was being lifted. But no — surely DAS were on our side? Not only were we training the bodyguard for them; we'd now got caught up in the fight against the narcos, and so were in a position to give them help.

This was not a peaceful environment. Outside the big condos, all protected by high wire fences, bodyguards openly flaunted sub-machine-guns. My driver — young, swarthy, grey-uniformed — handled the car well but with amazing arrogance. Twice he went straight over red lights, and at every opportunity he blasted pedestrians out of the way with his horn. No doubt he was immune from prosecution.

Soon we arrived at a pair of high wire gates, set in a twelve-foot wall of concrete blocks topped with broken glass. Except that I couldn't see any closed-circuit TV cameras, the compound was unpleasantly similar to the RUC stations in Belfast. The gates were opened mechanically by some unseen person, and we drew up outside a brand-new office block. The Merc had hardly come to rest before a man stepped forward, opened the door beside me and ushered me into the building.

In the passage he muttered, *"Disculpe,"* and ran his

290

hands over me in a swift, skilled frisk, which instantly brought to light my Sig, which I was carrying in a pancake holster on my waist. *"Disculpe,"* he repeated as he removed the weapon. Then he led the way up a shallow flight of stairs and knocked on a door.

General Nariño was short and stocky, with a broad forehead, greying hair swept across it, and slightly hooded eyes. His appearance immediately made me think of Marlon Brando — a dangerously sleek version of the actor, but a look-alike all the same. He was wearing an expensive-looking sky-blue suit and a black tie with a lightning strike down the centre. As I came in he got up from behind his desk and came forward to greet me. His hand was soft and gentle.

"Sergeant Sharp? Pleased to meet you," he said. "Take a seat."

"Thanks."

As Egerton had said, the General's English — or rather, American — was perfect. But in spite of his superficial geniality I felt he was hard and cold.

Whatever else, he had a magnificent office. Because the building was perched high on the side of the mountain, the windows commanded a panoramic view of the city. His king-sized desk and long, oval conference table were both made from some fine, rich-coloured wood like mahogany, but not so dark. The floor was made of wood as well, with a couple of bright rugs to give colour. No linoleum or chrome or glass-topped tables here. As I sat down, a tray with a cup of coffee on it appeared at my elbow. Again it crossed my mind that the coffee could be laced with the drug we'd heard about in Hereford — *burundanga* — which removes your will to resist; but again I thought, No, this is all above board.

"You have a problem, I think," the General began.

"That's right. These three people have been lifted."

"And you think the IRA is involved?"

"I know it is." I gave him a short run-down on Farrell, without explaining my personal connection. I simply said that I'd worked in Belfast and seen him there.

"Well, it sounds as if your group has been flown to a site on the Rio Caquetá."

"I gather that's very remote."

"It sure is. Look." He stood up and went over to the end wall, where he switched on a spotlight to illuminate a huge map of the country. Using a billiard cue, he began to point out details.

"We're here, in Bogatá, nearly in the centre of Colombia. Away down south is this vast area known as Los Amazonas. It's part of the Amazon basin. As you can see, it's one hell of a size. Eight hundred kilometres from here to here. No roads, just thousands of square kilometres of rainforest.

"Now, for some weeks past we've been getting rumours of a new laboratory on the bank of the Rio Caquetá — here." He ran the tip of the billiard cue along a river flowing in a big curve towards the Amazon itself. "It's here —" he drew a circle — "downstream of a settlement called Puerto Pizarro. A few days ago, American satellites picked up a new construction site."

He came back and sat down again. "The reasons the narcos set up in places like that are simple. First, it gives them protection — we don't have the resources to find them. Second, they can bring in their raw supplies by boat upriver from the Amazon. Third, they're close to the Peruvian border, and in a few minutes they can flip across by light plane.

"In the past they built the labs right beside airstrips, but lately they've gotten more sophisticated. Now they put the buildings some distance from the strip, which makes them harder to find. Communication between the two may be by road, but it could also be by water. Say by a tributary of the main waterway.

"We expect Caquetá to conform to this new pattern. There's an army airstrip at Puerto Pizarro, fairly close by, and a military outpost. But we're not too struck on low-level air reconnaissance. First, the distances are very big. Second, if the facility's a few kilometres off the river, you're probably going to miss it on a single pass. Third, the narcos are more than capable of shooting down a low-flying aircraft. They have all modern weapons, including surface-to-air missiles."

I nodded. An awkward silence followed. I wanted to propose a plan of action, but at the same time I didn't want this guy to think I was teaching him to suck eggs. In the end I said, "Do you mind if I make a suggestion?"

"Go right ahead."

"If a major assault went in on the facility — say by helicopter gunships — the narcos would top the hostages and throw them in the river before any incoming troops could get on the ground. Now in a way this problem is of our own making. If possible we'd like to crack it ourselves. I have a team of ten men, all highly trained. We're used to working together. We operate best as a self-contained unit, and our speciality is covert approach. We'd aim to infiltrate the area without being detected, find out the camp routine, and strike at whatever moment seemed most advantageous. We're most effective in that covert kind of role. If we can be sure the hostages have been taken to this place, and you can lift us to within a reasonable distance of it, we'll recover them on our own."

The General looked at me steadily, as if he was sizing up my fighting potential. Then he said, "Your men have won a lot of respect down at Santa Rosa."

"We're jungle trained," I said.

"We have helicopters — Hueys."

"Where are they?"

"All over."

"Could you get a couple down to Puerto . . . Puerto Pizarro today?"

"I expect so, yes."

"We'll need some logistics back-up, too."

"Such as?"

"Mosquito nets, hammocks, DPMs, medical packs. Ropes, in case we have to rope down out of a chopper. Inflatable boats, too, by the sound of it. Normally, we'd have all this as a matter of routine. But we didn't come equipped for an operation of this kind. Rations, also. We brought a small amount of food with us, for emergencies, but not enough to deploy with."

"All that can be arranged." Nariño had been making some notes, and now looked coolly at me.

294

"I'm sorry to break the training course. That's going well."

"Too bad. Maybe you can pick it up again when this is over."

Once more I nodded. Then I said, "The immediate problem is, we left most of our stuff in the camp at Santa Rosa. We need to get back there fast to pick up our kit and weapons."

"Of course. One moment." He picked up a telephone, pressed a single button and began to speak, quietly but firmly. I could pick up the gist of it; he was giving orders for an aircraft to be made available. I sat looking at the big map, and the ocean of green, denoting jungle, that lay in the far south.

The General put his hand over the mouthpiece of the phone and asked, "Where are your men now?"

"At the Hostal Bonavento."

He spoke into the receiver again, then turned back to me and said, "A truck will collect them at eleven o'clock and lift them out to the military airfield. The flight down will take less than an hour. The aircraft can refuel at Santa Rosa, and then fly you on to Puerto Pizarro."

"Thank you," I replied. "I appreciate your quick response." As soon as I'd said that, I thought it sounded phoney — but I didn't want to seem too effusive. To appear a bit warmer I added, "Bill Egerton at the embassy asked me to give you his best wishes."

For the first time a slight smile lit up the broad, impassive face. With his right elbow on the desk he held out his hand, palm down and fingers extended, and in a curious gesture rocked it slightly to right and left, as if to express that a certain amount of give-and-take went on between the DAS and the embassy. "Yes," he said. "Bill is a good friend of ours."

As I got up to go, he brought out a card, scribbled a number on the back, and handed it to me. "This is my direct line, here or at home. You can call me any time," he said. "I'm glad to help."

Back at the embassy I found Tony talking on the satcom telephone. He was giving, or checking, some coordinates. "Yeah," he said, "that's seventy-three fifty west, zero degrees fifty south. OK."

Seeing me come in, he turned and raised a thumb, then said into the mouthpiece, "Call back when you've seen the next one. Fine. Thanks."

He hung up and said, "We got it!"

"What?"

"The hostage location."

"How?"

"Satellites. I called my guys in Fort Worth, and they went right through to Langley, Virginia. One satellite or another is passing over here every twenty minutes. They checked their records and found that a new construction site's been growing during the past few weeks on a big bend of the Rio Caquetá —"

I held up a hand. "Don't think I'm trying to take the piss, Tony, but I know all that already."

I told what I'd heard from the general.

"OK," he said equably. "Anyway, the controllers are

going for a high-resolution shot of it on one of the next passes."

"Brilliant!"

Our only map was too small-scale to be much use, but Tony had marked a dot in the green area just north of the river, about eighty ks east of the settlement. No road of any kind approached the township, or whatever it was.

Already it was after 10.30. Time was zipping past. I phoned the hotel to warn the guys to be ready for the off at eleven. Then I called Hereford to update the boss on the situation. I said we were planning to set up a forward mounting base at Puerto Pizarro, and play it from there. I told him I'd leave Tony Lopez as anchor-man in the embassy, and report in on our portable satcom phone as soon as I got back to it.

I was on the point of leaving when Tony's mate in Langley came through again to say that the close-up satellite shot showed details of the new workings at the Caquetá site. There were now three buildings, as opposed to two a week ago, and the snap-shot, taken twenty minutes earlier, showed a twin-engined aircraft sitting on a strip carved out of the jungle alongside the river about one k away.

"That's got to be the aircraft which took our party in," I said. "That clinches it."

Getting up to go, I tried to thank Bill Egerton for all he'd done. "I'm sorry. This has wrecked your weekend."

"Not a bit. If I wasn't here, I'd only be sitting in the garden reading *The Times* weekly edition. This is much more entertaining!"

Tony came down in the lift with me. "Listen," I said. "I'm really sorry to be leaving you here."

"No sweat, Geordie. I'm having a ball. Playing ambassadors is great."

"Yep, but if there's some action, you'll want to be part of it."

"Sure. But who knows where the action's gonna be? Take care, anyway."

A battered army three-ton truck clattered up to the hotel a couple of minutes before eleven. I checked that all bills were paid and all rooms clear, then we bundled into the back and rode out to the airfield, a short run of less than fifteen minutes.

The military field proved to be one side of the El Dorado civilian airport. A Herc, painted drab olive green, without markings, stood on the pan. A military truck was parked beside the tail-ramp, and guys were loading stores into it like ants. Our driver drew up alongside it and we piled out. Inside the back of the plane there was already a fair stack of kit, and as we arrived some of the loadies were starting to lash it down.

The Colombian head-loadie came down from the flight-deck for a rapid conference with the boss of the logistic party, ticking items off a list. Then he turned to me with a cheerful grin and said, *"Por favor,"* waving us to go aboard. He followed us in, checking that we'd all belted up into the canvas sling-seats along the sides. He said, "Fly one hour." Then he spoke to the pilot on the intercom, and hit the button to raise the tail ramp. The engines began to turn, and that dreaded whine built up to full strength as the big aircraft lumbered forward.

298

The flight lasted no more than fifty minutes, but it gave me time to think. If we did manage to launch an operation against the new drugs complex, everything would depend on surprise. If the narcos got wind of a rescue attempt, or thought an attack was coming in, they'd top the hostages for sure. This meant that we had to get in covertly, establish an OP, discover the routine of the place, and take the defenders by surprise.

The pilot never bothered to gain any great altitude, and air currents coming off the mountains made the flight pretty rough. I was glad when the plane banged down hard on the dirt runway at Santa Rosa, and there was Sparky, waving like a lunatic from the edge of the strip. I thought he was taking the piss out of us for coming back early, and spending all our money while he'd been hoarding his. Not at all. He was frantic for me to get on the satcom link to Tony in Bogatá.

"But I've only just left the bugger," I protested.

"I know, but there's been a development. He says you're to call immediately."

"OK, guys." I looked round. "Leave the Colombian stores on board. Everyone get their personal kit packed up and ready for the off. We need to load all our ammunition and PE, as well. Make sure we don't leave anything behind."

"Aren't we coming back?" somebody asked.

"Might be. Might not. It depends how things go. Anyway, we're off in a few minutes."

Sparky had the spike of the little dish aerial stuck into the ground outside our accommodation block, but the satellite had wandered out of range, and for a couple of minutes we couldn't make any contact. Then, having checked with his compass and reset the elevation, he suddenly hit it spot-on. The call went through, the line clear as clear.

"Tony — hi. What's on?"

"The bastards have split the party. We got two separate reports from the toads within a few minutes of your leaving. One party's gone to the Caquetá, all right. But the other's in Cartagena."

"Jesus! Where's that?"

"It's a port on the north coast."

"Fucking hell. Who's where?"

"One toad said that the *gringa* and four *gringos*, one old and three young, have been taken to the Rio Caquetá."

"That sounds like our party, with a couple of PIRA in tow."

"Yeah — but listen to this. The other toad said that a *gringo con cabellos rubios* had been put on board a ship at Cartagena."

"Jesus Christ! Fair hair — that must mean Peter, the Rupert."

"Exactly."

"Do we know what ship it is?"

"Yep. It's a cargo vessel called the *Santa Maria de la Mar*. Nine thousand tons. Panamanian registered. It's making ready to sail for Amsterdam."

"God almighty. They're trying to get him out of the country. The PIRA must have found out he's from the Regiment."

"Right. They'll beat the shit out of him to make him talk."

"Maybe they're aiming to get him back to Northern Ireland. Tony, we need to hit that ship. Maybe we'd better turn round and come back." I thought for a moment. Then I realized that what we needed were the special skills of the Boat Troop. We could undertake more or less any operation on land, and a couple of us had trained for short periods with the boat guys. But if it came to a ship assault we were neither fully trained nor properly equipped.

I said as much to Tony, then added, "We'll carry on with our own operation. But I'm going to call Hereford and get the Boat Troop put on standby."

"Wait a bit. It's not that easy. If we're going to hit the ship we've got to hit the lab at the same time. And vice versa. We need two operations, co-ordinated down to the last few seconds. Otherwise the narcos will top the other half of the equation."

"OK. Two operations. But, Christ — when's the ship due to sail?"

"Some time tomorrow. Our information is that she's heading for an offshore island, to trans-ship drugs. Our best tactic will be to hit her there, when the crew's not expecting anything. But we need to know where she's going. The toad said Amsterdam. That could be right, in the end, but it could be disinformation. She could head in any goddamn direction. What we've got to do is get a tracking device on board her before she sails."

Even as he talked, in my mind I was seeing the guys in the Boat Troop. I knew several of them well: Steve, Roger, Merv — all first-class operators. This looked like an ideal task for them.

"The trouble is," I said, "our lot will never get here in time. They have to go round about four stops on the way, like we did, spread over several days."

"No," replied Tony. "But mine will. The SEALs'll get there. There's a team on standby in Florida all the time. Your government will have to clear it from England, but I'm going to call my guys right away and give them advance warning that they're gonna go stick a device on the ship while she's still in port. A hit out at sea or at an island would be another matter. That would stir the diplomatic shit, and it might need clearance from the Pentagon. But we can get a bleeper in place without anyone knowing."

"Great! Go ahead with that. I'll speak to the head-shed in Hereford and tell them the score."

"Listen," Tony said. "You got a pencil and paper? I did a couple of calculations, based on the satellite information. On your jungle location: you need to chopper in towards the target without getting close enough to alert anybody. The best thing will be to cut straight across from the base at Puerto Pizarro to the north of the target. Aim for the tributary and come down that. That way, you won't fly closer to the laboratory than eight or nine ks, and nobody's going to hear you. If you head out from the base on zero-eight-seven degrees, you'll hit the Rio Cuemani ten ks north of the new airstrip."

"OK," I said. "I got a note of that."

"South of the big river," he went on, "there's a solitary mountain. I guess it'll stand right out of the flat jungle. Looks like it's got a conical peak. You're never going to be closer to it than fifty ks, but you'll see it away to your right. When you get level with it, you'll be coming to your tributary."

He went on to describe the precise layout of the landing-strip, the link road (which didn't run straight, but wound through the forest) and the buildings of the laboratory itself. As he talked I wrote and sketched details in my note-book.

"Thanks, Tony. Zero-eight-seven will be our heading. I'll get on to Hereford now."

I was about to line up the call when I saw Captain Jaime heading towards us. Pretending I felt happy, I said, "¡Hola, Capitán! Embarrada." A big problem.

He seemed a bit disgruntled, and wanted some explanation. I gave it, itching to be on the move. "How many days will you be away?" he asked.

"One or two," I said casually. "That should do it."

Of course I hadn't a clue. But I could see that he was getting the shits worrying how to keep forty-odd men occupied.

Sparky tuned his dish again, and we got through to Hereford. Again they put me on to the CO. I briefed him on the situation, then said, "Boss, this has the makings of a first-class international fuck-up."

"Don't worry," said the Colonel. "We've got the diplomatic side well under control. I don't think there's going to be any attempt to stop you. We've already cleared the SEALs' involvement with the US government. It's great that Tony Lopez is there to liaise."

"A big stroke of luck, I know."

"Wait one," said the CO. "Straighten me out on the different locations. I've got a map in front of me."

"OK. We're calling them Green One, Two, Three and Four. Green One's Tony, in Bogatá. I'm now on Green Two, at the training camp at Santa Rosa, about 250 ks south of Bogatá. But it's only a camp and a village, so probably it won't be on your map. The ship that we think Peter Black's been put on is at Cartagena, on the north coast, about eleven o'clock from Bogatá. We're calling the ship Blue One."

"Right," went the boss. "I have that."

"Green Three is an army outpost at Puerto Pizarro, on the Rio Caquetá, about seven o'clock from Bogatá, 400 ks further south from my present location, and right out in the Amazon basin. Again, you probably haven't got that marked — it's pretty small. Green Four is the other hostage location, fifty ks east of Pizarro, on the north side of the river, where it swings round in a big bend."

"Pizarro. Can't see that either. What's your plan, anyway?"

"There's a landing strip at the army outpost. DAS have put a Herc at our disposal, and we're off down there in a few minutes. We'll be there in a couple of hours. We'll make the camp our forward mounting base. Then we'll chopper out, establish an FOB, and put in an OP on the laboratory, to work out a recovery."

"You're definitely going to need back-up."

"That's right. We're short of all assets, weapons particularly. Apart from pistols, we've only got two G3s and two 203s. The trouble is, it'll take you bloody days to get here. It took us three days just to reach Colombia."

"Don't worry. There's a mountain of war stores sitting

in Belize. We can organize some of that down to you in a matter of hours. So — more 203s. More grenades. What else?"

"Basically, jungle gear for ten. Ponchos, mozzie nets, boots, hats. I think DAS have sorted some stuff out for us, but I don't know how good it is."

"What about rations?"

"We've got a few with us, and DAS have given us some more. Christ knows what they are, but they're on board."

"Boats?"

"Yep. They've lent us a few rubber dinghies. We haven't unpacked them yet."

"OK, then. We'll try to line up a couple more. Happy landings. Report when you're on your new location."

"Roger. We'll speak soon."

Inside the accommodation block I threw my stuff into kit-bag and bergen. By the time I went out again, Captain Jaime had already organized the loading of our ammunition. In less than half an hour we had everything squared away on board the Herc. As I looked round the camp, with its pool and dusty football field, I felt sorry to be leaving so soon.

"*Adios, Capitán.*" Although I was hatless, I gave him a stylish salute. "I hope we'll be back in a couple of days."

Aboard the Herc, I went up on to the flight-deck to make sure we all agreed about where we were heading. There was no problem, but I stayed in the upper cabin to soak up a bit of Colombian geography. From down in the back you could see practically nothing, unless you stood up with your eye at one of the portholes; from up front there was a great view as the ridges and spurs of the *Cordillera Oriental* fell away behind us and an endless vista of dark green spread out ahead, with bright silver veins of rivers running through it towards the east. The vast emptiness of the land was enough to scare the shit out of you. I felt for my little silver medallion, on its chain, and thought of home.

Compared with most hostage rescues, this one looked extremely dicey. For one thing, we were short of assets — we were certain to be out-numbered and out-gunned. On the SP team and in Northern Ireland we'd trained daily for house assault and hostage release but normally we had superior firepower, and major reinforcements at our disposal. Besides, the hostages were almost always close at hand. Here the opposite was true. Distances were immense, chances of reinforcement minimal. Our own firepower was strictly limited. We had no casevac facilities. We were going into the unknown, to a destination we hadn't even identified precisely. Basically, ten guys were attempting to do a job that would have taxed a squadron. Further, we knew from our various briefs how ruthless the enemy were — if any of us got captured, we could expect no mercy.

My mind kept returning to Black. Was he still alive? And if he was, how much had he already given away? We'd been trained, in the event of capture, to try to hold out for twenty-four hours, and then, if possible, to fall back on controlled release, giving away only low-grade information. But everybody knew that this was easier said than done. What had Black told Farrell? What about the animosity between Black, me and Tracy? Had he said anything about me? Had he revealed that I had been lifted from above Farrell's farm? I was speculating wildly, I knew, but it was impossible not to.

The pilot, a friendly guy, occasionally called out a name and pointed, but I wasn't concentrating too much on the scenery; all I could think about was how stretched we were going to be, how dependent we were on our satcom. If that freaked out, we'd have real problems. Then I became aware that the pilot was repeating some word insistently, and when I focused on him I realized he was saying, "*Caquetá, Caquetá.*"

There below us a vast river was snaking through the jungle, winding on for ever in coils through that terrific expanse of trees. For a whole half-hour we followed its course, and nothing below us changed. Occasionally, on the bank of a tributary, I saw a tiny cleared area of lighter green, with what looked like wooden huts along the edge. Obviously people were living there, and I wondered whether they were Indians. What a life! The isolation was something I could hardly imagine. The surface of the rainforest was never smooth and uniform, like that of a cultivated plantation; rather, it was rough and ragged, with trees of all different heights. There was something alien about the colour of it, too: the green wasn't anything like an English green, but darker and heavier.

At last, right on the nose, the outline of the mountain Tony had mentioned began to show through the haze ahead, and soon afterwards the pilot began his descent.

307

As we came down, the river grew until it seemed as wide as the English Channel. From a high altitude it had shone dully like pewter, but at low level it turned muddy brown, with occasional swirls that showed the strength of the current. In the last couple of minutes we saw a huddle of shacks on the north bank, with a few more substantial buildings behind them, and a couple of boats moored alongside a jetty.

Then we were over the perimeter of the camp, which looked much the same as the one we'd just left: a dirt strip, a high boundary fence, two lines of single-storey white buildings, one small warehouse, and goalposts with sagging crossbars at either end of a dusty football field. The best thing about it was the sight of a Huey helicopter parked on the pan outside the warehouse.

As we debussed, the heat hit us. Down at this level the air was ten times hotter and stickier. We were greeted by an army lieutenant, with circles of sweat spreading out from under the arms of his khaki fatigues, and wearing big shades. His English was even sketchier than my Spanish, so I had to make a real effort to communicate. After struggling for a while, and establishing that the chopper was out of action with a gearbox defect, I had an inspiration: call Tony and get him to interpret. I needed to speak to him anyway.

"We made it to Puerto Pizarro," I told him.

"What's it like?"

"Hot as hell. Just a little camp surrounded by jungle. There's one Huey here, but it's gone US. Spare parts are supposed to be on the way. What news your end?"

"The SEALs are deploying. They're going in tonight

to stick a tracking device on the *Santa Maria*. Then it doesn't matter where she sails — we can go get her to coincide with your operation."

"Great!"

"Your Boat Troop guys are on their way, too. I don't know how he hacked it, but the CO's got an RAF TriStar held back, and they're flying direct to Belize tonight. One hop only. They'll be there at 0100 local time." He paused, then said, "Hey — I got you some pretty good detail from the satellite station. You have a pencil and paper?"

"Wait one." I brought out the little notebook I always carry in the breast-pocket of my shirt, with a miniature pencil down the spine. "OK. Fire away."

"The new lab complex is near that big bend of the river, like we said. But it's four ks north of the Caquetá. The airstrip's confirmed along the bank of the tributary, and some kind of jetty's been built there, on the west bank. The buildings are grouped round a small compound one k west of the airstrip. There's a road of sorts connecting the two, probably earth. It snakes around through the trees."

As he talked, I was drawing a sketch. "D'you have the layout of the building?"

"Sure. There's two rectangular structures that look finished, each about fifty metres long. They're set out in a line, running east-west. The third building, across the end of the compound, is still under construction."

"Tony," I said, "I've been thinking the best way to make a covert approach would be to come down the tributary at night in a rubber dinghy, then slide in for a CTR. What about that?"

"Sounds good. I confirm. Chopper out of your present location on zero-eight-seven, dead straight for sixty ks. Then you hit the Cuemani, coming down from your left across your front. The alignment of the tributary's very nearly north-south. It's coming from three-five-zero and heading to one-seven-zero. Famous last words, but you really can't miss it. OK, Geordie? But for Pete's sake don't try swimming. Those rivers are full of crocs."

"Right," I said. "I'm calling this Operation Crocodile. Op Croc. Listen, the lieutenant here doesn't speak much English. Could you run through the plan with him? Thanks."

I handed the receiver over. Suddenly I began to feel rather good. We were within spitting distance of some action. Things were about to become interesting.

The lieutenant listened to Tony for a while, asked a few questions, and said, *"Si,"* a great many times. When he seemed to have finished, I beckoned for him to hand the receiver back. "Tony," I said, tell him for Christ's sake to get the Huey airworthy. I don't know what's wrong with it — I think it's a gearbox problem. He's supposed to be flying parts in, but I'm not too sure."

The guys were humping the stores out of the Herc and loading them on to a trailer pulled by a Willys jeep, vintage about 1942. "As you value your bollocks," I told them, "no swimming in the river. It's heaving with crocodiles." I turned to the beshaded lieutenant and made extravagant jaw-snapping motions with my arms. *"¡Si, si!"* he confirmed. *"¡Cocodrilos-muchísimos!"*

"Fucking great!" said Murdo. "That's all we want. If

the Amazon's the arsehole of the world, I reckon we're about 5,000 ks up it."

Murdo had a point. The facilities the Colombians offered us were as crappy as could be. They themselves looked to be fairly well set up in the better of the two barrack-blocks, with a generator, mozzie screens and fridges — and I didn't grudge them whatever comforts they'd been able to devise. If you had to spend any length of time in that hell-hole, you'd need everything you could get to stay sane. The block they gave us was another matter: no electricity, bare concrete rooms without doors, the iron bedsteads all rusted, no water in the showers, the bog an open hole in the floor.

When we unpacked the stores, things looked up a bit, because the General had done us well: there were four dinghy packs, two outboards, hammocks, mozzie nets, waterbottles, machetes and twenty sets of jungle DPMs. Once we'd sorted them out, everyone got a size that more or less fitted him, with another set in reserve. There were also four big boxes of MREs — US forces' standard-issue Meals Ready to Eat, or, as they'd been known in the Gulf, Meals Rejected by Ethiopians. In fact they were pretty good, especially the things like corned-beef hash and chilli con carne. The guys soon got brews going with their hexi cookers, and after some sort of a meal, spirits picked up.

In the usual way, we planned our tactics at an O-group that took the form of a Chinese parliament, with everyone sitting round in a circle on the ground. Obviously we weren't going anywhere that night, but there was no harm in having a plan ready. The sun was already sinking towards the jungle in a thick haze, and the temperature was dropping slightly. Even so, we were all still sweating like pigs.

Even if the Huey became airworthy, its maximum load, besides the pilot and navigator, would be three guys plus kit, one dinghy kit plus engine, and skeleton equipment and stores.

I offered to stay back, but everyone agreed I should lead from the front. That made me one of the three to fly. The second had to be Sparky Springer, as he was our radio specialist. For the third, I nominated Murdo McFarlane. Provided he left his blasted pipes behind, he'd be as good as anyone in the jungle.

The next wave — which would follow us in the next evening by the same route, provided the Huey was serviceable — would consist of Johnny Ellis, Stew McQuarrie and Mel Scott.

CHAPTER
THIRTEEN

Author's Note
Because I was in the jungle at the time, I could not witness the SEALs' approach to the Santa Maria del Mar, *or the Boat Troop's assault on the island of Desierto. I have therefore built my account of the actions on the reports of men who took part. All were well known either to Tony Lopez or to me, and I am satisfied that the account is substantially accurate.*

The SEAL team landed at a military airfield outside the old colonial town and port of Cartagena. The unmarked Herc which brought them from Florida touched down at 1600 local time, leaving them enough daylight for a quick scout round the port. As Tony later emphasized, they would normally have carried out a much more thorough reconnaissance, watching their target for several days to establish the routine on board and looking for weak spots; but this was a fastball, and left no time for niceties.

DAS had laid on two nondescript vans to transport the team and their gear. They also provided a local liaison officer to brief Master Sergeant Al Layton, the team leader. The Colombian informed him that the ship was lying in berth No. 7 on No. 1 Pier, the western of the two main arms at the *Terminal Maritimo* on Manga Island, at the north side of the bay. The dock gates were guarded by regular police, and there was no chance of gaining access through them, but the ship could be seen from the south side of the bay. Al therefore had the team driven to an observation point on the southern shore.

Casual clothes did much to disguise the physiques of the eight team members. Al was twenty-six, and although of only medium height he was extremely powerful, with particular strength in his upper body. His colleagues were all much the same, built up by years of swimming, running and work in the gym. Had they all stripped off on the beach they would have started a riot.

The vans parked on the south-east side of the bay, on a stretch of the shore that nobody had yet got around to developing. Other vehicles were already scattered along it, so that the new arrivals attracted no attention, and Al's guys were able to carry out covert observation without hindrance. The Old Town, out on the point beyond the harbour, did not interest them. Nor did the new high-rise blocks in the smart suburb of Bocagrande, away to their left. They wasted no time looking at the tourist boats drifting in and out of the harbour as they plied to the coral reefs offshore. Their attention was focused exclusively on the *Santa Maria*.

The ship was a fair distance across the bay, but through binoculars and a 30-power telescope they were able to make out useful details. She was moored with her bow facing the bay and her starboard side to the quay, so that they were looking at her port bow. She was second in line on that side of the harbour, with other ships moored close up fore and aft. Her hull was black and her upperworks white, but showing rusty patches, and she was flying the Panamanian flag. She looked scruffy, at least twenty years old. As Al and his men watched, she was still being loaded; two tall dock cranes were swinging nets over her deck and lowering them into the forward hold. According to DAS information, her cargo was officially coffee, but almost certainly included cocaine, probably several tons of it. With a street value in the United States of $35,000 a kilo, the illicit element in her holds could well have been worth over a hundred million.

For the SEAL team, the position of the ship was ideal. From where they were, they could swim straight to her without coming close to any other vessel or the dockside. At their normal average speed of a hundred metres in three minutes, it would take them just under half an hour to cross the bay. They decided that their best access point was forward of the accommodation, and beside the third hold; the hatch-cover stood three or four feet proud of the deck, and would help conceal them as they came over the rail. Having sized things up, Al opted for a midnight departure; because she was still loading, it was clear that the *Santa Maria* wasn't on the point of sailing, and if they reached her well after midnight there was a good chance that all the crew except the gangplank guard would be in their bunks.

During the interval, the team repaired to an empty warehouse which DAS had taken over. There they had plenty of room to lay their gear out and check it through. As usual, Al split his party into two four-man teams,

A and B, each of two pairs. Team A would do the swim and place the device, with Team B in reserve, keeping a lookout and ready to go after them or stage a diversion, should the need arise.

By 2345 both teams were back on the dockside at their launch point, clad in their black Spandex wetsuits. Working in pairs, each man checking his buddy, they squeezed out all the excess air and breathed themselves down until the suits were clinging to their bodies. Over the neoprene suits went their ops waistcoats, loaded with weapons and ammunition. Each man had an MP 5 and three spare magazines, besides a Browning and two spare mags for that. The weapons had all been soaked in Silverspeed and thoroughly oiled; immersion in water would make no difference to them. For safety's sake each man clipped his shooters to him with nylon lanyards and small karabiners.

Working with his buddy, Gus Ford, Al breathed down all his equipment to clear the air from it, then lashed a hooligan bar — an angled jemmy with a spike on one end to the middle of Gus's back. Each man checked the other off

"MP 5?"

"Yep."

"Magazines?"

"Three."

"Lanyard?"

"Yep."

"Hooligan bar?"

"Yep."

"Respirator?"

"OK."

Al was also carrying the transponder, sealed in polythene and attached by a lanyard to a ring on his waist. Normally, in salt water, he needed eight kilograms of extra weight to stop him bobbing on the surface. The transponder, together with its magnetic fastener, weighed one kilo, so he loaded one more kilo weight into a spare pocket. Finally the men pulled on their Drega rebreathing kits — cumbersome, heavy outfits incorporating mask, hood and oxygen bottle, that use a sealed circuit so that they let out no bubbles. Again each buddy checked his partner, then the supervisor said, "OK, guys. Go on gas."

To purge his lungs of extra nitrogen, Al took three deep breaths of oxygen, in through the mouth, out through the nose. His mask misted up immediately, and he was uncomfortably aware that he had thirty ks of equipment slung round his neck. Even though he'd been diving for ten years, he still hated this moment. If he was going to get an O_2 hit, this was when it would come. He himself had never gone down with oxygen poisoning, but he'd seen other guys go into spasm and then arc back, rigid. The cure was plenty of fresh air, quickly — but the experience was one he could do without.

Once in the water, everything changed. He felt comfortable and secure in a world with which he was completely familiar. After one last check to make sure his three companions were ready he set off, swimming on a bearing of 305 degrees.

The night was very dark. There was no moon, and hazy cloud was blocking the starlight. The water of the bay lay still as black ink, with the distant lights of the harbour and the town reflected in it. For the first half of the journey Al judged it safe to remain on the surface. He swam gently, keeping well within his capabilities, and watching the compass, depth-gauge and timer on the swim board held out ahead of him.

After fifteen minutes, with the party out in the middle of the bay, an offshore breeze started up, putting a ripple on the water. Then Al heard a speedboat approaching from behind his left shoulder. It could have been narcos, running a consignment of drugs across from Bocagrande to one of the ships in the harbour. It could have been late-night revellers taking a short-cut home. Whatever, he was taking no chances, so he and the others dived — and the speedboat passed harmlessly above them.

Thereafter he swam at a depth of four metres, coming up at the end of every three minutes to check his position. At twenty-one minutes the harbour lights were much closer, but still it was impossible to tell which ship was which, and he had to rely on the compass bearing to keep him oriented. All the time Gus was one man's length behind him, guided by the phosphorescence which Al's passage through the water was creating. The other two followed at similar intervals behind.

At twenty-seven minutes he slowed, and when Gus came alongside he gave him one squeeze on the arm to indicate that he was surfacing for another observe. This time he found a big hulk of ship right in front of him, but he could tell by the outline of her bow against the sky that she was the first in the line. They had drifted slightly to the left of their target. The tide must have been going out faster than they'd expected. Sinking back, he gave Gus two squeezes to indicate that they were approaching the target, then swam on, heading right. Three minutes later he surfaced again. This time he was just off the bow of the *Santa Maria*. The big white letters of her name stood out boldly from the sweep of the black hull.

Diving again, he gave Gus three presses to tell him they'd arrived. Gus passed the message back to the other pair. All four men surfaced and swam gently to their right, observing from a distance. Apart from one light showing through an open doorway in the accommodation block, and one naked bulb dangling from a cargo derrick, the ship was dark.

Satisfied that their plan was good, Al swam in and clamped himself to the side with two magnets. Now he was close, a faint hum of generators told him that the ship was alive. There was also the usual background noise of water slapping gently against the hull. Four presses, passed back through the team, confirmed that they were at the entry point. Al pulled off his rebreathing kit and magneted it on to the side, out of the way, and the others did the same. If anything went wrong while they were on board, they could jump over the rail and recover the sets from this temporary storage. Peering up, Al was glad to see that the curve of the hull put them out of sight — and range — of anyone looking down.

It took Gus only a few seconds to assemble the telescopic pole which had travelled strapped to his back. As he fitted the lengths together, the No. 3 swimmer, Jack Ashby, was unrolling the thirty-foot kevlar ladder. Then, with two of the others holding him steady on short ropes,

Gus swam out a few feet, hoisted the pole and hooked the ladder over the ship's rail.

Al was the first up. His jungle boots made only faint scuffling sounds on the ship's side. When his head reached deck level he paused, listening. Then with a quick scramble he was over the rail and against the hatch cover, Browning in hand. A moment later he holstered the pistol and brought his MP 5 to the ready. A tug on the ladder: two up. Another tug: three up. The fourth man, Sonny Mitchell, came up and took station to secure their entry point.

The other three moved cautiously aft, keeping in the deep shadows thrown by the single light high on the derrick. Al was thinking to himself, "Now we've got this far, why don't we go in and rescue the hostage?" The trouble was, they didn't know which part of the ship the poor bastard was in — he could have been down in one of the holds — and in any case, he was bound to be guarded.

The night air was hot and moist. Inside his suit Al was sweating freely. Creeping aft, he came level with the start of the accommodation block. The first doorway stood open. Beyond it was a porthole, also open. Through it Al could hear the hiss of water moving through pipes. The john. Just the place, except that he wanted somewhere higher, on an upper deck. It was odds on that all the plumbing systems were stacked on top of each other.

A metal companionway led upwards. Leaving Jack to guard the base of it, Al and Gus went up. Another open doorway. Another porthole in a similar position. There was one more deck above them, but there was no more external companionway, and this was the highest they could go without penetrating into the heart of the accommodation.

Al pointed to the porthole and stuck up a thumb, meaning "This will do". Gus stood guard with his MP 5 at the ready while he stepped carefully over the sill. The metal door of the john was ajar. He applied pressure very gently, in case it squeaked, but the hinges gave silently. With the door open, there was enough light for him to see all he needed: a cistern above the twin urinals on the outside bulkhead.

The metal lid was held in place by small bolts with wing-nuts on them, one at either end. The threads of the bolts had been painted over, and he couldn't shift the nuts with finger and thumb. Pulling out a pair of pliers, he unclipped them from their lanyard, reached up, and got the nuts moving. In a few more seconds he had lifted off the metal lid and laid it carefully on the floor. Then he drew his knife from its sheath, slit the wrappings of the transponder, pulled out the pin to activate the device and held it firmly to prevent any sudden jerk as its powerful circular plate-magnet clamped itself to the underside of the lid. A moment later he had the lid back in position. It was fractionally tilted forward by the aerial wire leading out over the rim and propping the back up, but no Colombian seaman was going to notice that. He screwed the wing-nuts back down by hand, leaving the upper threads of the bolts bare of paint. Nothing he could do about that — but again, it was highly unlikely that anyone would notice so small a change. Providentially, a metal pipe ran up and down the bulkhead behind the cistern, giving him an ideal conductor. He wound the naked end of the wire round it, and pushed the rest of the coil down out of sight.

Out in the open again, he faced in the direction of the rear party, onshore across the bay, and turned on an infrared torch, invisible to the naked eye, but instantly detectable to someone with the correct receiver. Seconds later a voice in his earpiece said, "OK, Al. We're just going to check your signal strength with base. Stand by."

He waited, thinking of the satellites passing overhead, and reflecting on how extraordinary it was that the little device he'd just stuck in the john could communicate with them. Then came the voice from the shore again. "OK, Al. They have you loud and clear. Signal strength six. That's as good as you're gonna get."

He doused the torch and raised a thumb to Gus. The two of them checked each other in whispers:

"Pliers?"

"Yeah."

"Knife?"

"Yeah."

"All screws back in position?"

"Two screws back."

Both knew full well that the slightest trace of their presence, the smallest alien object, could destroy the secrecy of their visit. Satisfied that all was well, they crept down the companionway to the main deck. Back at their entry point, they unhooked the ladder and secured it temporarily with long lines of paracord tied in slip-knots, which would fall away when pulled from below. Al saw the other three down, then went over the side. Two tugs on the cords brought the ladder splashing softly down on them. With their rebreathing kits back on, they sank away into the black depths of the harbour, and the *Santa Maria* bore no more trace of their entry than if she had been visited by a ghost.

CHAPTER
FOURTEEN

Most of the time I was worrying about Peter Black. The poor bastard was going to get skinned alive by the PIRA. I tried to stop myself thinking of all the things they'd do to him to make him talk.

It was good to hear that the SEALs had successfully planted the transponder, and that satellites were picking up its signals. Then Tony came through to say that the ship had sailed from Cartagena at 0830, and that she was heading north into the Caribbean. The head-shed in Hereford told us that a consignment of stores was on its way down to us from Belize, and that a quick-reaction force put together from B and G Squadrons was standing by to fly in.

We unpacked the dinghies and inflated them to make sure they weren't punctured. All day, on and off, I nagged the local boss about the Huey spares, and he made radio calls about them. But it wasn't till 1500 that at last an aged Dakota came droning in from the west, bringing the parts and a couple of mechanics. We watched from a distance as they went to work, and we could hardly believe it when, around 1630, they announced that they'd cured the problem. The pilot and navigator walked out, started up, and took the Huey for a test flight around the area. Back on the deck, they reported that everything was fine.

At 1700 I held a final O-group to confirm details. By then I'd drawn out a bigger plan on the side of a cardboard ration box, and I used it for reference. Also we had a fairly good map that the DAS had provided. "Operation Crocodile," I began. "Voice comms out of the forward operating base will be insecure, so we'll refer to locations by call-signs only. OK? Our locations are as follows. The Bogotá Embassy is Green One. The training camp at Santa Rosa's Green Two. This forward mounting base here is Green Three. And finally, the FOB, close to or on the target, is Green Four. It's easy to remember, because the locations are numbered in the order we've been through them, or will be through them."

"Green!" exclaimed Murdo sarcastically. "Everything's fucking green, as far as the eye can fucking see."

"OK," I went on. "So it's the four greens. Now, personnel. Murdo, Sparky and I will chopper in to a point approximately here." I indicated a spot on the bank of the Cuemani. "If the Huey can land, so much the better. Otherwise we'll fast-rope down. We'll identify the spot by displaying the cloth, either pegged down in the open or tied to a tree. Then we'll launch the boat, proceed downriver and get ourselves in position for a CTR. During tomorrow, the second wave of three will chopper out to the same point and come downriver to join us. After that, we'll have to play things by ear."

A few questions, and everything was wrapped up.

By 1720 we were hot to trot. We took one G3, two 203s and three pistols, plus ammunition and a box of PE. Luckily I'd thrown an ops waistcoat into my lacon box before leaving the UK, so that accommodated a lot of my personal kit, including the Magellan.

The pilot, Pedro, and his navigator were both young fellows with short, spiky black hair. Neither spoke more than a few words of English, so I went through everything several times, making certain they'd got the right bearing — zero-eight-seven — firmly in their heads. I also impressed on the pilot that it was essential he memorize the spot at which he put us down, so that he could find it again next day. Also, after he'd dropped us, he had to swing out to the north and return to base in a wide arc, as though he was searching the jungle for lost persons.

He started up and took off without fuss, and in a few seconds we were over the forest-sea, skimming through the hot dusk just clear of the highest trees. I caught an occasional flash of emerald, red or yellow as some brilliantly coloured bird took off in fright, but otherwise our whole world was drab grey-green. Looking forward over the pilot's shoulder, I watched the needle of the compass sitting steadily on the correct heading.

Apprehension crept up on me. Why were we going in on this crazy operation? Because my first loyalty was to the Regiment, I'd far rather have been in on the plan to rescue Peter Black. Maybe we should have devoted all our resources to that. Then again, I thought, even if we'd turned around at Santa Rosa and headed back north, so that we could go in to storm the boat in harbour at Cartagena, the narcos would probably have topped their

326

captive before we could reach him. Better leave things there to the SEALs or the Boat Troop. Meanwhile, down here in the jungle . . . I had no strong feelings about the DA. I didn't care too much about what happened to him. But Luisa was a different matter. The idea of a beautiful, intelligent woman getting roughly handled, maybe raped or killed, through no fault of her own, was difficult to live with. Maybe it sounds sexist, but for me at any rate she was the main reason for going in.

The navigator and I had calculated that, cruising at 120 knots, we would reach the Cuemani in twenty-three minutes. Twenty-one minutes into the flight, the pilot began to lift up to gain a wider view of our surroundings. Already the light was going, and the forest beneath us had turned from grey-green to nearly black. Then suddenly ahead was the gleam of the river, across our line of approach.

In seconds we were over the near bank. I motioned to Pedro to slow down and turn right, over the water. I was prepared to fly about two ks downstream, towards the airstrip, but no nearer. Within that distance we'd have to find a landing zone of some sort.

As he hovered, we searched in vain for an opening in the cover. The forest grew right to the bank of the river, the trees overhanging the stream. I'd started to think we would have to fast-rope through the canopy when suddenly I spotted a slight rise in the ground, an outcrop of rock, which formed a little cliff. The chopper could have landed on it, but for a single tree growing out of a cleft.

I gave a shout and pointed down. Pedro went straight

in and hovered at a good height. We lowered the pack containing the dinghy, and then our three bergens in a single bundle. Finally we ourselves slid down individual ropes and signalled we were clear. Up went the Huey with our lines trailing from its belly. It swung off to the north as instructed, and in a minute the noise of its engine had died away.

The occasional bird was still calling, perhaps stirred up by the aircraft, and frogs were croaking; but apart from those natural noises, there wasn't a sound. In the last of the light we took stock of our surroundings. On three sides the jungle stretched away unbroken. On the fourth, right below us, ran the river. We were on top of the small cliff, maybe thirty feet high, but the face of it was not vertical: it had enough of a slope and enough hand-holds for us to scramble down. I pulled out the strip of pale-coloured cloth which I'd borrowed from the Colombians, spread it over the rock and weighted it down with three or four loose stones.

I took out my Magellan, set it up, and waited for it to lock on to a passing satellite. When I got an accurate reading, I wrote it in my notebook, so that we could pass back the precise location of the landing zone when Sparky got his 319 going. Then we broke out the rubber dinghy from its pack, inflated it with the hand-pump and lowered it over the cliff, followed by the outboard on a separate tether. Within ten minutes of landing, we were drifting downriver, steering with the paddles and letting our eyes become accustomed to the gathering dusk.

Except where there was a rock-face similar to the one we had come down, the jungle pressed in to the very edge of the banks, overhanging the water. The river was at least two hundred yards wide, and I could see from the bare face of the banks that it was below its highest level. Because we were out in mid-stream, and the forest was so uniform, with few landmarks, we found it hard to tell what speed we were making; but when we augmented the current by paddling, we reckoned we were doing at least three knots, or about five k.p.h. At that rate, we'd be at the airstrip within two hours.

Occasionally a loud slap and a splash would sound from the stream. In fact I think most of the disturbances came from fish, but several times I felt the hair come up on my neck just from the thought of crocodiles. The pilot of the Herc had told me that the Caquetá was over two thousand kilometres long. Even though we were only on a tributary, our own river was big enough — and here we were, going down it in a tiny rubber boat to an unknown destination in the heart of the biggest rainforest on earth.

We must have been travelling faster than we thought, because after only one hour forty I suddenly realized that there was no longer a wall of jungle on the right bank. We had come to a place where the trees had been cut away. Further downstream I made out a long, grey shape which could only be the landing jetty.

"Look out!" I whispered. "Back up! Paddle for the bank."

Murdo and Sparky spun the dinghy and headed across the current for the shore. A few trees still clung to the edge of the water, and we came in under them among a mass of roots. Standing up in the back of the little rubber boat, I got hold of an overhanging branch and pulled us in.

The roots, over which we had to scramble ashore, were treacherous in the extreme: invisible, uneven, and slippery as ice. Getting wet up to mid-thigh hardly mattered though, as the night was so warm; more serious was the noise we made floundering about. We tethered the boat temporarily to a branch and scrabbled up the steep earth bank, to find ourselves on the edge of a flat, clear space: the new airstrip. Away to our left, glimmering like a big, white moth, was a twin-engined plane, a square-bodied Islander.

Immediately we had a problem: what to do with the boat? To drag it ashore, through the mat of roots and branches, would be impossible. An alternative was to climb back on board and let it drift downstream, bringing it ashore on the new wharf. The trouble with that one was that the jetty might be guarded — and if we got the dinghy on land, what would we do with it then? A third alterative was to head back upstream and cache the boat on the edge of the virgin jungle; but, given the strength of the current, I doubted we'd make any headway with paddles alone, and I didn't want to risk starting up the outboard. In the end, after a rapid Chinese parliament, we decided to leave the dinghy where it was. It was well hidden from boats passing on the river by overhanging branches, and the chances of anyone searching the bank along the perimeter of the airstrip seemed infinitesimal. Once on the airfield, we took a note of the boat's position by reference to a single tree that stood taller than the rest.

Pepperpotting was the order of the night. By luck we'd come ashore near the northern end of the landing strip. The plane was parked at the south end, about six hundred metres away. While one of us went forward to check our immediate surroundings, the other two covered him from a distance. Then, at a low whistle, they moved up, and one of them took over the lead. We stalked the aircraft with extreme care, moving silently over the raw, scraped earth of the runway. We expected to find at least one guard stationed by it, or in it, and we were surprised to find the Islander deserted. The temptation to booby-trap it was almost overwhelming: we had the explosive and detonators. But I had to keep reminding myself that our mission was one of covert approach and extraction, not one of sabotage.

In the dark it was difficult to tell whether or not we were leaving any tracks; but as we moved round the plane in single file, Murdo, at the back, was swishing a branch of big leaves back and forth across our trail.

Leaving the plane, we headed for the wall of forest to the west, aiming for the corner of the field. Sure enough, there was the road, leading off into the jungle, a pale strip just visible. Dark as the night was out in the open, it was still blacker under the trees, and I paused before entering the tunnel.

"Give us your branch, Murdo," I said quietly. "It looks to me as though security's very lax. They're so far from civilization that they don't reckon there's any threat. They're relying on the isolation to protect them. But I'm not taking any chances."

I stripped the leaves and side-shoots off the branch,

until I was left with a springy stick about four feet long, and I moved down the road with this held out at an angle in front of me, in case we came on a trip wire connected to an alarm. But the track was clear.

As Tony had described, the track wound in curves between the trees. It could have been made like that for reasons of camouflage — to preserve as much tree-cover as possible — or for reasons of economy, to save shifting obstructions unnecessarily. Probably the engineers had chosen the easiest route, which involved the minimum of clearing.

We moved in bursts. I'd go on a hundred steps, then stop in the middle of the road. The other two waited a couple of minutes, then closed on me. The darkness was such that twice they went past me, only a few feet away, without seeing me, and I had to hiss at them to stop.

At that erratic pace it took us half an hour to cover a kilometre. Several times I froze, hearing movements on the edge of the jungle to right or left, but after a while I realized that the disturbances were caused by animals, possibly jaguars, more likely snakes.

By about 10.30 the moon was rising. The sky was growing lighter, and we could see the tree canopy silhouetted in black against it. Then we began to hear the hum of a machine — probably a generator — in the distance ahead. Finally we made out lights showing through the trees.

It was after 11 p.m. when we reached the edge of the clearing, and from the lack of movement we reckoned the place had settled down for the night. Hanging back under the trees, we scanned the new settlement. The approach road opened out into a clearing perhaps seventy metres wide and two hundred long. On the left-hand side, as we looked, two long, low buildings were laid out end to end, running away from us and continuing the line of the road. Beyond them, at right-angles across the far end of the clearing, a third building was still under construction, the skeleton of its roof showing up white in the moonlight. In front of it several vehicles were parked: a couple of bulldozer diggers, two or three dump-trucks, and two jeeps.

The nearest building looked like the accommodation block. It had doors and windows, and the walls went right up to the eaves of the corrugated iron roof. The second building was not much more than a roof on pillars — part of the side we could see had a wall about head-high, but the rest of it was open. That, I guessed, was the laboratory. Somewhere at the back of that a generator was drumming, and a couple of bare electric bulbs flickered erratically.

"How the fuck did they get the stuff here to build all this?" whispered Sparky.

"By water," I told him. "A boat comes upriver. An army of guys with power-saws goes ashore. Next they land a bulldozer to clear the road, and the site. Then some trucks to carry concrete blocks, cement and so on. In about a week, it's cocaine city."

Skirting the open ground, we moved forward and to our right to get a closer view. I wished to hell we had PNGs or kite-sights. As it was, we had to make do with one pair of binoculars, which gathered light well but was no substitute for real night-vision equipment.

On the right-hand side of the clearing we found a high rampart of logs, roots and earth. Everything bulldozed off the site had been pushed up into a heap about twenty feet tall and over a hundred yards long. Immediately behind it was a tangle of virgin forest. In fact, all the debris had been pushed back and piled up into and around the first of the standing trees, so that when we tried to creep round the back of it, we found it impossible to make progress. But when we scrambled up the back of the long mound, we discovered that we had a view of the whole clearing, a naturally commanding position.

"This is the place for the OP," I whispered.

"It's bloody close to the buildings," said Sparky. "We're right on top of them. It can't be more than sixty or seventy metres straight across. If we're caught here, we're fucking history."

"I know. But if we get any farther away, we'll be in the trees, and able to see fuck-all. Listen: I'm going to recce round the back of the buildings. You guys stay here and cover me. Sparky, rig an aerial and see if you can get a sitrep through to base. Report that we're on Green Four, and find out if they've got any news of the Boat Troop. If it goes noisy, RV back at the dingy. I just hope to hell these bastards haven't got any dogs."

I scrambled along the back of the heap, working my way left-handed to the airstrip end. Back on the side of the road I paused, listening, then crossed to the rear corner of the accommodation block. Behind it I found a strip of cleared ground maybe ten metres wide, so that walking up it was easy. There were no windows in the back of the building, which was made of bare concrete blocks, only narrow ventilation slits high in the walls. As I crept along I was thinking. If Luisa and the DA are here, they could be right beside me, the other side of that wall. At the far end of the block I again stood still for two or three minutes, but I heard nothing except the cicadas at a distance, the drumming of the generator close at hand, and the mosquitoes aiming for my neck.

As we had guessed, the second building was the laboratory. It was fifty metres long, and above a shoulder-high wall of blocks it was open to the outside air. Looking over the wall I could see long working surfaces, or possibly vats, and there was a chemical smell in the air. At the far end, a collection of 55-gallon drums stood in one corner, stacked two-high. These would be the ether.

Beyond the laboratory I came to the end of the new building, and beyond that I found myself on the bank of a small river, which ran past the end of the site.

I'd started along the back of the unfinished structure when suddenly I smelled woodsmoke. Somewhere ahead of me there was a fire. Maybe people were camping in the open. Then, within a few feet, I heard a noise that made me freeze: a man snoring. The sound came from head level. There was somebody in a hammock almost within arm's length. Inching backwards, a quarter-step at a time, I retraced my route to the corner of the lab. Earlier, I'd been considering the idea of making my way back along the front of the buildings and getting a look at the doors. Now I decided that any such manoeuvre was out of the question; there were too many people on the site.

By midnight I was back in our OP at the top of the rampart. Sparky had got no joy out of his 319; he'd run an aerial up, but probably it needed to go higher. It wasn't on to go tree-climbing in the dark, so I told him to wait for first light. In the meantime, we needed to get our heads down.

Slinging hammocks at midnight in the jungle was something at which we had had a good deal of practice. If you sleep on the ground, you not only put yourself at the mercy of all the creepy-crawlies on the forest floor; you also advertise your presence by leaving signs — impressions in the earth and dead leaves. The correct procedure is to wrap a length of hessian round the trunk of a tree, so that your support rope doesn't mark the bark, and then lash on.

Soon two of us were swinging gently under our mozzie nets, while the third stayed on stag. I don't think any of us slept.

CHAPTER
FIFTEEN

Even by their own swift standards, the Boat Troop had made a fast getaway. The ops officer put out a call at 1715 on Saturday evening, when most of the guys were at home or around the town. The commander, Staff Sergeant Merv Mason, an Aussie famous for his walrus moustache, was in his local Tesco when the bleeper went off in his pocket. Hearing the summons, he cut short his shopping, made a dash for the rapid checkout, and hurtled home to pick up his kit on his way into camp. In under two hours of frantic activity his team had got itself together and lined up the stores and equipment they would need for a drop into the sea and an assault on the *Santa Maria*.

In the background, Merv knew, urgent talks were in progress. The boss was negotiating to get the party aboard an RAF TriStar which was leaving Lyneham that evening. The basic need was to lift the team to Belize with the minimum delay, and have them there ready to deploy as things developed. A Herc plodding round the northern route would be far too slow. After pressure from the Director of the SAS in London, the wing commander in charge of air movements at Lyneham had been prevailed upon to hold the TriStar for two hours, and to throw off a dozen less urgent passengers. In the end a Chinook lifted the team from Hereford to Lyneham, together with their kit, and they flew out at 2200.

Eight hours later, at 0100 local time, they landed in the hot darkness at Airport Camp, Belize. Three four-ton trucks drove out to the aircraft to collect them; leaving the plane before anyone else, they and their kit were whisked away to a holding area in one of the warehouses, where Keith Marshall, their liaison officer, had set up a standby ops room. The rest of the guys got their heads down in transit accommodation, but he was up for the rest of the night, fielding the messages that came in by secure fax from Hereford and Regimental Headquarters in London.

From the faxes Keith could see that diplomatic negotiations had been going on at the highest level. No matter that in North America it was the early hours of Sunday morning; it was Prime-Minister-to-President stuff as Whitehall urgently requested assistance in lifting the Boat Troop to within striking distance of their objective, wherever that might turn out to be.

When the *Santa Maria* sailed from Cartagena at 0830 local time — 1330 in London — an emergency meeting was called at the COBR, the Cabinet Office Briefing Room, underground in Whitehall, which was opened up and manned to act as the control centre. There the SAS Director met senior officials from the Ministry of Defence and the Foreign Office and a representative from the United States Embassy. After an initial conference, as satellite surveillance showed the ship heading north, they stood down the meeting until her destination could be established. When she put into Desierto at 2000 local (0100 in London), the senior officers were routed out of bed by telephone calls, and sleepily reassembled. Later that morning, at the US Embassy in Grosvenor Square, the American Defence Attaché called the duty officer in the Operations Center at the Pentagon and confirmed that help was going to be needed again, this time in the form of a warship to put the Boat Troop within range of their target. "The British Prime Minister's been talking with the President," he confirmed. "The orders are to give every possible assistance."

None of this background activity concerned Merv Mason and his men in Belize. All they knew was that they had to prepare for Operation Gannet. By midday on Sunday they were ready to parachute into the sea, with their two twenty-five-foot Geminis fully inflated and secured on platforms with all their gear inside them, including the forty-horsepower Mariner engines. The stream of secure faxes, which continued all morning, told them that the Pentagon had agreed to divert a nuclear attack submarine, the USS *Endeavor*, from its exercise in the Caribbean so that it could pick them up and take them covertly into the target area. The planners assumed that the *Santa Maria*, although by no means new, must have effective radar; and this meant that the approach of any large surface vessel or unidentified aircraft would warn the narcos of an impending attack. A submarine was therefore by far the safest option.

Shortly after 2000 on Sunday evening, messages reaching the standby ops room in Belize began to give information about Desierto. The northernmost of a group of small islands which were the tops of extinct volcanoes, it had never been permanently inhabited. Although the others supported small communities of fishermen, Desierto was deserted because it had no reliable fresh water supply. Intelligence routed from the United States Drug Enforcement Agency revealed that in the 1960s a bauxite mining company had built a quay on the shore of a creek on the western side of the island, but that the venture had gone bankrupt and the port had been abandoned. Recently big-time drug-runners had begun to use it again as a safe haven and transit base, cross-decking consignments from one ship to another, and flying small planeloads into Mexico.

In the old days the team commander and signaller at Belize would have spent an anxious hour working out latitudes, longitudes, distances and courses to create a rendezvous between aircraft and submarine in the middle of the Caribbean. Now computers made the calculations in seconds, and then did them again, so that their human operators could feel confident they were right. The upshot was that the Boat Troop boarded a Hercules at 2100 on Sunday evening, for a flight of two hours forty minutes on a bearing of 112 degrees for a rendezvous with USS *Endeavor* thirty miles off the west coast of Desierto.

As the plane droned through the night, Merv looked round his nine men. All were asleep, or nearly so, and certainly none looked worried. A night jump into the sea was routine for them. Gannet was exactly the kind of operation they had spent years training for. Far from being scared, they were positively looking forward to some action. Merv at thirty-two, was the oldest in the party — although with his short, curly fair hair and pock-marked face he didn't look it. He eased a finger inside the collar of his black wetsuit and settled himself into a more comfortable position.

Once, at about 2230, he went up to the flight-deck for a chat with the captain and a last check of the coordinates. As everyone seemed happy, he moved back down and concentrated his mind on the task ahead. The rendezvous with the sub should be routine; it was the landing on the island which would demand quick assessment and positive decisions. Maps faxed across during the day had given him an idea of the shape of the coast around the creek, but there hadn't been time to send photographs, so a lot would depend on the nature of the shore where they landed.

At 2300 the captain began a gentle descent, easing down from 20,000 feet. Merv plugged in one of the headsets hanging along the sides of the hold and listened in. At 2330 an American voice suddenly came up on the compatible radio channel. "Alpha Two to X-ray One. How do you read me? Over."

"X-ray One, loud and clear. Running in on one-one-two. Estimate nine minutes to DZ overhead."

"Roger. We'll give you a white light buoy on our starboard side, your port."

"X-ray One. Thanks."

"Alpha Two. Happy landings, and please not to drop your goddamn boats on top of us."

Merv knew that, to have comms with the aircraft, the sub must have her periscope above the surface. By the time they reached her she would have surfaced.

"Four minutes to DZ overhead," the pilot called. "Stand by."

The head-loadie held up four fingers. The Herc had levelled off and was flying steadily at 1200 feet. All round the hold guys were adjusting and checking their harnesses. The rest of the hold crew were snapping off the fastenings and removing the nets that had held the boats down. At D minus two the head-loadie hit the button to lower the tailgate ramp. Warm, fresh air rushed in as the broad platform descended and the back of the plane yawned open to reveal black water glittering below.

The head-loadie held up one finger. Merv counted down the sixty seconds to himself. Then they were into the familiar sequence: "Red on. Green on. GO!"

First out were the boats. One big shove, and their platforms slid quickly backwards over the steel rollers in the deck until they toppled clear. The team immediately followed, in two sticks of five.

As his chute snapped out, Merv saw the brilliant light shining up out of the sea, and beyond it he made out the long, dark shape of the sub's upper hull. Then he steered for the boats, which were hitting the water with a big double splash three hundred yards away to the east.

Ten minutes later each team was clustered round its boat, still trussed on the platform. Cutting the tie-cords was a dicey business, because if anyone got entangled he could easily go down deep six when the platform fell away. With most of the cords severed, all but two men backed off and they severed the final bonds in unison.

With both Geminis fully operational, they motored

gently towards the long, low hulk of the sub. The crew had already opened up the main hatch above the forward torpedo room — a huge, empty space on the front of the ship — and all the gear went into that; the boats were deflated, rolled up and packed into valises, the engines sealed inside waterproof bags. The guys changed into dry gear and went down into the heart of the ship. The hatches were sealed, buzzers sounded and the crew prepared to dive.

Merv introduced himself as the commander, and met the officer of the watch. He'd been in submarines before, but they had all been small and cramped. This one was mega, with four decks, passages running for a hundred feet or more, and a luxurious amount of space. The whole ship was very quiet, and only the faintest hum of air-conditioning was detectable. It was also spotlessly clean, with fresh pastel colours on the bulkheads. The temperature was a comfortable 68 degrees, the air fresh, and the crew were in shirt-sleeves. The facilities in the enlisted men's mess included a TV screen, a whole library of videos, and a bar at which the visitors were encouraged to make themselves tea and coffee. Their American hosts must have been curious about their mission, but they showed professional restraint. Apart from a few cracks such as, "What's it like out there?" they asked no questions.

In any case, the visitors were going to be on board for no more than a couple of hours. While the rest of the team relaxed, Merv went along to the CIC, or Combat Information Center, beneath the conning tower, to check details of their approach to Desierto. The island was only thirty miles off, and the sub was closing on it at twelve knots.

For a layman, the CIC was an eerie sight: a circular room, almost dark, full of men monitoring low-lit dials with dark-red figures flickering on them. Since the whole principle of a submarine is that it does not advertise its presence, the *Endeavor* was operating on passive sonar only, sending out no emissions that other vessels could detect. At a bank of complex arrays five men were listening for transmissions at different ranges — distant, medium and close.

"Don't think me a prick," said Merv to the cheerful first duty officer, "but if you don't use radar, how do you know where you are?"

"We have very precise inertial navigation systems," was the answer. "Gyroscopes — yes? Right now I can tell you where we are to within a few feet. If we have to, we can put up an aerial now and then to get a fix off a satellite, but most times we're happy to stay down. We can hear a lot, too. Listen in."

The officer handed Merv a pair of headphones, and he found they were full of mysterious swishing, booming noises.

"Hear that?" said his companion. "That's a shoal of barracuda giving us the time of day. When we close on this island of yours, we're gonna be hearing the surf on the shore from about four miles out. Now, you call the shots. Just say where you want to go, and we'll squirt you out."

"Can you give us a sub-surface release?"

"Sure can. In fact, that's all the better for us. If we

don't break the surface, we don't break international law. Until we break the surface, we don't become a ship."

By 0345 they could hear the surf ahead of them. The sub came up to periscope depth and sat there, moving gently forward, five ks off the coast. In the cavernous forward torpedo room the team pulled on their full diving kit and checked each other methodically, then went two at a time into the escape hatch. Merv always found that an unnerving moment: once you're sealed in the hatch in total blackness and the chamber is filling with water, there's no turning back. If anything goes wrong then, you could be written off.

Having released a float with a steel hawser attached, the first pair swam up the cable, popped the air-bottle to inflate the No. 1 boat, and scrambled aboard. Humping the 175-lb engine out of the water and on to the back of the boat was no picnic, but they managed it, and moved away from the buoy. Up came the second team and the second boat. Last to the surface were their bergens full of kit, their weapons and explosives, all done up in Ellison bags. With everyone and everything on board, Merv counted heads, made the total ten, and with a torch flashed a clearing signal to the officer observing them through the periscope.

The time was 0405. The moon had set, leaving the night very dark, and only a gentle wind was blowing from the west, so the sea was calm. The sub had put the boats out west of their target, and they set off on a course of ninety degrees, due eastwards, cruising easily downwind at eight knots.

Soon the coast of the island was showing as a dark line on the horizon ahead. The coxswains reduced speed and continued until, one kilometre out, Merv signalled a halt. With the boats hove to, he and another swimmer slipped over the side and went in alone for a beach reconnaissance. Thirty minutes later they were bobbing in the swell and touching bottom, a few yards offshore, only to find that their navigation had been almost too precise. No more than 300 metres in front of them, a big cargo vessel was moored alongside a jetty, her upperworks showing white in the starlight.

"Too fucking close," said Merv. "Let's get round the corner."

The Int guys at Hereford had faxed him a map of the island. It was only a photocopy, but it gave a reasonable idea of the layout round the port, and Merv had memorized the details. He remembered that the jetty lay along the inner edge of a small bay, and that the bay was sheltered by a hook of headland. He also remembered that the airstrip was inland to the south — about one k away to their right as they faced in from the sea.

Pushing off again, they swam to their right for twelve minutes until they rounded the headland and discovered a second, much smaller bay backed by low cliffs. Coming ashore, they landed on a steep little sandy beach, no more than thirty yards from front to rear. At the back was an overhang of cliff, and centuries of rock-falls had divided up the beach with a series of natural partitions. As a lying-up point, it was ideal. Even in the dark they could tell that it must be out of sight of the jetty, and the combination of overhang and rock-falls would help conceal the boats from any aircraft that might come in. Furthermore, the carry from water to cache-point, was the shortest they were ever likely to get.

Over his covert radio Merv sent the message: "OK. We've moved 400 metres to the right of our original approach line. Beach clear." Then he cracked out a cyalume chemical light, placed it in an empty tin can, brought for the purpose, and laid the can horizontally on a rock so that the green glow could be seen by the crews but by nobody on land.

A few minutes later, the boats purred in out of the night. The cache was so close to the water that there was scarcely any need to post sentries to secure their landing-point, but the team went through the drill anyway. They carried the boats the few yards to the base of the cliff, dismantled them under the overhang, and pitched scrim nets over them. Finally they changed out of their diving gear into DPMs and got a brew on.

"Watch the water, guys," Roger Alton, the second-in-command, warned them. "It's going to be bloody hot later on, and if anything goes wrong in the jungle we may have to hang around here for a couple of days. So we'll need all we've got. The other thing's sunburn. For Christ's sake keep your heads and arms covered."

The tide was coming in, and would soon cover the beach. But Roger was taking no chances. He went back to the edge of the water and, working backwards, scuffed away their tracks with a paddle.

"It's like Robinson fucking Crusoe," he exclaimed. "I don't reckon anybody's ever landed here before."

Leaving two sentries to guard the base, the rest

climbed warily to the ridge above them. They could see the odd palm tree outlined against the stars, but on the ground there was little vegetation, apart from tussocks of grass.

Everything seemed to be in miniature. The whole island was only about three ks in diameter, and the top level of the headland was no more than thirty metres above sea level. It was still dark when they reached it, but against the paling sky they saw the outline of Mount Desierto, rising to a short, blunt peak ahead of them. The upperworks of the ship showed white against the land opposite; she was moored with her bows to their right, and three or four hundred metres ahead of her, on the inland end of the quay, they could make out a huddle of pale-coloured buildings.

As they lay on the ridge, Merv checked off features he remembered from the map. "It's a dry creek," he said, pointing down to the right. "Comes to a point just below us here. No river. The airstrip's down there, round the corner, and the old bauxite workings are at the back of it. There's a road from the port to the strip, but that's the only one. No other habitation. What we need is cover for an OP."

Moving along the ridge to their left, they soon found some. A palm-tree had blown over in a gale, bringing up a big plate of earth on its roots, but it was still alive, and its tumble of branches offered excellent shelter, not only from aircraft but also from the sun. When dawn broke they realized that their OP had one bad feature: the sun came up just to the right of the mountain, in their faces, and they were looking straight into the light. Otherwise, they were ideally placed, not least because the seaward flank of their headland, behind them, was out of sight of the port, and guys could move up and down between OP and base quite freely.

At 0645, as soon as they'd established that the ship was the *Santa Maria*, they got through to Tony in Bogotá on the satcom.

"Blue Team on location," Merv reported. "The target's here."

"Roger. Have you identified the hostage?"

"Not yet. The locals are only just starting to move."

"OK. Keep me informed. And well done. The Red Team's ready when you are."

"Roger. We'll let you know."

Merv established a rota of two men on stag at the top, two at the bottom, and the rest crashed out, cooking or whatever. He and Roger took the first stag, to gauge the strength of the opposition and work out a plan.

One of the first things they realized was that the buildings at the end of the quay were inhabited. Doors started opening while it was still half light, and people went in and out. The watchers saw that a good deal of work had recently been done, both to the buildings and to the quay. Patches of fresh-looking cement showed up on the dock wall, and some of the buildings had had a new coat of paint or whitewash.

Soon the narcos' plan of action was apparent. Machinery started up on board the ship, and the derricks began lifting nets full of bales ashore. The cranes landed each load in the open back of a decrepit four-ton truck, which drove off down the airstrip road, disappearing round the bend of the hill to the OP's right.

"They must have an air-lift going to the mainland," said Roger — and soon his assessment was proved right by the arrival of a twin-engined Cessna, which came in from the north-west, over their left shoulders, took one sweep to the south, turned back towards them, into the wind, sank out of sight and landed. Half an hour later they heard its engine wind up again for take off and got themselves well tucked down among the palm leaves, knowing that it would come low overhead. Sure enough, it cleared them by no more than a couple of hundred feet, struggling for height under a heavy load.

"Easy enough to make sure the ship never leaves," said Roger.

"Swim out and put a charge on the props?"

"Exactly. The trouble is, they'd still have plenty of time to top the Rupert. Somehow, we've got to cut him out first. If that poor bastard's in one of those cabins, he's going to bloody bake when the sun gets up. The ship looks that crappy I bet she hasn't got air-conditioning."

Two more flights came and left. By then another team had taken over the OP. As Steve was scanning through binoculars, he suddenly said, "Jesus! There he is!"

Jerry, his companion, whipped up his own pair of glasses and watched as Black emerged from the building they'd christened No. 2, with his hands cuffed together in front of him, followed by a guard wearing DPM fatigues and armed with an MP 5. He'd been ashore all the time. He was wearing a white shirt and dark trousers, but he looked in bad shape: his clothes were filthy, and his face had a dark, puffy appearance.

Steve gave a double tug on the communication cord which ran down to the base of the cliff, and Roger came scrambling up. "That's him, isn't it?"

Roger, who'd never worked with Black, but had seen him often about the camp at Hereford, gave an exclamation of disgust. "It's him, all right. But they've been hitting him about. Bastards."

Black and his escort walked a couple of hundred yards along the airport road, then turned and came back. Exercise time. They went out and back three times, Black walking slowly and awkwardly because of his handcuffs. Then for a few minutes both prisoner and gaoler sat in the sun on a low wall. Two more guards appeared and sat with them. Then all four disappeared into the building.

"OK," said Roger. "We know where he is. But why have they got him there, I wonder?"

"The heat, probably," said Steve. "In such a sheltered position, the ship must be like an oven."

"He must have spent the night there — otherwise we'd have seen him come ashore. If they're going to keep him in the same place tonight as well, all the better. Much easier to grab him from there than on board."

By sundown they had their plan. The prisoner was still inside building No. 2. During the afternoon, guards had come in and out, but Black had stayed put. Everything pointed to a night hit — and there would be no better time than 0300, when everybody concerned should be in the deepest trough of sleep.

At 0130 two men would swim out and place a charge of explosive on one of the ship's propellers, with a timer set to detonate at 0300. At 0230 four men would work their way round right-handed, overland, to cross the road and come in on the buildings, taking with them a couple of made-up door charges in case they had to blast their way into the gaol-house. By 0255 they'd be in position for an assault on the building, but they'd wait for the ship to go up, and then give it a few seconds to see if the explosion would flush anybody from the buildings. If anyone ran out, they'd drop them, and then go in. Having lifted their quarry, they'd make their way back to the boat cache, but one of them would create a diversion by running off along the airfield road and putting down some rounds towards the strip, as if the rescue party were fighting a battle in that direction. Then, with most of the locals distracted by the fire on shipboard, they'd slip out to sea in the Geminis for a rendezvous with the *Endeavor* at pre-arranged coordinates.

At 1730 Merv called Tony on the satcom.

"All set," he reported. "We've got it hacked. We'll go in at zero-three-zero-zero local, if that suits."

"That'll suit just fine," Tony answered. "I'll pass the word along."

"Thanks. And maybe you can ask our cabbies to be at the rendezvous by zero-four-three-zero."

"Your cabbies?"

"Our cab-drivers."

"OK. They'll be there. Happy landings."

CHAPTER
SIXTEEN

Down in the jungle we were almost on the equator, so the dawn came up quickly, with none of the long-drawn-out twilight we're used to in the far north. At 0600 we suddenly felt we were under attack from a deafening chorus of insects. It started in the tree canopy with a kind of moaning twang from what we called the stand-to beetle, and spread down to the crickets and other creatures at lower levels. All at once the clearing was bright as day, and we only had a few minutes to settle the details of our OP as well as get the aerial aloft.

Murdo and I moved a few yards along the top of the rampart until we found a spot where some branches which still carried dying leaves formed a natural screen. Behind them we shifted lumps of wood and kicked away earth to make a comfortable hollow. As soon as we were settled, Sparky went climbing with his wire, aligning it east to west, with the east end ten feet higher. The standing trees gave us overhead cover, and by the time it was full daylight, we were well set. Unless somebody came walking along the top of the mound — which seemed highly unlikely, because the heap of trees and roots was so rough — we'd be perfectly safe. All the same, I reckoned we were too close to the enemy to risk any cooking, so we had a cold breakfast of corned-beef hash and lemonade out of our waterbottles.

As I expected, the locals were up early. Soon after 6 a.m. people came out of the buildings and began moving about. We arranged the stags so that two of us were watching the compound all the time. Most of the earliest activity occurred at the far end; evidently the cookhouse had been set up in the right-hand end of the unfinished block. We soon realized that at least some of the people present were native Indians — tiny, grey-skinned people, wearing nothing but grass skirts. There were also some Colombian guards in DPM fatigues; we couldn't tell the exact number, as they kept disappearing and reappearing, but we guessed there were about ten in all.

It was at 6.30 that a door opened towards our end of the accommodation block and out came a man who was manifestly neither Indian nor Colombian — a carrot-haired, freckled fellow in a dirty white T-shirt and jeans, carrying a towel.

"Jesus!" I whispered to Murdo. "One of the players."

Murdo's hair and moustache were dark red, but this guy was practically orange. He slouched off to a door at the far end of the block: the ablutions or shit-house, for sure. As he returned a few minutes later, the door of his room opened again, and out came Farrell.

I went into momentary shock. Somehow I'd made up my mind that he was on board the ship, knocking hell out of Black. Not at all. Here he was, stretching and looking round.

"Don't move," I breathed. "This is the fucker I've been after."

So, for the second time, I had a perfect chance to drop him. My mind flashed back to the scene outside the barn in Ulster. Now, as then, I had only to pull the trigger. But if I fired now, Farrell's mates would surely panic and try to kill their hostages. Even if we dropped all the players, the guards were on hand to carry out whatever orders they'd been given.

Farrell appeared to be looking straight at us, but in fact he was only getting his bearings, and after a moment he too moved off for a piss, with that characteristic dip on the left foot. I let my breath out and turned to Murdo with a shake of my head. Close on Farrell's heels came a third player, shorter than him, also dark-haired. I recognized him immediately from the restaurant in Bogotá. At about seven o'clock all three moved off in a bunch towards the far end of the compound, heading for the cookhouse.

It was Murdo who drew my attention to the end door of the accommodation block, the left-hand one as we looked across. Like the others it was made of metal, but this one was fastened with a hasp and padlock. "I bet that's where they are," he whispered. "It's the only secure room in the place."

Ten minutes later two of the guards came strolling along. They looked a slovenly pair. They carried sub-machine-guns that could have been Uzis, or the American version, Ingrams. At the door one produced a key and undid the padlock while the other covered him. The door opened, and out came a handcuffed man also wearing DPMs. For a few seconds I stared in consternation. Who was this? Had we made a mega cock-up and come chasing after the wrong hostage? Had the toads got their wires crossed? Then I clicked. With a jolt I saw that this scruffy character was the DA. He looked filthy and dishevelled and utterly different from when I'd last seen him.

I felt my temper rising as he was taken off under close escort to the ablution area, and then brought back. Where the hell was Luisa? In some other cell, I supposed. As the DA came back towards us I could see that his face was pale and drawn. He looked as though he'd shed ten kilos.

The subsequent events of that day were few and far between. At 8 a.m. a man brought the DA some food in what looked like a couple of mess-tins. At the same time construction work started up on the new building. Cement mixers began churning, and files of Indians portered stuff around. We could also see action in the laboratory, and a glint of bright blue from the stack of drums confirmed my diagnosis that they contained ether.

Not long after work had started, a single shot cracked out from the jungle near the far end of the compound.

"Jesus!" I said. "They've topped somebody." I didn't think it could be one of ours; the DA was certainly inside the gaol-block, and we presumed Luisa was too. We speculated intensely for a few minutes. Could it have been a punishment shooting — the PIRA extending their home methods to the jungle? All was made clear when a commotion broke out in the cookhouse area, and four or five Indians came into view dragging some heavy animal.

There was a lot of jabbering and shouting as they pulleyed it up with ropes and hung it on the scaffolding, where they started to skin and butcher it; although we had a fair view of it, we couldn't make out what the hell it was. From its thick brown coat it could have been a bear, but it looked more like a king-sized beaver. Not until we'd left the jungle altogether did I discover that it must have been a capybara, the biggest rodent in the world.

Around nine the PIRA crowd joined forces with some of the guys in DPMs, sorting out weapons and boxes of ammunition, and the whole lot drove off down the track to the airstrip in a decrepit old truck which backfired viciously. Soon we could hear the rattle of small-arms fire in the distance, and it was obvious that the PIRA guys were into training the locals. Their fame as professional terrorists had spread to the jungle, and here they were using the airfield as a range. Then we heard the odd loud *crump* as well, as if demolition instruction was being thrown in.

With them temporarily out of the way, I felt that the air had cleared. This would have been a good moment to launch our attack, if we hadn't been constrained by the need to co-ordinate with the Boat Troop. I almost decided that one of us could slip round through the jungle, scurry across the road, and creep up behind the accommodation block to whisper through the ventilation slits and let the hostages know that help was at hand. Then it seemed better to wait until dark, and until we were organized to strike.

A plan was forming in my mind. One 203 grenade into the store of ether drums would cause a major explosion and put the lab on fire in seconds. But better still, a timed charge of PE; if things began with a big bang from the back corner of the camp, the narco forces might be bluffed into thinking that the attack was coming in from that quarter, rather than from the direction of the airfield. If, during the initial confusion, we blew the bolt of the cell room with another small charge, we could get the DA out. He could tell us where Luisa was, and we should be able to spirit the hostages away down the airfield road without much of a firefight. At least we'd get a start. If we could somehow block or booby-trap the road we might get clear. Then it would be into the dinghy and away upriver with the outboards. If the Islander was still on the field, we'd put enough rounds through it as we went past to make sure it couldn't take off.

Talking quietly, I put the plan to the others.

"The idea of starting it with a bang's good," said Murdo, "but we still need more firepower."

"Well, the other guys will be here this evening."

"We'll be better off when it's dark, too."

"Agreed. But let's confirm what's happening on the ship. Sparky, get that fucking radio going."

Luckily, as Sparky began fiddling his dials, the bulldozer started up. Its noise was so loud we could have yelled at the tops of our voices without being heard, and voice communication became by far the most satisfactory option. In a minute or two we got through to the base at Puerto Pizarro. Johnny Ellis must have been right beside the Colombian signaller, because he came on within seconds of our making contact.

"Green Four," I told him. "I confirm one hostage is

on site. Second hostage presumed here also. Not the one with blond hair. Three PIRA also on site. Plus maybe ten local guards. Onpass to head-shed. Over."

"Green Three. Roger." He told us that the Blue team were on their objective. Also, the head-shed had reiterated that any assault we planned must be synchronized with theirs.

"We're ready when they are," I told him. "Any time after dark, provided you guys can get here. Is the chopper operational?"

"Green Two, affirmative."

"Green Four. In that case, we'll expect you this evening. Tell the pilot to fly to the same place as yesterday. You'll need to rope down. But see if you can borrow a chain-saw. There's one tree that prevents the chopper landing. Cut that down if you can, and bring the saw with you. Then launch your dinghy and drift. Don't use the engine. There's no need to paddle, except to steer, because the current's quite fast. Aim to launch at 1800 hours. After one hour forty, watch the right bank for a big clearing. We'll be there to meet you. We'll give you double flashes from a torch. Over."

"Green Three. Roger. We'll see you there."

"Green Four. Try for a pair of bolt-cutters, also. And inform Green One we're in good order. Anything else? Over."

"Green Three. Yes. The narcos are demanding a ransom of one billion pesos for the return of the British hostages."

"Green Four. Billion or million? Over."

"Green Three. Bravo for billion. Over."

"Green Four. That's peanuts. Emphasize that recovery is fully possible, and keep the negotiators talking. Out." I turned to Murdo and said, "A billion. That's about a million quid."

"Bollocks to them. They can whistle for it. Pity Johnny can't line up a fucking great tin-opener and bring it with him. Then we'd just carve open the roof of the shed and lift our two out."

The day seemed to last for ever. By noon, with the sun dead overhead, the heat was overpowering. Back under the jungle canopy it wasn't quite so bad, but out in the open it hit you like a blow over the head. I kept thinking that under the tin roof of the accommodation block it must be fearsome. We still had to go easy with our water; we'd brought two bottles apiece, and could have drunk twice as much. After dark we'd be able to refill them from the river — we had Stereotabs to kill the bugs. I wondered what the narcos were doing about their own supply. Getting it from the small river and boiling it, I supposed.

The shooting party came back and debussed into the cookhouse area for lunch and, we presumed, a siesta. A man brought food and drink to the DA's cell. Construction work stopped, and silence fell on the compound. What with the heat, the mosquitoes, and processions of inch-long ants marching into our OP, we didn't have that comfortable an afternoon.

The highlight was the appearance of a decidedly unwelcome visitor. I was dozing when Murdo suddenly nudged me and said, "Hey! Look at this!"

I rolled over and peered out through the leaves. Half-way across the open ground was a monstrous snake, slithering towards us from the far side. If I said it was the length of a cricket pitch, I'd be exaggerating. But I'm sure it was twenty feet at least, and a foot in diameter at the thickest point.

"Fucking python!" Murdo whispered.

"No, it's an anaconda."

"How d'you know?"

"No pythons in South America. I read it somewhere."

"Whatever it is, it could swallow a bloody goat."

"And crush you like an egg. Thin out, snake."

As if it had heard me, the huge reptile hung a right turn and headed away down the approach road, leaving a trail as deep as if a heavy log had been dragged through the dust. With the binoculars I could see its tongue flickering in and out.

Around four o'clock thunder began to rumble in the distance, and the sky darkened as a big storm built up. Back at Santa Rosa somebody had mentioned that the dry season was about to end, so maybe this was the beginning of the rain? The forest birds, which had been screeching away merrily all day, went quiet. Then the trees began to stir in a hot wind, and the storm came steadily closer, the noise growing all the time, until at about five o'clock it burst over us.

Being so close to the enemy, we didn't want to pitch our ponchos, which shine like hell, so we simply had to endure the rain, which came hammering down with such force that in a couple of minutes everything was flooded; cascades started running down the side of our rampart, and every hollow was full of water. When I looked across the compound, I couldn't see the far end for the sheer volume of rain falling. What I could see was that the deluge was raising a kind of brown froth several inches from the ground as the incoming drops beat air into the dust soup. The noise was phenomenal: a background roar of rain as loud as a train in a tunnel, and through it sizzling crackles of lightning, instantly followed by earth-shaking thunderclaps.

Within half an hour the storm had rolled on. It left us soaked through and miserable, but at least it cooled the air by a few degrees, and enabled us to fill our bottles with fresh water: I'd sent Sparky back into the jungle to spread a poncho and use it as a miniature catchment.

As soon as full darkness had fallen, Murdo and I set out to meet the incoming parry, leaving Sparky to man the OP. The storm had turned the dust to mud, and we couldn't help leaving tracks, but we kept to the edge of the road to make our trails as inconspicuous as possible. When we reached the airstrip we stopped for ten minutes' observation. The Islander still sat in the same place and, except for the insects and the sound of water dripping, everything was quiet. Skirting the edge of the open area, we made our way to the river bank, identified our cache by the high tree, and came down on to the dinghy first time.

From its mooring among the roots there was no view out over the water, because the outer branches of the trees hung down to the surface, so we cast off and pulled ourselves out until we were in the very fringe, then made fast to the end of a branch to hold ourselves against the current.

By then it was 7.30. "What do we do?" asked Murdo. "Start flashing?"

"Yeah. I reckon so. If there's been heavy rain upstream, the river could be running faster. They could be here any minute."

So we sat in the dark and waited, with Murdo giving a double flash upstream every thirty seconds. There was time to think of a hundred things that could have gone wrong. The helicopter could have gone US again and never taken off. It could have taken off and been forced to turn back. The pilot could have failed to find the rock outcrop. The dinghy could have got punctured. My mind flew to the propaganda tower in Bogotá, and Tony cooped up there on the fourth floor. I imagined wretched Peter Black, sweating in some oven of a cabin on board the *Santa Maria*. I saw Tracy and Tim in England. What time was it there? Two-thirty. They'd just have had lunch. Maybe they were walking in the spinney behind the cottage. I hoped they'd had no more strange phone calls . . .

Suddenly, from out on the water to our right, came a low whistle, which Murdo returned. Seconds later a black lump with heads sticking up out of it bore down at us out of the dark. Murdo kept the torch on to guide them in, and the second dinghy bounced gently into ours.

"How's that for fucking navigation?" said a Scots voice, which I recognized as Stewart McQuarrie's.

"Shit hot," I told him. "Good on yer, Stew. Who's with you?"

"Me," said Johnny Ellis.

"Me," said another voice.

"Who's that?"

"Mel. Who else?"

"Great!" I said. "Welcome to Shitsville."

"Can't be. We've just come from there."

"This is another."

"What's it like?"

"Fucking horrible. But you'll get used to it. Did you bring a power saw?"

"Sure did. We cut down that prick of a tree, too."

"Brilliant. What about bolt-shears?"

"Nothing doing. None to be had."

"Too bad. Any news from the north?"

"Yeah. The Boat Troop are still on target. What's the plan, then?"

"The boat guys' operation's going down at 0300. I told Tony we'd go in then too, unless we tell him different."

"Christ! We'd better shift our arses. What weapons have you got?"

"Only the one 203, and MP 5s. There's supposed to be a load of stuff coming down from Belize, but the Colombian aircraft went US somewhere up country."

"¡Carajo! What about ammunition?"

"Loads." Somebody tapped on a metal box.

"Good. Let's get ashore, anyway. Watch yourselves on these tree roots. They're slippery as hell."

We pulled both dinghies in, secured them deep among the root tangle, and hid the engines about twenty yards along the bank.

Up on the edge of the airstrip I gave a quick briefing to bring the new guys up to speed. It was easier to talk out there in the open, well away from the compound. I had to choose words carefully to give them a good idea of the layout without drawing any diagrams, but they got it well enough. I repeated the outline of my rescue plan.

"How many guys are there on the site?" asked Johnny.

"There's the three PIRA, maybe ten guards — guerrillas, or whatever they are — and some technicians, brewing the coke. Plus a few Indians. The bank we've established the OP on is a natural strongpoint. It commands the whole open area. From there, I'd say we could drop most of the guys on the spot, as they react to the explosions and run out into the compound. Now we've got the saw we can also fell a tree across the road, so they won't be able to follow by vehicle. If we put rounds into the plane as well, they'll be grounded. Then we motor upriver to the LZ, and have ourselves choppered out."

"What about their comms?" asked Stew. "It would be good to knock them out, so they can't report what was happening."

"We haven't identified any VHF mast or aerial, so we assume they've got satcoms — and the same on the ship. The bastards are probably comparing notes all the time." I paused, then added: "The sooner we get out of here, the better."

Back at the ranch, I settled everyone on the rampart, and in whispers explained the layout again, this time pointing to the various locations. Members of the garrison were on the move, but the centre of activity was the cookhouse.

After the rain, the mozzies were out in force, and even with liberal smearings of repellent, everybody was swatting and cursing.

I decided that Murdo should be the man to hit the stack of ether drums, so, when movement in the compound had died down, I took him with me on a recce beyond the buildings.

This time, as we crept behind the accommodation block, I looked up at the first ventilation slot — a horizontal slatted opening about eight feet off the ground. It was only six feet from the end of the building, so it must go through into the room where the DA was held.

At the far back corner of the lab, I pointed out the stack of drums, and we briefly discussed possible approaches. In fact only one spot was practicable — where we were.

"No problem," Murdo breathed. "This'll do just fine."

As we were returning, I said, "Listen, I'm going to make contact with the DA. Give me a platform."

Under the ventilation slot Murdo bent over and braced himself against the wall. With a bit of a jump I was up on his back, my head level with the opening. The stink that came out was anything but reassuring.

"Hey!" I hissed. "Major Palmer!"

For a moment there was no answer, but I heard movement inside.

"Major Palmer!" I hissed again.

"Who is it?"

"Geordie Sharp. SAS. We've come to get you out."

The DA gave a kind of grunt. "Thank God! When?"

"Three o'clock in the morning. Listen — where's Luisa?"

"I don't know. They took her away."

"When was that?"

"Can't remember. I heard her screaming."

"Oh. Shit! Are you tied up?"

"Only handcuffs."

"Not chained to anything?"

"No."

"OK."

I tried to think. It wasn't on to stay where we were any longer, I just said, "All right. I'll tap on the door just before three. It'll start with a big bang from the far end of the compound. A few seconds after that we'll blow the lock on your door. When you hear the first explosion, get your hands over your ears and keep them there until your door comes in — but be prepared for take-off. OK?"

"Yes, yes."

"Keep away from the door. After I've knocked, keep on the front wall, at the far end from the door. OK?"

"All right."

"Hang in there, then."

Back on the mound, we speculated furiously about what had happened to the woman. As far as we could see, there was no other room in which she could be held. Could she have been flown out to some other narco hideaway?

There was no way we could do any more recces. The chances of being compromised were too high. The operation had to go down.

I assigned everyone a role. Whilst Murdo would hit the ether, I would see to the door-charge, and escort the hostages when they came out. Sparky would help me with them; obviously they'd be disorientated and need close supervision. Johnny would be away down the approach road with the chain-saw. The moment the ether went up, he'd start cutting, with the aim of dropping a good-sized tree. Once he had a barrier in position, he'd jettison the saw. Stew and Mel would give covering fire from the top of the rampart for as long as they could, or as long as seemed necessary. As soon as the whole party was on the move, we'd pepperpot our way back to the boats.

"Easy peasy," said Stew.

CHAPTER
SEVENTEEN

We'd synchronized our watches down to the last second. I stood back round the end of the accommodation block. My watch read 0259. One minute till things went noisy. The night had been long. Those of us not on stag had tried to get our heads down for a couple of hours, but sleep had been elusive. The locals had held some form of piss-up round the cookhouse fire, and there'd been a good deal of drunken shouting. We'd seen the three players go into their room at 11.30. At least we knew where they were; but we weren't so certain about the guards. We reckoned that some of them were living in the far end of the accommodation block, but a few must have been sleeping somewhere else. I kept thinking about Farrell and I kept thinking about Luisa.

At midnight Sparky had sent his last sitrep back to our forward mounting base at Puerto Pizarro, confirming that our operation would go down at 0300, and that after it we'd make our way out to the airstrip, then upriver to the LZ.

0259 and everyone in position. Murdo was up at the ether store with a one-pound charge of PE, already made up with a detonator pushed into it, and a thirty-metre length of black Don Ten wire for cracking it off from a distance. I'd already crept along the front of the building and placed a tiny charge no bigger than my little fingernail on the padlock of the DA's door. I'd also given a couple of gentle warning taps.

Now I held the clacker in my left hand, MP 5 in my right. Sparky was with me, to give covering fire and help propel the hostages in the right direction. Johnny was away down the road to a tree that he'd selected in a midnight recce, and the other two were on the rampart, ready to put rounds down if the defenders started to come forward. They'd done useful work up there, clearing out a second position about ten metres along from our OP so that they could open the firing from there, and then move along if anyone started to shoot back.

Another storm was brewing. Big bangs of thunder were rolling gradually closer, and the darkness was intense. The usual two bulbs were burning in the lab area, and in their glow I saw Murdo slinking up the side of the building. He was moving carefully, with his MP 5 slung over his back and the made-up charge in his hand.

Then I caught my breath. In a sudden flurry of movement a figure rushed out at Murdo from the right. Murdo obviously had his mind on planting the explosive, and was taken by surprise. But the assailant had picked the wrong man; before he could even grapple, Murdo had let go his charge and dropped the attacker with a kick in the groin. Next second he was on top of him, arms round his neck. The man didn't even have time to scream. One of those big, tattooed hands had clamped over his mouth, and with a violent jerk his neck was broken. The whole incident was over so quickly that our timing remained as planned.

I saw Murdo pick up the charge, go forward, place it and move back out of sight. Fifteen seconds to go. If we'd been properly kitted up, with covert comms, I'd have been giving a countdown into the guys' earpieces. In the absence of radios, I was counting to myself. "Seven, six, five, four." I closed my eyes. "Standby . . . standby . . . GO!"

BOOM!

I'd been expecting a good bang, but this was mega. It was nuclear. The whole compound twitched and juddered under the shockwave. As I opened my eyes again, a fireball fifty feet wide exploded into the air and continued up in a searing pillar of fire. Suddenly the jungle all round was lit by a ruddy glare. Pieces of debris rained down all over the place.

My heart was pounding, but I forced myself to wait — wait for doors to open, wait for the locals to run away from me towards the fire. There they went: the guards first, then the PIRA. Three guys out of the PIRA room in a flurry of movement. In the dark it was hard to see if they were carrying weapons; they were just ragged silhouettes against the leaping flames.

One more shout wouldn't matter now. "Block your ears!" I yelled. Then I closed the clacker. *Boof!* went the lock charge. I ran forwards. The door was swinging outwards. I leapt into the room and found the DA standing dazed right inside.

"Come on!" I yelled. I knew he'd be deafened and

disorientated, so I grabbed hold of his arm and started dragging him.

"RUN!" I roared. "RUN! RUN! COME ON!"

In the glare of the fire at the far end of the compound, men were racing all ways. One started to run in our direction, but a burst ripped out from the top of the rampart, stopping him in his tracks and swivelling him round. As he went down, he tried to bring his Uzi to bear, but another short burst nailed him to the floor of the compound, and he lay still.

I could see the DA was in deep shock. He tripped over the door and half-fell — he felt like a sack of suet. I grabbed him tighter and held him up. "Listen!" I screamed. "WHERE'S LUISA?"

All he did was shake his head. We had to go. The flames had built up to such an intensity that steam was hissing out of the leaves of the nearest trees, and some of them were catching fire. More rounds rattled off the rampart. Then came another explosion and another. First I thought that isolated drums of ether were going up. Then I realized that either Stew or Mel, or both, were putting 203 grenades into the transport.

In a few seconds we were on the road and under the trees. Sparky was at our heels, turning to put down the odd burst from his MP 5. Murdo appeared from behind the accommodation block, running fast.

"I found her!" he yelled. "She's dead. Go for it!"

He started to run with us. The other two were still on the rampart. Ahead of us I heard the chain-saw screaming, then a crash as Johnny dropped his tree.

Light from the fire penetrated only a short way down

the road; further under the trees the night was intensely black. Now we'd have to be bloody careful not to score own-goals by shooting each other.

"You OK?" I shouted to the DA. He was still so shattered he didn't answer. From the smell I knew he'd shat himself.

"We haven't far to go," I told him. "Only to the airstrip."

We came to Johnny's barrier. He'd seen us approaching, silhouetted against the fire. "This end," he called softly. "It's easier here."

Our own covering fire had died down. Looking back, we saw Stew and Mel running like hares to join us. I rapped out a warning so that they didn't go arse-over-tip into the felled tree. Just as they reached us, rounds began to crack past and smash their way into the jungle farther down the road. Our guys hit the deck, but the DA just stood there.

"Down!" I snapped. "For fuck's sake get down."

I grappled him to the ground. More rounds cracked past overhead.

"Don't fire back!" I called. By shooting back we'd give away our position — and in any case, for the moment no targets were visible.

The compound was a fantastic sight — flames leaping and smoke billowing in a framework of primeval jungle.

"So much for your billion fucking pesos," Murdo cried.

"We're not out of it yet," I told him. "Stew — you and Mel hang on here while we go ahead. If you see anyone coming, drop them, but don't fire without a good target. RV at the dinghies as soon as we can."

"Fair enough."

I turned to the DA and said, "Right — we're off."

We started down the road at a fast walk. The darkness was such that at the first bend we walked straight off the track and into a patch of undergrowth without seeing it. Suddenly I found myself caught up in those bloody awful thorns known as "wait-a-while" which dig into you like barbed fish-hooks and rip you to shreds if you try to pull away.

I was struggling to disentangle myself when a sudden, rushing roar ripped past us, instantly followed by a flash and an explosion in the tree canopy beyond. I dropped to the ground, oblivious of the thorns tearing at my arms.

"Fucking hell!" shouted Murdo. "They've got an RPG."

I got up again and shouted, "Keep going!"

No harm to use a torch now. I switched mine on, taking care not to flash it backwards. On we went, more quickly.

Small-arms fire rattled out behind us — our own guys were keeping the enemy pinned in the compound — then we got some incoming rounds cracking past us into the trees. Then another rocket — but this time we weren't so lucky.

The missile must have hit a tree trunk right beside us. All at once I was on the deck, knocked down by the blast and temporarily blinded by the flash. I got up, my ears ringing, and I knew straight away that I wasn't hurt.

"Everyone OK? Murdo?"

374

"Yeah."

"Johnny?"

"OK."

"Sparky?" I waited. "Sparky?"

I shone the torch towards where I'd last seen him. He was still on the deck, stretched straight out, face down. I ran across. A pool of blood glistened darkly beside his head. I moved the torch closer and saw more blood welling from a hole at the base of his right ear. Instinctively I started struggling out of my bergen to get at the med pack, but before I'd even slipped the straps I knew it was too late. Sparky's eyes were shut. His face was dead white. I'd hardly begun to feel his pulse before I knew the answer: nothing. A piece of shrapnel had driven deep into his head, severing the jugular. Gently I turned his head over. It moved without any resistance in the neck, and I knew the top of the spinal column had been smashed.

"He's gone," I said. "We'll have to take him with us."

Behind us, the firing had died down.

I turned to the DA. "You all right?"

"Fine." At last he'd found his voice.

"Can you carry this?" Holding Sparky's torso upright, I disengaged the 319 in its webbing cover and straps, and handed it over. "It's heavy, but we haven't far to go."

"I'll manage it."

"Good."

I took Sparky's bergen and slung it over my left shoulder. The other two were pulling out a hammock, which had handles on the side and could double as a stretcher. They just about had Sparky in it when we heard movement on the road behind us.

"Stew," I called softly.

"Hello."

"We've got a casualty."

"Oh Christ — who is it?"

"Sparky. He copped it from that RPG."

"Dead?"

"Yep. We've got to get him to the boats."

"Shit!"

"What's happening back there?"

"We dropped at least six of them. Couldn't tell which. The 203s may have done for more. Ditto the big bang. The survivors are thinking things over. The lab's destroyed, anyway."

"Come on, then."

We went on as fast as we could, weaving along the road, with four guys lugging Sparky's body. We reached the airstrip without further harassment. It was a tremendous relief to come out of the claustrophobic blackness of the forest and into the open. Thunder still rumbled in the distance, but the clouds seemed to have lifted and the night was slightly less dark.

The plane was still in the same position. It offered a tempting target — but I didn't feel like making more noise by firing at it. We had enough trouble already.

"Wait one while I whip over and slash its tyres," I said. "At least, no, you lot carry on, and I'll meet you above the cache."

The others picked up their limp burden and continued diagonally across the open strip, heading for the tall single tree. On my own, I ran to the plane, not bothering about the tracks I was making. By the time anybody followed up in daylight, we'd be well away upriver.

It took all of ten seconds to drive the point of my Commando knife into the side of each tyre, and as I made away the air was still hissing out.

I caught up with the others as Murdo scrambled down to check the dinghies. Then from below came a curse and an exclamation.

"What's the matter?"

"The boats have gone!"

"Don't be stupid."

"They fucking have."

In a flash I was down on the edge of the roots beside him. I shone the torch at the bank. There were the blue painters, still tied to branches.

"It's OK," I said. "They haven't gone. They've swamped, that's all."

I pulled on one of the ropes and got a soggy response. When the dinghy at last came to the surface, we were shattered. The rubber skin had been slashed all over, ripped to shreds.

"Fucking crocodiles!" exclaimed Murdo. "Can you believe it!"

The other dinghy was the same. We had repair kits, but this damage was far beyond anything they could cover. God only knew why the croc had taken exception to the rubber crafts — but he'd torn them to kingdom come.

We didn't look for the engines — there was no point. Back on top of the bank we held a little O-group.

"There's basically two alternatives," I said. "Either

we make our way to the LZ overland, or we call in help and lie up somewhere close."

"How far to the LZ?" asked Mel.

"Maybe nine ks."

"We'll never make it through the jungle."

It didn't need to be said that, without the extra burden of the hostage and the dead man, we could have done it.

"Let's get on the radio, then. Murdo — you're our signaller now."

"Where's the 319?"

"The DA's got it. Here." I moved across, took the radio pack off him, and handed it over.

Murdo began to open it up, but a moment later he said, "We'll not get many messages out with this thing."

"Why not?"

"It's fucked."

He held the set up, shining his torch on it, to show that a piece of shrapnel had blown its guts out.

By 0200 a fresh westerly breeze had sprung up round the island of Desierto.

"That's great," said Merv as he breathed down his diving gear on the little beach. "This ripple on the water will suit us fine."

He and his partner, Terry Llewellyn, checked each other off, pulled on their rebreathing kits, went through their routine against possible oxygen hits, checked again, and slipped into the water. Besides his usual gear Merv was carrying two five-pound charges of plastic explosive in waterproof bags, already made up, with detonators embedded in them. In another bag he had det cord and timers.

The pair swam out round the point of the headland. The sky was overcast, and no lights were showing, either from the ship or from the quay. The chances of being spotted seemed minute, but Merv was not one to take risks. As soon as they came in line of sight of the *Santa Maria* he dived, and swam in at three-metre depth on a bearing of eighty-two degrees, surfacing every three minutes to check his line of advance.

Five lots of three brought him under the stern of the vessel. She was moving gently in the swell, and waves were slapping against her side. He gave Terry's arm four squeezes to indicate that they were on target, then felt his way down the swept-out curve of the hull until his gloved hand bumped gently against one blade of the starboard propeller. Down there, well underneath the ship, they were far out of sight of anyone on deck, so he switched on his helmet lamp, and in less than five minutes he had the first charge in place, tied round the prop-shaft at the point where it disappeared into the hull. Then, paying out the white det cord as he went, he swam down, under the end of the keel, and back up to the other prop. By the time he had the second charge in position and wired up his watch said 0235; so he set the timer for twenty-five minutes and swam quickly away.

Twenty minutes later he and Terry were back on the beach. Freddie Taylor, the single guy on stag at the boats, welcomed them in as they peeled off their kit.

"No problems?" he asked.

"Piece of cake," Merv answered. "We'll whip up to watch the fireworks."

Freddie had the boats fully inflated, ready for the quick carry to the water. Merv and Terry just had time to scramble to the top of the headland ridge.

"Blue One to other Blues," he said quietly over the covert radio. "All go at our end."

He didn't expect, or get, any answer. By then the assault party was at close quarters, and nobody would want to speak. In the event Roger had taken six men with him. One of them was to head out along the airstrip road before things went noisy, so that he'd be well placed to put down diversionary rounds without having to outsprint everyone else.

As the watchers lay on top of the ridge, the wind was coming from behind them, blowing onshore. Through 8 x 56 binoculars the buildings were clearly visible. A Russian-built Gaz jeep was parked outside, a few yards to the left of the objective.

"There!" said Terry suddenly. "Somebody crossed the front of No. 2. And another. They're on the target, all right."

"Thirty seconds to go," said Merv over the radio link. "Twenty. Standby, Standby. Fifteen. Ten. Five. Four, three, two . . ."

Before he could finish, a heavy, dull thump sounded from across the water. A fountain of water and spray flew into the air at the *Santa Maria*'s stern, and the whole ship gave a heave, a kind of slow flip from stern to bow. Then she settled back to her normal attitude, as if nothing had happened.

Lights went on in the ship's accommodation. Men began shouting. Merv and Terry saw people running aft along the cargo decks — but they didn't care too much about what was happening on board, their attention was focused on House No. 2. Now two men were visible outside, backed up against the wall, five or six yards apart, either side of the entrance.

"They're going to blow the door," said Merv tersely. "There she goes."

A flash sparked out from the front of the house, and seconds later the boom of an explosion reached them. White smoke and dust billowed out in a ragged cloud. The assaulters disappeared. Then came two short bursts of automatic fire, the first and loudest in the watchers' earpieces, the second more muffled and through the air.

Suddenly they heard Roger call, "Bolt-cutters!" A moment later they picked up a *snap*, followed by clinking noises.

At that instant Merv saw a dark figure running up the road from the left.

"Blue One," he snapped. "Watch out. One X-ray approaching from direction ship."

Roger must have had a man outside on stag, because two more bursts rattled out, and the running figure dropped. Immediately afterwards they heard Roger say, "Let's go. Run!"

Men poured out of the doorway — one, two, three, four, five. A sixth sprinted from the left to join them. Four ran to the right, while two temporarily vanished, having gone down to give covering fire. Then the two were on their feet and running. Hardly had they passed out of sight to the watchers' right when a far louder explosion — the loudest of the night — took House No. 2 apart. In a few seconds the structure was on fire, flames pouring from the roof. More men appeared, running from the ship, but the sight of the blazing house brought them to a halt. The last radio call Merv heard was Roger telling Charlie — his man down the airstrip road — not to stage any diversion, because none was necessary, but to head for base.

The watchers were about to pull back to the beach when Merv took one more look at the *Santa Maria*.

"Jesus!" he cried. "She's down at the stern. She's sinking."

"Arse on the bottom, anyway," Terry agreed. "Let's go."

Five minutes later the assault group tumbled on to the beach, panting but elated. Peter Black still had a shackle and a few links of chain dangling from his left wrist; for the past forty-eight hours he'd been chained to the structure of whatever gaol he'd been in — one night in a safe house used by the narcos in Bogotá, then in a cabin on the ship, then in the island building. He was still in his party gear, or at least the remains of it: the jacket of his suit had disappeared somewhere along the way, and his shirt, once white, was now filthy and torn. But his dark city trousers and black shoes looked ridiculously out of place. He was holding a pistol that Roger had thrust into his hand in case of emergency.

"Good to see you, boss," Merv said cheerily. "Had a nice holiday?"

"Charming, thanks. Five-star treatment."

"Seriously — are you OK?"

"Absolutely. But, Christ, am I glad to see you guys. What a fantastic effort!"

"All part of the service. Now let's go for a little voyage."

After a quick sweep to make sure they'd left nothing behind, they fitted the engines, launched the Geminis, and motored out into the wind. As they cleared the headland, well out to sea, they looked back and saw flames rising high above the creek. Merv switched on the satcom and went through to Tony Lopez in Bogotá to report the success of the operation.

Somebody lent Black a sweater, because the night was quite cool, and once he'd got some food and drink down him, he seemed pretty much himself. As the party headed out to sea, they filled him in on their side of the operation, but he seemed desperately eager to find out what had happened to "the others".

"Who are they, boss?" Merv asked.

"You don't know?"

"No. We came out so bloody fast, we never got a full briefing. All we knew was that we had to lift you, off the boat or wherever it stopped."

"Well . . ." Black seemed at a loss for words. "It was the DA from the embassy, and the . . . woman who runs the comms office."

"They're at some location in the jungle, and the training team from D Squadron's gone after them. Their operation was due to go down at the same time as ours.

"Let's ask the embassy what's happened, then."

They went through again on the satcom, and Black talked to Tony direct — but all the anchor-man could report was that no news had come up from the south.

"What about the 319?" Black asked Merv. "Can't we raise them on that?"

"We can try."

The radio was in the other boat, so they closed on it and called across. But presently the answer came back: no contact.

At 0440 Merv took one last fix with his Magellan and saw that they were almost on their rendezvous, a few minutes early, so both coxswains throttled back their engines and cruised gently forward into the swell. Then a couple of men in each boat dangled their triangle-like signalling devices in the water, fishing for the submarine.

In fact the *Endeavor* had been listening to their engines for the past half-hour, and had been shadowing them. By the time they began to signal, she was almost underneath them. A couple of minutes later they saw her periscope break the surface a hundred metres to their east; next the conning tower hove into view and finally the long, gleaming whale-like upper body. Within quarter of an hour they, together with all their kit, were safe in the belly of the leviathan.

It can't have been long after that we at last managed to separate the DA's handcuffs. All we had to sever a link of the chain between them was a hacksaw blade I'd been carrying in my ops waistcoat. Taking turns, concentrating so as not to break the blade by exerting too much pressure, we gradually cut through the link.

At the time that seemed a bit of an achievement. Certainly it was better that he could use his hands independently. Apart from having chewed-up wrists, he didn't seem much the worse, but he was exhausted and in shock. At any rate, he was very quiet, and it was only when I asked how he'd been lifted that he at last became articulate.

"My fault entirely," he said. "We'd had a few drinks, you remember. I was driving. I stopped outside the door of the restaurant, and we stared in. Then we drove off, came back, and did the same again. The next thing we knew, we were cut out by two cars full of armed men — and that was it."

"And they brought you and Luisa here?"

"Yes, but we got separated as soon as we arrived."

"Then what?"

"I'm afraid they gave her a bad time. I could hear her screaming . . ." His voice faltered and stopped.

"It's all right," I said. "You needn't go on."

"I can," said Murdo. "Her body was lying on the floor in another room. She was naked, and it looked like she'd been badly beaten."

I didn't answer, but I was thinking one name only: Farrell. That was his hallmark: rape and torture. Probably he'd been trying to make her divulge what SAS forces there were in the country. Once again my resolution to avoid personal vendettas had been blown to the winds, and I bitterly regretted my failure to take the bastard out while I'd had the chance.

We'd withdrawn into a small open area just inside the jungle at the north end of the airstrip. The rain had held off, but the mosquitoes were a major pain. The DA was still wearing the DPMs that the Colombians had given him, so that at least his arms were covered; but he had no hat, and the only way to protect his head was to drape himself in a little tent of netting.

We sat around miserably in the dark, debating our options. One faction, led by Murdo, was in favour of going back for a second hit on the compound. He argued that surprise would be on our side once again. The narcos and the PIRA — however many were left of them — must think that we'd somehow slipped away downriver, and they wouldn't be expecting a repeat performance.

"Listen," I said. "We came to lift the hostages. Now we've got one, and the other's dead, we want to get the hell out. We've lost one guy already. We don't want to risk any more. If any PIRA have survived, they'll be well into the jungle by now."

"In that case," said Murdo, "for fuck's sake let's get back to the LZ, so that the chopper can pick us up."

That made good sense — and I didn't think we'd have much difficulty navigating. Our basic need would be to head due north. Obviously we'd have to weave about, taking the easiest route through the jungle, probably along animal tracks. But if ever we seemed in danger of getting lost, we could make our way back to the river and steer by that. The trouble was the physical difficulty of making progress. As I knew from past exercises, the jungle grows thickest along river banks, and our best hope would probably be to keep in the thinner areas, further inland.

Bitter experience, on training and previous operations, had taught us that it was impossible to move through the jungle in the dark. All the same, Murdo insisted on having a try, and he set off in company with Mel, announcing that they would move on a northerly heading. They never made more than a couple of hundred metres. For the next twenty minutes we could hear them cursing quite close to us as they tried to push their way through the undergrowth, and in half an hour they were back, with skin and DPMs ripped into shreds by the wait-a-while thorns. We agreed that we'd start trying to blaze a trail north as soon as it was light. In the meantime, at 0500, we pulled out the pin from one of our TACBE beacons, hoping that the international distress call it put out would be picked up at Puerto Pizarro and alert our rear-party to the fact that we were in the shit.

Thereafter, all we could do was sit and wait for the light. As we were in thick cover, we got a brew on, and that cheered things a bit, but time seemed to be moving at the pace of a constipated snail. I kept looking at the wretched bundle in the hammocks, all that was left of Sparky. You poor bugger, I was thinking. All your money-saving didn't do you much good in the end. Also on my mind was Luisa's naked body, lying on the floor, with flies and ants getting at it.

"Let's hope the Boat Troop have had better luck," I said, and everyone grunted assent.

Eventually dawn broke, retarded by the fact that the

sky was still overcast. Grey light filtered down through the tree canopy, and we were just sorting ourselves out for the off when, to our consternation, we heard an engine splutter and start up out on the strip.

"Jesus!" I cried. "The plane!"

In twenty seconds we were out on the edge of the cleared ground. The Islander was some 600 metres off, at the other end of the strip and facing away from us, but even in the half-light we could see that both its props were turning.

"They're nuts!" I shouted. "I fixed the tyres. They'll never get off."

"If they do, we can drop them," said Murdo. "They'll have to take off this way. They'll be right over our heads. Just go on automatic and give the plane plenty of lead."

I watched, half-hypnotized, as the Islander started to move. Was it possible that someone had come down to the field and changed the wheels during the past couple of hours? Or was the pilot in such a panic that he hadn't checked the tyres before he went aboard?

Slowly the plane turned right-handed and straightened. We heard the pilot winding up his engines. But then we heard something else.

My TACBE, which had been beeping quietly for the past hour, sending out the emergency beacon, suddenly came to life. An English voice was saying, "Green Four, this is the QRF, Do you read me? Over."

I seized the set and switched to the voice channel. "Authenticate!" I shouted. "Authenticate!"

"Operation Crocodile," came the answer. "Op Croc."

"Green Four, roger. You're loud and clear. Where are you?"

"Estimate zero eight ks from your location. We're airborne towards you."

"Roger. We're on the north end, repeat north end, of the new airstrip beside the river. There's an Islander trying to take off at this moment. It's the narcos' transport. If it gets airborne, shoot it down."

"Roger. We have eyes on the river. Turning downstream now. There's smoke rising from the jungle to the west. Is that you?"

"Negative. That's the laboratory. We hit it during the night. We're one k east of the smoke, right by the river. Repeat. One k east of smoke."

"Roger. We'll be with you in two minutes. Wait out."

I put the set down, hardly able to believe my ears.

"Bloody hell!" shouted Murdo. "Who is it?"

"QRF from the Regiment. For fuck's sake let's not have a blue-on-blue."

"Green Four," I called again. "I confirm, our location is on the northern end of the airstrip, on the edge of the forest."

"Roger," called the QRF leader. "Location coming in sight. We have eyes on the aircraft."

On the ground the Islander was still teeing itself up, engines screaming at full revs. At last it started forward, towards us, but not accelerating quickly, as it should have been. Rather, it began weaving from side to side in a sluggish, drunken stagger. After no more than a couple of hundred yards of that, it veered off to its left, coming to a halt a few yards from the jungle wall.

As the pilot doused the engines, we became aware of another sound: the heavy thudding of helicopter blades and the scream of turbines. A second later two Hueys swept overhead, with side-gunners sitting in the open doorways. We waved frantically, and one of the pair went into a hover above us. The other carried straight on, to land well beyond the stranded aircraft.

The Islander's door had popped open. Two men jumped to the ground and began to run. One was aiming for the end of the road, the other came our way, heading for the jungle on our right. Instantly the machine-gun overhead opened up with a heavy hammer. A line of bullets flickered across the strip, kicking up puffs of dirt ahead of the farthest runner. No warning could have been clearer: stop or you die. The man continued to run, and within seconds he'd been cut down by another burst.

At the same moment rounds came snapping across the tops of our heads. Belatedly I saw a group of two or three Colombians way down the field. As we returned fire I suddenly realized that the single figure disappearing to our right was running with a limp. Farrell! I swung round and put in a burst from the MP 5 just as he disappeared into the trees.

"Stay with the DA!" I yelled, throwing Murdo my spare magazines. "Keep them off. I'm going after him."

Incoming fire was still cracking past, but I was possessed by the realization that this was my last chance, and I gave no thought to the rounds going past. In a few seconds I was on the edge of the jungle at the spot where I'd last seen the fugitive. There, on a big leaf, was a splash of fresh blood. He was wounded, at least. Possibly dead, but anyway wounded.

I dropped on one knee, listening for sounds of movement. Behind me rounds were still going down, and I could hear the choppers landing, but my whole attention was focused on the wall of vegetation ahead. A wounded animal is the most dangerous of all. What weapon was Farrell carrying? I hadn't seen any long, but he could well have a pistol.

There was more blood on a plant ahead. On the forest floor some dead leaves had been turned over. Further on, at the edge of a clearing, I saw threads torn out of a shirt and hanging on the wait-a-while thorns. I guessed he wasn't far in front.

Twenty yards across the clearing, a bush moved. I whipped a burst into the foliage and heard a yell. The branches thrashed about and Farrell half fell into the open. I raised my weapon to engage him again, but when I pulled the trigger, nothing happened. With a sickening lurch of the stomach I knew I was out of rounds — and I'd given Murdo my spare magazines.

Farrell was on all fours, struggling to stand up. I raced straight for him and kicked him full belt in the ribs. The blow sent him flying on to his back. I saw blood all down his right side — one burst had got him in the arm and flank.

Never before in my life had I lost control, but I did then. Holding the MP 5 in both hands, I smashed the butt down on to Farrell's jaw. With his good hand he grabbed my sleeve and tried to drag me down on to him. Caught off-balance, I toppled and landed with all my weight on my left forearm, right on the old break. A stab of pain shot through me, like a shot from my recurring nightmare.

I gave a yell, drew back, kneed him in the bollocks, ripped free and stood up, panting. Blood had started to trickle from his mouth. I kicked him again in the side of the head and knocked him flat sideways — but still he was trying to get up. I was on the point of using the MP 5 on him again when I felt a touch on my arm. I whipped round, and there was Murdo, offering me his weapon.

"Shoot the bastard, Geordie. It's easier."

I took the MP 5 and levelled it at Farrell's head. Still he was struggling to prop himself on his left elbow. He looked straight at me and spat. Then, in a snarl, he said, "Don't fucking miss."

"Go on!" snapped Murdo. "Top him!"

"No." I handed the weapon back. The hatred had suddenly drained out of me. "No," I repeated, "the cunt's far more valuable alive."

Back on the airstrip, the occupants of the plane had given themselves up. Everybody had been searched and lined up in the open. The second Huey had landed; six more armed SAS troops in full combat kit rapidly debussed, and the pilot shut down the engine. Silence fell over the airfield.

Murdo and I propelled our prisoner towards the commander of the QRF whom I recognized as Billy Bracewell — big, blond, muscular, a staff sergeant with G Squadron.

"Geordie!" he shouted. "Are you all right?"

"Fine. Let's get the fuck out of here."

"Who's this?"

"Declan Farrell. One of the key members of the PIRA. He's volunteered to come back with us, to help the police with their inquiries."

"OK. Hand him over to two of those guys there. What about the hostages?"

"That's the DA. He's all right." I pointed to our group behind me. "But they killed the woman. You'll find her body in the concrete building. Sparky's dead as well. That's him there." I gestured to a little mound under a poncho.

A minute later, as people were milling around, I got Billy to one side and whispered fiercely: "Farrell. That's the fucker who killed my wife." I felt choked. Suddenly I was hit by everything at once: the let-down of tension, lack of sleep, frustration over Farrell, grief over the loss of Sparky. I sat down on the deck with my head in my hands and tried to get myself together.

Presently I felt a hand on my shoulder. There was Murdo, with his moustache drooping fearsomely in the grey dawn light.

"Come on, Geordie," he said. "Let's have a proper brew and a bloody great breakfast. Then we'll all feel better."

CHAPTER
EIGHTEEN

They couldn't get us out of the country fast enough. It was as if we'd created too much of a disturbance already, and the authorities feared that the narco bosses would order a revenge strike if they could find out where we were. The other worry was that the media would latch on to us and start bringing out wild stories. The big essential was that we kept our heads down, and as a result our feet hardly touched the ground.

Landed back at Puerto Pizarro by the Hueys in the second of two lifts, we found that the prisoners, including Farrell, had been taken on ahead to some holding centre. A Herc was awaiting us, and we flew straight back to Bogotá. We weren't allowed into the embassy, but at least we got a proper shower, a change of clothes and a decent meal at an army barracks outside the city. Also, I managed to phone Tony, and asked him to call Tracy, to say we were on our way home. He filled me in on the success of the Boat Troop's operation, but said that the guys were still on board the *Endeavor*, heading for Florida.

Then, that same night, it was into an RAF VC10, which had come in after dark with a reserve crew on board, and

394

turned straight round as soon as it had refuelled. At the last moment Tony joined us, so that we had plenty to talk about during the flight. He told me he'd been through to Tracy, and she was fine.

Missing out Belize, we went north to Gander, to refuel, then across to Brize, and landed there feeling more dead than alive at 2200, after a total of fourteen hours in transit. As we waited for our baggage to come off I dialled home, and was puzzled to find the answerphone switched on. Oh well, I thought. The plane was late. Maybe she's come to camp to meet me?

All the same, worry began needling me. No, I was thinking, surely she'd never take Tim into camp at ten o'clock at night. There was something odd going on.

Because the operation had turned out a big success, the camp helicopter came up to meet us, and we had an immediate debrief on the aircraft as we flew down. When we reached Hereford, we found everything set for a big celebration. The ops officer was there, the CO, even the Director, who'd come down from London in the middle of the night. They cracked open bottles of champagne, and it was all congratulations and back-slapping until one o'clock in the morning. I tried to enter into the spirit, but I was too wound up to get the party feeling, especially after I'd slipped out, rung home again, and once more got the answerphone.

At last, around 0145, the duty driver took me out to Keeper's Cottage. To someone fresh in from the jungle, the April night air seemed very cold, and I shuddered as I got out of the car outside our door. As far as I could see in the dark, everything was neat and shipshape. The

Cavalier was parked on the gravel, and Tim's miniature mountain bike was leaning against the wall. But why were all the windows dark? Why hadn't she left the hall light on for me?

I didn't have a key, and was about to press the door buzzer when I thought, No — she's expecting me, so she'll have left it open.

Sure enough, the door gave when I turned the handle. I switched on the light and looked round. Everything seemed normal. I put down my bergen and holdall and called up the stairs, "Trace — hi! It's me."

No answer.

Must be fast asleep, I thought. But a loud alarm was clanging in my head. I ran up the stairs three at a time and switched on the landing light. Our bedroom door stood open. I flipped on the light in there. The bed was made up, un-slept in. I rushed into Tim's room. The same.

Back downstairs I tried the kitchen. There too everything was immaculate, neatly squared away. Panic threatened to choke me. I stood holding the handle of the kitchen door, rooted by fright. Then I shook myself free and went into the living room. As the light flicked on, my eye went straight to an alien object on the rug in front of the wood-burning stove.

I dived and picked it up: a Polaroid colour print, five by three. It showed Tracy, holding Tim on her hip, in front of the fireplace, and, on either side of her, a man in a black balaclava armed with a pistol. They were standing in the mock-heroic attitudes always shown in the IRA murals in Belfast.

I sat down hard on the arm of a chair, breathless with

shock. How did they know? I thought desperately. How did they connect her with me? And then in a flash I remembered. That man I'd chatted to so innocently about fishing in the Spanish Galleon, the pub on the coast of County Antrim. The man who'd come round to the cottage next morning. That one contact had been enough.

My hand was shaking. I stared at the photograph, and the expression on Tracy's face. A stranger might have thought she was smiling, but I could see how scared she'd been when the flash went off.

The publishers hope that this large print book has brought you pleasurable reading. Each title is designed to make the text as comfortable to read as possible.

For further information on backlist or future titles please write or telephone:

Australian Large Print Audio & Video Pty Ltd
17 Mohr Street
Tullamarine, Victoria 3043
AUSTRALIA
Tel: (03) 9338 0666
Fax: (03) 9335 1903
For Vic. Country & Interstate:
Toll Free Tel: 1800 335 364
Toll Free Fax: 1800 671 411

In the British Isles and its territories customers should contact:
Isis Publishing Ltd
7 Centremead
Osney Mead
Oxford OX2 0ES
ENGLAND
Tel: (01865) 250333
Fax: (01865) 790358

45%
5 5 5 4 6